SEEDS
AND OTHER STORIES

We gratefully acknowledge the support of the Canada Council for the Arts and the Ontario Arts Council for our publishing program. We also acknowledge the financial support of the Government of Canada.

Cover design: Val Fullard

Library and Archives Canada Cataloguing in Publication

Title: Seeds and other stories / Ursula Pflug.
Names: Pflug, Ursula, 1958– author.
Series: Inanna poetry & fiction series.
Description: Series statement: Inanna poetry & fiction series
Identifiers: Canadiana (print) 20200203444 | Canadiana (ebook) 20200203754 | ISBN 9781771337458 (softcover) | ISBN 9781771337465 (epub) | ISBN 9781771337472 (Kindle) | ISBN 9781771337489 (pdf)
Classification: LCC PS8581.F58 S44 2020 | DDC C813/.6—dc23

Printed and bound in Canada
Inanna Publications and Education Inc.
210 Founders College, York University
4700 Keele Street, Toronto, Ontario M3J 1P3 Canada
Telephone: (416) 736-5356 Fax (416) 736-5765
Email: inanna.publications@inanna.ca Website: www.inanna.ca

SEEDS
AND OTHER STORIES

URSULA PFLUG

inanna poetry & fiction series

INANNA PUBLICATIONS AND EDUCATION INC.
TORONTO, CANADA

To Keemo, with love and spaceships

Table of Contents

Mother Down the Well

I WANTED MORE THAN ANYTHING to keep a stone tablet, but they always slipped out of my grasp back into the water. I felt there must be some rule I was missing. They were covered with inscriptions of course; that was the whole point of tablets. Without inscriptions they'd just have been meaningless slabs of stone. Once they'd slid back into the pond I couldn't remember the inscriptions anyway, so it was just the same as if they'd been blank, as if I hadn't read them, hadn't held so much wonder in my hands. Finally, one day a tablet stayed in my hands without being pulled back into the water, as if there was a giant down there tugging with all her might. Needless to say I felt stoked, pretty much like Moses, in fact. I wasn't expecting proclamations that I could share with multitudes though, or even just my village, but hoping for something more personal. A fortune cookie, a horoscope. Some light thing to cheer and sustain me when all else had failed.

I had trouble making out the engraved words, what with all the slime and chipping, so I left the tablet by the pond and went up to the house to get the wheelbarrow. My friend Blue was sitting on my back steps; he asked me what was up.

"I have a tablet," I said. "It's heavy so I'm going to get it into the wheelbarrow and bring it up to the well and scour it so I can read what it says."

Blue smiled. "I don't believe in that whole stone tablets business," he said, "but even if I did, aren't you supposed to get them up on mountaintops and not out of the lake?"

"Pond," I said. "Siena got hers out of the water too. She found it upriver. Maybe some places it's mountains, but here it's water."

When he was around, Blue stopped by fairly regularly to see if I needed his muscles for anything. He is a big strong man with long blond hair and dark roots.

"They're just so tantalizing. Siena got one that said…"

Blue smiled as though now that I'd cloaked it as a bit of neighbourly competitiveness, my craziness made all kinds of newfound sense. "What did Siena's tablet say?" he asked.

"It said her third child would be a great leader of his people. Siena is confused because she couldn't have any more after her second daughter; all the doctors said so."

"She could always adapt a third one," Blue said, "in hopes of fulfilling the prophecy."

"You mean adopt," I said.

"I try very hard to mean what I say," Blue said, "and say what I mean."

He followed me back to the pond where my tablet lay in the grass. A long crack running through its middle, right where the words were.

"Tricky," he said.

"No doubt."

We headed back to the barnyard to get the wheelbarrow. It was between the well and the house, and I avoided the well like I always do, giving a little shudder.

"Why do you always avoid the well," Blue asked, "giving a little shudder?"

"My mother fell in before I was born."

"Really, Clarissa? You never told me you had a mother. I didn't want to pry so I didn't ask but I always assumed you'd grown up without one."

I looked at Blue. He is a friend I can stand. Most people really just want to take advantage of your kind heart, should you be lucky enough to be in possession of one. They want to complain and borrow things and not return them and call that poor assemblage friendship, when really what you've been praying for is the friend who can help you map it all out, say the insightful thing, help you disentangle the sheets of fabric softener from the wash as it were. Help get your mom out of the well she fell in before you were born.

"I have spent my whole life coming up with ways to try and fish her out," I said.

"I take it none worked," Blue said.

"So it would seem."

"Getting mothers out of wells is something I have a little experience with, actually," he said.

"Really?" I asked, casually as I could so as not to give away the as-yet-unfounded hope I felt.

Talking about such things, we took the wheelbarrow down to the pond. Blue and I tried to lift the tablet but it was too heavy, even with him on one end. That made me wonder whether the giantess who lived at the bottom of the pond hadn't pushed a little to help me get my tablet out onto the grass. The grass was wet, the tablet was wet. It was late October and the sky was overcast. I'd worn thick socks and rubber boots so my feet were okay but I needed an extra sweater under my sweater. I wanted to get this thing done so I could get back inside and have homemade squash soup and tea, perennial favourites for dinner.

"We'll lay the wheelbarrow on its side," I said, "then we'll tug the tablet into it; then you'll right the wheelbarrow with me holding the tablet to prevent it from slipping out again."

Blue rolled his eyes as if I might find this much exertion and coordination a stretch, but he didn't offer an alternate plan so we went ahead with mine, which turned out to be successful. We took turns pushing; Blue's turns were longer than mine. It was hard going through the long wet grass; there hasn't been much of a path down to the pond since I sold the last of the cows.

By the time we got to the barnyard we were so exhausted we dumped the tablet out of the wheelbarrow instead of gently laying it on its side, and even more gently sliding the tablet out onto the gritty dirt. Because of our carelessness it split in half right along the big diagonal crack, making an inordinately loud cracking sound as it did so, almost like thunder.

I thought I might cry, it was all so pitiful: the old well, the split tablet, the dirty barnyard. I'd tried planting flowers but even tansy and comfrey hadn't taken.

To cheer me up Blue said, "I told you I don't believe in tablets. I also don't believe in divine messages being accompanied by cracks of thunder."

"I'll just run up to the house and get a brush and some scouring powder," I said.

"Scouring powder?" Blue asked.

"You don't believe in scouring powder?" I asked.

"Just the syntax is unfamiliar. I call it Comet Cleanser or Old Dutch."

I came back from the house clutching a wire brush and a bottle brush and a brush for floors. The truth is I hate brushes now, the way the bristles are all shoddy and made of plastic.

"I'd go gentle with the wire one," Blue said. "That tablet is made of limestone and flakes easily. I wouldn't want to brush away what's left of the words."

"No ma'am," I said. I say this all the time, to anyone and everyone, including small girls and grandfathers. It is true I particularly like saying it to big strong young men like Blue, because that makes it funnier.

I cleaned out the carved words on my stone tablet as gently as I could with the sharp corner of a scraper and the wire brush. The well itself is open and level with the ground; no wonder, I sometimes think, that my mother fell in. There used to be a wall around it, a fieldstone-and-muck deal made a hundred years ago. Its crumbling accelerated at some point and I worried all the crumbles would make the water gritty so I took it down.

More truthfully, I called Blue and he came over and helped.

We teamed up to push the two halves of the tablet back together.

"Did you hear a clicking sound when they snicked together?" I asked.

"Clicking and snicking sounds we believe in," he said.

"The crack didn't disappear, though. The halves didn't melt back together."

"Accompanied by a hissing sealing sound," Blue said.

"And maybe some smoke," I laughed.

"I can make it out okay now but I think you should be the one to read it aloud," Blue said.

"Raise Your Mother," I said after first reading it inside my head a couple of times to make sure I'd gotten it right.

"Well, that's kind of anticlimactic, isn't it?" he asked.

"Come in for soup and tea?" I shrugged.

"I would, Clarissa, but I've got a dinner date," Blue said.

After he had gone I stayed a moment alone by the well and thought about my mother. Trying to get her out of the well was a project that made me feel stupid so much more than it ever made me feel smart. I'd turn over stones and ask them what I should do and they'd answer me with a stony silence. I'd make tea and forget to drink it. I'd walk until my legs ached. I spent as much time as I could outside, communing with nature, with tree spirits; seeing myself or the fate of the world in the flight of a bird or the curve of the current around a submerged rock.

I'd wear necklaces that had once belonged to my mother or her mother or my beloved aunt, sometimes all three at once, thinking it would help. I'd stay up late worrying about my brother Dave, alone across the continent. After Father died I was alone too, but I stayed on at the family farm in eastern Ontario, so it was as if everyone was still there even when they weren't, Grandma and Grandpa and Father. And of course Mother was still alive, just living down the well. I've only ever heard her voice the once, although Dave, who was there, has never been a hundred per cent sure it was even hers.

◆◆◆

After I retrieved the stone tablet, a doe came out of the woods every sunset for a fortnight to raid the gardens along the river, eating our lettuces. She was so pretty that we mainly forgave her foraging and just gathered on our verandahs to watch. My friend Siena kept her garden right up near the house, and after a couple of days the doe overcame her shyness and investigated Siena's kale. We stood together drinking tea and Siena pointed, showing me how the deer's left ear was split. We discussed whether this was the result of a wound or whether she'd been born that way. Siena also told me she had named the deer Georgia O'Keefe. She seemed relieved when I didn't laugh at this affectation and was even familiar with the famous artist's work. I suggested that Georgia—the deer not the artist—was skilled like me and my mother at bridging dimensions and that if I could only teach her to speak English we could have the nicest conversation about our metaphysical work.

"Or you could learn to talk deer," Siena nodded agreeably. "And how do you know Georgia-the-artist didn't know how to bridge dimensions? Many artists and writers do, you know."

"Of course. And equally many, or almost equally many, don't know that's what they're actually doing when they create. I just can't ask her, because she's dead, and wherever she is now is a place I don't know how to get to and ask things."

"How do you know your mother could, then?"

"For starters, she had another name for it. She called it exploring portals. It's why my grandparents bought the place next door. My mother said there was a particularly powerful portal in the well."

"Well, that explains a lot," Siena said.

"Agreed," I said.

"If it's true. Maybe she's been dead all this time and you're just telling yourself otherwise."

I laughed at Siena's joke and said goodbye so I could go home and plant. I expanded the gardens so much I didn't know what to do with all the food I grew. It was an earwiggy summer because of the damp but the insects left my crops alone. This seemed a boon from nature I had to repay and so I hugged trees on a daily basis, whispered to them to tell Ms. O'Keefe to stop raiding our gardens. I can speak tree but not deer, but you gotta figure a tree and a deer could likely converse.

Lovely as Georgia was, I was worried come November deer season someone upriver would kill her in revenge for eating all their succulent young beans, which would make her flesh so very tasty and tender. Maybe the trees told her this advice of mine for she did eat all my beet tops, but my beet tops only, and I was able to push the dark red globes back into the ground where they simply grew new leaves, palest green streaked with crimson. She also ate my beet tops in a pattern, leaving interesting designs in my rows. At first I thought my eyes were fooling me but after the third time I realized she was mimicking her famous namesake, leaving art behind everywhere she went.

It was because of this succession of events that I felt closer than ever before to raising my mother. It wasn't just retrieving a stone tablet and reading its self-evident yet powerful message, or my special relationship with Georgia O'Keefe that gave me hope, but the fact that sometimes now when I called down the well my mother answered back, a cool burbling cry that let me know she was submerged but employing some method she knew for breathing underwater.

My aunt's and grandmother's necklaces were beautiful, green jade and red carnelian respectively, but my mother's was the nicest, opulently beaded from coral and amber and finely wrought silver filigree. I knew that once she emerged from the well I would have to give it back. I didn't mind because I was looking forward to the conversations we would have.

"Have you ever noticed how people may be called Blue or Red, but rarely Green or Purple and certainly never Orange?" I imagined asking her. "Why is that?"

"What did you think the tablets were for?" I imagined her asking back, while putting on the necklace I'd been so careful not to lose. The only time she ever spoke aloud was twenty years ago. She said, "Magic is a skill that can take generations to learn, and many incarnations."

Dave and I had turned thirty and thirty-one that year. We stared at the speaker we had set up beside the well, astonished, waiting for more. Then Dave proposed that maybe someone had hacked the transmitter and interposed a recording of a woman's voice uttering these cryptic words, just to embitter us. After all, we didn't know what her voice actually sounded like, did we? I felt that it indeed was our Mother, and that she was trying to explain how she had abandoned us in favour of the study of magic, so compelling a task she couldn't give it up, not even for us.

Dave nodded when I told him my opinion, but still he was gone west before Easter and only returned three Christmases out of ten. He's invited me to Vancouver Island but I've always used the excuse that it's too hard to find someone reliable to look after the livestock. Of course the last cow has been sold for some years now so I wonder what is still holding me back?

I think maybe my mother didn't throw herself in the well; I think maybe she jumped. Everyone knows there is an inter-dimensional portal down there. Before he died, my grandfather even told me it was a selling point. Perennial gardens; good barn; older farmhouse with new 200-amp service; steel roof; wood/oil furnace; portal.

"What's this?" my mother apparently asked. She was just a young unmarried lady back then.

"I don't know," the real estate rep said. "It must be a typo. I've never heard of a portal before. I'll go home and check the master listing."

"I know what a portal is," my eighteen-year-old mother allegedly said. "Magic, of course, is not at heart either wand waving or spell weaving or the gathering by moonlight of certain types of nuts, berries, and owl innards, but a form of thought," she apparently continued. "The other things in the aforementioned or any other list are just supports, but without mastering the type of thinking that is called magical, all your crystals and ceremonies may be worse than useless."

My grandmother fished a pen out of her purse and wrote it down right away. This speech was the first, and almost the last, clue that there was anything different about my mother. Whether Grandma got my mother's words right or not we have no way of knowing, because our grandfather didn't also copy down this strange proclamation. And my mother certainly didn't write down her channeled wisdom. Maybe if she had, she'd have had the strength of will to stay out of wells. She might've written books and inspirational tracts she could've sold and bought me and Dave new school clothes come September, instead of the church sale and Value Village rags Pa was able to provide.

And so they bought the place. Sometimes people assume we've been living here for generations, beneficiaries of a land grant. It is true that during the Irish famine the local government gave away lots of hundred acre tracts of swamp and brush and bush to starving farmers from Ireland. That was what the Williams Treaty was all about, swindling the local Michi Saagiig out of what they had left, so it could be given away for free to white folk. Blue and his cousins still complain about it and why wouldn't they?

Mainly, the only people who think we're a land grant family are newcomers, for the old timers around here still know exactly who is who and some of them are old enough to find it a point of scorn that my best friend is Indigenous. I figure that along with a lot of other things that is their problem more than it is mine.

My mother jumped down the well the day after her wedding to a local settler boy. Everyone thought her young husband must just have been awful until a beautiful baby girl floated to the surface nine months later. That would've been me. Dave followed a year later although how Pa impregnated Ma once she was living down the well I was too shy to ever ask.

Pa did a fine job raising us. I think he missed my mother a lot and wished he had been able to provide whatever it was she got suckling at the portal down the well, but of course he could not. Special as he may have been he couldn't provide her with whatever other dimensional flavour it was she loved best, for it simply doesn't exist here on Earth, not now and probably never. Ma never did tell me what it was either.

◆◆◆

This year's harvest was a bumper crop in everything the earwigs didn't eat, although I've had better-tasting tomatoes; they prefer things on the dry side. Siena and I bottled for weeks. Come November, Blue went hunting; he said it was how he gardened. Successful on the second day, he brought me half a deer for my freezer once they'd done cutting and wrapping it at the organic abattoir. I thanked him and he asked whether he could tan the hide in my barnyard. He lives in a little apartment in town, so there is nowhere to tan a hide unless he does it in the parking lot of his building, which wouldn't work for a number of reasons.

I said okay. Once he was done with the hide he nailed it up in my barn and said I was welcome to it. This seemed puzzling to me but I figured he had his own reasons for doing things, as well as his own ways. When I went and checked I saw the hide had a telltale slit in its ear. This made me sad. Would I be able to eat this beautiful wild creature we had fed all summer? Had Georgia been easy to kill because she was half tame from snacking on our carrots while we stood by and watched? Had my whispered warnings to the trees gone unheard after all? I didn't know whether to tell Blue the story or not. I didn't want to make him feel bad, for the food and the skin were beautiful gifts, and he would not have shot her had he known she was our pet. As to the mother raising operation he suggested we try sinking rare earth magnets into the well.

◆◆◆

We worked most of the morning and half the afternoon with a complicated assemblage of pulleys and ropes, magnets, delicious snacks, and photographs of my brother and me when we were babies. The snacks were for us, not for my mother. Like a baby in amniotic fluid, we figured she had been nourished by the earth herself while she was sunk. When we finally got her up we stood discussing how to get her back to the farmhouse. It was because she was too heavy to carry. Blue is a really big and really strong man but he couldn't lift her, not even a few inches off the ground. We finally got her into the wheelbarrow, but it took the two of us. I am as shrimpy as they come but was still able to help with the leverage. It all seemed like a rerun of our tablets adventure except so much more important. Would she split in half if I dumped her accidentally? And what would her insides look like if that happened?

We trundled her up to the house. Blue kept saying he'd never seen anything like it, and he'd gotten a few women up out of wells.

"Anything like what?" I asked.

"The amount of water," he said. "The wheelbarrow keeps filling. We've had to empty it four times between the well and the house."

"True. It's as much water each time as a king-size duvet you've just removed from a machine where the spinner doesn't work," I said.

"It's got to be magic on that count," Blue pointed out.

"How so?" I asked.

"More water than the body of one small woman can contain," he said.

"It must be some portal down there."

"That's what they've always said," he agreed.

Artificial respiration. They used to teach it to all the children at swimming class. Maybe it was so that should their mothers throw themselves down wells, the children could perform this trick once they were fished out. And once they were able to breathe by themselves again, their mothers' eyes would open. That was my hope anyway.

We got her up onto the table in the farmhouse, an old varnished job, slightly better than the one you use for slaughtering chickens on. Then I pinched her nose shut tight and pushed air into her lungs, over and over and over. You are supposed to give up after three minutes, or is it twenty? When do you make that decision, and how? Blue said I should just keep going, since magic was involved. I said I didn't believe in magic.

"Portals then," he said. "Call it portals."

Those I believe in. I kept going, breathing into her mouth and then the moment came when her chest started to rise and fall, rise and fall.

Rise and fall, rise and fall.

"Well, that'll be that then," Blue said, making for the door.

"Stay for soup and tea?"

"Dinner date, Clarissa."

I meant to thank him profusely but he was already gone.

I sat and looked at my mother whom I had never seen before, even though she had carried me for nine months and given birth to me from inside the bottom of a well. It was the original water birth.

Her eyes were open and she was breathing. I put pillows under her but left her on the table as she was still too heavy to move. The pillows soaked through immediately. She was dribbling big puddles all the time as if she were an unending source of water.

"For the last fifty years I have been sure my life would have been different if I had only had a normal mother like other folks, and not a drowned one," I told her. "Waterlogged, silent, unmoving. Your hands waving feebly, not that Dave and I could even see them except when we attached waterproof video cameras to poles and stuck them down the well."

I think that is what sent my little brother to Vic in the end. He couldn't stand Christmas after first our grandparents and then Pa died. Just me and Dave left, sending cameras and mics down the well, hoping Ma would wave and offer Christmas greetings.

"Why are people never called Orange?" I asked after trying to help her sit up for the fourth time.

"Give me back my necklace," she gurgled.

I went and got it from the bathroom and clasped it around her neck, gently as I could. She didn't thank me. She fingered the necklace as if she knew each bead from memory but didn't look down at it. She didn't speak again either. Mainly she dripped and dribbled.

After a couple of days I got tired of all the mopping. I put her back in the wheelbarrow and took her to the barn. She had drained so much water I could push her on my own now. Even in the barn she was still spitting water. Finally I hung her up, thinking it might help. Thin rivulets streamed out of her fingers and her feet. I began to realize she had probably been drowned all this time, after all. While our resuscitative methods seemed to have worked, her breathing and even her speech weren't breathing and speech per se, so much as some kind of enteric nervous system response.

♦♦♦

Blue has been scarce. Maybe getting mothers out of wells is more exhausting than he makes it look. No one calls anymore except the telemarketers. I keep making lists and forgetting them. I make tea and forget to drink it. I stay up late worrying about my brother. I wear my grandmother's and my aunt's necklaces, but I don't think they're helping.

When I go down to check on Ma she blinks at me, or maybe I just think she is. She fingers her own necklace almost constantly, wearing away the filigree. Georgia O'Keefe's skin is nailed to the wall beside her. I think one day I will use it to make a coat for my mother. She would like a deerskin coat I think, after having spent decades down a well. The damp must have seeped into her bones something fierce.

The Lonely Planet Guide to Other Dimensions

RACHEL CLIMBED THE SECOND HALF of the dirty stairs to the upstairs hall, half-empty Tiger beer in hand. The Red Arcade Hotel, she suddenly felt, existed in another dimension. Although it didn't, not really, of course not. But it felt out of time or out of place or both, as if it was all there was to the universe and her life. No past, no future, no world at all, just this hotel and time to write. The hotelier, a young queer songwriter from Toronto called Berndt, was a big supporter of the arts. Maybe he had bought the hotel because he too, could intimate the presence of the portal even if, unlike Rachel, he didn't have the word for what it was.

Although you never knew.

Rachel knew about the portal because her fingers were tingling. She loved portals even though like menopause they caused or maybe just worsened ADHD. Portals felt prickly, like electricity, and whooshy, like white water canoeing, and delicious, like arousal or an amazing book or the first beer. She knew not to go looking. You couldn't rush a portal. Like inspiration it would come when it was ready.

She had booked a week at The Red Arcade on a self-directed residency in the hopes that the hotel would be a place where she could recapture her youth. She was broke and Berndt had told her she could swap workshops for her room rate. She didn't care about her crow's feet and laugh lines, but she wanted to be able to write like a young person, without a deadline, without tweeting about what she was working on, without rephrasing the cover letter twice after dinner. Although nowadays, maybe all young writers did those things and it was the old ones who didn't.

Her fantasy trilogy had done well enough as these things went, but she had lost part of herself along the way. She had lost the first writer, the youthful creator who loved William Burroughs and feminist science fiction and black American women writers and French symbolists, and wanted her writing to be the purest possible expression of who she was and believed that doing so made the world a better place, opening doors to spirituality and imagination in a post-capitalist world, not just for herself but for her readers.

Yeah, whatever.

Rachel unlocked her door with an actual key, instead of putting a card in a slot. The room smelled of old carpet and rotting plaster. She wrenched at the window in its wooden frame. A stick was called for, not a memory stick but the old kind of stick, the kind one threw to dogs and started fires with and used to prop windows open. Hotels like this, Rachel thought, should provide a window-propping implement. At last she thought to try an upright pencil; amazingly, it didn't snap. Rachel was relieved. It was summer, too hot to sleep without an open window in a musty old hotel with no AC. She fell into bed. There were two, both twins with godawful mattresses. She chose the opposite one from the one she slept in the night before after staying up late with Berndt talking about anarchism and music and literature. She had only slim hopes that it would be better.

Rachel closed her eyes, still thinking about writing, which of course was much different from actually writing.

At a certain point it had gone flat. She'd start something new and in no time at all the main characters became words, the settings became obvious strings of words, the plot became words. Fiction writing only ever worked when the people were real and the colours of the tea cups were as bright or brighter than the colours in this world.

She couldn't sort it. She went to sleep.

◆◆◆

The bus that travelled the coastal highway no longer made the turn into the village. It was already getting dark when Esme asked the driver to let her off at the dusty crossroads.

"Do you have anything underneath?" he asked.

She shook her head. She carried one bag, a big flowered tote, and wore only her jean jacket and a straw hat with her dress. He wouldn't need to get out and open the luggage compartment.

"You know people there."

"Sure." It wasn't actually true, unless Margit still ran the hotel. "When will you be back?" she asked. Esme knew the bus would follow the water to one more town, before looping back and making the long trip back to the city.

"I turn around here."

"It didn't used to be like that," she said, and she wondered. How did one get to the last town now, by walking? Was there any vehicular traffic? Could one hitchhike? "The bus used to go to the actual last town."

"There isn't another town."

"There was the last time I came," Esme said.

"And when was that?" the driver asked.

"Ten years ago."

"You came here ten years ago?"

"With my aunt."

"I wonder if I knew her. Not that I was driving this route then."

Esme was going to volunteer her aunt's name but then thought she had better not. You never knew what people were saying. "And where is your aunt now?" the driver persisted.

Esme picked up her bag and started down the stairs. "In town."

"This town."

"No, the last town," she said.

"No one lives there now," he said.

Not even Annielle? But suddenly Esme was afraid to ask. What could have happened?

At least he had finally admitted it existed, even if he hadn't mentioned it by name, but then neither had she.

The town renamed Dream long ago by the woman Annielle many said was crazy.

Esme climbed the rest of the way out of the bus hauling her canvas bag with the orange flowers. "Where is the hotel?" she asked from the road.

He pointed. It was the right turn as she had thought. But you had to ask—sometimes the hotel moved, especially in the summer. "It's just past the bend, that's why you can't see it."

"I was going to bring my suitcase, the one with wheels. This bag is heavy."

He shook his head. "They'd just have gotten stuck in the potholes. It's closer than you think." He hesitated. "Closer than it used to be. Sometimes we used to stay overnight. I liked that. I could have a drink with John."

♦♦♦

Rachel woke an hour after she'd gone to bed, her body vibrating like a tuning fork.

Three twenty a.m. What else could it be?

She opened her computer. Might as well grind away at her story for a while. Three twenty almost always meant not getting back to sleep at least for a couple of hours.

Turn the internet off, she told herself. *If you piss away the night on "research," Youtube and Twitter, you won't get your shitty story finished. In addition, you will miss the information oozing through the portal. Right now. As we speak. So shut the fuck up, shut the computer, pay attention.*

She had first felt the portal on the stairs, its presence making her skin prickle and her mind light up with some kind of caffeine much better than caffeine. It had taken Rachel most of her life to understand that she really could feel the presence of portals and sometimes even stick her head through them. She might have crow's feet and be afraid she'd lost her flow as a writer but being able to unequivocally identify portals was a fairly snazzy trade.

Portals were usually formed because of the confluence of various geophysical factors combining. Here, Rachel wagered, it was the high mineral content. People came to this area from all over the world to hack smoky quartz and tourmaline out of the road cuts every summer; they stumbled over big amethyst geodes just going for a stroll in the woods. There were stores and festivals catering to the phenomenon. Little did the crystal-crazed know what was actually going on around here; so few of the people who claimed to be "sensitives" ever actually were.

When Rachel next woke up it was daybreak. Was it late enough to go to the upstairs kitchen and make coffee? She was afraid of waking the young Norwegians who stayed in the top floor dorm. Like a lot of northern Europeans who were a little obsessed with the Canadian wilderness, they had come to hike in Algonquin Park. The hotel was close to the eastern gate and a good starting point.

◆◆◆

It was good to put down her bag. The walk from the corner to the hotel was less than a mile but it was hot. It was called the coastal highway but Esme hadn't actually seen the sea except briefly though the trees early in the morning.

The lobby was empty but there was a round silver bell on the desk. Esme pushed the button and waited, popping a mint from the pink cut-glass candy dish into her mouth. She immediately wished she hadn't; the mints were unwrapped, slightly dusty and sticky.

A wide curved staircase swept up to the right. Against the walls philodendrons in big pots struggled in the low light that snuck in from the windows, still shuttered to ward off the afternoon heat. Most of the woodwork was painted bright red, peeling in places. The floors were cracked black and white linoleum tile, real linoleum too from the looks of things, made out of linseed oil and not petroleum.

Margit came out from the door behind the desk, which led to a small suite she shared with her husband and their daughter. "Welcome!" she beamed. "It has been so long!"

"Yes." Esme peered. Could Margit really remember her? It seemed unlikely. Ten years were after all ten years. And she had been little more than a child when she had stayed here before. Maybe Margit was mistaking her for someone else.

"I'm Esme."

"Of course you are Esme. Who else would you be? Esme Templetree."

"Thank you, Margit. I didn't know if you'd still be here and I didn't know whether you'd remember me. You look amazing." Margit did look good. She was short and rotund, and only a little more of the second than before. Her hair still framed her pleasing face in thick dark waves.

"Oh, shush. None of us are young anymore," Margit said. "Except you and my daughter, of course."

"And how is your husband?" Esme remembered the dinner parties, the acidic white wine from Dream that her aunt had given up after it made her vomit twice in a row.

"John is passed on several years now. I don't know if you remember he was ill."

"I'm so sorry to hear, Margit. John was always kind to us."

"And our daughter—she went away." Esme didn't ask in case it was something bad. "Annielle is still here though. She looks so good for her age."

"I was afraid to ask. Of course it is my aunt I came to see. I just came to the hotel first, because I wasn't sure."

"She doesn't live here. We haven't been much in touch in a long time, not because I didn't want to be."

Esme nodded, and again she didn't ask. "I thought maybe I could stay a week, go back with the next bus. The driver doesn't go to Dream anymore. Could I hire a taxi? Some local man with a truck?"

Margit beamed. "Local woman. Jeannie goes to pick up fish and she's friendly."

"Do I know her?"

So few people lived at the bottom of the peninsula and of those who did, many, like Margit, never left. When you knew everyone it was hard to go to a place where you didn't. Hard to go to a city. Some of the young of course wanted nothing more than to run, but others—it was as if the sand itself was sticky.

"We can talk about all of this tomorrow. First I will show you to your room. You would like your old room, yes?"

"My old room?"

"You and Annielle's old room. The big one at the back."

Their room had overlooked a field full of salt grass in which a few old ribby horses munched. A corner room, with shabby furniture and tall windows on two walls, their opened shutters filling the room with light. Strange that Esme had forgotten and Margit had remembered.

"I'll help you with your bag." Margit came out from behind the desk and with a sprightly step lifted the bag.

"When does the dining room open?" Esme looked at her watch. She'd had to find one in a drawer.

"I'm sorry. My daughter had so many plans to reopen it, hire local chefs, source local food. That's why Jeannie started bringing the fish, but now it's mostly just us who eats it."

Us? Who lived in the hotel other than Margit? In the town? It seemed even more de-populated than the last time. "What do I do about dinner?" she asked.

"Sometimes I cook, but not tonight. There's a good soup

place down the street." Margit hefted the floral bag and edged it up the stairs, setting it down and resting a moment every few steps. Esme felt guilty but didn't intervene. The walk from the corner in the scorching heat had exhausted her.

A woman passed them, heading down. She carried a laptop under her arm and gave Margit only the palest of nods. She barely glanced at Esme.

"Who is that?" Esme whispered.

"She's staying across the hall from you. She's not from here."

"Who even is? It's a hotel."

"I rent a few rooms on a monthly basis. But I meant she's staying in the other hotel."

"Oh?" Esme asked.

"The hotel is a node. People from another dimension can stay here. What I mean is. The hotel exists in two dimensions at once, and in the other one it's called The Red Arcade."

They had reached the landing. "My across-the-hall-neighbour, does she have a name?"

"It's Rachel. I don't know her last name. And I can't check the register. She's booked into The Red Arcade, but she can use this hotel too. Sometimes she breakfasts with us."

"Wow," Esme said. "What a good deal."

"Yes," Margit said. "Two hotels for the price of one. It's part of why people come here. The ones who can stand it."

"I beg your pardon?"

"It makes some people a little nauseous."

"Ah. Like altitude sickness or seasickness."

"A bit."

♦♦♦

When it was light enough Rachel went downstairs to get takeout coffee at the general store across the road. On the way back she saw the charming owner standing on the steps. "Why did you choose to buy this hotel?" she asked. "There's something magic here. It's hard to explain."

She didn't tell him about the portal. Cool as he was, Berndt didn't seem ready for that message.

He stood there vaping nicotine, looking thoughtful. "How do you write the ending?" he asked, instead of answering her question.

She thought of inviting Berndt to her writing workshop, promising they'd cover that, but he probably had hotelier paperwork to do. "This morning I woke up remembering a failed story," she told him. "Sometimes I still want to go back and finish them."

"See? Endings are hard."

"Are they hard in songs too?" Esme asked. Berndt wrote beautiful songs when he could scrounge a little time for it.

"Yes. But in a song you can cheat and just reprise the chorus again."

"The story takes place in a hotel, funnily enough. Maybe that's why it's the one I looked at when I couldn't sleep. I never thought of that."

Berndt, Rachel noticed, was also drinking takeout coffee from across the road.

He noticed her glance and looked sheepish. "I'd make coffee upstairs but what if the Norwegians are light sleepers? They pay my bills after all."

Rachel nodded. "That's what I thought too. You know, I've always wondered."

"What?"

"Why is it called The Red Arcade Hotel?"

"It was called that when I bought it." Berndt said. "No one could ever tell me why. It isn't red and there are no arcades."

"You'd think someone would know," she said. "There's always a history to these old buildings."

"I know, right? Once I had a dream of red arcades, blind arcades on the outside of a building, cinder block like this one. But instead of being at the edge of the forest it was in an arid place by the sea, with a big windswept sandy yard."

Ah. So the building did have a history but only in dreams. Maybe she could use that.

Never able to construct an ending to the hotel story that satisfied her, Rachel hadn't been able to give it up either and had transferred it through decades and an entire succession of computers. She remembered where she had lived when she began the story. The apartment downstairs was empty; her friend had moved out and the new tenant hadn't moved in yet. For some reason the door was unlocked. Her musician partner Adam was out of work and so Rachel would go downstairs to write.

Maybe she liked Berndt because he reminded her of Adam. Adam with only the good parts: the charm, the talent, the finger-picking. But because they weren't involved, she could skip the bad parts. The drug abuse, the philandering, the financial drain. But maybe Berndt wouldn't have been guilty of any of those things. Except the philandering, but he'd only do that with men. It wasn't like he could pretend he didn't like men. That was what people used to do, and it caused all sorts of problems. And if it was okay with her, then it wasn't philandering.

She remembered how, on Saturday mornings, she'd force herself to stop on the second floor landing instead of going out to visit a friend or go to a café. She'd go into the apartment, empty except for one chair at the table, and slog away. There was a typewriter on the table, a Selectric with a spinning ball. You could buy spare spheres with different fonts. It seemed unthinkable now, to have physical fonts, but at the time Selectrics had seemed modern. Most typewriters back then were Courier, and that was the end of it.

Even though Rachel had struggled to stay in her chair, one of the things, other than the still unfinished hotel story she worked at that weekend, turned out better than she expected and eventually became part of a novel that she sold.

It was a good anecdote, Rachel told herself. Inspiring. Teachable. She ought to share it with her students later in the morning.

It was a different struggle now.

If she could somehow go back to that room, replete with colour and light and poetic descriptions. If she could retrieve both her stubbornness and her enchantment, maybe she could still write something good while she was here. She wanted to write for its own sake. She wanted to write something that felt like dipping a bucket into a well brimming with colours and secrets and raise it, ever so slowly, to the top.

♦♦♦

Esme woke very early and swept the leaves in the sandy yard. Her sweeping was a going away present. It was so much harder for Margit without John and their daughter helping. The bus was due today, and Margit had told her this time the driver was coming right to the door. There were passengers with hotel reservations, more than there had been in a long time, and they didn't want to drag their luggage through the potholes.

Her bag was packed and she had paid her bill. Esme was getting on the bus even though she hadn't gone to Dream with Jeannie the fish-monger, hadn't seen her aunt. Her blue dress stuck to her legs, her skin damp with sweat in the heat and now coated with a thin film of dust as well. The sand from the dunes was constantly blown across the highway by the itinerant winds.

Behind her the hotel stood, anomalous as though it was the last vestige of a town that had been razed by some catastrophe either environmental or perhaps spillover from an uprising. She had never questioned it, just as she had never questioned the hotel moving a few miles up and down the highway that everyone agreed it periodically did. Maybe the impossibility of it moving made its other oddnesses pale in comparison and so they were ignored. Why for instance did a three-storey hotel stand near a lonely crossroads with only a few scattered dwellings nearby? Why did the hotel have blind arcades on the east wall, painted and re-painted red long ago, much of the paint now scaled off by the sea wind?

Jeannie had told her she wouldn't want to see Annielle, not the way she was now. And probably she shouldn't even go to Dream. Reality wasn't stable there, maybe even a side effect of Annielle's madness, as though ripples of unreality spread out from her like waves from a stone thrown into a still pond. The fish in Dream was the best but Jeannie hardly went herself anymore. She was afraid she'd fall into a breach or get caught in a vortex and not be able to come back. The shredding was getting worse.

There had been other disappointments for Esme, including never speaking with Rachel. Esme felt the stranger was a lot like her; they were both drawn to this isolated hotel for reasons no one else would understand. She had hoped that one day Rachel would stop on the stairs and say hello.

This morning Rachel had sat with them and drunk coffee and eaten toast but she hadn't spoken much, immersed in her screen. She had wavered a little as though she was only partly there. And Esme had once again felt too shy to start the conversation.

She went inside to rest. They'd all have lunch together at the makeshift dining table they'd set up in the lobby and covered with a red checkered oil cloth to hide the splits in the wood. They'd feast on fish from Jeannie's last, and she said final, trip to the tip of the peninsula. Esme had gathered wild mint for tea, and there was grated carrot salad from the little garden in the back; carrots and peas liked the sandy soil.

On her way back upstairs she noticed a laptop on the table. The computer belonged to Rachel. Esme glanced around. There was no sign of Margit or Rachel. Esme gently opened the lid. There was text on the screen. It looked like a story or a memoir. Maybe Margit had told her Rachel was a writer. She couldn't remember.

The bus that travelled the coastal highway no longer made

the turn into the village. It was already getting dark when Esme asked the driver to let her off at the dusty crossroads.

"I turn around here anyway," the driver said. "Do you know people there?"

"Sure," Esme said. It wasn't actually true, unless Margit still ran the hotel. "The bus used to go farther. It followed the water to one more town before looping back."

"There isn't another town."

"There was when I came ten years ago with my aunt."

"Did I know her? What was her name?"

But Esme didn't say. She knew how people talked, probably now more than ever.

◆◆◆

Maybe if Rachel had written her aunt's name, Annielle would still be sane. Esme ran upstairs and pounded on her door.

Rachel opened it. She looked more solid, as though she'd brought more of herself across.

"You must write Annielle being well. Only you can do it. You must write the rifts in the fabric of reality closed."

Rachel looked honestly puzzled. "You should say tears in the fabric. It can't be a rift in fabric. A rift can appear in the clouds or the continental shelf or a relationship, but not in fabric."

Esme stared at her. Rachel didn't know the power she held in her hands.

But at least this time she saw her. Often she didn't, passing Esme on the stairs or ignoring her at breakfast as if she didn't exist. "Take me back with you," Esme said. "I need to see what your world is like. You have access to my world but I can't go to The Red Arcade." Esme felt slipshod and no-account in comparison, but maybe it was like music. Maybe if you were tone deaf no matter how much you practised you'd never be more than a mediocre singer.

"I don't know if I can take you back but we can try," Rachel said.

"After lunch. You'll come to lunch, won't you?"

She went back downstairs to help Margit cook. She knew she wouldn't get on the bus back north because everything had changed. It was a heartbreak, but to be a character in a stranger's story was so much better than not existing at all.

There was the mahi-mahi Jeannie had brought from Dream, and sautéed wild greens all three had gathered together early in the morning. Margit had discovered three dusty bottles of white wine in the back of the pantry.

"Yuck," Esme said. "Remember how it used to make Annielle throw up?"

"She was just allergic. And maybe ten years have improved it. I don't have anything else. I don't drink anymore."

When she heard the bus pull in Esme went out to meet it.

"Did you go to Dream yet?" the driver asked, opening the door.

"No, I didn't." She stepped aside so everyone could get out.

"I thought that's why you came," he said. "I thought you needed to go to Dream and see Annielle."

"You said her name. I wasn't sure you knew it."

He opened the baggage compartment for the passengers before he replied. "Everyone knows it. Even if we don't know her, we know her name."

"Everyone says she is really crazy now and that it would hurt me to see her."

"We should go in and have lunch," the driver said. "We can talk more then."

Esme's broom was lying on the ground beside the door. She picked it up and propped it against the side of the building, in the corner of an arcade. The passengers followed them inside. One dreadlocked young man with only a knapsack had preceded them and was already seated at the table.

Margit hugged the driver. "It's so nice that you came all the way. I'm so sorry."

"But why?"

"John isn't here. He passed on two years ago."

He shrugged. "We must go on, all of us."

"I need to check people in." Margit held the door open for the stragglers. "I haven't got any staff, I'm sorry."

"We'll eat first," Esme said, showing the guests to the table. "Everyone's starving."

The young man's guidebook was propped open on the oil cloth in front of him.

"In the future," he said, "Lonely Planet will include listings of destinations in other dimensions."

Esme nodded, wondering where he was from. The past or the future, here or there? In one way it didn't even matter. Maybe that's what staying here taught you.

Rachel hadn't come to lunch and Esme ran up the stairs again to knock. The door was ajar and Esme, presumptuously, poked her head in. The bed was rumpled but there was no one in it. The stranger had snuck out for a walk or she had disappeared, sucked back to her home world.

When Esme rejoined the others the driver poured her wine she sipped at desultorily and asked her where she'd been.

"There is a woman," she said. "Every day she passes me on the stairs. She's carrying a computer. She uses it to write. At first I thought she was real, but then Margit told me she's not. I mean, she is, but she's not real here. She is working on a story. And, it's about me. So, I worry. Do I only exist because she is writing me? I wanted desperately to talk to her even before I found out, I wasn't sure why. And now, I am afraid. If I go back to the city, she might forget about me. She might stop writing about me. And then..."

"Very Chuang Tzu," the young man said.

"But what if it's the opposite?" the driver asked. "What if it's we who are the originals, the writers, and she is the character. What if you are writing her writing you?"

"Maybe," Esme said. "But it's one of the reasons I'm not getting on the return bus tomorrow. Maybe next week. Rachel is looking for an ending, she said in her notes. She has worked on this story for decades and she is tired of it. But she doesn't understand. If she walks away from the story, or even if she finds an ending, then we will all die. We only live because she writes."

"You don't know that," the young man said.

"Be careful," Margit said. "You sound like her."

"Rachel?" Esme asked.

"No. Annielle before she left for Dream."

"I wouldn't be afraid to go to find my aunt if I didn't have to go alone."

"But maybe if you go to find Annielle we will all die. Isn't there another possible ending?" the driver asked.

◆◆◆

Every morning after breakfast they would read their work and share notes at a big table Berndt had set up in the cavernous bar and covered with a red cloth. On the way downstairs Rachel passed a tall blonde in a blue floral dress and frayed straw hat.

She must have just checked in, Rachel told herself. *I've never seen her here before.*

Then the woman wavered a little, and Rachel could see through her. Which was weird enough, but she also seemed incredibly familiar.

Even though vaping was legal indoors, Berndt couldn't break the habit of smoking outside. He liked standing on the little concrete porch to see who was coming and going in his town.

She told him about the apparition. "Are there ghosts here?" she asked.

Berndt said, "I've never heard of one. But you've been working hard and you haven't been sleeping well."

"How do you know?"

"People in the three-twenty club can all hear each other in the halls, back and forth, to and fro from the bathroom. My guess is the ghostly woman is somehow a part of you."

"Busted about the three-twenty club," Rachel laughed. "But I don't think she's a projection or an alter ego. While indistinct she was definitely exterior, not in my mind's eye. And she seemed familiar."

Berndt said, "Do you know Ursula LeGuin wrote about Lao Tzu and translated him? She said he was an anarchist. You can't keep working on your hotel story and you can't end it either. You've told me this more than once. This woman is the key, I'm sure of it."

"That's interesting but it doesn't help me understand what just happened."

"It's just a feeling I have, that she is the clue to your ending. Just a feeling, but a strong one. "

"Maybe it's the crystals, I don't know," Rachel said. "I forgot my laptop upstairs."

"Really?" Berndt raised a gently mocking eyebrow. "How could you forget a thing like that?"

They went back inside. Climbing the stairs to get her computer Rachel noticed the grime more than usual. She opened her door with a key, not a card, and instead of her pokey room she was in a big panelled corner room full of light. She crossed the room to look out one of the windows set into the red-painted walls. It looked out at a fenced field where skinny horses stood munching grass. Really their corral was just posts driven into a dune.

"Forget something?" a woman asked behind her.

Rachel turned. A straw hat with holes in it cast a shadow over her face but Rachel could still see that she was beautiful.

On the bed was a big canvas tote, orange flowers with stitched leather handles. "Do you like the bag?" Rachel asked idiotically. "I could change the colour. Maybe you'd like fish instead of flowers."

Esme smiled and handed her her laptop.

"How can my computer be in your room?" Rachel asked and then she laughed, a little hysterically.

"How can you see me on your stairs? Go teach your class," Esme said.

"I will. I just want to look out the window a moment longer."

The ribby horses munched grass. Rachel traced her finger along the carved woodwork around the window where the red paint peeled and peeled.

"It isn't called The Red Arcade here," Esme said at last.

"Why not?"

"The name moved across to your hotel years ago. Even though it is here that there are blind arcades on the outside of the building, painted red. The arcades are symbols. Each arcade represents a different dimension, a doorway to another hotel. Although right now there are only two. At other times there were more."

"Can you show me? I'd love to see the building from the outside."

"You already know what it looks like," Esme said.

Rachel nodded. "The front yard is mainly sand. You swept this morning, to spruce things up for when the bus comes. Leaves blow in from the trees that edge the sea."

Esme nodded. "I have to help Margit serve the lunch. The driver hasn't stayed over in years and she is so excited. Did you get all that?" she laughed.

"I think so. Can't I come to lunch too?" Rachel asked. "It feels like somewhere I've always wanted to live only I didn't know it."

"If you stay, you'll become like Annielle."

"The driver said she went mad because she left the hotel to go to Dream."

Esme shook her head. "It's the staying that makes you crazy, not the going."

"It just feels so amazing, so much like what we all long for over there. We can sense it but we can't quite touch it and it breaks our hearts."

"But you can," Esme said.

"I can what?"

"Touch it."

Esme placed her hand over Rachel's hand, still on the peeling red window frame. She exerted a little pressure.

"You feel it, yes?"

"Yes."

"Then that is what you must go back and teach."

Big Ears

JOEY WANTED TO GO HOME. He wanted to go home so bad it made his teeth ache, but home was back with Sally, balanced on a tightrope wire he didn't have the shoes for, and the thing that frightened Joey most was large and very hairy and had just taken up residence on the opposite bench. It leered, drooling. Joey tried his best to ignore it, warming his hands around his coffee cup.

Joey did not notice Rickie when she walked in. He didn't look up when she ran off a long complicated order at the take-out counter, inverting syllables like a dyslexic push-me-pull-you. Then Rickie did a Python 007 routine and slithered over to his table. She snuck in beside the drooling hairy thing, scaring it half to death. It was none the wiser for it. Those types never are.

She cleared her throat and lowered her voice as far as it would go, which was a fair distance. "I believe the Sourpuss Parade just turned left on Main Street," she said, staring him right in the eye. "It was no more than five minutes and change ago. You can still make it if you're quick."

"It isn't funny."

"It isn't? Tell me what isn't?" She did look like the sort of person who laughed a lot; a big round face nestled in large quantities of cheerful black curls.

"Me. Right now." He felt too tired and beaten for the old game: extract female sympathy for your miserable condition and go on from there. So what were his motives in telling her the truth?

"You catch on quick," she replied, "for a turtle on reds that is," and went to wait for her order.

And why was she bothering? She'd been up all night; he knew that already. The mix of beer and bennies that had propelled her this far not yet worn off; the mile a minute chatter she'd entertained her friends with all night had just enough gas left in it to spill over onto him. She didn't really care, and he didn't hold it against her. But she was cute, very cute. "All you got to do is ask," she said, coming back with an enormous paper bag. Mind reading powers as well, it looked like.

Joey spoke up, pride notwithstanding. "Okay, okay, I'm asking."

Rickie gave him a Camel filter. "When you're finished you can have one of these." She reached into the bag and brought out a cheeseburger.

"That's a pretty good hat trick," he admitted, lighting the cigarette greedily, "considering when I ate last."

"It is," she boasted, "although I know a few others."

"It shows," he said. Joey wastefully put out his Camel only half smoked and carefully unwrapped his burger, took an enormous bite. It tasted almost as good as a brand new reed would have, for his exiled saxophone. Almost.

Half the burger gone, the drooling hairy thing shrank a little, its ugly grimace distending into an almost smile, appeased by Rickie's gifts. Joey managed to ask, "Where're you having so much fun, anyway?"

She gave him the card to a private club, and he asked, because she seemed more than just a club kid, what she played, and she said, "I just sing, but I'm learning the guitar, although I haven't taken it on stage yet. But it's a cool place; Mojo comes every Thursday, and you should come."

"What makes you think I'm a player?"

"I've seen your picture in the trade papers, Joey."

"You mean you read?"

She rolled her eyes, pulling the card away, but Joey took it back and put it in his pocket.

Mojo. Mojo's first derivative world beat recording had sustained a moderate success, and Joey felt bitter. If he went to this place, Joey guessed, he'd be surrounded by musicians ten to fifteen years younger, and a few of them, like Mojo, who was white, would have better club dates and recording contracts under their belts than he'd ever had, even with his twenty years of dues. He thought he wouldn't show. "I'd love to come," he said, surprising himself, "but my best lady's in hock, and I wouldn't want to show with a lesser companion."

"How much?" she asked.

"Seventy-five bones," he replied wearily, wiping cheeseburger grease off his chin.

She did something miraculous then. Reached into her jeans pocket, and pulled four crumpled twenties off a roll. "Here," she said, "don't spend it at the bar. Show by eleven. By sun-up you'll have enough to pay me back."

He took the card out again. The Rainbow Bridge. Prop: Carlos Cienfuego. "You mean you actually get paid at this place?" He was revealing everything now, and to a girl who couldn't be more than twenty-eight. So much for sounding older, wise, cooler than hell. But she seemed the one with all the wisdom this morning. Maybe they're like that now, he marvelled.

"Ten dollar cover at the door, and people come, because the music's real good and doesn't stop till morning. At least some nights it's real good."

He stared at her. "How come you got so wise?"

"I want to get to heaven," she said. "You have to save one life. That's the entry fee, I heard."

"I knew there was a catch."

"Don't screw up," she said, as if only now, the first daylight streaming in the front windows, could she see how broken he really was. She left in a hurry, crashing into the door on her way out, sounding like a platoon of armadillos wearing rings on their fingers and doorbells on their toes.

He hated her for just a second: a girl, afraid he might embarrass her. Didn't she know who he was? But she did. It was why she'd invited him. And why she was afraid.

And he walked across town in the snow to save the bus fare, brought his beauty home, bought a loaf of bread and a jar of peanut butter at the Latino convenience store on the ground floor of his Avenue C walk-up with the leftover five dollars. He practised for four hours before he ate and went to sleep, and when he played that night at Carlos's he didn't embarrass Rickie at all. He'd completely forgotten the rush of applause; he'd done only session work for so long. Jingles. But this was real.

♦♦♦

After they'd made music four nights a week for a fortnight his landlord turfed him out for non-payment, and Rickie, reading his mind again, invited him to share her First Avenue one bedroom, use the fold-out. How foolishly idealistic the young are, he thought. How does she know I won't screw up my share of the rent, won't come on to her, won't deal heroin out of her crib? Rickie stared into his eyes, still too knowing, said, "Because I believe in music. Because you're not as good as you used to be."

"No, I'm not," he answered, ready to call his old supplier, have her come to the apartment while Rickie was out at work, make indiscreet phone calls, leave the bathroom full of needles and bent blackened spoons.

"No," she said. "You're not as good as before. The last two nights you were better. Whatever happened to you, and I know it wasn't good, you've finally turned it into something good. I'm just a girl who believes, but you're a real musician."

It was true, he thought. "I believe too," he said.

And she said, "Of course you do. Why else would you have stayed in the game so long? Not gone into real estate, software, whatever?"

Could be I wasn't good for anything else, he thought, but agreed instead. "Whatever. But you know too much."

"Only when I've been singing," she replied.

And they went to Orchard Street and shopped for sheets for the pull-out, and he thought perhaps she'd teach him to love New York all over again. "Get an extra set," she said, "for your beastie." She leaned down to pet it but it snarled, snapping at her fingers. He winced, full of remorse. Why did it have to follow him everywhere, looking like that?

But Rickie only said, "I've never met anyone who has one before. I've heard of them of course, seen them on TV, but I've never met a real person who's got one. Even Mojo."

No kidding, he thought, you can't be a copy-cat and expect an animal to come to you, but said instead, "I know you don't have one, I would've seen it by now. But don't you ever feel one waiting for you, wanting to come?"

"I dream of a bird sometimes. It's golden and very beautiful."

"Dream more," he said, and looked at his creature in shame, dragging her peeling yellowed talons along the cement. She hadn't always looked like this.

He remembered the beginning, when he'd first moved here, when it had meant so much to live in the East Village. Meant everything; that he'd honed his craft so lovingly he had a creature to prove it, a beautiful gryphon with yellow eyes who sat behind him when he played. That had been worth more than gold. He looked at Rickie. That must be what she felt like still, waiting patiently for her animal, calling it with her passion, her attention, her discipline. Life's biggest dream was about to happen to her. That anyone could still feel like that. His monster drooled and shuddered beside him, shedding feathers and fur. He wished he could kill it, start all over. But of course it didn't work that way.

◆◆◆

Three months into their arrangement a girl came to the door when Rickie was at her four night a week waitressing gig. Pale pale face, short dark hair, a hollow wooden look. Rickie was such a survivor, so efficient and competent, he'd forgotten there was another kind of girl, this kind. Stick figure, bird bones, puppet. Marionette, he thought, who's pulling the strings? And then wondered at the thought, its flash of unasked-for intuition. He checked to see if she had an animal. She didn't, unless it was very small, hiding in a pocket. She stared right back, looking past him at his monster who'd come skulking down the stairs after him. A bag of feathers and fur, matted, shedding.

The girl asked for Rickie, but Rickie was at work, and Joey too had to leave to record his tracks for a jingle, so he couldn't invite her in for coffee, not that he wanted to.

"What should I tell her?" he asked.

"Just say Phoebe dropped by," the girl said. "We're real good friends," but Joey had never heard Rickie mention any Phoebe.

"You come back some other time," he said, hoping she wouldn't. Phoebe sighed heavily, as though he was such a drag not to invite her up, stared past him, slyly, at his creature, smirked.

He shut the door in her face, hating himself again for being so old, for knowing too much in a different way than Rickie did, Rickie whom he owed rent. He hated himself for his cynicism, but knew without a doubt that friends like this didn't come to the door unless they wanted something: food, a share of the stash, a place to stay, money. He knew he was being unfair, but he'd been around too long not to peg the type when he saw it. He'd had that look himself, for over a decade, frightening people, or arousing their contempt. Probably still had it. Only Rickie had seen through to something else, a brightness buried deep within, almost winked out. Maybe he was an alley cat, protecting his turf, jealously guarding Rickie's generosity for himself. What if Rickie kicked him out, invited Phoebe to share the flat instead? Those cat eyes, he could feel them staring through the door even as he climbed the stairs. Telling him he wasn't an alley cat at all; no, he was a monster. Had to be: he had one, didn't he?

A street door that locked. Windows that didn't look at an air shaft. That's what First Avenue did for you, even if it was a cheap rent control she'd paid key money for, borrowed from her parents. Sally was still in the one Joey had had. Heat that worked. Three months and he still couldn't get used to it. It had been years. He thought he wouldn't mention the girl.

He didn't tell, but Phoebe showed up when he was out, and Rickie home. And when he got in, Phoebe was asleep on what he'd come to think of as "his" sofa bed, blue shadows in the white sheets, under her eyes. He sighed and slept on the floor. In the morning, when Phoebe was still asleep, and Rickie had just gotten in from Carlos's, she said, "You take the bedroom tonight, it's only got a twin. I'll share the pull-out with her."

And he wanted to say, it's because she was here I didn't show up at the club. I was afraid she'd rob you, friend or no. I know her type too well. I was one, but at least I got an animal first. But Rickie stared at him with a look that said, it's my apartment and that's the end of it, and so Phoebe stayed.

♦♦♦

Phoebe would come to Carlos's too. She always sat alone, a shadow in shadowy corners, drumming her hands impatiently on the table, scowling at anyone who tried to join her. Sometimes he thought she'd melt, disappear, and sometimes she did: disappear for an hour, come back darker, more shadowy still. He'd pay for her beer without knowing why. She'd make cat eyes at him. He'd wonder what she was thinking. With Rickie always reading his thoughts he'd come to think of communication that way: fluid, easy. But Phoebe was the other kind of girl. You didn't know, and she didn't tell. It made you want to know. It was her game. He'd be angry, and then he'd remember. All his games, and bring her a second beer so she wouldn't have to ask. Rickie always spent her breaks sitting with her, happy she'd come. He couldn't figure it.

She worked in a St. Mark's Place vintage clothing store, making minimum wage. This wreaked havoc with her newly acquired Rainbow Bridge hours, and, she confessed she sometimes took naps on the old blue velvet couch that was part of the store's decor, on slow afternoons. He wondered she wasn't fired when she told him that, but Rickie said her window displays were the best, and he had to admit they were darkly hip.

Every so often, if it was promising to be a lame night at Carlos's, and neither Rickie nor Joey had work they stayed home instead, talking into the early hours.

Somehow long detailed conversations required the presence of all three: they never happened otherwise. Once when Phoebe went out, visiting friends she said, Joey finally asked.

"You never mentioned her before she showed up."

Rickie swigged her Coors, sorted seeds, stared at him. "Mention me one good friend you told me about."

"Of mine?" He was flabbergasted. "I don't have any. I pissed them all away."

"So make one out of her."

"She's not like you. She's not together. She has no drive, no passion."

"She cooks and cleans," Rickie said. "She's an amazing cook." He shrugged, wondering why Rickie suddenly thought these were important; she lived on take-out and dry-cleaning.

"We never used to stay in and talk till she came. I didn't even know you. You just lived here, and we played music together."

"We're not friends?" he asked, astonished. He thought they'd been so close.

"Of course we are." She gave him her signature comradely hug, said, "but people have different qualities. Why shouldn't I have a friend who isn't brilliant, talented? She starts the conversations about life, feelings. Something you and I never bother to do."

"We don't have to," he said. "We have music."

"Don't ever let her know you think she's nothing. Talking is communication too. We're just not very good at it."

"No," he said, "we're musicians, naturally telepathic."

"Right," Rickie said. "Remember you telling me once why Sally said she left you. Something about no talking? Maybe we should learn. Maybe Phoebe will teach us."

"She doesn't talk to me. It's only when we're all three together."

"Nobody's perfect."

"S'pose not," he said, relenting. But he thought, you don't know what she's really like. And then: but you took me in, and you weren't wrong. At least not yet.

♦♦♦

It was all right when Rickie was there, making a bridge between them. But when he was alone with Phoebe they prowled around one another; those were the times the one bedroom felt too small. Phoebe would do her nails yet again, a new shade of green, and answer in monosyllables when Joey tried to make conversation, draw her out. She'd laugh, as if it was pointless, the effort at talking. He asked her once what she wanted from life and she said, "I like it, I like my job, I know it doesn't pay well but I like old clothes."

"What else?" he asked.

"I used to really like math."

"What else d'you like?"

"I like music."

"You don't want to play, though?"

"Not everyone plays. I don't have talent." She glared at him, sneered at his monster. Who'd want talent, she was thinking. He could tell.

"The years'll go by, you have to have something you care about, some way to get ahead, make progress."

"I like my life," she said. "What's wrong with just living?" She stared at him as if she thought he was very very old to have forgotten this. She looked at her watch. "Time to go to the club. You'll be late. The others are expecting you." She scooped his creature off the floor, handed it to him. It looked like a winged rat, but he was grateful it was small tonight. She looked spiteful. "Forgetting something?" And it was true, he'd rather leave it home, if it were only possible. It was embarrassing having it sit next to him on stage, so ugly.

♦♦♦

She shrugged too much. He should've known. You only shrug that much if there's a payoff: the secret comfort, the thing that matters, makes the other things not matter. Shruggable.

Carlos's, being private, got away with a unisex john and that was the night Joey saw the needle imperfectly hidden under damp paper towels in the waste basket under the sink. He confronted her. And she stared at him, her eyes huge, purple shadowed. "Big deal," she said. "It wasn't mine." And he left it at that, having no proof.

♦♦♦

He wasn't sleeping with either of the women. Sally was years over by now, and while there'd been women since, none of them had been real. If he got involved with Rickie, it would have to be real, she'd stand for nothing less. And if he got involved with Phoebe, it wouldn't be real, and he'd chance blowing his friendship with Rickie.

He smiled at himself: the things you knew at forty you hadn't at thirty. If only he'd been so circumspect with Sally. And now he was living with two women, and not doing either of them. Hard to figure. In time he'd even stopped being hopelessly aroused by their long sexy if unshaven legs propped on the coffee table, balancing coffee cups. He wondered if they'd known.

He wasn't in love with either of them. It was more as if he was in love with their life, and it was something about being three: just one and he knew the inevitable outcome. Two were safer. When they weren't working or at Carlos's, they spent their time watching old black and white movies on television at two am, eating Phoebe's incredible sandwiches, doing crossword puzzles or reading in the big perpetually messy bed. He'd never had female roommates before, not without being romantically involved. It was like a revelation to him, what girls were like when they lived together. He got to listen to them talk about clothes and make-up; Rickie'd never revealed that side to him.

Sometimes he woke in the morning with a strange, sickly, unfamiliar sensation. At first blink he'd figure it for a hangover and then he'd realize it was hope. Joey felt he'd been given a reprieve. He was forty-two, and the girls were in their late twenties, even Carlos only thirty-one. One day, he suspected, it would be over and he'd have to reassume his real age. Plodding towards middle-aged failure.

He wanted to warn Rickie, protect her. So few made it, in spite of talent or hard work, or even an animal, and she hadn't one yet, not one that he'd seen. Why not?

Why was it taking her so long to grow a creature? They were the only true solace; they made everything possible. His, for instance, was busy pulling the stuffing out of their only arm-chair, spreading it over the carpet in an even unvacuumable static coating.

"Have a back-up," he said. "Not cocktailing, even if you're in a good place, the tips are good. Go to school for something more practical than music, more worthwhile than waitressing. Have continuity, friendships or partners that last for years and years."

All the things I didn't do, he wanted to add, but Rickie, as always, already knew the unspoken things. She walked over to his creature, picked it up, put it in his arms.

"Be kind to her," she said, but the gryphon bit his ear. Maybe he'd give it to Phoebe. If only he could. Where was she?

But he knew.

Out.

◆◆◆

He lived with them with great pleasure, feeling each day a little more healed, knowing still it wasn't really his life, but theirs. Or Rickie's. Phoebe he knew had already given herself up to the shadows, just making a good secret of it. And who was he to judge?

One day when she was leaving he asked, "Where are you going?"

"To the racetrack."

"Isn't that a euphemism for your dealer?"

She smiled, seemingly not taking offense. He'd never seen her smile. "Actually not."

"Yeah, right."

"Come see for yourself then, if you're so sure."

He had nothing else to do, so he put on his coat and accompanied her on the subway, all the way to Queens. They drank ice cold beer and chatted. Phoebe read the racing forms with a determined focus that startled Joey, and moreover won sixty dollars, which wasn't bad considering. Perennially broke, her original stake had only been ten.

"I'm impressed," he said, meaning it.

"You can't go to off track," she explained earnestly. "It's not the same thing. You have to see the horses, the jockeys; if you look at them carefully you can see whether it's a good day for them or not. But mostly you have to be very analytical: judging, weighing, measuring everything."

"Analytical," he said on the ride home. "What a concept."

He was careful not to sound snide, but she only said, "Thanks for coming with me, Joey. It's more fun when you're not alone."

"Isn't everything?"

It seemed she liked it that he was impressed. She went more often, dragging him along when he wasn't busy. She took to bringing the racing form home and studying it for hours, pointedly, in front of him. So much for thinking she didn't care whether he lived or died. She stopped cleaning up after them, stopped doing their laundry. At least her incredible Italian sandwiches didn't stop.

There were fewer needles in the bathroom suddenly, the needles that he always hid before Rickie came home, the ones Phoebe had been too gone to hide.

"One junkie always knows another," she said. "You stopped; I'll stop. Just let me do it my way; please don't tell Rickie. Remember when no one could tell you anything?"

She didn't say, "not even Sally." Rickie would have said that, but Joey was grateful Phoebe didn't, thought it showed a remarkable discernment, a finely discriminating tact. He even forgot to think it was more game. And so he conspired in her secret with her, and prayed no harm would come to any of them because of it. It went against his better instincts, but it was all he could do. Her big shadowy eyes: *give me this one chance.* And Rickie had given him that chance, and so he couldn't say no.

He remembered what Rickie had said, that first morning, when he'd asked why she was bothering with him. *To get to heaven, you have to save one life. It's the entry fee.* He'd thought she was being facetious, but now it gave him pause. Phoebe's sandwiches were delicious, but food for thought is the best kind. He took the trash out often, and went so far as buying Phoebe needles so she'd use new, and clean. He didn't think that was what it would take, to save her life, but it was all he could come up with. Buying time.

But now there were horses in Phoebe's life, and fewer syringes in the trash. She emerged a little from the shadows. He thought it was the winning, which she did often, in small amounts, but she laughed when he called her a gambling junkie. "I like winning," she said. "It's a reward, but it's the figuring I really like."

He remembered again when she'd shyly admitted that in high school she'd loved math, as though, in their musicians' crowd, it was something to be ashamed of. And it was true; it was so foreign to him it was as if he hadn't heard her. And now, some nights when she got that slippery look again, as though she was going to disappear, make phone calls in alleyways, he'd get off stage, apologize to Carlos, take her by the arm and say, "Let's go. We're going to the races."

♦♦♦

Mojo asked him to lay sax tracks for his new CD, said it would be an honour.

Joey was astounded, and Rickie laughed at him. "You really haven't a clue, have you?"

"A clue?"

"We all think it's an honour. You're one of the best."

"People my age don't think that," he said, grateful for her all over again.

"Fuck 'em," she said. "We need you."

"Maybe you just haven't seen me screw up real bad."

"Oh," she said charmingly, "but you're reborn now. You're over all that, whatever it was."

He'd never told her. She didn't know. He was amazed at her faith in him. She didn't know how tempted he was. Phoebe. A door that swung two ways. What if he only threw out Phoebe's needles so he could handle them again, a tiny illicit thrill? It would be so easy to fall, such a comfort.

Then he realized if he fell, he might fall alone, for Phoebe was changing, or just showing him more of her hidden good side. They all went to the recording studio together, and Mojo, who loved to play but had only learned MIDI because you had to, was struggling with the code, grinding his teeth in frustration. And Phoebe leaned over his shoulder, took the pencil from his hand and scribbled down a new version.

Mojo stared from under his dreadlocks, blinked.

"That's it, Phoebe. How'd you do that?"

"I don't know, really. I went out with a guy who understood MIDI, and I paid attention, a bit."

Mojo looked at Joey, dumbstruck. "So much for Phoebe as the junkie groupie," he said later, when the girls were out getting food.

"So much for. Not that she ever slept with me; isn't that part of that particular package?"

"Me either," Mojo said a little wistfully, and Joey had to suppress a laugh. He'd cut off his own dreads around the same time white kids like Mojo started growing them, but he liked him in spite of himself.

"She should go to school, stop wasting her brains."

"And her veins."

"That too."

So Mojo knew. But he was pretty sure Rickie still didn't.

♦♦♦

Sometimes, coming home from an ecstasy-stained midnight tour of Carlos's club, they'd fall asleep, all three, fully clothed on the pull-out. As had just happened. But Rickie woke again, got up alone. The peace of it. She looked at Phoebe and Joey, curled around one another, her hand sheltering his cheek. Joey's rough years vanished when he slept. And Phoebe wasn't old enough for hers to show, not that Rickie knew much about them, had always loved her friend too much to see the shadows that were drawn to her, collecting at her feet like black puddles. She rearranged the duvet, pulling them down where Joey's long feet emerged like curious platypi. Spring had come, and with it the heat prematurely turned down as always. The dawn chill had set in.

She re-boxed the coloured felt pens that Phoebe used, with a complicated system of colour coding that neither she nor Joey understood, to annotate her racing sheet. She replaced Joey's sax into its case. She liked that Joey played with her, thought she was good enough now, on her guitar. And the few older musicians in the city's club circuit who occasionally dropped in at The Bridge no longer treated her like a flighty wannabe. She knew, too, that the session guys gave her points for trying to pull Joey together, when they'd turned away, frightened or angry, contemptuous or apathetic. So many lose everything in this town.

It had all seemed easy that morning: being funny, giving him Carlos's card.

She'd just wanted to play with him. Was honoured by the thought. Didn't know his peers stayed away from him as if he had the plague. She hadn't even thought he'd show up, especially in light of that risky eighty-dollar loan. After all, she was just a girl who couldn't play, and he was a small legend, a firefly.

Did she want him, she wondered? Did Phoebe? They'd discussed it and both agreed that while he grew more attractive with each day that he cheered up, he was too good a friend to risk losing as a lover. And really, his heart was still Sally's. One day she'd have to ask about Sally. Some people just never got over a person.

She pulled on her boots and her coat, closed the door softly behind her, heard the lock click into place, walked towards her river.

In the street everything was dawn grey, the pigeons and the newspapers, even the sky, now. When she reached the water it was grey also. She knew it was dangerous, walking alone to the East River at dawn, past burned out tenements, but she never felt threatened. She loved it. It was her most church-like moment.

◆◆◆

When she got back they were already gone. Rickie set up the mike stand in the middle of the floor. She plugged it in and turned on the tape deck, playing back her previous attempt from what was, after all, only three days before. She listened carefully, and could name the place where her voice lost its resonance, where her gut drew back and hesitated. When the song was finished she fast-forwarded to Joey's new instrumental track, the cries of his saxophone, Carlos's punctuating drums. She switched over to the voice track and touched the record button; the familiar little red light went on. She listened to the music, feeling for an opening, hoping for her bird to flutter from her throat—a strange bird she'd seen, alone, three times. She'd been afraid to tell, even Joey. What if it didn't stay? Its moods were still too unpredictable. Perhaps if she made her bird feel welcome it would visit more often. Her voice grew and filled the confines of the small room, as her song rose and fell, then something larger grew from behind, pressing her voice outward, expanding it even more. It was that something she could never explain nor define, that fleeting spirit of her music. Her voice would always, she knew, be her first and best instrument. The guitar was just so the guys wouldn't make fun of her, call her just a singer.

The bird sang into the room, and with its appearance Rickie suddenly knew what the other two were thinking, food shopping at Phoebe's favourite Little Italy stores, far across town. Joey was trying to shrink his monster as usual, and his shame made her feel a brief sudden hatred, a flare of it. What was the point of trying to make his creature small if it was still so ugly?

Gryphons were supposed to be large, proud, beautiful. She knew then that his monster was her bird transformed. He'd drowned his gryphon so long it had died, been reborn earthbound, ugly. His muse transformed, darkened, grown teeth and hair and misshapen.

That was when he'd become a drunk, when he'd given up the needle. It hit her like a truck. How could she not have seen it? It wasn't like he hadn't hinted enough times. She hung around with musicians half her waking hours and thought they spent their time eating pie. So focused on the music she never even noticed all the attendant lifestyle pitfalls. Carlos could murder his mother under her nose and she'd say, "Good solo, dude." A fresh faced kid from Ithaca, that's what she was. Unspeakably naive.

Her bird, she knew, was so shy because it was terrified of his monster, terrified it would be drowned by proximity: stained, destroyed. "But what if you can heal?" she asked. "What if?"

And the bird said, "I'm not strong enough."

And Rickie said, "Oh, but birdie, you might have to be."

It was about Sally. Six years they'd been married, Joey promising he'd quit. And finally when he gave it up she'd left anyway, too tired. And he'd reached for the bottle, replacing one comfort with another. It only happened when Rickie sang, that she could know like this, so richly and full of detail, and she was as always both afraid and full of wonder.

And birdie said, "Sing more."

◆◆◆

Rickie, in homage to the first summer heat was wearing a white strapless dress. She removed the huge white flower from the tiny cut glass vase on the club table to tuck behind her ear.

"Very Billie," Joey said admiringly, wishing he remembered what kind of flower she'd worn.

"Who's Billie?" Rickie asked, and Joey groaned. What was the world coming to? Rickie was mixed race but she was a small town girl whose parents probably listened to Belafonte. Or Zep. But what had it been? A camellia? A gardenia? One of the facts he'd once known, dissolved by heroin, by alcohol. Or just aging, if he was kinder to himself. Or even, if he was kinder still, simply for lack of use. Use it or lose it. Our lady of the flowers, he thought, our lady of sorrows. Suddenly he knew what this girl needed, what to offer her next, in his unofficial role as her musical educator.

Yet how long was it since he himself had thought much about the blues, his first love, the one that had compelled him, at seventeen, to pick up a saxophone unlike his white friends who, listening to Zep, had saved up their pennies for Strats? And Rickie had more range then she knew. Range she'd yearn for if she listened to the greats.

A midtown west side bar. It was an open mike night they'd gone to, promising friends. The bar was still almost empty so Joey got up on stage and did Strange Fruit, just on his sax.

"What is that?" Rickie asked when he came back. The usual wannabes were shuffling in, complete with their built in audience of girlfriends, boyfriends, roadies, and partners in crime. But Joey went up first, before the manager had even had time to write down a lineup. Joey could do that; he knew the guy forever. Sometimes having been around the block a few times was still an advantage.

And Rickie came up this time too. He began the haunting song again, she reached for words that didn't come; she didn't know them. But the music called for song and so she let her voice out; a vocal improvisation made not of words but of sound. Her voice was a bird let loose in the room, and they could all see it then, a bird golden and black.

"What's with this eagle?" Phoebe asked herself, softly so it wasn't heard above the music, all alone at their table under the stage. There were no other creatures in the room, except Joey's, snivelling and drooling. Phoebe winced, couldn't help but compare. Rickie's eagle was golden, shining so bright it hurt their eyes, swinging under the lighting before it headed out to the darkness of the barn-like room. Wanting room to soar. As though it could, here. And Phoebe knew at that moment what Rickie would become, felt exquisitely pained by it.

His monster's gotten smaller the last few months, she thought, and he drinks a little less; somehow we've been a good influence on him. It curled at his feet, seemingly warming him, almost kindly. Phoebe knew from having shared the sofa bed that Joey's feet could use a little warming, were ice cold even in summer. And clearly Joey was good for Rickie too. If his gift to Rickie had been her voice, could he extract a like miracle from her? As if there might be a genius worth a creature hidden within; it was too good and too hopeless a dream to consider. She looked at Joey's monster again to remind herself what little use talent was, but at that moment it was beautiful, its yellow eyes blinking. It was being fed, was already a little larger. She'd have sworn it was purring, as if she could hear it above their music.

But supposing she could have a creature, what would it be? Not everyone needs to hack an arty muse; some people were more inclined to be logicians. I wouldn't have a bird, Phoebe thought, I'd have scissors. Scissors. What kind of creature is that? Something toothy, can make nice clean cuts, discriminate. Perhaps a lizard of some sort, or a big cat. But that's always been for other people. The bright lights, the smart ones, the ones who know who they are. Not for people like me.

Her friends were still on stage, jamming Strange Fruit. The bird circled the room, its wingspan three feet now. Phoebe thought, how will she ever fit it back in her mouth, and laughed at herself. She stared from Rickie to her golden bird, a mixture of pride and envy. I think I'm happy in this scene but heroin eats more musicians than it lets go. Phoebe snagged the waiter walking past; he set down eight drafts. She wanted the refreshments there for Rickie and Joey when they got back down. Her train of thought was making her lonely.

Rickie and Joey were finished now, and the room filled with applause. More than Rickie had ever had. She turned to Joey and hugged him, tears in her eyes. The applause was for both of them, and she couldn't have done it without him. How she loved this man, who could make such a thing with her. A golden bird. A healed gryphon. A room full of hands clapping. Music.

"Billie paid for your sins so you wouldn't have to repeat them," Joey said pointedly when he sat back down. "I've seen it too often. You're too smart to waste. Not that I expect you to listen to an old man," and Phoebe noticed a glimmer of understanding in Rickie's eyes. But she didn't want Rickie to know, not yet.

"How d'you like her Billie then?" Phoebe asked to change the uncomfortable subject.

"Unconventionally brilliant," Joey remarked. "But then what could one expect from a woman like that?"

"But Mr. Joey, you've got big ears," Rickie said, "always have had."

"It's Rickie who's got the big ears," Joey said. "She can hear people think, especially, she says, when she's singing."

"Now there's an unusual talent," Phoebe said mildly.

"The street eats hangers-on even faster than musicians," Joey said, back on track and Phoebe winced again.

"Perhaps," she said, mostly just to placate him, "I should study computers, make a new kind of instrument, never been done."

But Joey looked more than interested, said, "Logician, magician. I want to see this instrument of yours; my fingers are getting arthritic. You know Rickie, even if you're a rocker born and bred, you'll only get better by having learned them. Billie, Sarah, Aretha, the rest, the best."

"But you already told me all that on stage," Rickie laughed, "with your saxophone and much more eloquently. Why bother with English?"

Phoebe stared at his fingers. "You never said."

"No."

"Did you really used to be a junkie, Joey?" Rickie asked and Phoebe thought with huge relief, it's not me she's guessed about at last, but him. Still she wanted to run away, to hide, to hit up in the bathroom. Anything to make the shame go away.

But Joey winked at her, comforting, promising silence all over again, said blithely, "Mojo told you that? Now you won't like me anymore."

Rickie asked, "What's it like?" and Phoebe was so grateful

for his foot beneath the table brushing hers.

"Better than Billie," he whispered. "The only thing."

"Why did you stop then?"

"Why d'you think? For just that reason. Better than Billie. At first I thought it fed my music but in not too long it was bigger; it ate my marriage, ate my music, shamed my animal, yet still seemed like the only thing. One day you wake up and realize maybe your woman, your proud creature, and your work were more important after all, that you chose the lesser thing. Seems obvious I know."

Phoebe remembered that comfort went both ways, reaching out to pat his hand with its swollen joints. How could she not have noticed? She was so selfish; he'd noticed her secret, as careful as she thought she'd been, and kept it for her. This was a different kind of shame, these distended knuckles. Why not share a thing like that? It was the shame of growing old.

Joey reached for the last beer, and Rickie thought again how he'd replaced one comfort with another. We all drink but there's a difference in the way he does it. Desperately. "Here's your friend, miss," he said, and there it was. Rickie's voice, shrunken to pigeon size, settled on her shoulder. It cooed and billed her cheek, glittering.

"And yours, sir," Phoebe picked up the winged mouse, proffered it in her outstretched hand. He nuzzled it briefly and tucked it in his jacket.

"I've never seen it so friendly," Phoebe said. "But it should be bigger."

"Will be," Joey said. "If Rickie lets me go with her where she's going. Only small now so it can ride home in my pocket."

"Of course you're coming," Rickie said, still brimming with elation. "I won't get there unless you come too. I'll remember this night for the rest of my life."

Management locked the door on the last club kid and came over to chat, but Joey wasn't up to it, not tonight. "Okay ladies, let's hit the road."

On the street, walking towards Seventh Avenue to catch a Checker downtown, Joey linked one elbow through Rickie's and one through Phoebe's. And Phoebe, meaning it this time, said, "I'd give almost anything for an animal of my own. As original as Phoebe's bird, as persevering as your gryphon mouse. It's hard to tell what shape it's going to settle into, Joey, now that it's not a monster anymore."

"I think a gryphon mouse is a monster," he said. "There's benevolent monsters too, you know. Benign demons. For some people nothing less than a monster will do. Something with teeth."

"Or scissors. Perhaps a dragon," Phoebe said, wondering.

"There's only one way for you to find out what your creature might be, and you know what it is."

"What?" Rickie asked and Phoebe kicked Joey in the shin and he laughed, but still she wondered what her choice would be and knew for the first time it would never be any easier, that she would always be standing on exactly this fulcrum, this moment. She might never grow a creature, be able to call its strength and beauty to her, but she had to try. What else was there? Even Rickie, who seemed so enviable, stood always at this same crossroads, choosing, choosing, again and again and again. There was no other place, ever, not in Manhattan, or on all of Earth. Only this one locus, this one choice. Whether to desecrate one's light or shine it.

A Room of His Own

CASSIDY WAS RIVETED BY HIS HANDS. They were trying to disengage what looked like yellow gauze from the torn screen of the door to her new potting shed. He was picking at the gauze with those long fingers, at once sensual and gnarled, an expression of great intentness and some worry creasing his long handsome face. She thought perhaps it was his favourite scarf. She herself might wear just such an expression if her favourite scarf, a fine purple silk brought from Rome by her sister Mara, had caught on a protruding nail.

But how had the screen torn in the first place? It looked like he'd been trying to break into her new shed, tearing the screen to unlock the door from the inside. It served him right for catching his scarf on the snags. It had taken Cassidy so long to get the shed in the first place. She re-potted plants in it, and kept her gardening tools neatly organized. Henry had little use for trowels and spades and cultivators and wasn't likely to pinch and then lose them.

"Could you help?" the man asked. He had a low fluty voice; it sounded a little foreign.

Cassidy began to unhook the yellow gauze from the tiny, clawed metal ends of screen. He made a face when she did that, and twisted his entire body quickly. Cassidy saw his back then, saw how the yellow gauze was attached to his shoulder blade. How the other shoulder had a matching scarf, this one draped magnificently over his arm, almost alight. Not moving but capable of movement, she was sure.

She unhooked ten or twenty tiny metal ends of torn screen from the yellow gauze. She thought he might have nerve endings there, and so she was as careful as could be, as if removing slivers from a young child's tender feet. Not that she knew much about that.

The stranger craned his neck; trust in his pale grey green eyes. Puce, his eyes are puce coloured, Cassidy thought, using a decorating word from one of her magazines. He moaned a little, and turned back around. Perhaps it had hurt him to face her, twisting the yellow gauze that was heavily veined as if by the finest of tendons, the softest of cartilage. More like a bird or a bat than a butterfly.

At last he was free. "Mind if I stay here for a couple of days?" he asked. "I can't quite leave yet."

"Shall I bring you food?" Cassidy asked.

"A bit of honey might be nice," he said. "Otherwise I can graze."

"Graze?"

"Not like a cow," he said. "More like a hummingbird or a bee."

"Oh," Cassidy said. "I'll look for honey and if we're out I'll buy some."

He nodded. "Unpasteurized if you can find it."

And Cassidy went back to the house and read decorating magazines. There was nothing wrong with their house that several thousand dollars wouldn't fix, but now that they were semi-retired, they needed to hold on to their savings.

"This dresser," she told Henry when he emerged from his basement, "would look quite nice with a coat of white or palest yellow."

"Or puce," Henry said.

"Why puce?"

"It's a funny word, that's all," Henry said. "Like chartreuse. What colour is chartreuse again?"

"A kind of yellow-green," Cassidy replied to Henry's back. He was already receding, having poured himself fresh coffee. Soon she'd hear his footsteps on the basement stairs. He was refurbishing old tube radios. The tubes were dangerous to work with, he'd once explained. He mostly did it to occupy his time, and because he enjoyed it. Luckily, because his skill was rare he was occasionally paid nicely. He only worked in the hardware store a couple of afternoons a week now, doing the ordering and such.

"And a vase of fresh flowers," Cassidy said to no one in particular.

She'd meant to spend the day in the potting shed drawing. She'd recently bought a good sketchbook and watercolours, and real coloured pencils, not the cheap ones children used. She'd had to drive forty minutes each way, because Brookside only had a crafts store. The art supplies store in Stony Creek boasted a little espresso machine. The owner made her a cup before she rang up Cassidy's things. Cassidy downed the tiny cup, and drove home very fast.

She'd make notes instead of painting right away, just as she did for her decorating projects. She would plan her paintings in advance. A vase of flowers first, she thought, and then a bowl of fruit. And on the third day, a tall thin man with puce-coloured eyes, his yellow wings caught on the torn screen door of her shed. Thinking about him, she felt a little giddy. She was afraid to go down to see whether he was still there, or even to peek at her art supplies, which she'd stashed under the bench after she got home from Stony Creek.

Cassidy called goodnight down the basement stairs to Henry. She went up to bed, holding her glamorous feeling for the stranger close to her heart.

In the morning she hunted through cupboards till she found a dusty unopened jar of honey. She and Henry put sugar in their tea and coffee; she must've bought the honey to use in a recipe she'd clipped. She remembered it then: orange honey cake, supposedly a traditional rural cake, although she'd never heard of it till she'd read the article. She'd clearly never attempted it either; the unopened jar of honey was proof.

He was sitting on her stool, bent over her new sketchbook. His antennae bobbed; they were so fine she hadn't noticed them yesterday. A delicate smile played about his lips, secretive and knowing. It reminded Cassidy of the woman in that famous painting. His twin yellow scarves draped decoratively down his back.

She set the honey down on the poured concrete threshold. Had it taken the whole night for the impossibility of him to sink in? Yesterday she'd instinctively helped him as she might a hurt child. Just because she wasn't a mother didn't mean she had no protective feelings.

He licked his lips in concentration, dipping her best brush into an empty tuna can full of water. The sable brush had been the most expensive of her purchases, too fine to ever be used for stenciling borders, or découpage. She'd looked forward to being the first to use it. Cassidy turned and hurried back up the field stone path to her house.

She'd expected her feelings to stay outside with the sky, the garden, the shed, him. But they hadn't.

His puce eyes. She wanted to look into them.

Henry came into the kitchen and put the kettle on. As so often, he wore his brown corduroys, his safety glasses perched on his dark tousled head.

"I thought you'd be painting in your new shed," he said.

"The screen in the door is already torn."

Henry nodded. "I've got lots of spare screen. It won't take me more than a few minutes. I wonder how it happened?"

"Maybe a raccoon or a porcupine," Cassidy said. "I've got some bulbs in there. Even people can eat tulip bulbs, you know."

"I do know," Henry said. "My mother's family in Holland ate them during the war."

"You never offer to do anything right away."

"I am now."

"Now I don't want you to."

"Why?"

"You built the shed," Cassidy said. "It took time away from your radios. You shouldn't have to fix it yet."

"You haven't used it even once and it's been finished for a week," Henry said.

"It doesn't matter. Mosquito season's almost over since we had those cold nights. You have to work tomorrow. You should go somewhere."

"Where?" Henry asked.

"I don't know. Somewhere."

"To the basement then," Henry said and headed for the stairs.

Cassidy looked around the kitchen. The new curtains, though pretty, were no huge improvement over the blue blinds that had hung there previously. Not if she took into account how long they'd taken her to make.

She took a piece of paper towel off the roll that always stood beside the sink and sat down at the kitchen table, picked up the red permanent fine tip so fortuitously lying there, and drew a screaming face. It had no antennae so maybe it didn't belong to the stranger. And she'd never seen him scream; he didn't seem a screamer, somehow, although she supposed everyone and anyone might turn out to be a screamer if pushed hard enough.

♦♦♦

She wondered what the stranger painted in her book, with her Windsor Newtons. In his hands her book would just fill, as if by itself. And no one would wonder why he wasn't decorating instead. Or gardening or cooking. No one would wonder at all.

He was still there the next morning, and the morning after that. Cassidy knew because she checked before she left for her bookkeeping job. He never noticed her standing at the shed door even if she coughed, or wore her heavy plastic gardening clogs and thumped a little on her way.

On the third day she cleared her throat and said, "You wouldn't even have art supplies or a studio if it weren't for me."

He didn't look up, not even to mutely show her what he was working on. He hadn't torn pages out to prop against the vintage goose-neck lamp or pin to the walls, so Cassidy couldn't see what he'd done. But he was a good way through the book, almost half, and wore the same beatific smile as yesterday. It was as if, drawing, he'd uncovered the secrets of the universe. Her pencils had grown short; her paint tubes were twisted and rolled at the bottoms.

Back in her kitchen, Cassidy picked up the same red fine point marker she'd used to draw on the paper towel and wondered about its provenance. She used these markers to write on the little plastic tabs she pushed into her flats to identify seedlings or seedlings to be. Somehow the marker had migrated from the potting shed to the house. It was the kind of thing that might happen to Henry, but not to her. She was the organized one. Not that it mattered much. She opened her decorating magazine and uncapped the marker once more.

She drew a screaming person seated on a full-page photograph of a white couch. Was it an advertisement for the couch, or for the flooring beneath the couch, Cassidy briefly wondered, but she didn't take the time to scan the text and find out. Instead, she plunged into her drawing as if it were a pond, and she diving underwater. When Cassidy re-emerged she realized the screaming person she'd drawn had wings. And the wings were tangled in the lamp stand behind the couch, so that he couldn't escape.

No wonder she'd hidden her art supplies beneath the bench. This was neither a bowl of fruit nor a vase of flowers but a depiction of cruelty. She was sadistic, this excursion into her own creativity made clear. Cassidy felt dirty. Still, the drawing was good, even scribbled as it was with a gardening marker in a decorating magazine. It was quite a likeness. In spite of her deep confusion, Cassidy felt a little proud of what she'd done. In school they'd always said she had talent. She'd set it aside; she wasn't sure where or why. It wasn't as if she could blame the children she'd never had for taking up all her time.

But Henry touched her shoulder. He had crept up at some point, come and stood behind her. "You better let him go," he said.

"But I did let him go," Cassidy said. "The very first day."

"He won't leave till you ask for your things back," Henry said.

How long exactly, had Henry known her secret? But then, that had been the point of Henry, right from the beginning, hadn't it? Someone who could know her all the way through and not judge. She sat, still staring at her drawing. She didn't say anything more to her husband, but she definitely didn't want him taking his gently kneading hands from her shoulders.

"You don't think I'm a bad person because I drew him like this?" she finally asked.

"I'll bet you anything he drew you too. I'll bet you he drew you drawing." Henry caressed her hair and for some reason Cassidy was swept back to their beginning. She'd known Henry for a long time but one day had been different. There'd been a storm, and she'd turned the sign so it read "Closed" and locked the door in the dusty comfortable bookstore where she worked. Afterward they'd held each other in a different way, each needing reassurance they were still real, still separate, still had names.

Drawing made her feel a bit like that.

"I'll make a stew," Cassidy said, getting up. She'd wash the floor; she'd spend what remained of the weekend at flea markets looking for a new table for the guest room. The one there now was ugly, even after she'd painted it in a complicated faux finish, precisely following the instructions in her magazine. She'd already forgotten what the carefully rendered surface had supposedly been an imitation of.

"No," Henry said. "Why do you think I built you a studio?"

"It's just for plants," Cassidy said.

"It is not," he said, prodding her gently in the ribs.

She knew he was right. Cassidy got up and marched out the kitchen door and down to the shed. This time, she didn't stand timorously peering through the screen, mumbling accusations and hoping the stranger would notice her. Instead, she opened the door and spoke loudly.

"Give me back my stuff," she said. "It's not yours."

"I know," he said.

"What did you draw?" Cassidy demanded.

"See for yourself," he said, and turned the book around to face her.

Trembling, she opened the door and stepped inside.

It was just as Henry had said. The stranger had drawn her drawing. And unlike in her drawing of him, he'd pictured her happy, if a little transported.

He handed her the sable brush. "It's your turn," he said. "You already know you can do it."

"I do?" Cassidy asked.

"Remember how you drew me?"

She lowered her head, ashamed. "I didn't mean…"

"You were ashamed of me," the stranger said. "That's why you made a hurtful drawing. You were afraid and wanted me to suffer because of it."

"Why should I be ashamed of you?" Cassidy asked.

"Because I'm not grape vine stencils. Or faux marble stipple effect. I'm not any of those things."

She looked at his hands. There was the same fine veining in them as in his yellow wings; more like the veins in a leaf, she thought now, than anything else. "What should I paint?" she asked.

"What did you plan?"

"Flowers," she said, after thinking for a moment.

"Then paint those."

Cassidy took the brush from him and dipped it in a pool of aquamarine on the ceramic palette. With the wet brush she conjured outlines of flowers on the nubby white expanse of Arches paper. The brush swooped this way and then that, and before long Cassidy felt it again, that pull, a loss of self as intense as sex, but of a different kind.

◆◆◆

When she surfaced she saw pistils, stamens, petals; florid, penile, fluted, scalloped, rippling, tumescent. She observed these qualities scattered throughout her painting, again disturbed by her own work. It was true flowers were the sexual organs of plants, hell bent on attracting pollinators. So why had she never seen it before? Except, of course, she had, or she wouldn't have just painted them that way. Maybe she'd always pretended not to notice, afraid to be unladylike, and it was only in her art that her vision re-emerged, bypassing her filters.

But like her drawing of the visitor tangled in the lamp, the intensity scared her. If she had a show, all the neighbours would see what she was really like.

Not like them. Not one bit.

"It's so good," the stranger whispered. "Like Georgia O'Keefe."

"Who?"

"Look her up. She's your soul sister."

"It's not the sort of thing I can submit to the annual Water Colour Society exhibition," Cassidy said.

His puce eyes met and held hers. They were fathomless and deep. "I'm not like a grape stencil on the bathroom wall," he said again.

Cassidy felt a little swoony.

"What happens if I don't?" she asked. She tried to give him back the sable brush but he didn't take it.

"Then I die," he said.

"Really?" It seemed so extreme. Again, she tried to give the brush back.

He fluttered his hands, no no no. Pleading. "Please," the stranger said.

She began to cry, shaking her head. Her flowers resembled open mouths, open vulvas. It was too much! She knew now why she'd stopped drawing. She couldn't look at what emerged. She could even less consider putting her visions out into the world for others to see.

He took her by the shoulders, tucked his long slender finger under her chin.

Forced it up.

His gentle puce eyes were whirlpools. She'd drown in them forever; she knew it for a fact, but better than gasping for air every hour of every day.

Washing Lady's Hair

"**I**HEARD YOU COULD GET Rick Sutton's sculptures here," the woman said, "for half the Yorkville price." Coiffed and slender, she wore an equally slim black suit that smelled like money. Feeling shabby, Karen wished she'd gotten properly dressed, but maybe her vintage flowered dressing gown, smudged mascara, and vaguely matted hair could actually help. Shadow always said people came to the gallery just to feel they were a part of something.

"You can," Karen said. Maybe the woman thought if she had one of Rick's animals, her life might change, just a little bit. She might be right too; Rick's work was that amazing. Karen knew it wasn't just because Rick was her boyfriend that she thought so—his work actually sold, and not for pennies. Well, sometimes anyway.

"Show me," the woman said, and Karen had only to point to the ceiling where a manta ray, three feet in circumference, hung from a chain.

"It's six hundred dollars," Karen said. "Which is half of what you'd pay uptown. And it's his newest, so truthfully he wanted to keep it a bit longer, but..." She made an ingratiating gesture.

"I'll have to think about it," the woman said, "Not that it isn't gorgeous." She hesitated before asking, "Do you happen to know where I can get any Green?"

Karen just shook her head no, as Shadow had instructed. Green wasn't scheduled, but it wasn't exactly legal either. Shadow and Rick had both tried explaining the difference between selling and personal use, between synthetic and leaf, between last year and this year—a bristling confusion of facts that, just when it was about to cohere in Karen's mind, always chose to disintegrate instead. Like a sea urchin she'd just stepped on, but not before it poked her sharply in the soft sole of her foot.

The woman gave her a disbelieving look. "But I heard."

Karen just shrugged, returned to the desk, leaving the woman to browse. She opened the little metal box that served as cash register, sorted change into appropriate compartments. The box was dependable in times of power outage, which was often. Everyone was dumping their smart phones in favour of stacks of clipped together file cards, and email, no longer reliable, was out. Green Magic sported a meeting area consisting of a spotty Wi-Fi connection and more importantly, comfortable seating. There was no charge for use of the embroidered couch and the connection; people who met at the store sometimes ended up buying clothes or art.

Beside the couch, a metal stand housed fabric paints, mason jars of brushes, and a stack of white tees Shadow had liberated from the dumpster behind a Spadina jobber. Karen took the top shirt and stretched it over a painting board. She'd let an arty customer try her hand at painting a shirt to take home the week before, and now Shadow charged people for the pleasure. Karen figured it was the first thing she'd come up with that her boss had approved of.

Karen sighed, staring at the shirt. People who had never dived could hardly be better painters than her; they didn't have a wealth of undersea imagery in their heads to draw upon.

The door chimes rang, startling her. The woman had finally left. Karen wouldn't tell Shadow; he'd complain she could have closed the sale.

No sea here. Karen missed the Pacific Ocean. Occasionally she took the streetcar to Cherry Beach, just to sit there looking at water. Lake Ontario was so big you couldn't see the other

side, but there were no breakers and no jellyfish and it didn't
smell of salt. Of course, the Strait of Georgia didn't have much
in the way of breakers either. She'd grown up in Vancouver but
she'd never spent much time on the island, outside of Victoria.
Some friends of Rick's had told her it wasn't really the ocean
till you'd built a bonfire on Long Beach, brought hand drums
and tents or—if it was summer—just curled up in a sleeping
bag. No one else around for miles. It wasn't really Green till
you'd done that. Back then, she still thought her life would
change just by being with Rick. It had, too, but not quite in
the way she'd hoped.

Still, they'd been in Toronto, now, for over two years, and
some things were definitely better.

◆◆◆

Back in Vancouver they'd mostly sat in their east side basement
apartment heating little pots of green paste on their hot plate.
Once it was warmed, they rubbed the paste gently into each
other's skin where it was thinnest: temples, neck, the insides
of elbows and knees. Waiting for it to begin, staring into each
other's eyes, smiles of delight deepening and widening. And
there it was: a popping sound, like squelching through soft
clean river bottom mud. But it was more than that; it was a
popping feeling, her skin transmogrifying. Karen would look
then, just to make sure what she felt was also what she saw:
Rick's hand wasn't just a hand anymore but also a whale's
flipper, the flipper brushing her own, that of a green sea turtle.

Shape shifting. It was electrifying.

Rick never disappeared entirely when Orca arrived. Karen
still felt the warmth of primate skin, the hardness of the bones
within, the slender bird feet tendons. She knew if she pressed
just so, his tendons would move, just a little, and at the same
time she'd be touching skin that was slick and rubbery and
wet, so alien it left her breathless. Cetacean skin.

Sometimes the change arrived mere moments after dosing,

sometimes it took hours to achieve. They chanted and drummed to bring it nearer. They closed their eyes and tuned into the process with every scrap of energy and will, and—something like love. Definitely something like passion. Wasn't prayer in the end just that, an expression of passion for the divine?

Walking, they'd talk about everything that was wrong with the world. If it was up to Rick, he'd have been born as a pre-industrial revolution European peasant. Then, even if his land wasn't his and most of the products of his work, whether it was a lamb or a vegetable or a loaf of bread, went to the owner, well, at least he and his woman could sit on the broken back step peeling apples and looking at the moon. They'd tell folk tales to the little ones, and someone would get out an instrument and someone else would sing, and the apples would be organic because no one had ever even heard of pesticides back then, let alone invented them.

Karen had shared Rick's daydream about a feudal existence with a Green Magic customer once and he'd told her she was romanticizing a brutal existence. Which was probably true but you had to hope there was a better life somewhere. Maybe for some, the implausible fantasy lay in the future.

The present was no help at all.

Nowadays you had to work forty or more hours per week at a call centre, told how to dress and what to say. Everything mapped out bit by bit, piece by piece, all of it, until you got home and there was nothing left, no *you* anymore. Every part of you remodeled by them and for them, for the privilege of an evening can of soup or a box of take-out and a thriller on the DVD.

And there it was, her mother's life. To prove it, Karen noticed she'd painted not a whale or a turtle on the T-shirt as she'd intended, but a flower sporting Thelma's face.

Rick had always told her art was a kind of therapy.

Thelma stared at her reproachfully.

Why was her mother mad at her this time?

Why was she still so mad at her mother?

It wasn't Thelma she ought to be mad at, anyway, but Thelma's boyfriend Syd.

Rick's manta ray sculpture swung just a little on its chain. She ought to wake him up but if she did he might just dive again. These days, Rick spent most of his time awake upstairs in the bedroom, diving. Not working on his art at all. It was worrisome. Green wasn't addictive; many users said their physical and psychological health improved when they did a little Green now and again. But lately Rick returned to Green Lady over and over, withdrawing from real life.

Karen dabbed away at her mother's face. It had been Shadow's idea that she painted shirts. Green Magic didn't do much business; the weekends were their big days, but it still made sense to open during the week—you just never knew. If she painted "Greenstyle" T-shirts while she clerked she might make a little money and create additional stock for the store.

She didn't think the painting of the flower with her mother's face was "Greenstyle"—she ought to be painting visionary fish, sharks, manta rays, even jellyfish. Still, the likeness was better than she had any right to expect. She'd actually taken more art lessons than Rick ever had, and only now did she remember her instructor telling her she had a talent for portraiture.

She'd painted Thelma with a mournful cast to her face, and while Karen definitely hated Syd, she couldn't hate her mom. Even back in Van she hadn't blamed Thelma—she'd just needed to get out of harm's way. She understood why her mom would want to get tipsy on Friday nights, forget everything for a few sweet hours, even her daughter, who it was ostensibly all for. The supervisor with his creepy surveillance, the landlord who didn't fix the washing machines in the basement, the spiraling costs of gas and food and rent and insurance and fear.

"Relax, Thelma, just relax, I'm here. Take off your shoes, I'll rub your feet for you."

Karen felt ill, hearing Syd say that. But why should she deny her poor overworked mother a pleasure that, after all, Karen indulged in with Rick as often as she could?

Well, they used to, anyway. Nowadays Rick dove so much it had affected his libido.

"Darling, Karen hasn't eaten," Thelma said. "I'll just run down to the corner and pick us up a bucket of chicken. And then we can pick up where we left off."

Karen hated the taste of KFC, never mind that the cost of the bucket would've paid for a sack of organic brown rice Thelma could've made with vegetables: better tasting food that might just help to keep her encroaching cancer at bay. But who had the time, or the energy? It was Rick who had taught Karen about natural foods, how to make kombucha tea and grow herbs on the windowsill and sprout grains and pulses.

"Of course," Syd said and grinned at Karen, meaningfully. She knew what was coming, and awful chicken was the least of it.

And just like the other times, she hadn't told Syd to stop. She'd frozen. She couldn't understand why; she hated herself for freezing. No, that was wrong: she actually had tried telling him to stop. He'd grinned at her, a grin with just the tiniest, shocking hint of menace in it.

There were footsteps outside in the hall. Syd stopped. Karen moved away from him and adjusted her clothes. He smiled, a weird mix of gratitude and again, menace.

Don't tell. He didn't have to say it out loud.

Thelma came in, looking happy to see them, but especially, it was unarguable, Syd. He got up and took the takeout bag from her and assembled food onto three plates. Thelma laughed and Syd kissed the top of her head. No, he buried his face in her hair and Karen watched in some horror as her mother melted, as if this was the one good thing that happened in her week. She'd never give it up. How could she?

Syd winked at Karen over her mother's shoulder and said, "It smells delicious."

"We'll sit and eat, the three of us," Thelma said happily,

and Syd, serving the chicken, said, "I brought a movie over."

The chicken smelled rotten.

Everything had smelled rotten for a long, long time.

The part that, oddly, creeped Karen out the most was that Syd didn't even behave as if he were hiding anything. Maybe he thought it was normal, even fun, for the three of them to sit down together and watch the latest sex and violence thriller bordering on porn and eat chicken bred with no heads, right after he felt her up.

Did the chickens really have no heads? Karen wasn't sure if it was true or Greenie apocrypha but it didn't really matter. It could've been true; if it wasn't true now, it would be soon.

It felt like it was true now.

She left without eating her chicken. She never told Thelma. She went to Rick's. Her schoolbooks were all in her locker at the high school. She wore Rick's clothes, and bought a few more at the St. Vincent de Paul, which was a lot cheaper than Value Village. She went on student assistance so she could help Rick pay his bills. He welcomed the windfall and spent a lot of it on art supplies. And Green.

Diving and phone calls were activities inimical to one another. And Karen wouldn't have called her mother once they'd resurfaced; after diving, sleep always seemed of the utmost importance, leaving pesky to-dos like letting family know you're safe to be left till morning. Anyway, Thelma wouldn't have worried, not right away; she'd have known Karen was at Rick's.

Problem was, she'd never called. And it was two years later.

Shit. No wonder Thelma was melancholic.

Karen picked up the store phone, looked at it.

Put it back. Shadow would hate it if she used long distance.

She left her painting to get up and re-arrange the crab in the window. It was slipping a little from its perch in a pink velvet Victorian armchair. If it fell forward to the floor it might break; papier mâché was hardly the hardiest of materials. Beautiful and rose-hued, the crab's huge claws were painted with an eerie life-like verisimilitude. Light-shadows of waves floated across its back as though it were underwater, and prisms swirled in its eyes. Most visionary art was wall art painted on canvas and the fact that Rick's was 3-D gained him an extra cachet. Even his early attempts back in Vancouver had been clearly better than average. It was why she'd crushed on him in the first place, more than his looks or his charm which were, truthfully, somewhat nonexistent. Karen had still been living at her mom's, going to high school and hating her mom's creepster boyfriend. Dropping in at the café where Rick worked part-time and hung his sea creatures had been her one solace. The dreamy oceanic peace in his work implied another world was possible, in a way nothing else ever had.

◆◆◆

Rick hadn't gone to Emily Carr. Green Lady, he used to tell her, earnestly mixing adhesive in their basement apartment, woke the neurons in his brain. He'd stay up all night studying and reading and making big slurries of smelly papier mâché. He spent their money on wire to make the armatures and flour to make glue. Karen wouldn't have thought it possible to burn through a cheque buying flour, the cheapest of all possible supplies, and he probably wouldn't have, if it weren't for the infestation. One day when she went to close the big twenty-five kilo bag of flour Rick had left open, she was greeted by the tiny smiling faces of countless little white wriggling worms. She didn't want to see what they turned into after they pupated, so she dumped the flour out in the alley, under the surprising winter-blooming hollyhocks, the uncollected pumpkins planted by forgetful guerrilla gardeners, caved in now and covered with the slightest dusting of snow.

Rick told her she was hallucinating.

"Hallucinating the faces, Rick, but not the worms."

She remembered looking at his sculptures and wondering whether she should drop in on Thelma and ask if her mother could get her a job at the call centre. She could work in the evenings after school. It might work except she already got so tired. Algebra seemed especially strange when they'd dived the night before, never mind the regularly scheduled day-after exhaustion. Maybe if she'd had a nutritious breakfast more often, she could've concentrated. Maybe if Rick had cleaned up the apartment now and again.

And that smell. It had rained for months on end and Karen told Rick she thought the half-finished sculptures were rotting instead of drying out.

Smell pulled you back like nothing else. Was it just the Vancouver damp? Mould was supposed to be so very bad for you.

Mould. The smell had come from mould. But it wasn't mould in the walls.

Gathering up the laundry after school one afternoon, she'd lost her footing and fallen into an unfinished orca sculpture, and the ghastly smell had suddenly been everywhere. Enveloping her, touching her, clothing her. The smell was like Syd's hands. It gave her the same feeling of shocked humiliation, as though the mouldy whale was raping her, as Syd, technically, hadn't. There'd been a knock at the door then; the landlord asking for the cheque.

"I thought Rick paid it," Karen said, looking down at the smelly goo on her sneaker. Syd's smell was suddenly still on her too, in spite of all the baths and showers she'd had in the interim. But there it unarguably was: the smell of lavender oil and alcohol and cheap cigarettes, intermingled with the smell of rotting papier mâché—a smell not entirely dissimilar to the smell of normally drying papier mâché but more sour, more vile, more loathsome, more Syd-like.

It was as if Syd's hands were still under her shirt while she waited for Thelma to come home, while she waited for Syd to notice he was crazy and offensive and stop.

While she waited.

While the landlord stared at her, smelling that smell.

Karen finally said, "No, Rick didn't give me the rent." Greenies always said one shouldn't spend too much time thinking about such bullshit, and the truth was, chronic divers were forever having their hydro cut off. Even in the rare instances when they had the money, they often forgot to pay.

Maybe welfare had found out she wasn't at school much anymore. She'd been cut off and that was why there was no money for food. It wasn't, as she'd thought, that Rick had spent it all on art supplies. Karen wasn't sure. She stood there blankly looking at the landlord, just as she'd sat there blankly while Syd felt her up.

Neither moment had any intention of ending; worse yet, they were merging. Maybe they'd go away if she swore at them. Karen was tempted, but she didn't. Both the landlord and Syd remained where they were. At least the landlord's hands weren't under her shirt.

The landlord stood staring at her goo-coated foot and then he turned around and shut the door on her in a final sort of way, more or less as she had done to her mother that night. Karen sat down on the unmade bed and cried. She was afraid of being charged with welfare fraud.

Perhaps she cried, then as now, because she hadn't eaten or maybe because of the overpowering smell of mould and of Syd's breath which still, even now, clung to her.

Mouldier even than the mould. They were given their eviction notice two days later.

Rick insisted Green Lady would fix things. She was magic, mistress of synchronicity, of providential solutions appearing as if out of nowhere to solve even seemingly insoluble problems.

"Why didn't Lady help us before?" Karen dared to ask. "We've never seen her, not even once." Green Lady was an aquatic goddess vision who appeared occasionally to divers. Rick and Karen had been waiting a long time. "Because we didn't ask for her help before we dove," Rick replied, the perfect logic of it creasing his face into a delighted elven grin.

♦♦♦

Green Lady's hair. There had been so much of it.

They'd gone walking after their dive, thinking they'd resurfaced and it was safe to do so, oddly not exhausted as was usual, and saw her hair emerging from the sewer grates. It was made of weeds. Living weeds, dead weeds, grass with clumps of mud in it, bits of stones and seashells and the tiny legs of crabs' shed exoskeletons.

And really a lot of garbage.

Karen sat down on the street and plucked bits of broken glass and bits of Styrofoam, bits of plastic bags, bread tags and surprisingly many tiny oval fruit stickers out of the goddess's hair. The Styrofoam was the worst. Of course it didn't decompose, but why did it have to convert to pellet form? There were beads and beads and beads of it stuck in Green Lady's rampant hair, flowing now, not just along the gutters but over the curb and along the street.

Karen sat there for what felt like hours, cleaning Lady's hair. It felt like stringy mud in her fingers, muddy and slimy and maybe some of those clumps weren't mud at all. Her hair was coming up, out of a storm grate, after all, and the recent storms had wreaked havoc with the city's plumbing. Karen understood suddenly that the mould from the rotting carcass of orca and the smell of Syd's breath and Syd putting his hands on her all stemmed from this simple undeniable fact: they hadn't looked after Lady's hair, hadn't kept it clean.

Rick sat down beside her, crying and threading the condoms and syringes out of her hair, careful, so careful not to stick himself. In no time they had a big heap going. Rick doused it with lighter fluid. They burned it, burned all the garbage that had been stuck in Green Lady's hair.

"Thank you for helping," Karen said.

"I wouldn't even have seen it, if you hadn't pointed it out," Rick said. "It was here all the time, her filthy hair. She was begging us to clean it for her. I've walked past it a million times and never even dreamt it was there. Maybe now my life can change."

"How come we see the same thing at the same time, any-way?" Karen asked.

"That always happens on Green," Rick said.

"But we resurfaced hours ago," Karen said.

"Maybe this time it's real," Rick said, "Maybe it's the next level." He pointed at Lady's hair, which, now it was clean, began to move, sparkling and shining and flowing down the sidewalk, an endless green wave, smelling of beauty and the sea.

They stood there, holding hands by the little fire of burning plastic that made a worse smell, Karen had to admit, than Syd's breath and mouldy papier mâché put together. But at least they were getting rid of it at last, the pollution in Lady's beautiful hair and in their own souls, it felt like. And then they heard sirens.

"Let's go," Rick said, and still holding hands they ran down alleyways only he knew. Hiding in the unused entryway of a brick building, they waited and waited for the cops to find them, but they didn't.

The phone rang the second they got in the door to their base-ment flat. Rick talked for an hour. It was his friend Shadow, long distance from Toronto.

The Green thing was catching on. There were people who went dancing after they did Green. Green visionary art was needed to hang in the clubs. The sea creature sculptures were perfect. Shadow would introduce him to the club owners. But of course Rick was good. Shadow knew that. He'd always been talented. Those drawings he'd done in his binders at school instead of his chemistry; they'd been amazing: hauntingly beautiful and sad and masterfully drawn. "Greenstyle." It was clothes too; maybe Karen could get into that, or she could work in Shadow's gallery and clothing store, Green Magic. They could live upstairs.

Rick got off the phone and stared at Karen. "I told you so."

"What, what, what?" Karen asked, and so Rick told her all of it.

"I told you Lady would fix it up," he said, but not in a mean way, just as if he was a little boy who had finally met his fairy godmother.

My mother couldn't take care of me properly. I couldn't tell her about Syd. Thelma needed him too much and it was too weird, I just couldn't voice it, and maybe Lady will be our mother now.

"It's not even our mothers' fault," Rick said, "they did what they could, the world being what it is. Their own lives are so lost after all, lost from themselves, how could they mother us any better than they did?"

"You knew what I was thinking."

"Lady makes that possible," Rick said, it had to be admitted, a little smugly.

"I was so mad at Thelma for leaving me alone with him, for not noticing Syd was that kind of guy. She was so starved for anyone who'd be even a little nice to her. He rubbed her poor feet in real lavender oil," and Karen started to cry.

"Yes, but now it doesn't hurt so much anymore, does it?"

"That's true," Karen said, because it suddenly was. "Why?" she asked.

"Because we have a real mother now."

All moments go on forever, Karen thought, not one of them ever ends, either the bad ones, or, more usefully, the good ones.

She'd never told Rick about Syd, and about her mother before. And he'd been kind.

◆◆◆

It was time to close. Karen, after taking out the garbage that smelled more than a little, locked the street door and turned out all the lights. Slowly, she made her way up the stairs, wondering what to make for dinner. She should make rice and vegetables, but she was so tired. Maybe a can of soup. Almost anything, so long as it wasn't KFC.

For once there were no dark circles under Rick's eyes. Still, she looked at her boyfriend's sleeping form a little reproachfully and said, "What happened to my dreams?" She didn't ask what had happened to Rick's dreams, because, implausibly, they were coming true.

Maybe Karen didn't believe in Green Lady as much as he did. Or maybe she should figure out what her dreams even were.

It would beat a lot of the other things she had planned for tomorrow.

Seeds

I DON'T KNOW HOW IT IS I came to have no parents and no name. I hear this is a place you can come, if you lookin' for a name.

I have nothing. But I have had nothing before, and now I am glad to be free of it.

It is in the city. There are five of us, or maybe ten or thirty. The building is an empty one, gutted by fire. We have been sleeping on the floors, on found mattresses. I sprayed them all with a can of bug juice I bought. I do not like fleas or bedbugs.

Since I came here, last week, I have been planting flowers. I dig the earth out of the central courtyard. An empty yard. Probably it is full of lead, but eventually that too will be washed away by rain. The rain is cleaner now.

When I came, there was no one here. Now there are sometimes ten, sometimes twenty of us.

I have planted sunflowers in the yard. Their big heads turn, slowly, throughout the day.

I make window boxes out of some panelling ripped out of a wall. In them I plant geraniums, herbs, and tomatoes. The seeds are seeds I brought from the West. The soil is not good, this soil dug out of the yard. It is not really a yard.

One day I wake up and there are chickens in it. Where did the chickens come from? It doesn't matter. They lay eggs, and they will be good to eat, when winter comes.

I gather the chicken dung and dilute it with water, and carefully pour it into the pots of plants. The tomatoes are doing fine. When someone new comes, I make them eat tomatoes.

"Vitamin C," I say. They look at me strange, their eyes wide and dark, blank as stones.

"Eat your tomatoes," I say.

They are young, most of them. They are young and frightened and ready to fight, and yet their mouths are all open, as though they were expecting something wonderful to come out of nowhere, to fly in.

They gather from the edges of the burnt city, hearing.

What do they hear?

That there is a place, a place you can come.

My sadness is that I am alone, that I am older than everyone here, that I must look after them all. They play with each other, giggling and combing one another's hair.

They are like children, really. They run up and down the halls of the building, delighted, discovering things. Exploring. They like to rearrange, to take things apart and rearrange them. I remember I did that too. It is necessary, if they are to learn. Why we are here and not somewhere else.

I look after the plants and make the children eat them. I hope that none of them will get sick with something I cannot cure. I make them eat garlic and drink tea brewed from nettles and chamomile flowers. So they will be strong, will not get sick. I dream of someone coming over the hill. A man. He will be here soon. He will help me in my work.

I do not mind anymore, being always alone, being lonely. I no longer look for anyone to fall into, to carry me. I make them drink their teas. I make them wash. I watch as they play their secret, whispering games. I do not mind any more. Now I can do this; now I don't mind not being one of them, but one of the others.

The man coming over the hill. I realize he isn't coming over the hill, but is one of the ones here. He says his name is Stephen. He is maybe nineteen. He is very strong. I lean out the window, watching him. He is leading the children. Shit in the pit, he says, not in the sunflowers. Wash your hands before you eat. Here, drink this tea. He yells at them sometimes but they do not really mind. As he becomes stronger, I disappear into the shadows. I lurk in the hallways, disappearing. I can, now. Now it isn't so much responsibility; now someone has grown, like a sunflower ... he is almost ready to harvest for seed. Ready to be an adult, come to help me shoulder the weight. I am glad. He does not speak to me, Stephen, but I can hear his voice in my mind, asking questions. I answer, from my room hidden in the dim corridors. Yes, you can do this and this and this.

Yes, the windmill on the roof is good. They will help you. You must make them work, teach them it is important. Energy and power. Their own. At first they won't believe you, will not understand why, just as you did not understand, thought it was enough just to drift, to be asleep to your own power. Yes, you can do it.

"Will you help?" he asks me in my mind.

"Yes," I say. "I will."

Now they can hardly see me anymore. Stephen sees me, but only dimly, like something half forgotten, like a dream. He has already forgotten that I used to be a real person. He has forgotten I used to be flesh and blood like him, that I too suffered, hated to be so alone. I watch him cry, alone, sometimes at night.

"I cannot do it," he cries, calling out my name. "I cannot do it, I cannot. You must help me. You say you love me, so you must help. You don't know what it's like he says, to work so hard for so little. Everything is darkness here, and I cannot see."

"You can see," I say. "There is a little light inside you, and if you turn it on, you will see everything, everything."

He does then, at first tentatively, like an experiment, and then the whole yard is shining, illuminated, and he can see the faces of the children, some sleeping, some waking. They cannot see his light, but they know something has changed. They stir in their sleep, smiling, cuddling one another.

"You aren't a human being," he says. "You cannot know how it hurts."

"Oh?" I say, but my heart hurts for him, for his hurt.

Then he is better again, and happy.

How I love him.

One day I will come back for him, and then we will be together.

At night, when they are all sleeping, I make the rounds of all my window boxes, gathering seeds. Seeds from tomatoes, from echinacea, cucumber, geranium, hyssop, basil. Parsley, garlic. Valerian, bergamot, mint. Sunflowers, zinnia, sweet pea. And of course, the beans and corn.

I dry the seeds on the roof, under the sun.

Then I climb the stairs again, at night. Up up up the stairs, all around the shadowy building, leaving it behind: its weight, its solidity. Each floor I go up, I look at the sleeping faces, bless them all. Each floor I go up, I feel a lightness, a greater freedom.

On the roof there are stars.

One of the stars moves and comes closer. In a great swoop of the mind I am lifted up up up among them. They welcome me, princes of peace. I recognize them all.

We skim over the night, looking for lights. Where we see lights, we hover and send our minds down into their dreams, the sleeping children. They do not know we have been there, but they feel a presence, a kindness, a benevolent intent. We are happy and shining.

◆◆◆

Far below I see a girl, walking over a hill. In her knapsack she holds a packet of seeds and a bottle of water. Through the canvas of the knapsack I can see the seeds, the life inside them glowing like light bulbs

And on another hill, there is a man. He is making something, a new kind of machine. He will put it on the roof, and it will spin light and energy down from the stars.

One day they will be together, and then my work will be complete.

Unsichtbarkeit

IHAD SOME MONEY PUT ASIDE by October, and went to Paris to continue my work without distraction.

My work. Your work. Our work.

It has to stop, you used to say. And I agreed with you. Agreed with you that it had to stop, and believed you when you said we were helping.

Helping what?

Helping to stop it.

I did not write to you after I arrived in Paris. By spring I had finished the coding but when I tried to get in touch so I could deliver, it was as if you had disappeared. Vanished from the net, and your various emails and phone numbers didn't work either. Maybe that was a clue.

If you are going to do this work, you will have to know how to disappear.

We used to practise disappearing. I was better at it than you. Once high on a ridge in Hawai'i I leaned against an ancient temple wall and watched Japanese tourists walk past me so they could look out over the ocean. Hoping for whales, getting boats. The little group went back and forth a few times making bathroom forays and fetching forgotten binoculars and cameras. I guess the *heiau* itself had studied as we had, for it couldn't be seen from the road unless one knew what to look for.

When the tourists were heading back to the parking lot for the final time, I made myself visible again and one of them cried out. "Were you there all along?" a man asked in heavily accented English. It was his wife, presumably, who had shrieked. Or maybe she was his sister. I don't think it matters. What mattered was the invisibility spell had worked.

"Yes," I told the man, "I've been here all along."

Where is here?

All places and times exist at once.

That isn't really useful information though, is it?

Following online trails I came across someone who said he had talked to you recently. The past tense made me anxious. A small grey fear began to grow inside me, from mouse to cat and eventually to dog, although there was no reason why it should. It just seemed strange that you should be careless, that if you were disappearing you had done so only partially. No one should have heard of you at all. It shouldn't have been so easy to find your footprints. But maybe the person who said he had known you (in Athens, he said, over the winter) was lying. Maybe he posted on the internet to catch people like me, people who really had known you, and actually might know where you were.

Sometimes the same people who say they are helping you are actually trying to hurt you.

Sometimes you're actually hurting the people you're trying to help.

Did I inadvertently lead people to you?

But if that was true I would at some point have been captured and tortured so I would give it up. Your location. Your plans. And I wasn't helping them, I was trying to find you, so that I could give you the work I'd done on invisibility.

And Karina? She told me the day they found you she was driving—not that that means anything.

In hindsight so much seems crazy dangerous, both of us making unwise choices—at least if we were interested in keeping not just body but soul together—we were like people in a le Carré only it was our lives.

Yes, it was ironic. I had been working on software to make you better at what you were already doing.

Disappearing. *Verschwinden.*

But there are different kinds.

How to erase one's traces, achieve *unsichtbarkeit.* Invisibility, the program. Sure to be a giant seller if I'd gone commercial, but then they could have used it too. The people who were watching us could have become invisible, so that we wouldn't know they were watching. You wanted it just to be for us. For people like us.

What are people like us like?

People who agree it has to stop. Invisibility Spell, the program. VPN was just the beginning.

Because of the cat-sized fear I wrote you a letter one friend writes another when they don't want them to die. I copied it several times and sent the same letter to snail mail addresses in three countries and to your German cousins. All six identical letters were returned unopened. The three sent to Germany, the one to London, even the one sent to a new address, one I'd never seen before, in Athens, that the stranger I met online when I was staying in Montmartre had given me. But the return of the letters didn't necessarily mean you'd really disappeared. It might have just meant you were practising. We used to practise all the time. It was the most important exercise we could do, you said.

How do you know when the other person has stopped practising disappearing and disappeared for real? How do you know when you yourself have stopped?

Somewhat rhetorically, I asked these and other things of the person who had known you over the winter in Athens. But was it one person, or three, or was it Karina?

They were kind, the person who said he was a man and had known you. Too kind, I thought, to be lying to me, but they also did not agree to meet me in the flesh. He said he had not seen you since early March, and that no one else he knew (that you knew too) had seen you since then either.

I tried to visualize these people in Greece, whom you had spent the winter amongst, while I laboured on Invisibility Spell, alone in Paris. You, in Athens, where it was warm, sitting in Exarchia cafés late at night, unmaking and remaking the world in conversation. You never tired of it.

I didn't write you from Paris. It never occurred to me you might not have been able to find me. You were you, after all.

I moved back to Berlin. I waited for you to get in touch. For no particular reason, my fear grew to dog-size. If I wasn't by your side I could not protect you, I could not change things. I was the wrong person to practise disappearing from.

When I heard something again (and it was a whole other year), it was that you had killed yourself before they found you. I suppose it seemed better than them getting hold of you. I was strangely comforted to hear you had used a gun. Fast and painless. One hopes.

It has to stop, you used to say.

What has to stop? In the end it was *you* who stopped, not *it.*

In the end it was *they* who stopped *you.*

Maybe you let them find you. Maybe you were tired. Maybe it wasn't suicide at all. Maybe letting them find you was a form of suicide. Maybe hounding you till you killed yourself was a form of murder.

In Berlin, after I heard, I did not contact anyone, out of perversity. And knowing there was nothing anyone could say. More than once I "accidentally" walked by your building, where I had often stayed, overlooking the Admiralbrücke over the canal. It was strange to see your building in the spring sunlight. I had only known it in winter, known its courtyard full of bicycles, its steep narrow stairs leading to your top floor flat. I still had a key to the arched wooden street door but I didn't take it out of my pocket to see if it still worked in the sticky lock.

It was only much later that I understood. Perhaps you were trying to protect me from what you saw as inevitable in yourself. You would slip through my fingers like a fish, back into the ocean. You had an appointment there with someone, and it wasn't me. I lived in a different ocean altogether. I wanted to go with you, but you wouldn't let me. You knew the appointment was for yourself alone.

Once I knew I would never try the key it was time to leave Berlin again. I went back to Paris, briefly. But I'd gone to Paris to finish the work, and with it done, and you gone, Paris was haunted. I went to New York. Home. It had been decades.

I didn't want to call anyone, neither family nor friends, not right away, maybe not ever. I stayed in a hotel.

♦♦♦

When you go back to New York City (which is where I'd begun) it is as though no time has passed, as though the person you left there decades ago has been waiting for you all along. She is the person you would have become if you had stayed there. You wonder if you made a mistake, if you can still find her.

Who is she? She is the person who never knew you.

It's as if you are a tattoo I can never remove. But growing up in New York I hadn't met you yet.

In New York I went to the Met and looked at *Toledo*. It wasn't after all in the room the docents told me it was in and so I had to run from room to room quickly before closing; it had taken me all day to get uptown, what with this and that.

You had cousins not only in Germany but also in Greece and had always wanted to see the El Greco but had never been to New York, never in fact, to North America at all. It is a much different thing, seeing a painting in "real life." There is a certain frisson that happens, looking at a painting in the flesh as it were and not in reproduction. It's a form of time travel, sharing space with brush strokes done hundreds of years ago. I looked at that haunted green square for both of us. I wished you could also see it, could look out through my eyes. I pretended there was a little part of you that didn't leave this planet and stayed inside me. Kept our pact, to go to my hometown together one day, and look at *Toledo* in the Met. Maybe it was even true.

That night I dreamed it was I who had died and that you and Karina were at my funeral.

You were both drunk, and danced around my coffin waving empty liquor bottles full of flowers you had picked in public gardens. I lay in my open casket, trying very hard not to wink.

I woke up sad. It was fall again and I began to think that I could never forget you. I had crossed the Atlantic to forget the beating of your heart but in the end what is the difference— Berlin, Paris, New York? Some would say a great deal and they are right of course but I began to see my delusion. I was bleeding my life away in cold northern cities telling myself you would find me one day. More than a little part of me believed you'd faked your death, covered your trail.

Practised invisibility, even from me. Or especially from me. I'd written Invisibility after all, so that if you could hide from me you could hide from anyone. Even, presumably, them.

It is hard to breathe in the northern hemisphere, the summers so brief one is never without fear of the cold, of freezing somehow, alone in the night. I would go somewhere warm, I told myself, somewhere nearer the equator, where people did not think so much, where they dream more, where it is easier to forget time, the hand of time.

Or maybe it was hard to breathe anywhere you had breathed.

And then, on the subway, someone called my name. Who could be calling my name? It was Karina, our Berlin cabdriver. She was so happy to see me, it too made me sad.

We went to an old bar close to my hotel. The Ear Inn is ungentrified, old school and full of neighbourhood types. Why, I asked, was she in New York? Was she going to NYU for graduate work?

She asked me about you, and once again a cold wave of fear (what size animal?) came over me. It was not fear that they would find you, it was the other fear: that they would find me. It was partly because of this fear that I left Berlin for Paris in the first place, even though I did not leave the work. I would make myself invisible, and work on Invisibility. I did not want to be found before I finished. And in this plan, at least, I succeeded.

I think.

One grows too weary for fear.

Karina had known all along, she confessed, she had always worked with us. She just hadn't been able to tell us, so that we could all be safer. She had kept her involvement invisible, even from us. She beat us at our own game.

Maybe.

Involvement in what?

In stopping it.

In helping us stay invisible.

At least that is what she said.

She also spoke my thoughts aloud: I came to New York because it is hard to breathe anywhere he breathed.

Was she reading my mind or had I spoken it, written it somewhere? And is there already a technology for mind reading that I don't know about yet? Or did we just feel the same way?

Yes, she slept with you too. I didn't mind. You were like that. Many women could sleep with you and not only did we not hate each other we also didn't hate you.

Maybe she didn't come to New York for the reason she said but to keep tabs on me. Taxi driver, yeah right.

She was wearing the jacket like yours. Did I ever tell about the jacket? It was like this:

Leaving Paradise and trying to hail a cab, we often got Karina, you and I. At first it was coincidence. But the coincidence, after repeating itself so many times, like links in a chain, transmuted into pattern, and she would come looking for us.

Paradise would close, and we would pour out the gates, waves in the deluge of aftermath. We would ignore the line of taxis waiting like vultures, looking for Karina, and if she wasn't there we would wait, knowing she would be soon. Seeing us she would honk her horn like a trumpet and we would limp over to her, a collective Jonah to his whale, a killer to the hangman of his choice. You, me and your hangers on. Movement people, artists, lawyers.

And she would take us home.

Why did we let her?

I met her once outside of her work. It was in January, during the Winter Schluss Verkauf at KaDeWe, the year-end sales. It was in the men's department. There was a jacket of the softest black leather. There were others of course but it was the only one of such an exquisite cut, so masterfully sewn together. Reaching for it at the same time we found unexpectedly one another's hands. Our fingers brushed and strangely I took her hand instead of withdrawing from the awkwardness, the transgression, touching a stranger in public. Maybe some part of me knew that I knew her. Maybe my fingers knew.

And we looked up, away from the jackets, and into each other's eyes, mine blue, hers green. Strangely we did not let go, not immediately, even though we did not know one another yet. I couldn't place her, this red-haired girl with a clear strong face wearing, I now saw, a look of such confused recognition it could only have mirrored my own. I felt (or maybe my fingers felt) the connection to be more than the superficial circumstances it generally turns out to be in such situations. I didn't think of the obvious which, by its plainness had assumed a cloak of—I must say it—invisibility.

"*Ich kenne dich,*" I said, as people do.

"*Ja näturlich, aber von wo?*"

As people do, we listed all the places we might possibly have met. It gave us no clue, for of course she and I could never both be in the same place on any given night—if she was at the same play or art opening or party or just drinking at Paradise then she wouldn't be available to drive us home and listen to every word we said. Finally, as I should have at first, I asked her what she did. She told me she was a taxi driver and only then did I exclaim, "*Du! Du! Du fährst uns nachhause vom Paradise!*"

It all seems so obvious now—she always drove us; she was in KaDeWe that day. She saw me on the L train in lower Manhattan, going back to the west side. It seems strange, *erstaunlich,* that I didn't see it sooner, not just who she was in the department store in West Berlin that winter day now years ago, but all of it. And as to her? Who knows?

When she drove taxi she wore makeup and her hair pulled away from her face but in the department store it spilled down the shoulders of her scruffy sweater in waves; some women dress up to shop but she was not one of them. And of course, the context was unusual. My second excuse, or maybe she knew an invisibility spell I didn't know. If we're not recognized, it's as good as being invisible, isn't it? At least to those who do in fact know us.

There were always certain things I saw that you didn't see, and I realize now it is why you kept me close. That and you liked my coding. That and you liked me in bed. But if you kept me close, I'd help to keep you safe, because I saw things you didn't see. Like so many leaders, it was hard for you to find people who didn't need to put you on a pedestal. Many leaders of course, wish for this, for adulation. But you had been saved once or twice or three times by women and men who didn't worship you particularly but saw things coming you didn't see. And so you kept us close. None of us were trained bodyguards or agents. We were just people with a good eye for things, with good minds that noticed.

At the Ear Inn Karina said, "Of course I listened, why would I not? I could not help you erase your steps if I didn't know what you were doing."

"And where we were doing it."

"They buried him in the jacket."

I hadn't known and wondered if she had a photo, one in any case I wouldn't have wanted to look at. "There were two," I said, "on the same hanger, one on top of the other, the same size, it was so odd."

"Yes, I remember. In KaDeWe in Berlin im Winter," she said in the Deutschlich we both affected. "The year after *die Wende*."

After the wall came down we migrated to the east, young people from all over the world, and rented acres of loft in Prenzlauer Berg without amenities or heating for pennies and pretended we were making art.

I remember I didn't try the jacket on. I was tired and wanted to go home. (I was living in your flat at that time.) If it didn't fit you, or you didn't like it, you could bring it back. But Karina tried one on. "Is it for your husband?" I asked, for I noticed she wore a ring.

"No," she beamed. "*Nür für mich allein.*" A beautiful present for herself. Blue angel, she looked good in a man's jacket, so good. "If the second one doesn't fit him, you can wear it and then we can be twins."

"I was just thinking that." As if I could touch the mirror and merge with her.

They buried you in the second one. In East Berlin. I wasn't there because no one could find me in Paris. I'd wanted complete quiet, radio silence while I finished the work. But because of it I can't be sure. And I don't ask for a photograph.

Now I can never go back to Germany, although why should it matter? The day I met you, that is the tattoo that unlike the others I can never have removed.

Karina.

What side is she on?

But she may too forever wonder the same thing about me, and in the end we can never know the truth of one another, but perhaps the only truth is this—maybe we both just want to be with someone who knew you, who had touched you, who had let you in.

We will go to Mexico together, to Oaxaca. Taking turns wearing the remaining jacket until it is worn through in many places. And then I will find somewhere else to go. *Zusammen, oder vielleicht allein.*

As If Leaves Could
Hide Invisible Beings

ANGELIQUE DOES IT ALONE once a week, winter and summer. In summer she takes off all her clothes, wades through the mud, shoots off into the middle where she can no longer stand, treads water for a few moments, then turns around and swims back. She looks for a grassy spot on which to dry off, one not shaded by cedars, relatively free of rocks and deadfall. She smokes one cigarette before she gets dressed. She likes being naked in nature too much to give it up. Still, the thought always niggles: what if a strange man comes across her lying naked on the grass beside the Ouse, far from shouting distance? Not likely; deer season is in November.

Once when she arrived at the river there was a black bear on the other side, investigating something in the shallows. Angelique knew the bear probably wouldn't cross to attack her, but all the same she ran all the way back. The trail was knotted with deadfall, rocks, and roots. She only slowed for breath when she'd reached the back pasture, out in the open again. Her heart hammering, she listened for the dog, didn't hear him. The bear could eat her dog instead of her. That would be okay.

Angelique used to think the bear chased her all the way to the village. It was time to leave the farm, the bear was telling her.

Or maybe it was the fairies.

They were not a thing you saw, but a thing you felt. Angelique acknowledged their presence with an organ she'd never known she had, as if a gigantic eye had just been blasted open by their presence. Part mockery, part dare, there they were, hiding under the cabbage leaves. Full of shame, stooped and bent and dirty and poor and tiny and magic and otherworldly, they shaded their eyes with their hands, staring up at this giantess who had so rudely interrupted them.

"Go away," they said.

But how could she, for it was her garden after all and needed weeding?

They tried to hide under the leaves. It was pathetic really, as if leaves could hide invisible beings, which of course they can't.

"We don't want to be seen," they said. "Not yet, and not by you."

"Too bad," Angelique said.

What she meant was: *I couldn't stop seeing you if I wanted. Now that I can, it's not like I can put the ability back in its lock box for you must understand that's quite impossible.* Shutting her new enormous eye, her ear, for she couldn't really see them and they spoke not in words but in meanings and feelings sent from one to another and now to Angelique as well by some kind of faerie short wave radio. Angelique stared and stared, felt and felt with whatever the new organ was. Went inside and put on a soup to simmer. Set out dinner for the family. Read the children Tolkien before bed.

Pretending things were normal didn't really work, because as almost everyone knows, you can't go back if there is no back to go to. It had been erased, back had. Permanently. Or so it felt, for they were still there the next day and the day after and the day after that. At times Angelique even admitted she liked it, because at least this feeling of strange and fertile newness was, well, new, if quite impossible and a little creepy, but things had after all been boring for longer than she could remember.

◆◆◆

In the dream she came to a village where a ring of beautiful old houses shared a huge common garden. The garden was wild and overgrown and better because of it, at its heart a deep still enchantment. Angelique approached a house and knocked with a brass knocker and the door opened and she went in and then it swung shut behind her. The door swung shut and then they were there as they'd always been; she'd felt them a moment before they'd made themselves known: a door opening, an eye beginning to open, another eye closing to make way for the first. They advanced from all sides, imprisoning Angelique in a sleep so deep and old she knew the door would never open again; she'd never ever be able to leave. This was a spell as binding as being born: once invoked it could never be broken except by dying. It was over now. Everything she'd ever thought life was for was over, irrevocably and forever. A spell as deep as dream, as sleep, no, deeper, a sleep perhaps which had two doors: first, the door into ordinary waking life, now slammed irrevocably shut, and then the other. The one they'd taken her through, locking the first.

And so Angelique and Mort picked up and moved. Angelique built a new garden and planted it and then they came, and there were more of them than there had ever been at the farm. Eventually she got used to them and didn't worry about being crazy anymore and even got to like them and as she did they seemed to change, but it was Angelique who was changing.

◆◆◆

Since their move she wonders whether men still snowmobile on the Ouse, whether the ice ever gets thick enough anymore. Angelique always went the day after, when their trails had not yet been covered by new snow. Once she found part of a deer carcass on the frozen river, half eaten by coyotes. Farther on, a loose leg, its knee socket gruesomely mobile, which her dog found fascinating. On the way home she came upon a little hunting shack, barely larger than an outhouse, but with a window and a chimney. Angelique was afraid to look into the window. What if someone was inside? And why was she both brave and foolish enough to leave the trail?

Angelique still goes on long walks alone, except on the country roads around the village. The Ouse runs through her backyard now, home to blue herons, snapping turtles, otters and a beaver which, like the Pleistocene Castoroides, is almost the size of a sub-compact car. In the village she doesn't have to worry about people raping her or shooting her accidentally, even in deer season.

Smoking; skinny dipping alone; walking off trail; bears: it seems these things don't frighten Angelique as much as they do other women, even if they should. What frightens Angelique is something else. Like Angelique's mother, only in England, Virginia sunk stones into her pockets, submerged herself in the first Ouse.

Home from her walks, Angelique removes stones from her pockets and lines them up on the windowsill beside the post-cards of her mother's drawings. The stones are not from here, not from now; they tell the story of a different kind of life. Angelique counts the stones sometimes. One for each child, one for herself, one for Mort. Because of this, one day the river's name will have a new meaning, the meaning of a stream that winds its way between worlds.

The Dreams of Trees

THERE WERE SEVERAL PAIRS of knee-high green rubber boots on the mat, including a pair that belonged to Sandrine and three that were Randy's. They were the kind of boots people wore to go fishing or hunting, with a felt lining. It wasn't possible to buy them in the city at all. She took her own shoes off by the door as she always did. Because of this almost universal rural habit, Sandrine thought, country houses generally had clean floors even when inhabited almost entirely by men.

Changing from boots into slippers, Sandrine remembered with some dismay that her husband's name wasn't Randy at all; it was Mike. Said husband was sitting at the table working on the crossword puzzle. He looked up and measured her with a lingering elevator glance from head to toe and toe to head. He didn't say a word but gave her the slightest of nods, after which he got up and put on the kettle for tea. When it was done they sat at the table and drank it.

Watching him work on his crossword she knew with a dead certainty he wasn't called Mike—not Mike nor Randy, either. She wished he would speak and give away his name. How could she forget such a thing? It wasn't as if she was eighty-two and had dementia. She was a young woman, thirty-four, in possession of a nice house in a small Ontario town and two beautiful small children who were away for the weekend, visiting their paternal grandmother two towns over.

She also had an unusually attractive husband whose name she'd forgotten. How could that be? She knew he'd been grating on her nerves lately, to the point where she'd been indulging in escape fantasies. Was forgetting his name some kind of karmic retribution for her unkind thoughts? Sandrine did a quick mental check: had she been in a car accident or recently suffered some other serious bump to her head? Was her aphasia caused by a concussion? Alas, none of these seemed true. She simply didn't know.

Just as strangely and suddenly as her husband's name had fled, Sandrine saw in her mind's eye diagonals of green lozenges printed onto the back of the upholstery of the seat in front of her. It was a childhood memory. She'd been on the train with her father in North Africa. She didn't think of the trip often and wondered why the memory was chasing her now, taking over, hanging on, not giving up. Looking out the window at the purple-black watchman hollyhocks guarding the vegetable beds, Sandrine wondered whether she would ever remember the trip again. Memory was a strange and fickle thing. She should make a note before the image fled, perhaps on the back of the phone bill that sat on the kitchen table, with its varnished veneer top and white lacquered legs.

Sandrine looked at her husband and smiled; he was so gorgeous it was hard not to. He smiled back and bent over his crossword as if he welcomed the silence. That's what being married for a long time got you: the possibility of making and drinking tea all without needing to speak. Sandrine figured it for a good thing, most days.

She remembered camels she'd seen, slurping out of buckets at an oasis near Djerba. At some point her father had gotten off to go on an important visit alone, and the train had sped on through the night without him. Sandrine remembered sitting alone in her seat, trying to converse with strangers in languages she didn't know well, wishing for blankets, more money, apples, friends, all of the above. In the end she'd fallen asleep counting lozenges, noticing their patterns, how they repeated. She'd written in her journal, but not about pomegranates or camels or the magical train ride itself. Instead she'd described the strange upholstery on the back of the seat in front of her. Sandrine had been so young at the time, a child really, thirteen or so, scribbling in a notebook that might still be in a carton in the attic. If she saw it, would she even recognize the book? Why was she thinking of it now?

She'd learned that often enough the timing and content of certain thoughts had significance. Djerba, the Island of Dreams, was in Tunisia, a country she had visited at thirteen with her father. He had wanted her to see the place of her birth and after her mother had died had used part of the insurance money to pay for the trip. Had their train really crossed the old Roman causeway to Djerba, or had they taken a bus or taxi for this last leg of the journey? It was all so long ago she wasn't sure. Maybe the train had been a dream train, just as Djerba had been Ulysses's Isle of the Lotus Eaters.

How could Sandrine even know such obscure literary trivia? Maybe, sitting on the train, she'd read a tourist brochure whose useless facts were now emerging from her subconscious like flotsam escaped from lengthy entrapment beneath the waves. Maybe some kind of mischievous metaphysical imp had taken up residence in her brain, excising important data, such as her husband's name, and replacing them with dreamy poetic child-hood memories whose relevance, if any, she couldn't fathom. At least not now, not yet.

Was it even a real memory? And if false memories weren't inserted by evil therapists and hypnotists, as often alleged, where in fact did they come from? Anyway, evil therapists usually inserted memories of childhood abuse, and the train memory, while dripping with anxious feelings of abandonment, wasn't about abuse.

Sandrine felt tempted to haul a stepladder into the bedroom and unfold it under the trapdoor. She'd climb to the top step, tea in hand. It was the kind of minor eccentricity she liked to indulge in. She told people she was practising for menopause. She'd even walked the streets of her village carrying a coffee mug, and not the stainless travel kind but a proper ceramic mug with daisies and ewes on it.

She looked at her husband meditatively chewing on his pencil end. All she had to do was ask. Was his name Ethan? Or maybe Karl Johan? If it wasn't either of those, then what was it? Maybe she'd written his name in one of her notebooks. In fact, that was highly likely.

Very quietly, so as not to disturb his chewing, she got up and tiptoed down the hall. The bedroom closet was capacious enough to hold large objects such as the stepladder in addition to their meagre supply of clothing. Leveraging the ladder out through a selection of her man's plaid shirts, she opened it beneath the pink trapdoor in the ceiling. The trapdoor was pink because Sandrine had once painted the walls and ceiling, rebelling against her husband's blues and browns and camo. It was his house; he'd inherited it along with two or three other nearby properties both large (a swampy hunt camp) and small (a cottage on one of the lakes), and every damn wall or floor or roof or exterior wall on or in each of his houses, sheds, and barns was either green or blue or brown. Sandrine remembered how when they'd begun dating she'd taken whatshisname for financially struggling because of his frayed shirts and ailing trucks. She was used to city signifiers of prosperity: clever phones and name-brand clothing. His little white clapboard house near the Brookside canal, the one she'd moved into after they'd married, had been so unassuming she'd felt a little sorry for him. Later she'd found out it was a country thing; folks had houses and plots of swamp and cedar bush tucked away all over the county, bits and pieces that had been in the family for generations. Many families were cash poor but land rich, their various parcels having been acquired during earlier times when land had been cheap to come by, having then been recently expropriated from the local Michi Saagiig. It was still cheap, comparatively speaking, tucked away in this forgotten Eastern Ontario township.

Sandrine stopped in mid-thought halfway up the ladder, imagining a house painted in camouflage. She smiled. It could be quite wonderful, certainly a talking point. Would she use the green-and-brown kind or the greyscale kind? The different types of camo had different names; Sandrine just didn't know what they were. What she did know was that she had once painted the bedroom not camo but a flaming flamingo pink. She'd done it when her husband was away hunting, just to prove that she had some say, to prove that pink was a good colour. If he hated pink so much he shouldn't have married a girl; a moose would've done just fine. Moose, after all, were brown.

Still parked halfway up, Sandrine pictured Mike's winsome moose wife and giggled. Then she climbed back down to retrieve the flashlight that always sat on her nightstand in case of a power failure; there were lots of those in the country, just as there was lots of camo. Truth was the pink had gotten to her, too—the much and suchness of it; maybe a paler pink would've done the trick just as well, proved the point, made her husband laugh instead of groan.

Once back at the top she pushed the trap door out of the way. It wasn't hinged, just a loose slab of wood squared a little irregularly to fit the slightly irregular square someone had long, long ago cut into the ceiling. Sandrine hoisted herself up and turned on the flashlight.

She'd bring the box of books down, she figured, or she'd sit up there all night, opening one book after another, trying to find the passage about the lozenges woven into or printed onto the train upholstery. If she were smart, once she'd found it she wouldn't slip the book, unlabeled, back into its box. She'd slap a sticky note on the page, or she'd get a fine-point marker and write on the cover, or she might even take the book and carry it down the ladder to keep on her night table until it drove her crazy and she could no longer stand the presence of this chapter from an earlier life, recorded in neat cursive hailing from the days before her handwriting had gone to hell.

Amazingly, the box was right near the hatch, as if someone had pushed it there for her perusal. Or else she'd had this same idea a month ago, and forgotten. Just like her husband's name.

She selected a book from the top layer, opened it in the middle and read aloud. *Over the course of a lifetime I have found that random thoughts, like dreams, can be cryptic messages from the soul, disguised or veiled, yes, but requiring only a bit of personal pondering, inspection or introspection, to parse their meaning and significance.*

Not the passage about the lozenges, not at all, but maybe there was a connection nevertheless. For instance, hadn't she just been thinking that often enough the timing of certain thoughts was significant? Did that mean there was a reason she was thinking about the train in Africa on which her father had left her, promising to meet her in Tunis the next day while he went to visit an old French girlfriend living in the south, in Tataouine?

What happened, Sandrine? Did something happen on the train that you've shut out? Is that why you're thinking so much about the damn train suddenly? Djerba's other name was the Isle of Forgetting, after all. Or is it the feeling of abandonment by your father that you're still, decades later, trying to heal? Maybe nothing beyond his departure had to have happened for you to feel so neglected. Maybe the train voyage was perfectly innocent and nice, if a little bit frightening as you spoke neither Arabic nor French well, and Tunisia isn't the sort of country in which young teen girls travel alone, then or now. Did something happen on the train, Sandrine? Think a little harder. Maybe, like her husband's name, she'd written it down in one of the notebooks, whatever it was, if there had even been anything. There were so many books in the box. Layers and layers of books, not in any kind of order. She looked at the one she held in her hand with its green cover and creamy lined pages, not all of them full. She hated wasting journals. She could resume writing in this one, just to confuse the hell out of herself when, in another ten years, she got it out of the box so she could look for her husband's forgotten name again.

What was the point of even having a husband if you couldn't even remember his name from one moment to the next? She closed the book again, looked at the cover, which all by itself ought to offer clues. Without perusing the interior, she ought to be able to discern both the approximate year and her place of residence at the time of writing. Maybe even where she'd gotten the journal itself, whether it had been a gift or something she'd purchased in a stationery store, unable to help herself, knowing she shouldn't buy it, not really, because it was expensive and the rent was due.

She opened the book to a random page.

The café I am sitting in is like the café on Sixth Street, she read. *That one was a basement café with nice white cups and healthy carrot bread. She would leave her apartment and walk there during the day. The clerks were supercilious. She felt her loneliness and her poverty were both recognized and snickered at, a little. She was cute enough and her thrift-store coat was of good wool and a becoming cut; with a church-sale silk scarf she thought she looked quite good. And yet anyone must be able to tell that she was poor and lonely, bored and aimless.*

Sandrine couldn't remember having written this, nor could she remember the café, but there had been a lot of those over a span beginning approximately at the time of the trip to Tunisia and ending when she moved into her husband's house and started a family. She never went to those sorts of cafés anymore, mainly because there weren't any in Brookside or Stony Creek, villages that favoured Canadian Chinese and breakfast specials. She examined the handwriting. It was undeniably her own, evoking the long-gone days before her cursive had gone to hell. She felt a little regretful looking at her beautiful penmanship, wondering whether she could relearn it. Trying to recover lost cursive would be sort of like going back to French or pottery, both skills she'd once been not half-bad at but had left by the wayside at some point.

Probably the same point at which she got pregnant, if not before. She'd taken up reading about nutrition and child development, consequently both French verb conjugations and wheel throwing had seemingly vanished—*poof!*—from her brain as if they'd never been there at all. Did it even matter? She wasn't with Mike or Randy or Euell or Darrel because of his name but because, with him, she no longer had to be that person, the one who scribbled obsessively in sad cafés, the one who had looked out the windows of a train that had seemed, forever, to pass through the North African night. On Djerba there were three-thousand-year-old olive trees, still living. What did trees that old dream of? An older dream than that of the Romans, by far.

What happened on the train, Sandrine? She had in the end tired of the years of lonely views and focused just on the upholstery, its patterns repeating, over and over. *Clack clack clackety clack*. Eventually the train had left North Africa and gone back to Canada as only dream trains can.

Sandrine heard her husband enter the bedroom. She listened to him sit down on the bed; it must be late, even by her standards. She began her descent, clutching the little green hardcover book with its descriptions of thought processes and sad cafés, if not train upholstery. Later she'd leaf through it again, and hopefully come across a list of lovers' names that would end with her husband's.

On Fire Bridge

I'M SURE NOW THAT YOU started the fires, that your desire called them into being.

I see you in our kitchen, your orange-stockinged legs up on the table, smoking cigarettes, pleased as punch. It's dawn and we haven't slept.

"We are like gods," you say, "playing marbles in space." I like you saying it; I like your arrogance. I like how you always push me to stay up late, when, if it was up to me, I'd have been in bed hours ago. But you need those sunrises, need what they give you.

We walked together so very far, little friend, much farther than I ever could've gone without you. I was so happy! We dreamed together, prying open all the doors in space, doors that were never supposed to be opened, at least not by us. The revolutions that occurred in far corners of the galaxy because of our pliers! That were never supposed to occur, at least not for that reason. In the very centre of things we found a gaping hole and fell into it. Time yawned. In its breath we were taken apart and reassembled, exquisitely, in a different way.

♦♦♦

In my memory I come with you till halfway across the bridge. It is so cold on your damn bridge, a shivering place, and underneath us the waters rage, a stormy winter current so strong I'm afraid it will carry me away, even when I'm just looking at it. I never thought for a moment you were planning a much longer journey, a journey you would never return from. I come up behind you, always the dawdler, going only because you have gone, sometimes you fool me, allowing me to believe it is I who leads.

On the bridge I stay back a few feet, watching, a little terrified, how you sit on the edge, your legs dangling, staring into the whirlpools. I like it, but it's very strong; enough of God's raw breath to last me a whole month. But you, you always want to stay. You call me a wimp. All the same, you want me with you. When we do leave, you explain, it's because of me, because you don't want to stay alone. I sigh. We go home together, home to breakfast specials and laundry and floors that always get dirty again. I am content just to be with you, but for you there is never enough; you are so hungry, always wanting to go back. Over morning coffees we argue, and the outcome is always the same. You will go alone, you say, if I don't come.

When I met you I thought I was the brave one, the adventurer; sometimes you even let me believe it, for a little while, so long as it meant I'd come a little further, stay a little longer. Until of course the time came I didn't go. And now I retrace our worn steps, calling, hoping to find you.

♦♦♦

The surface of the water rippling. Scudding smoke, embers. The fire is close by tonight. The rain turns cold, turns white. Pebbly stone rough under my hands. The bridge's railing. One hand, the right one, curled around a cigarette. Cigarettes change taste when it turns cold, when the snow comes. The new sharp smell reminds me of you. I smoke: the tips of my fingers go numb and tingly with clues. You are nearby.

And now this writing has led me to you, to a voice that seems to be yours, to a place like the places you loved, the bridges. "Isn't it good here?" you say in my mind. "Isn't it good?"

And I say, "God, how I've missed you, how I've missed this

strange feeling, as though my cells were electrified, as though I'd been drinking for a week, as though I hadn't slept in years. Oh God, oh God," I say.

You chide me, saying, "If only you'd come too, that last time, like you promised, everything would have been different."

Perhaps I did promise.

If only I'd had the courage to leap into the fire, then I would find you still alive, unsinged. I go in my mind, now, just for a moment, to be with you. You are always inside the fire now, dancing. It's as if I can see you through the flames; as though you come out and join me to say, "Hey, no burn marks."

We talk. I care about burned bridges, about writing, but you never have. "It doesn't matter," you say. "Death doesn't matter, appearances are a lie. They saw insanity, those others, but that was only the outer shell. I am where I have always been, dancing inside the fire." Ah, that strange feeling of being with you.

It's always night and sleeting on your bridge.

You turn to go. You smile, will I cross with you tonight? But I don't, not even this time, this second chance. If I did, they'd burn the bridge, and besides, I have to be somewhere in the morning, to write you into life. I stroke your leather jacket good-bye, with a tenderness born of fear, as though even in this dream our lives are so dangerous we might really never see one another again. As perhaps they are.

My footsteps ring on the empty bridge but you call me back one more time. "Kim?"

And I say, "Yes?" and you hand me a film can, full of wooden matches.

"You might need them later," you say, when I ask.

♦♦♦

In the morning the city is grey and full of rain; I walk through it bleakly, missing you. The newspaper is full of stories of fires, and I am jealous, knowing you caused them.

I go to the bridge, but in the morning it is just a bridge, snow swirling into the river. There is the smell of smoke, of fire, but I know that even if I crossed here, I'd never be able to find you; the snow has obscured your footsteps. Still, I hear you laughing at me, faint as a train whistle, very far away. Later on I sit in cafés and look out at the snow. I drink coffee and smoke endlessly, writing in notebooks, feeling I have failed.

♦♦♦

The forgetting begins, the loss of memory. For days that feel like centuries I sit in my diner by the river, reading my newspapers, watching the snow swirl. I forget what you look like; everyone becomes you. They build a highway, a busy one, between the diner and the river; all summer the bulldozers are hungry, tearing the earth. When winter comes again I have finished the front section, moved on to arts and entertainment. When the snow returns I am sure you will come back, will bloom again like a winter flower. I bring a boom box to the diner, and I listen to talk shows and to my favourite tapes while I wait for my pancakes. When they close up for the night they leave one light on for me, and let me help myself to coffee. I become a legend, a tourist attraction; bohemians and artsy types come and sit down beside me, hoping to catch some of my fire, hoping they, too, will become so free they will be allowed to stay in diners all night long, watching the fish swim around the room at purple morning, let out from their aquarium for an hour at dawn before the place opens for the nine-to-fivers to get their before work coffees.

♦♦♦

Purple chrysanthemums appear in my water glass, books on my table, television sets. Soon they move out the next table to replace it with a washer and dryer; after the showers are installed I never have to leave. Still I forget you. Still I see others. A man with long yellow hair tied back with a string shares my table for weeks; he shares my ability to go without sleep, or else he's the only one I know who can drink as much coffee as me. He makes tiny objects so small one needs a microscope to see them, but his hands are like laser beams and he can see without one, so one learns his trick and one's own eyes become microscopes too. Tiny sections of the table become very large, magnified a thousand times, until one can see them, the things he makes: intricate boxes full of electronic parts and food for the soul. They are beautiful, they are art.

Then, slowly, I begin to remember. I don't remember what it is I have forgotten, just a nagging sensation in the thighs. I stare at a man in the phone booth, his hand cupped around the receiver. Is it you? But the question is meaningless, because I *have* forgotten who you are supposed to be, what it is you do, only (and until recently I didn't know even this) that once you existed; now you do again. The blond man has moved on, but yet another stranger, this time with short dark hair, comes in and piles his knapsack on the floor under my table. He goes to the bathroom and I get up to do his laundry; in the pockets of his jeans I find maps, maps and names.

For the first time in three years I leave the diner. I call a number I found in the stranger's pocket, on the same page as a map of a bridge. A woman answers, her voice breezy and sincere. Suddenly I know where she lives; it is a house I once stayed in with you. She didn't live there then. There were others; we didn't know them well. We'd sit around the kitchen table reading science fiction books (everyone in that house read science fiction), comparing plots and styles of writing, bitching about the price of cigarettes, the price of time. Whenever I was with you, it was always someone else's kitchen. In this memory which is not a real one but one invented by the telephone wires, one which cannot exist independently of them, you are going away somewhere, and I am sad. Through the smoke of the cooking, the cigarettes, the people, you smile the smile of a brother and I am comforted.

"I'll be back," you say.

But you weren't. In that life you never came back. Or I waited for you in the wrong place, on the wrong bridge. When I hang up the phone I am released from the invented life, the life that never happened except in the electronic part of memory that exists because of telephones and computers, but I am still left with the nagging suspicion that you are real, that somewhere I will find a real memory of you. So I go to the bridge. It snows; I wait for you. I do not know if this is the right bridge, but it is the only bridge I know.

◆◆◆

You died in the fire. But that was in another city, and you and me both had different names then. Maybe in this city I have moved to, this emerald green city below the border, you will have a new name, one that doesn't burn so easily. Maybe in this city we will meet on the bridge. They do not know, those artists, that this freedom I have is not mine. They do not know I have it only because of you.

◆◆◆

I remember how I used to visit you in the hospital and you would tell me you wished for drugs and shock treatments, how it would make you better, because then you could no longer think and see and feel. "But that would mean being stupid," I said, and you said it would be better. "But that would mean happiness was only possible if you were stupid," and again you said it would be better.

Sometimes it is as though all of love died with you in that fire. I couldn't bear it, so I tried to escape, hoping even the memory of you could disappear in this fog. And now it begins to be not you I mourn, but someone else whose name I can never place, someone whose loss I mourn more than all the others, someone whom my human lovers can only approximate, be representations of.

Castoroides

1) IN MY VILLAGE the swollen creek lapped at the edge of the sidewalk. Your young friend and I squatted there, dipping our fingers in. It wasn't just plain water, lapping over the edge of the sidewalk; it contained secrets. The secret of where you were. The secret of why we missed you. Your friend and I dipped our fingers in and sucked off the secrets one at a time. Then I put my fingers in your friend's mouth and he put his in mine, and we sucked each other's secrets. Both my secrets and his secrets were about you. The secret of who you are. The secret of how to get you back. When we were done doing that I told him to go inside and iron your lace collars.

2) What with no ironing to do I swept the stairs from top to bottom and bottom to top. I went back into the bathroom and looked at the untouched stack of wrinkled white collars, at the iron, at the tiles on which you had painted animals. You and your friend and I used to keep busy painting broken dishes with birds and flowers, creating not fake antiquities but relics from a time not yet. "I'm not a good person," I remember telling you, "I'm a bad person with healing powers."

3) This story connects to all the other stories. Am I ready to finish it now? You had already been gone for a long time before I painted the stars. I could have told a different story. I could have picked a different staircase to follow down from the freshly painted stars. Out of this story. I could have sat at the sewing machine today and sewn words. I am making

a yellow quilt. It is hard work and time consuming. If only I could type on my sewing machine. The sun faded the curtains in streaks. I take them down and cut them into squares. The soft white stripes, irregularly shaped, were made by the sun. I lay these stripes crosswise to one another. I affix things to the squares. My mother's face. Transparent silk. Coyotes. Pine trees. The great grey owls. Your face.

4) We are the moment that we need. This time it's easier to repaint the stairs than to try and clean them yet again. Today I even abandoned my quilt and went outside to remind your friend he promised he'd help with your ironing but he was already gone, his big flat tail thwacking the water loudly to announce his submergence. Just before he dove I saw he wore one of your white lace collars. Underwater it wouldn't matter whether they were ironed or not.

One Day I'm Gonna Give Up the Blues for Good

L ITTLE DAVIS IS DEAD, his body dragged out of the river this dawn. He was murdered, his light snapped out by some jalloo who couldn't let him live for not giving it all. Jalloo. It's a word that means client, in our game. Benji made it up one night when she was drunk and high, and it stuck.

Me and Little worked together, down in the Clinic on River Street. The Clinic. To cure what ails you. Whatever it may be. Cure the blues with The Blues, I say. Clinic is the only place you can get the stuff. Little only started working here after he got his habit. Most people, it's where we got ours. But not poor Little. He had me to fuck him up.

Royally.

I come in to work tonight, even though Frankie tells me to stay home. I come in to sit in this chair, soft and grey and comfortable. I come in to look out this window, out onto the street, where I keep hoping I'll see Little dance around the corner, swing into the big glass doors to start shift. But I know he won't.

Because he's dead.

Outside, the blue CLINIC sign blinks off and on, its reflection flashing in the puddles below. The Clinic.

Everything begins here. Here is where it all ends.

At home his ghost sits on the stool under the factory windows, watching the ships on the river, looking for my face in the night crowds below.

But he won't find it.

Because I'm here. And because ghosts never find each other.

I am a ghost now, and The Blues have all of me, when nothing, and no one should ever have all.

All the time you think it's you that wants the drugs, when really it's the drugs that want you.

They got me now.

♦♦♦

Benji comes in, on break from her case. She dances with herself, in front of the mirror. She sings. "Who do you love?"

"Little Davis," I say, even though I know it's just a song she likes. Outside, the streetlight winks red.

Tells me he's dead.

Benji goes to the fridge, takes out two beers, brings me one. I suck on it, set it down next to the other, stare at the window.

She brings me her kimono, drapes it around my shoulders. "You'll catch your death," she says, and I think, no, I can't, I already caught someone else's. The kimono is turquoise, with dragons embroidered in silver and gold. Benji is beautiful: half black and half Italian. She wears her hair in long dreads; they dance around her thin face like dragons. Her dancing hair makes the room go quiet, all still like before the thunderclap. The stillness wraps around me, a second kimono. In my head I thank her for it.

Out loud I say: "Me and Little was gonna quit this year, give up The Blues for good. I don't know what to give up now."

Benji comes over, opens my mouth ever so gently, rests a cigarette between my lips.

I smoke it, thinking it doesn't matter if you die of cancer when you can't feel. "I used to be able to feel," I say to Benji.

"How could you tell?" she asks, dancing.

I remember the last time, but I can't talk about it to Benji. I couldn't even talk about it to Little. So I tell her about the time before that. "When Marianne left it felt like I was torn open and my guts pulled out and spread all over the floor and stepped on."

Benji laughs, and I can't really blame her.

Marianne is the first lover I ever lived with, and the only one, besides Little. I would say she was my first lover but she wasn't. She was the first one that counted. "My hands shook all the time. The skin under my eyes went grainy, like a photograph that's been blown up too much. Like those."

Wet rings on them now, from my beer bottles. Prints of the body they dragged out of the river. But blown up too much. The eyes look bad.

"Don't look at those, Ruby. That's asking for it."

The cops brought them in for identification purposes. I could identify them, all right. No, officer, that's not my sweetheart. My sweetie was beautiful, and what you got there is a piece of meat, all swelled up and ugly. Cops got no sense of humour.

Benji fishes around in her stuff piled up in the corner beside the mirror. She makes her piles of stuff wherever she goes, says it makes her feel at home. I wish I could do that. Feel at home. "You got an itch to look at pictures, you look at this one."

She kneels on the floor beside me, showing me the postcard. I look down at it. It's a photograph of a lot full of gravel, raked around a pile of rocks.

"So," I say.

"It's a garden. Chuckie sent it to me. It'd called Ryonji and it's in Japan. That's where he went."

"It's a dead quiet kind of place, Benji."

"Quiet, maybe, but no more dead than you right now."

"I wish it was me and not him. You know we were going to Japan? Right after we gave up The Blues. His buddy in Kyoto had a place for us to stay. The one who sends him oranges. You know Little was part Japanese."

"Yeah," says Benji, dancing. "I know." She turns around, dances to me now instead of the mirror. "Too bad it wasn't the right part."

"Yeah. Too bad."

I know she is dancing for me. To make me still, like Chuckie's garden. I wonder whether Benji can still feel, or whether all of her has learned this stillness.

I stare out the window.

◆◆◆

It was last Christmas. He was dancing on a table, juggling oranges. He wasn't wearing anything, and he was covered head to toe in silver body paint. He looked maybe seventeen. Later I learned he was twenty, but it was too late; by then he'd already made me feel old.

It was afternoon, the Ocean Club. I'd gone there to try and shake off this case that had left me more spooked than I'd been in years. Since Marianne. It's an arty bar—people who go there have weird hair and no money; they sit around a lot, waiting for life to turn dangerous on them. Because I never had that choice, the Ocean is a kind of vacation for me, and last Christmas it was as far away a place as I could think of from where I'd just been, the chamber of horrors that was my jalloo's mind.

Little ended his song by tossing his oranges into the crowd. There were six of them and the last one he kept for me. When I caught it he smiled. There are smiles, and then there are smiles. Little had the second kind. I got up and followed him into the dressing room. Eyes followed me all the way there, but I didn't mind; I liked the feel of them, tickling my neck.

He was sitting on a stool at the makeup mirror, just lighting up a joint. I closed the door behind me, sat down on the other one, peeled the orange. It's a trick I use on my jalloos; nonchalance gives me the upper hand.

"Mandarins," he said, passing me the number. "From Japan. I got a buddy there sends them to me every Christmas."

So we both knew the same game. I laughed. It was a beginning.

We smoked, ate mandarins. I wanted to sit there all afternoon, basking in his beauty. He was so beautiful: thin, slight even, his body still a boy's, legs dangling from the stool, graceful and bony. His black hair was cropped close to the skull, showing off his Asian cheekbones. The Ocean is a dive. Its dressing rooms are tatty: torn leopard upholstery with the foam bulging out. At River Street even the walls are broadloomed. It gets stifling. I liked the peeling paint, the bare bulb; they set him off, made me want him more. Made me want his startling blue eyes. More.

His smile made me happy to be alive; after this case, a scarce feeling, hopelessly precious. I wanted so bad to make him feel the same way. I wanted so bad for him to like me, but I didn't think he could, ever, like someone like me.

So I reached for the only way I knew would work for sure. Unzipped the pouch on my belt, took the little packet out. Poured blue powder out in a little heap onto the shelf under the mirror.

"Merry Christmas," I said.

◆◆◆

A jalloo like my father. Like him, a child molester. Like the leftover bits, the ones I couldn't kill. The bits of memory I couldn't wipe, no matter how long I worked Clinic, how long I lived The Blues. There's not many of them left, those daughter fuckers, thanks in part to us, to the Clinics. But the ones that don't get to us before they go bad, get sent to us after. Except this one just walked in off the street. He headed straight for me, like he was special ordered. They fit me like a glove, all his fuckups.

And so we worked it out.

Like my dad, he'd woken up one day, one eye at least. Taken a look around and realized it was not too cool, what he'd once been up too. Thought he could fix it, and in the worst way. He even found the creep who'd sell him the gun. But on his way home, this wiseacre passes the Clinic, like he does every day of his life. Only this time, something twigs and he comes walking in, straight into my waiting arms. Just lucky, I guess. I was probably the only one in the world who could fix him, aside from his daughter, and you can count her out.

Only to be of any help to him, I had to unlock all my boxes, and they were glued mighty shut. Yanking all those rusty nails out cost me more than it did him. It cost him too, but by the end of the week he'd gained some. He didn't even hate his mother anymore. Saw that where her handiwork left off, his had picked up. That surprised him. It always does.

It's like kindergarten, really; making animals out of clay. Just for the hell of it, you think you'll make a monster. Then when clay class is over, you're stuck with it, saying, "Where did this monster come from?" Like you hadn't made it all by your lonesome. But by the end of the week, he'd finally understood. That if you got the itch to make something, there are other things besides monsters. It's not like it's written in the rule book somewhere, that a monster is what you have to make. Only a lot of people see it that way. Some make big monsters, some make little ones. By the end of clay class, you've got one hell of a collection. And all those monsters, boy, do they have some party.

He told me about his daughter. Miranda. His stories of her felt like me. That's how come I could get at him; I knew her so well. After he left I had to call, explain things. It's policy. Dumbfuck policy, but you know how policy gets. It's stick to it or your job. It was just my luck she answered the phone.

"Hi," she said, all breathless, like I was her girlfriend or someone she'd been expecting.

I sat there in that grey-walled room, the telephone in one hand, his gun in the other. I'd made him leave it, but now I was wishing I hadn't. I was thinking I would shoot myself instead of talk to her. Not for her, you understand.

For me it would be easier. But I did. Tell her. I told her her daddy wasn't coming home anymore. Told her why, what it was he'd planned. Told her things he'd said, things no one in the world but her could've known. Things that made her breathing go funny over the telephone.

I hoped she wasn't crying. I wondered what it looked like, the room she was sitting in. Not grey. Please, for her sake, let it not be grey.

"I hate him," she said, when she could say something.

"I know, honey. I know. He won't hurt you now."

Now, if he hurts anyone, it'll be himself. But I didn't say that part, didn't tell her I couldn't get rid of the monster, could only turn it inside out.

"I only know your word that what you said he was gonna do is true. I know you said you made it so he's never coming back. I know I loved my daddy. I love him. Even right now I do."

His gun lay stupid in my lap, stupid and silent. I couldn't use it now. I never could have used it. On me. On anyone. I'm just not made that way. She'd led me to the spot, the one we come to, all of us, sooner or later. The spot that was my job. Take people there, take them out of it again. If you can. Everyone but me. For me the spot was made of memory, the feeling of a little girl I'd been, all crumpled up and thrown away. Was still. So I told her. I couldn't do anything else, just tell her and tell her, how it had been with me and him.

She listened to me, like the little trouper she was.

She was just a kid, like I'd been. Only for me there hadn't been anyone to explain. Why I survived, when my testimony sent my daddy away for good. That I loved him too, always would, no matter how much I hated him. That neither love nor hate would make me free.

That it was him who was bad, and not me.

And after I'd said goodbye to her his monster was still with me, sticky like glue. I felt like it was mine now, and not his. Even after four years, you sometimes forget how to let it go. His murderous heart was circling me, in orbit around my soul like a darkened moon.

♦♦♦

"Where'd you get that?"

"Only one place this comes from," I said, smearing a line of blue powder down my nose. "Help yourself."

But he was already painting it around his eyes, laughing at himself, a blue raccoon. That's how it works. It sinks into the skin, gets absorbed into the bloodstream.

Finds the heart, the brain.

"Thank you for loving me as much as you do," said Little Davis.

♦♦♦

Oh, The Blues, you learn to live The Blues. The Blues is what we call it because of its colour, little packets of blue powder, fringe benefits to the trade. If you have the habit, you're Living the Blues. Officially it's not habit forming but what else could it be for how it makes you feel. Like you're loved. Like you love. Love. That's our other name for it. Love and Blues, two opposite kind of names, for the paradox it is, the double-edged blade.

We're given an allotment to use in therapy on the clients where nothing else works; sometimes it can make people see the truth of themselves, but without violence, without pain. Makes them able to perform that open-heart surgery of the psyche that is necessary to their survival, to ours. Gives them a little light to travel their dark river. We are only their guides, and not always good ones. We suffice.

Ostensibly the government bureaucrats who administer the Clinics issue it to us for therapeutic use only, but they give us a lot more than we need to patch up all the broken suckers that walk in the door. It's an open secret that it's our danger pay. The breakdowns, the burnouts among therapists are so high they know the only way they can keep us is with The Blues. And by the time we realize how dangerous, how hard the work really is, and are ready to quit, we're hooked. By then we're strung out. 'Cause after you've emptied yourself, after you've torn yourself into tiny pieces leading some poor stranger home, you need a little solace for yourself as well, a little Love to get you through the night. And after a while you just need.

It took Little to teach me that as good as it works, it isn't the real thing. You lose that distinction. If you ever knew the difference, you forget. Little died, and I remembered. It's an imitation, and a cheap one, and the closest so many people ever get to love.

◆◆◆

"How much did it cost?"

"Did what cost?" asks Benji, rolling a joint.

"Your peace," I say. "I don't trust it. You got to tell me how much it cost."

Benji. For the first time I see what looks like an emotion on her face. A little half smile like a voice breaking. Since Chuckie went away, Benji has learned how to be still, how to be alone. But somewhere it still hurts. I can tell. In this business, you learn all the signs.

"It cost," says Benji. "It cost."

"You just like the wife killers, Benji." I say it through my teeth, slouching way down in the grey chair: "You just like the twisted fuckers you is paid to fix. You just ain't as far gone."

"How so?" asks Benji, supercilious, raising an eyebrow. In this business, we learn bad games. We even learn to like them.

"You just like them, Benji. Deep down all you want is to be loved."

She laughs. Benji's laugh. "And you, Ruby, what do you want?"

"That is so easy, Benji, so easy. I want Little to be alive again. I didn't love him enough. That's why he dead, Benji, because of me. His jalloo murdered him, but it could just as well have been me."

"But honey," she says, "you didn't even know what love was. How could you know, being what you are?"

◆◆◆

We went home to my place. We walked there, stopping in alleyways to paint ourselves with blue graffiti. I live in a loft, further down the river on Kenya Road. All the way there Little kept telling me he loved me. It got to be embarrassing. This guy is such a kid, I'd think, letting the stuff go to his head so much.

"I love you, Ruby," he said. "I really love you."

We were lying on the Chinese rug, listening to music, staring at the ceiling. Painting it Blue. "Yeah, honey, I know. I love you too." And I'd roll over to change the music, to reach for more. And I thought I did. He was so beautiful. His eyes like the ocean, washing through me. Telling me he loved me.

And I told him about Clinic. People love to hear that shit, why you work there, what it's really like. So you tell them, you give them some kicks. Cheap thrills for them, easy points for you. But with Little I somehow got it wrong. With Little I got it wrong right from the start.

"I don't want you to go crazy, Ruby," he said. "I love you too much." He was looking down at me, into my eyes. He was obstructing my view of the ceiling.

"What are you talking about, me going crazy?"

"All you people go crazy. I never met anyone before works River Street. I never thought I wanted to, heard you were all crazy. But you're not crazy at all, and now, I don't want you to be. You're different. You're not like I expected."

"Listen," I say, propping myself up on an elbow, "crazy is part of the job. Psychosis in a controlled environment. So it doesn't happen out on the street. But you got to go with them, to where they go. And keep one foot on the beach, so's you can lead them back out. Only sometimes you don't come back. Sometimes they pull you in and drown you. I've felt it happening. Benji got me out one time, cut me loose. Some

126

of them you got to let go. We're still human, we government workers. It's hard sometimes, to remember there's that one or two a year, you got to cut them loose. It becomes a point of pride, fixing people. But it's better to lose them than yourself as well. They put those ones on drugs, keep them locked up like they used to. There's not many anymore. Not nearly as many as there used to be. Because of us."

"But they don't pay you enough, Ruby. Even this," he says, stroking my arm, leaving blue trails there, "this is lovely, but it isn't enough."

"I love you too, baby."

And after that he just tried to make me laugh.

And he did. He made me laugh for weeks, while we stayed high. I didn't go in to work, except to pick up my ration of Blues. Because I'm good, Frankie put up with it. And because Benji told him I was in love. And every day Little made me feel younger.

I felt young again, and I felt evil. I kept turning my back on it, thought it was residue from my last jalloo I couldn't shake off. But it wouldn't rub off, wouldn't come off, no matter how much Blue I scrubbed at it with, how much Love. No matter how much of Little I used. But it was mine. It was my very own monster.

I didn't know that then. I didn't know it when we didn't have enough anymore to keep the two of us going and Little came home one day, telling me he'd filled out an application for a job at the Clinic. I didn't even suspect when I heard myself tell him how good he'd be. It's a No Experience Preferred type of gig. They train you; it's based on a personality profile they get from a bunch of tests they run on you. But I didn't need to see the test results. I knew they'd accept him. He'd be better than me, better than Benji even. He had the dotted line around him, could merge, join others; see with them.

The night before he was to start training we thought we'd celebrate, do up what we had left in one big bang. And when the sky outside turned the same colour with morning, Little told me he loved me again.

"I love you too, baby. I love you because you're so beautiful…"

Only this time, Little told me no.

"No," he said. "You don't love me. That's just The Blues talking, and now you've made me hear them too. They've fucked me up, and I'm hard to fuck. I got too much polish, most things just slide right off. But The Blues has stuck, has made me need what I thought was just a good time. Not like you. You I loved from the start, although you never would believe me. You tried to buy me, Ruby. Didn't think you were worth shit, didn't think I could love you for yourself."

I went to the bathroom and locked the door, looked at myself in the mirror. Listened to his footsteps follow me, stop outside. Listened how his voice had gone quiet. Scary quiet. Saying: "You don't love me. You think I'm just some dream The Blues dreamed up. You don't even know what love is."

I looked at myself in the mirror. Opened my mouth. Heard: "You never could handle your drugs. You're just a kid. Go to bed, get some sleep. We can talk about it in the morning, if you still want. If you remember." Then I turned the shower on, loud, so I wouldn't hear what else he might have to say. So he wouldn't hear me crying.

♦♦♦

He forgave me. To prove it he even moved his stuff into my place. He didn't have much. Some clothes. A photograph album of some family. I threw that out, jealous. The only pictures I still had of family were scratched onto my brain, no matter how hard I tried to get rid of them. But Little forgave me.

It was hard, always being forgiven. Before, he'd always made me laugh, but now he had me taking showers all the time. I was never cleaner.

He finished training, started his first case. Frankie started him on an easy one: a teenage girl who'd had her heart broke. But

Little was good, too good; he didn't just heal her, he left her singing. And maybe that is what healing is, after all.

But it wasn't just the first one; it was all his jalloos that followed. They all came away clean as spoons. Little spent himself for all of them like he was a stock market crash about to happen. When it came to throwing pearls before swine, he was the prince. And I thought it was just he was new to The Blues.

He said it was the money he liked. He did, too; money he had for the first time. He bought presents for his friends, vintage silk kimonos he had sent from Japan. For Benji, a turquoise one, with dragons embroidered in silver and gold.

For her to dance in. Little loved to watch Benji dance.

"When you dance," he told her, "I don't need much more in the world." And she danced more often, because of it.

Sometimes he gave money to strangers in the street. "I like to make people feel better," he'd say. It wasn't only the money. Little loved his work; he thought it mattered.

◆◆◆

Living The Blues with you. We'd come off case and go dancing in the clubs that line the river: The Ocean, 1001 Knights, Kenya. Little knew all the doors and bartenders from his days as a performance artist. We never paid covers, and our first rounds always came on the house. They welcomed him home, his people. With me it was different. Little introduced me as his best friend, as the love of his life, but they turned away, mouths sharpening at the corners. I was the magician, the one who'd disappeared him, brought him back transformed: a therapist at River Street. The job attracts rumour-mongering faster than illicit sex. I played mysterious woman for them. I know all the lines; for some jalloos, it's the only game in town, at least at the beginning.

When the clubs emptied at four there'd be parties, speakeasies, restaurants. And then we'd go home. Every morning between jobs we'd see the sun come up from my big factory windows.

We'd see the sky change colour, shift from black to violet to blue. Blue. Washes of Blue. Awash in Blue.

"It's good," he said. "You're very good."

"This is all I've ever wanted." And it was.

But the morning came that Little disappeared, lost me in the crowd of night faces, slipped away on the dance floor at Kenya.

I looked everywhere. I spent fortunes on a half-awake cab-driver, asking him to wait outside. He waited, and I always came out alone. He grumbled at me in his rear-view mirror, telling me I'd never learn. Finally he drove me home.

No Little there to kiss me to sleep, just a hollow in my gut where he'd been. The bed was big and grubby; the morning light too critical for the dust we were always too happy to clean. I got dressed again and walked over to the Fifth Street Deli, and on my way there clouds came, and it started to rain. With the rain, even the pigeons took cover.

◆◆◆

It was noon when he found me at my table, littered with newspapers, coffee cups, Kleenex. He ordered a tea and sat down across from me. He looked different. I was withered, shrunken, but the hours had changed Little the other way; he was more substantial. His body took up space, filled the room; I'd only seen him float before. But Little wasn't dancing any more.

"You shouldn't have done that, Little."

"Ruby."

"How come you done what you did?"

"We're going to quit."

"Quit? What are we going to quit? You don't want me anymore. Is that what you're trying to say?"

"No. No, it's not, stupid. You and I are going to quit our jobs at River Street. Preferably we are going to quit this town, this country. We are going to quit."

"You sure know how to ruin a good thing, baby."

It seems he'd seen a friend turn blue. The other kind. From lack of breath. They are always cooking up new drugs to dump on the street, and this one hadn't passed the test. Or it had. Whichever way you look at it.

"Drugs are thieves," Benji always said.

"The Blues is just the same, Ruby. Maybe it don't steal your breath but it numbs your soul. Just because it's government run doesn't mean it's exempt. Especially because. I don't need to see it, what's happening to us. To you, especially. I'm new to this game, but you, Ruby, are going nowhere fast."

Big deal, I figure. I've been going nowhere fast my whole life and I still haven't arrived. "Yeah sure, Little," I say. "We quit. You and me. You gonna go back to dancing on tables at The Ocean? That silver paint shit for your skin, Little. You know some other way to feel this good?"

"It doesn't look to me like you feel very good, Ruby." And then he looked tired. I'd never seen him look tired before. It made me feel sad to know even Little could get burned out. That he would get old. I put my hand over his.

"Come on," I said. "Let's go home."

◆◆◆

We're sitting at the big factory windows, looking down at the ships. I've told you we'll quit, but I'm afraid. I'm afraid if I take away The Blues this will be gone too, these moments with you. Without The Blues, you'll see me as I really am, and, having seen, you'll leave me. Why would you stay?

I remember what it was like here, before you came. I'd sit at this window for hours at a time, smoking cigarettes, watching the river. And towards dawn, when the loneliness got too sharp, when the memories of my father came crowding in, I'd reach for The Blues. I'd send him away again, send him drifting down the long blue river of forgetting. Then when he was gone, I'd be alone. And I would dance. And in the morning, there would be birds.

There's silences between us as we sit here, watching the river. Palpable silences I can touch, that I know will open, will draw apart like a curtain, giving birth to what?

Little hands me the joint, as though, holding it, I'll be defenceless, will have to listen.

And he tells me I am proud to be a scar.

I don't say anything, because the curtains are drawing apart, and they're taking my breath with them. I can't speak, so Little tells me what I'm saying.

"It's like you say to everyone, "You can't hurt me, see how hurt I am already." You do yourself in so there's only leftovers for the rest of the hyenas. You take all their glory away—and you think that's good enough—you think you've won. But you ain't. 'Cause when you're Blue you're stuck, you never get to rise above it, to where the real colours are. The colourful colours. There's always been people who really do love you, Ruby. There always will be. You're lucky that way. For some people, there really isn't anyone. You've met enough of them on the job. You should be able to tell the difference."

He gets up, goes over to the stereo, turns the music down. "You're right. Most people don't give a shit about you. But the ones who really do care, you should treat them well."

The curtains are all the way open now and I'm trying as hard as I can to feel what's there, what it is they've opened to. Because it can't be seen. You have to feel it.

And I think maybe it's love. The other kind I hadn't known existed. I think maybe this time I can finally afford to believe, that this time he's given me the currency I need to hear the words only love could make him speak. I wonder from who Little learned it. He's only twenty years old. I wonder who made Little get so wise.

He comes walking back towards me. He's wearing a red kimono. With birds of paradise. At least, I think that's what they are. "Treat yourself well, Ruby. You, more than anyone, deserve it."

But I don't. I don't deserve it. I don't deserve him. If I had, I wouldn't have tried to buy him. For a moment you get a glimpse of it, your chance at happiness, but it's not a real chance, because no one gets happiness, at least I've never met anyone who did. It's just a trick, to let you know what you're missing. So that it hurts more, when you wake up, and things are the same as they ever were.

"You're too smart," I say. "You're too good-looking. You make me feel old, and I'm only twenty-six. And you make me feel ugly, and dumb. You're too fucking good. You're too perfect. Let up a little, will ya? Give the rest of us gimps a chance."

He looks at me from so far away, as though the room just grew a million miles long. I can't make out his face and I don't know if it's because I'm crying or because he is.

"Go away," I say. "The Blues has scrambled your brains, baby. Leave me alone."

He goes. From far away across the room I watch him go, walk ever so slowly towards the bedroom door. I sit where I am, frozen to death. I want to call him back but I don't know how. I've never done it before. At the door he stops, then turns.

"I don't believe you," he says. "I can't believe you are really such an asshole, Ruby. A real live honest to goodness asshole."

"You just a kid," I say, from where I'm sitting, frozen. The words come out of my mouth like they're someone else's, but I can't stop them, I can't help what they say.

And because, after all he is just a kid who loves me, he goes.

And in the morning he gets up and goes to work on a case he never comes back from.

♦♦♦

Benji is gone now, and I am alone in this room. This room, made, like any other room, of walls. Grey and carpeted, soft to mute the sounds that fear makes.

Before she left, Benji told me about her case, a man who

said he'd come for sex. Somewhere he'd heard that's what we were. People hear things. It took her a long time to bring him round to seeing what his real problem was. Himself. As usual. You get so tired.

Hookers. We had a big laugh over that one, me and Benji. It's our souls we measure out here, one little piece at a time. Some nights I think I'd rather be out on the street, out there in the traffic, with the red tail lights.

We are inside, always inside, enclosed by soft grey walls of fear.

"I want to possess you," he kept telling her. A real jalloo. Benji laughed, imitating him. She left me, went back to finish him off, still laughing. Maybe it was always the same, but tonight her laugh seems colder, tonight it freezes me so solid I feel I'm made not of ice, but of stone.

Possession. Only death possesses you now, Little, neither I nor the man who wanted too much of you. I never meant to get this old, not with these eyes. I'm just a kid, really; it was easy to be tough when I had you to laugh with. Used to be your thin arms would encircle me from behind and my skin would be alive again, just for a moment, before I went to sleep. Like it wasn't for anyone else. Since Marianne.

Why do people want to buy sex? Sex is so easy to come by.

If I could, I would buy love.

If it were for sale.

No matter how much it cost.

I have seen the ugliest eyes. You get rubbed to raw in this place, ugliness rubbing itself up against you like sandpaper, jealous that you still hope. You get a habit to put up between you and them, you buy yourself designer eyes, fashionable and cold, empty as hell.

You was the best of all of us, Little. They couldn't shovel in the money or The Blues fast enough for what you gave them. And they knew it. It made them proud, the ugly ones.

The ugly ones. It took an ugly one to know what I couldn't, what you were worth. Made him so jealous he had to snap out that light if he couldn't make it his own. But it could never be owned, that light. Not by him, not by me. Not by The Blues.

Sentiment. When the feeling's gone, you replace it with sentiment. Cheap sentiment and superstition. No matter how many times you told me.

I really love you, Ruby, I really do.

And I survive. Used to wish I could die, used to wish I could get dead. Used to think I'd never live this long, not in this business. But since I've learned that you hang on, you hang on, dead as you might wish to get. I do not live so sharply anymore. My edges are worn and so I bounce, I don't clatter now, I don't shatter.

I remember one time me and you rode the bus together, going home to my place after we'd been out dancing all night. It was so late they were going to work already, the nine to fivers, and we started kissing, just to jack them up. It was easy to make them jealous of us, because we looked so happy; we were young and good looking and we made each other crazy.

I remember I used to mix my own colours of nail polish in those days and I used to try and get it to match your turquoise eyes. So we were sitting on this bus kissing and my hand was resting on your cheek and I took my tongue out of your mouth and pulled my face back just enough so I could see how well I'd matched it ... and I had, exactly, until we got off the bus, because under the sky your eyes looked like they were lit from the inside, and they haven't invented the nail polish yet that can do that.

I used to love to dress up with you and go out on the street and be stared at; it made me feel like a queen from another planet.

Now I think I'd like to be on an airplane with you. On the way to Japan, to a place like Kyoto: a raked garden, full of stillness.

Mostly I want not to be broken anymore, to no longer be afraid of winter because it makes everything come apart. I want to pull myself back towards the sun from this place where I am now; wherever it is, it's scary.

Kaolani, from Kaua'i

WE SPENT ANOTHER WEEK together after we camped in Haleakalā, staying in the spare room of a tin roofed, one-storey house on a back street in Lahaina; one of those gravel streets under bedraggled coco palms, *poi* dogs asleep under cars, a corrugated tin wall around the yard you'd throw your laundry on to dry, after you'd washed it by hand in the empty lion-clawed bathtub that sat in the centre of the yard. I asked you why you didn't just take it to the coin wash, and you said you hated laundromats; the reason being you used to go to the post office in Kaunakakai, years before when you lived on Moloka'i in the Hālawa Valley, to get your mail and read it while the laundry spun but nobody in your family wrote to you anymore, none of your friends back home in Canada, where we were both from. And so now laundromats reminded you of not having mail, of your abandonment.

The house belonged to a new acquaintance; you met Michael at May's and an hour later anyone watching the two of you talk would've thought you were the oldest of friends. Michael was hardly ever home, and gave us the room happily and for free, or else you offered a little work in exchange. You had nothing either but you knew how to trade. Because of this he respected you. Just like May, or is that Mei—the Chinese woman in the restaurant who gave us free food because you'd repaired her door.

It was in the fancy Lahaina bars that people sneered at your bare dirty feet although lots of people in there had plenty worse. Maybe those waitresses wanted to sleep with you and you wouldn't, and if that was the case I couldn't really blame them.

You'd come in on a sailboat days before, up from Tahiti. Your friends were taking their boat from Lahaina to a dry dock in a hick town on the 'Iao side to do necessary repairs to the hull; unlike sailing from Midway, they could do it two-handed. Why didn't you and I hike through the crater, you'd meet your friends after, I could come along if I wanted, re-caulk the boat with the three of you; it was up to me.

Michael was half Portuguese, half Hawai'ian. He had a fishing boat, but he didn't go out every day, and made the other half of his living by odd-jobbing and barter. In his yard he had a pomelo tree and an avocado tree, and he didn't eat from either of them. We went to the park and collected fallen mangoes. Michael laughed. "Mangoes for the pigs, avocados for the dogs." He had a friend across the road who used to take them to feed his animals. One night he came home with fresh mahi-mahi; you sliced it up sashimi-style and mixed wasabi for it, and I made a big bowl of guacamole out of Michael's avos, first going to the store and buying tortilla chips and tomato and garlic. I'd meant to buy lemons too, but found fallen limes in front of a tree on the way. A Chinese woman came out of the house and I felt bad, but she said, "Take them all, they'll just rot," and was only a little bit condescending.

We drank Primo and smoked local *pakalolo* that Michael had. We felt lucky: usually people smoked imported Mexican; the Hawai'ian was so costly most of it went to the mainland or else you couldn't afford it. Mexican was cheaper. I hated Primo and went back to the store for Kirin, using up almost all of the rest of the money I'd made working on the poultry farm with Lulu, but it was a celebration, although I'm not sure what we were celebrating. I suppose because we could. So quickly afterwards, celebration was no longer possible.

Almost certainly, you knew. After we'd smoked I sliced up the sweetest mangoes and even Michael liked them, and after that he ate pomelo and avocado every day.

"You have to eat the healthy food," you said to him, "not the junk food," and I wondered if you weren't being a bit patronizing.

When Michael was home with his girl we'd go out to Mei's restaurant. She had a back room for people like us, or at least, people like me. Mei understood immediately that you were different. I wonder how she did that? Maybe it was just her age—she was over forty and could read people as I couldn't. All the young backpackers would chat and gossip in the back room; Lulu had discovered the place.

It was all a game to me, an As If. I wasn't really living my life. But it's as though I left a part of myself in that time, waiting for the moment when I could become a part of a community, have a sense of belonging. And that time is now. But I'm afraid of failing again, just like I did then, at the difficult task of being human.

I'd tried, of course, thinking, "This is just like high school…" and ordered tea and enormous almond cookies like everybody else, and maybe, I think now, I was more successful than I thought, coming at the difficult problem of being human. In that room, before I left, I reached across the table and took the hand of the dark-haired girl you'd slept with even though we were ostensibly together, and smiled.

I'm grateful; you were witness to the brittleness of my youth. How vulnerable I was, wearing my solitude and harmed quality on my sleeve in place of a heart. That you got to see that side of me I will never be able to forgive you. It is better to have the distance, to write to you. It is so easy to idolize the past, but perhaps all I say here is true.

I'm on holiday with our old friend Lulu, on my first island, Kaua'i, and not Maui, where you and I spent time together. Still, just being in Hawai'i reminds me of you so much I feel compelled to write. Hawai'i has changed, much of its wildness paved over by indistinguishable malls and hotels, even on the outer islands. The old Japanese men no longer sit in the beach parks, playing *hanafuda*. I wonder where they are now? Remember we sat with them once and asked them to teach us how to play? We got the basics that afternoon, under the tattered palms, sitting at the name-and-fire scored picnic table. But the nuances were endless. They finally got rid of us by threatening to play the next game for money, and we ran off, needing what few bills we had for takeout tempura and Kirin beer.

I unfold the page, look at your drawing I've kept all these years. The mouse is still so lifelike, but it doesn't move. I'll keep it forever. I'm already forgetting what you look like, except that your forehead was broad and tanned and high, and your big knotted hands much gentler than my father's.

Before she left for her solitary hike through the Alaka'i swamp, Lulu looked at me. "Did you call?"

I shook my head. "I have to write, try and sort it out one more time."

"Don't write too long," Lulu said. "You know what the verdict was, not so bad."

"That doesn't mean he was innocent; his lawyer might've just been good."

"Tomorrow is his release date. If you don't call today he might be gone. There's no harm in it. If he's not what you thought, you can change your mind."

I do not know how to tell this story. Hence I will try writing it as if it were a story, in third person, with made-up names. For write it I must. If I don't, I won't be able to decide.

◆◆◆

His brown eyes met hers across the yard, across the fairy tale crowd at the free temple dinner. She had gone inside to help in the kitchen, but just as she looked towards the door she saw him coming out. He was deeply tanned and wore a white cotton shirt, loose and unironed. She noticed him immediately. They passed each other, but he only glanced at her. In the temple kitchen she arranged fruit on platters: lemons, apples, papaya, mango, pomelo, *liliko'i*. Apple bananas, each banana the size of a thumb so that a bunch of bananas, a hand as they are called here, really does look like a hand, being almost exactly the same size. Guavas. Small as tennis balls, they fit in your hand, brown on the outside, green and slushy on the inside. Strawberry guavas that are smaller, perhaps the size of huge farm grown strawberries, scarlet and smooth-skinned. She took the platters out and set them on the table and looked for him but he was gone.

After the dishes were done she caught her ride back to Baldwin Park, where, as most nights, there was a fire and drumming as Scorpio appeared in the sky. She watched the fire and then him, standing directly across the flames, noticed how his forehead was so smooth and large and his hands were large too, but very gentle as he took an offered drum.

He came to her campsite that night, a secret campsite Lulu knew, under ironwood trees a quarter mile from the park.

"Hello," she said.

"Are you awake?"

"Yes."

She turned on her flashlight. He had come through the woods without one. She was glad. She didn't want anyone knowing where she was camped.

He showed her a drawing he had made, of a mouse.

"How did you know I was here?"

"I just sort of knew."

His mouse was very mousy. It had soft brown hair and jumped off the page and under the covers with them. They made love right away, in silent relief. Afterwards they went to the Chinese restaurant to eat, walking across the cane fields to get to town, because it was shorter than taking the road. She didn't even wonder how Mei's restaurant, which was usually in Lahaina, was now in Pa'ia. Or perhaps they'd walked the dirt tracks through moonlit cane fields for hours, and it only felt like minutes. Maybe it was because the mouse came too. The mouse was a very good supper companion, making them like each other and feel good without saying very many words. They ate in the shadow of the mountain.

Hitchhiking up the mountain the next day, they walked between rides, along an unpaved road, a gravel track really, covered in yellow crescent shaped leaves; neither of them knew what the tree was called. She walked beside Jim. She didn't know him very well although they were new lovers; the leaves were like the fingernail clippings of a family of giants. She wanted to say something important to Jim, something that would make him remember her. She hadn't eaten any mushrooms herself. It began to rain. They were hungry and, passing through a village, went into a café to eat. The proprietor scowled at Jim, more than at her, but served them coffee and fried egg sandwiches nonetheless.

She'd feel this peculiar chagrin in restaurants with Jim. It was the only time they were ever in public together. The Chinese one in either Lahaina or Pa'ia was the exception. Was he barefoot? Did he smell? She didn't much care, but it was tiresome and she didn't understand it. In Mei's restaurant, the mouse had tea with them; in other restaurants it stayed in his pocket. It's always a tea party when you have a mouse along, even if you're not wearing your mad hat. Jim talked about nothing and she talked about nothing, both careful to obscure their pasts, to cloud their trail. But that wasn't it; it was as if they really didn't have pasts. On Maui, she often found herself telling people she was from Kaua'i, and realizing, in a shocked kind of way that it was true. She'd been on Kaua'i for eight months and then met Lulu; they'd come here together. She'd been in Hawai'i almost a year altogether. When you're so young that's a long time, and each experience in that year so vivid her father paled behind it, grew ghostlike. But not entirely.

She realized, years later with Lulu in Koke'e that she'd loved Jim, even though she hadn't known it at the time. She'd liked him a lot, the sex had been great, and she'd felt like they'd known each other, which almost never happened to Tanya. Somehow, though, she hadn't put this together as love.

♦♦♦

"Every time I bend over I have this major realization," she said, pulling her head back out of the waterfall. On a stone lay their toothbrushes, the expensive health food store shampoo. Her one luxury.

"Like what?" Jim had made a camp fire and she was drying her hair after swimming. They were going to eat breadfruit and coconut, both of which Tanya had found. Tanya could tell by looking at a coconut what stage it was inside, milky or hard, or the puddingy in-between stage called spoon meat that some people loved.

They'd done their hike through Haleakala, and now, on the way back out, they'd left the trail and were camping on parkland, or maybe it was private land. They didn't know; it was such a vast tract that nobody could possibly find them. Waterfall after waterfall came splashing down the mountain like a stairway from heaven; mist and rainbows crowning the treetops of the rainforest like damp halos. They had been there for three days; the crater hike itself had been another three.

"What if he kills me?" she wondered aimlessly, and reached up onto the cliff ledge and took down the rubber cervix-covering item and put it in.

"Never say how long you were anywhere. It breaks the spell, the way an alteration of memory can redeem everything," Tanya said, and Jim smiled. She took off her sandals she'd wet getting out of the pool. They were leather huaraches; she put them by the fire to dry. She had nothing on. She dried her hair; which was long and thin and brown, with the blue towel and then sat down at the fire and took over cleaning the seeds out of the dope, some kind of Maui Wowie given to her by one of her young Hawai'ian buddies. She had impressed Jim with this, that she knew how to score local dope from locals, although he'd pulled off the same trick, meeting Michael within days of his arrival from Midway. He'd explained he'd once lived on Moloka'i; most of his friends there had been Hawai'ian.

They made love and lay in the sun and baked and swam in the pools beneath waterfalls and occasionally Tanya wondered, when, as it must, it would end, and vaguely, whether he would kill her, although he had never given any indication. Perhaps she'd just seen too many horror movies as a child, horror movies on television and the other kind, the kind she hid in the laundry room to escape from. Now, here, it was only at this moment that they passed through her skin, her outer membrane, that they made her truly fearful. The terror she'd had to suppress at the time.

What if he kills me?

Yet even still she missed her father a little.

Jim gave her enough pleasure to match the pain, an equal and opposite force, until she was filled. Then the pleasure ousted the pain. You have to be filled with something. It's one or the other. Nature abhors a vacuum.

They collected avocados on a rainy day. Jim climbing high up into the tree and shaking the limbs, and Tanya standing underneath to catch them so that they fell, one after another, plump and somehow obscene, green and huge, fleshy and woman-shaped, into her hands.

The sky came down and settled on her shoulders and she cried. They went back through the forest to their camp.

Jim asked what was wrong. "Hey babe, you haven't missed your period, have you?"

She almost punched him. Anyway, it wasn't logical. They'd

just met. And she never hid her birth control from him. She didn't point any of this out.

She looked at Jim's hands, so much larger than her own, large and strong and hairy and yet oddly gentle and she thought, they are like my father's hands.

She didn't tell him. It seemed like a terrible thing to tell him as if it was some awful secret, and he would be mortally offended, and he rolled another joint and then she couldn't talk anymore even though it sat in her throat like a fat white dove struggling to break free: your hands are like my father's.

And they were. She'd always dated young men before, barely out of high school. Jim was in his late twenties and had sailed from Tahiti with his friends, who, he always assured her, they would go meet soon. He had a sailor's hands, rough and knotted as, well, knotted ropes.

She cried. It was obvious to think of the waterfalls, pooling in pools and then hurrying in streams to rattle down cliffs and eventually empty into the sea but she thought of it anyway.

"After we've finished patching the boat we have to go," he said.

"Where are you going?"

"B.C. The Queen Charlottes maybe. You'll love it. You'll learn how to sail well enough to crew anywhere." Maybe there didn't have to be an ending. But she liked the way he left it open-ended, too. *After you spend this time with me, you'll be able to go anywhere, for free.*

"Your friends won't like me," she said, knowing perfectly well what she meant was: I won't like your friends.

At last her father's voice when it came was an exception, rarely interjecting. It was a place he couldn't easily come, a place she was inviolate. For she'd always belonged to him; he was always in her head, telling her she just that. That was Jim's gift to her: to almost silence her father's voice so that she felt for the first time in her life free of him, and could be herself instead. Whatever herself was. A friend of Mouse.

Jim poked the fire with a stick. He took her face in his hands and kissed her, apologizing for his lack of tact, her tears that had prompted him to ask the one question his own fear had demanded of him. He read his book, Mark Twain or Tom Robbins or someone; he rolled another joint, he tried to make love to her. Finally he went for a walk up the valley by himself to get oranges, Valencias, he said, that legend had it some Mexican *paniolo* had planted at the turn of the century. Or was it Spanish? She loved those stories everyone was always telling in Hawai'i, about history, even if only half of them were true.

She realized her father was always there with them, just as the Mouse was. And what her father said was this: he isn't good enough for you. And, astonishingly, this was just what her father had told her, when, in spite of everything, she'd begun dating, the year before both she and her mother had left, setting off in opposite directions. Two years ago precisely. Her mother was living in the Peg.

Tanya herself had drifted around Canada and then come here. Someone had told her the living was easy, but more importantly, it was geographically as far a distance from her father as it was possible to get. She kept hearing him say it, over and over and over again, a hoarse yet insistent whisper, so that finally she got up and followed Jim up the pig trail to the orange tree. At last she motioned him down and climbed the tree herself, thinking this effort would silence her father's voice; and, throwing oranges like little suns down into Jim's waiting hands, big as baseball gloves, she wondered, what can my father possibly mean, what can be better than this? And then she wondered again whether Jim might kill her. They were camped in such a remote spot no one would ever know. Perhaps that was what her father meant. Over roast breadfruit she forgot her irrational fear. Mouse helped feed the fire, and she lay on her back, staring at the stars peeping out between the gaps in the canopy. Nothing of this would be possible without Mouse along. Mouse washed the dishes, he sewed, repaired her jeans she tore tree climbing. The next morning after her swim, she sat at the edge of the stream, watching her reflection in the clear water, her image streaming away, carried by the currents and eddies like the many tiny yellow leaves. She sat with no clothes on, just the piece of blue cloth wrapped around her hips, while her shirt she tore climbing a food tree was being mended. While she was being mended.

"My mother wants me to go Winnipeg and live with her, you know. Finish high school and so on."

"How old are you?"

"Seventeen."

"Do you want to?" Jim asked.

"Want what?"

"To live with your mom."

"No. But I feel sorry for her all the same."

Jim didn't pry, said only, "Don't let your compassion get in the way of your wisdom."

She looked down at her body. It was very brown, graceful, very young. She looked at it in a kind of fascination, as though she couldn't believe something so beautiful could be hers. She wore their only towel, the blue one, as a sarong. She remembered how she found it in the bushes at Seven Pools, gave it to Lulu to take back to the laundromat in Pa'ia when they got back. She and Jim made love on it that night they met, spreading it on the ground over the prickly layer of ironwood needles, soft as a bed, everything fine except for the palmetto bugs, huge tropical cockroaches scurrying over and sometimes into her sleeping bags; hence the big towel only. She hated the cockroaches, although in the forest they seemed almost benign, living in a relationship less parasitical to humans; no longer an indicator of their own failures: to be clean, to keep their lives in order, to hope for the future. In Hawai'i they were just beetles.

On the hike back down towards Hana she quailed from the sudden heat. They were unsure of the streams because of pack horses using the main trail sometimes. Jim gathered *liliko'i*, a type of passion fruit. They were perfectly spherical, their bright yellow skins the consistency of plastic. She'd always found them disgusting, their insides, while sweet, were also almost impossibly acidic, and resembled in appearance and texture, tapioca. That day she ate seven.

◆◆◆

Later, hitchhiking up the ranch side of the mountain again, after the scene at the courthouse, the landscape itself seemed buttoned by the same buttons that closed her soul, made it seem foreign even to herself. Except for the blooming jacarandas. How could anything be that purple?

"When will he kill me?" she remembered thinking. After he was gone it seemed funny. Yet those thoughts had occupied a space in her, space that had left no room for him after a time. Now, having thought them so often, they fluttered away, little bats. Too bad it was too late.

As before, Tanya was alone. Her natural state. Except they hadn't left yet. She could still go find him, agree to sail to Vancouver, whether his friends proved irksome or not. She ought to turn back. It was ridiculous to hike through the crater again so soon, and alone, although that wasn't the part that scared Tanya. What if he sailed away before she got back? She crossed the highway, faced the opposite direction.

She stuck out her thumb as the first car appeared. In her mind's eye Jim was wearing the red paisley shirt she didn't have the money to buy him, the one in the window of the store in Lahaina, so expensive it was frequented by visiting rock stars. He wouldn't have killed her, she thought. It would be as impossible for him to hurt her, as it would be for Mouse to do so.

After their camping trip, Jim went to visit his sailor friends at the dry dock up island. Again, he invited her to come meet them, but Lulu was at Baldwin Park, and so Tanya hung around there for a few days. Already Lulu felt like an old dear friend.

A sober young American woman, twenty-one years old, her buddy. The one she would turn to if she was in trouble. The one she talked to about what was really going on. Sometimes the irony of it struck her; for a best friend she had a woman she'd known three months to talk about a lover she'd had ten days. It heightened her sense of strength, and also fragility. There was no one in her present life who knew her from the previous years, years in which she had been known always by the same others: her parents, her siblings. Her old friends too: if they hadn't known her for years, they'd known someone who'd known her for years.

"We are a composite picture which is passed on to and entered into by any new person we meet, who may change the image but only in infinitesimal ways," she'd told Jim under the waterfall. He'd smiled. Anyway, here all of that broke off with a snap. And she didn't know herself anymore, who she was. She could say anything, and no one would think it out of character. She was Kaolani, from Kaua'i.

"Don't think you know me," Jim had said, an edge to his voice, after he'd finished smiling. The only time there had ever been even the slightest edge. I wonder when he'll kill me, Tanya had thought in reply.

Try and kill me was better. It wasn't as if she didn't intend to fight back.

There was no one like Lulu for doing her laundry. It was Tanya who didn't mind still wearing her grubby camping clothes even after her return. At last Lulu lent her a clean dress and took Tanya's as well as her own; they caught a ride from the park into Pa'ia. Tanya left her friend in the laundromat. Instead of helping she looked for Mei's restaurant, hoping to find Jim. She didn't find it; maybe it was in Lahaina that day. She went and sat on the courthouse steps and cried. Jim walked by then and looked at her, as though she was someone he didn't know very well, and finally, after some hesitation, came and sat down beside her on the stone steps. He put his hand over hers, tentatively, almost shyly, as if their hands didn't know each other so well.

"I wish I could help you," he said. "What is wrong?"

She could only shake her head mutely: *no no no, no no no. I cannot speak it; it cannot be spoken.*

My father my father my father. And even if she had spoken what would she have said? *It is he who has cut out my tongue.*

"I'm hungry," Jim said. "Let's go eat, and then we can talk."

"I'm hungry too." But she started to cry again, and pushed Jim away, physically too, until at last he got up and walked away.

She assumed he'd gone to his friends again and the next day hitchhiked up the mountain alone, then changed her mind and turned back. Two days later in the rich kids' Lahaina bar with Lulu he appeared. "I have a house for us," he said, and even though the bouncer was trying to kick him out for some reason Tanya didn't understand, Lulu had smiled encouragingly and so Tanya had gone to Michael's house with him.

Tanya and Jim couldn't make it together in town life, were both too conscious of being with someone weird, an outsider to the human flock. You need at least one who swims with the school, who has the right protective colouring, Tanya thought later. They were both from the UFO, problem was. It all fell apart after the party; they'd slept together in Michael's spare room. She'd thought they'd make love but they hadn't, and it had been her turn to ask what was wrong.

"I have something I have to tell you."

Her heart had begun hammering, for no reason at all.

She didn't ask, and he didn't tell her. At some point, they found itchy uncomfortable sleep. Just before she drifted off, Tanya thought, there's no stitching it back together.

The day after she was back on the courthouse steps, crying again. It had shown promise, she had to admit. Lulu had come to the party too, and slept on the couch. They'd all almost felt like a family. That night Tanya had even changed her name back to Tanya from Kaolani, because Michael's lady really was Hawai'ian and it seemed dumb.

No matter how long she sat on the stairs crying no one passed by: not Lulu, not Jim, not even Michael or Plumeria, which wasn't Michael's girl's real name either, but it suited her long black hair.

She hitchhiked back to Baldwin Park alone, before dark. She didn't mind hitchhiking alone, but not at night.

At her old campsite under the ironwood trees she found a little note, again with the same drawing of a mouse. "I'm sorry you're sad, little sister. I wish I could help you but I don't know how."

Had he seen her crying on the courthouse stairs again, and, feeling helpless, not spoken to her this time? What else could the note mean? Or had it been here since before they'd moved into Michael's? Tanya didn't know.

After you spend this time with me, you'll be able to go anywhere, for free.

She was barking up the wrong ironwood tree. Maybe there was still time.

◆◆◆

Three days later they were drinking coffee and eating almond cookies in the back room of the Chinese restaurant in Pa'ia. Lulu paid. Tanya was out of money and thinking of applying for food stamps. Most of the restaurants took them. She needed very little; the food stamps would feel like wealth.

"Do you know where that dry dock is? I know he told me the name but I can't remember. No one I've asked knows. It's not the kind of thing people like us know. I should ask Michael, or Kai." Kai was her *pakalolo* connection; he lived in Makawao, where a lot of Hawai'ians lived.

Lulu didn't hear. Passed her the front page of the Honolulu paper. "Isn't that him?"

There was a full-page photograph of a man diving off a

pier. To one side, she saw 'Iao needle. She remembered they'd thought of going there; no one hiked on mysterious 'Iao. They'd be cooler than everyone else.

But it was him.

Tanya passed the paper back. "You read it," she said. "I can't. What's it say?"

"They stole a fancy sailboat on Midway. They killed the owners, probably. They caught his friends, but he got away. The Ala Wai in Honolulu was the boat's home marina. What were his friends like?"

"I never met them. I never even saw the boat. He invited me, but after we went camping, I hung out with you instead of going with him. Remember?"

Lulu narrowed her eyes for a moment, and then kept reading.

"It was an unusual looking boat, kind of like a little galleon, wooden hulled, double masted. I guess they thought if they did their repairs here, the boat wouldn't be recognized. But as it happens, a friend of the owners had the same idea. Take their boat out of the water at the little dry dock, 'Iao side, way cheaper than O'ahu. No radio contact since Midway, six weeks ago. No SOS, nothing. Too fishy, so the guy called the cops before even going on deck to see what was up."

"He told me he sailed from Tahiti with friends. He said his friends were working on the boat and he had to go help them. But, until we came back from camping, he kept putting it off."

"To be with you."

"He did go for a few days to help after we got back from the crater, but then he came back and we moved into Michael's house for a few days. Remember?" She didn't mention the scene at the courthouse in Lahaina.

Lulu nodded. "The party was nice. It felt like we were a family. I've hardly ever felt that, and I've been travelling for years."

"If he'd helped them full-time they might've been done before now."

Lulu folded the paper shut, glanced around the restaurant,

lowered her voice. "Let's finish this conversation somewhere else."

On the beach Lulu said, "Imagine getting away from cops by diving off a dock and swimming." She laughed a little. "Who else could pull that off?"

"Everyone knows what he looks like now," Tanya said.

"He's at large. He might come looking for you. What will you do if he does?"

"It won't work. Even if he goes to the airport he'll be recognized now. He can't go to Mei's, anywhere."

"You don't know Mei. She's slippery. You could ask her."

"No. It's the same. Everyone saw us together. They all know I was with him. I have to leave."

"Why not wait and see if he makes contact?"

"No." Tanya took the folded up piece of paper out of her pocket, unfolded it, showed it to Lulu. "The mouse is back on the page. I knew the moment I saw it, everything was over."

She and Lulu lay low at Baldwin Park, expecting the police to appear at any moment. But they didn't. Probably because, two days later, Jim was apprehended, boarding a boat in Lahaina, as the owners prepared to leave for San Francisco. Offering to crew for nothing.

Just as Tanya had thought, everyone in the restaurant stared and whispered. Mei gave them a corner table, said softly, "They were watching. They knew he was a sailor, could crew for other people. That it would be how he'd try to avoid airports."

She offered no judgement either way. Tanya was grateful, ate enormous almond cookies and sipped green tea. When they tried to pay Mei waved their money away. "The police won't bother you now. Also, you don't know. See how the trial goes. They say they didn't kill the owners, that they found the boat abandoned on Midway, the dinghy overturned on the beach."

"It doesn't make sense. They should've radioed the harbour master in Honolulu. The boat's papers would've said the owner's names, their home marina."

Mei nodded. "They said they were too afraid. Their own boat was damaged; they barely made it from Tahiti. They were afraid to tell anyone, wanted to get here first."

Tanya nodded. "It's stupid for them to say so much before the trial."

But perhaps that meant they weren't real criminals.

Just inept thieves and murderers.

"It's not true," she told Lulu when they got to the beach. "If that was true they would've sailed her into the Ala Wai. He told me once the repairs were done they'd go to northern British Columbia."

"I don't want to know these things," Lulu said. And then, "Do you wish it had gone another way? If all of you had worked on the boat you might've been done and gone and in BC by now."

Tanya nodded. "The Queen Charlottes or somewhere even more remote."

"You didn't answer."

"We'd have gotten a few months, is all."

"Maybe years."

"Why are you and Mei both speaking in his defence?"

"You were a different person after your time with Jim. You were so obviously fucked up before, everyone noticed. Now you're kind of all right."

"Maybe I was his penance. Maybe after what they did on Midway, he knew he needed to help someone. Buy his life back from God. He wasn't a killer, in spite of his record."

"What was it for?" Tanya had been reading the papers too.

"Possession. Grand theft auto."

"A logical progression from there to grand theft boat."

"Am I supposed to laugh?"

"Do you good. What say you we blow this pop stand, fly to Seattle? I can borrow the money. I have a friend with a restaurant there; we can work. Even you, if I ask nicely. Unless you want to wait, see how the trial turns out. Visit him in jail.

Where is he?"

"Honolulu. No bail. Trial's not for months."

"Maybe his friends killed them, not Jim."

"Maybe."

It was possible. But she remembered again all the times under the waterfall when she'd wondered if he'd kill her. Maybe she was picking up on the boat owners' fear, their last thoughts clinging to him, ever since that rainy night on Midway when they'd lost everything.

"You know when we were camping and we got high I always worried he'd kill me, even though he seemed like a kind man right from the moment I met him."

"Where'd you meet him? You never said."

"At the temple feast. We didn't talk even though I noticed him right away. And then I got back to the park after and there was the usual fire. I was staring into the flames and then when I looked up, there was his face. I thought I was imagining things," Tanya laughed. "Anyways, like I said, maybe what I heard was their feelings coming off him, their fear of him, the couple who owned the boat. I always thought I could tell a killer, they'd give off a vibe. The thing is, even though we broke up, you're right, he was good to me. He got through to me like no one ever has, not even you, Lulu. I feel so much more myself than I did before. And no matter what he did on Midway, you can't take that away."

Tanya remembered now, how just before he'd walked away from her when she'd sat on the courthouse steps crying, he'd reached into his pocket, come out with Mouse, offered her the little animal. "You take him," she'd said.

"I can't."

"Why?"

"He's not the seafaring sort." He'd kissed her on the forehead. "Perhaps it's better this way." What did he mean? She hadn't asked. "No matter what happens, don't think too badly of me. I'll remember you always."

She remembered how complete strangers so often seemed to hate him. It wasn't just that he was unkempt and wore torn clothes; lots of people did that. Maybe they could smell it on him, what she couldn't. Grand theft boat. Murder. Almost all had looked at him this way, as if he weren't fit for human company. Except for Mei, and Michael, and Lulu, and Plumeria. But he'd had a chance to charm them, as he had her. Or else they'd been part of his penance too, part of his desire to take a new tack at this difficult problem of being human.

After their talk Lulu had gone into town again, back to the laundromat to fold, first telling her not to run away, but it was silly, really. Where was there to go? Tanya left the beach for the fire pit in its scraggly patch of lawn, started the night's bonfire. The backpackers would be arriving from their day trips soon, and those who knew who she was would want to ask her questions. She got the drums out of their hiding places in the bushes. Tonight, she'd drum so loud she wouldn't hear a thing.

◆◆◆

The door bangs; it's Lulu, returned from her hike. She looks at me, questioning. I put down this pen, pick up our room phone. Koke'e Lodge has room phones now, as it didn't back then. The mouse jumps off the page while I wait for someone to pick up. *Or we could go there together.* It's not too late to learn how to sail.

Fires Halfway

OUR FIRST NIGHT IN BERLIN I went out with Katie, the German label's A and R woman, to a pub called Die Ruine, in a bombed-out building near the Brandenburg Gate, never restored since the war. The second storey, roofless, crumbled upwards into the night sky, while in the tiny, one-roomed club itself, a trio of young women looked like they were falling asleep from terminal boredom.

I found myself staring and Katie nudged me. "They're junkies," she whispered. "Disgusting."

Still, I stared. I felt like I was in the bar at the end of time. In those days, before reunification, West Berlin residents received subsidies from the state, hence, all sorts were attracted to the city by the lure of easy living. And heroin was as popular with artists and musicians as among street people, unlike in Canada. So, of course, were Colours.

The bartender's name was Max; he wore a western shirt and a flowered tie. He sported slicked-back hair and a handlebar moustache, looking like a character in the Wenders film, *The American Friend*. There was a record player of elderly but good vintage, and Max played us Velvet Underground and early Rolling Stones. Everyone was dressed in black and very thin.

I watched an old gay derelict clean tables and empty ashtrays for a few minutes; Max pulled the man a pint in exchange for his trouble. He sat at a table alone after that, sipping beer, opening and eating a can of sardines with a clean fork he got out of his jacket pocket.

Katie and I were joined by one of her producer friends, but before we could be properly introduced a raven-haired woman extricated herself from the trio and offered to read our Tarot cards. Katie tried to get rid of her but she whined persistently, reeking of patchouli and layered in scarves. At last I gave in, making her promise that once she'd done my reading she'd leave us alone. Leni, for that was her name, agreed, laying out my hand after I'd shuffled. My question, which I didn't share, was whether Rudy's German tour would ensure greater success back home. In Canada to be famous you have to be famous somewhere else first.

Card fifteen, the Devil, came up. She asked me to re-shuffle, as if to want for me a kinder fate, but even when I did, there he was again, and the third time too. I thought Leni must be adept at sleight of hand, would promise to exorcize my devil for some large price, but instead she sighed, "What are you doing with him?"

I thought she knew I was Rudy's girlfriend. I was smug enough about his small-time fame to assume bar gossip had already labelled us his for-the-moment prince-less entourage, and told her truthfully: "Even back in high school, his music spoke to me more than any poetry ever had. I even changed my name to the same name as the girl in my favourite song. When we finally met last year, I asked who Kim was and he told me she didn't exist; he'd made her up. I said I'd changed my name to Kim because of the song and he said he'd hoped someone would do that, become Kim for him."

I was so busy delivering my monologue I didn't at first notice Leni staring as if I were a little mad, and Katie glancing from one to the other of us, suppressing giggles. I could have gone on, but I shut up. Scotch and jet lag, what can I say?

"Who are you talking about?" Leni asked.

"Rudy Mix, of course."

She tossed her locks. "I've never heard of him. Does he play with Lou?"

Katie elbowed me, whispered, "She means Lou Reed. He lives here now."

"I've met Lou," Leni said. "I've read his cards. Here. Right at this table."

Canadian that I was, I unashamedly glanced around the room to see if Lou was there, if I might have to call Rudy, get him to cab over, meet his maker. He'd thank me forever. But no Lou. Just his music pouring out of the speakers, changing us forever like the first time we'd heard it.

"Maybe he lied. Did you ever think of that?" Leni asked menacingly. "It would be a good way to get in your pants, yes? I bet you Kim is his first wife. It's your Rudy who's the devil, I see it now." Leni tossed her hair again.

"But the devil doesn't mean the devil personified," I said, explaining Leni's Tarot to her as if it was my profession and not hers. "It can mean addiction of the mind or body, any kind of enslavement."

"Precisely."

"I don't even believe in the devil," I said.

"No one said you had to," Leni said. "But you agree with me there exists real evil in the world?"

"Of course."

"Keep it symbolic then, if you prefer," Leni said.

I stubbornly kept defending my boyfriend. "Rudy's music is amazing. He's not rich but he is by my standards; I'd never have gotten to Europe on my own. What's devilish about any of that?"

"All the same," she said, peering at the rest of the layout, reading a meaning there that was, even with my superficial knowledge of the cards, completely opaque. "I see coming enslavement of a kind."

"How precise. You have real talent," Katie's friend sneered. I thought maybe he was trying to save face for our little group after I'd made us look like ingénues not knowing who they meant by Lou. Leni just shrugged him off, a piece of fluff, a beetle. Katie pushed several Deutschmarks in small denominations across the table, as if hoping once Leni had her money she'd find someone else to scam.

"He paid my airfare here," I said.

Katie looked alarmed; she hadn't thought I was taking this seriously. I hadn't thought so either. Scotch and jet lag, I told myself again, call it a night and get some sleep.

"That's worth your soul?"

"My soul isn't in danger," I pointed out, "it's my self-respect."

"How so?" Katie's sneering friend asked.

"I'm a fan, for God's sakes. I went backstage at a concert in Toronto and got him to autograph my programme. I gave him my number and he actually called. How pathetic is that?" I'd never seen myself as a groupie before then. I'd thought Rudy was in love too. "I should come up with an art of my own," I continued, "not just turn myself into a character in one of his songs."

"Don't be ridiculous," Katie said. "You'll do something worthwhile one day—or not. Not everyone should feel they have to. What's the point of it? And to be pretty and clever is more than most people ever get. Whether you worked for it or not you should enjoy what it brings you."

Katie's friend, whose name turned out to be Hans, agreed. "If a handsome young musician asked me to keep him company on his U.S. tour, you'd be sure I'd go. What if the chance only comes once?"

I nodded, trying to believe them. Leni reassembled her deck, wrapping it in a square of patterned blue silk with pretentious ritual. Katie and Hans rolled their eyes after she'd slunk off to another table to try her luck. The table was populated by regulars, not a rube like me among them, and she was waved away. Katie pointed and laughed at her as she sat down alone at the bar, nursing a glass of red wine and smoking; her friends had already left. Still, I said good-bye on our way out.

"It's through the wall for you then," she sighed with great import, and Katie laughed the entire taxi ride back to the hotel where she dropped me off.

I didn't see much more of Berlin.

◆◆◆

Rudy hadn't practised at all but he'd already scored some Purple. Of course I did a few lines with him, even though I was exhausted and more than a little drunk. I thought it was laced with something else, because when we disrobed I saw his penis had turned into a pretty blue candle. It looked like a regular candle, just blue, not one of those penis-shaped candles they have in sex shops, thank heavens.

Of course I lit it and turned off the lights. Instead of having sex, we watched for hours, his penis's flame the only blue light in the dark room. Just before it burned to its end we blew it out together: one two three, blow.

I meant to go to sleep then, but Rudy asked, "Kim, are you ever afraid of going insane?"

"Yes," I answered truthfully, "but not here, not now."

"What do you mean?"

"It isn't my time to go crazy yet," I answered. "This is yours." I didn't know where the words came from. Blame it on the Purple.

And I was right too. The next day Rudy had to check out the club and run through a few songs with his band. I stayed in our room and slept. When he came home I wanted to go out for Schnitzel but he wanted to order from room service and do more of the new Purple. Somewhat reluctantly I agreed. I was here on his dime.

A brand new candle appeared almost immediately.

"Where are we, Kim?" Rudy asked. "Have we gone too far in this time?"

I have no idea where he got the Purple. I know he'd tried

in Canada and hadn't been able to get any; we mostly had Green there, not the same animal at all. Maybe Katie got it for him—I wouldn't put it past her—or maybe he bumped into Lou on the street.

Who wouldn't take beautiful, exclusive, scary new drugs given to them by Lou Reed? I would have, then. I took them from Rudy after all, not nearly so glamorous. I guess he was to me what Lou was to him; Rudy was my Lou. I have no one to blame but myself, that and my age; I was only twenty-two, if clever and sophisticated as Katie and Hans liked to point out.

Most of the time, I was pretty happy about my life, knowing, as Hans said, it would likely only come once. Only now and then did I fret I was a mere groupie as I had that night in Die Ruine, or that I'd wake at forty, lonely and alone, in need of a long stay in rehab.

Like what happened to Rudy.

To answer my question to Leni: Rudy's little West German tour was the height of his fame. With the exception of "Fires Halfway," his next album was awful, and the one after that bombed. His contract wasn't renewed, but he still had habits, and they are harder to kick even than memories of failure. I only know this from hearsay, because after I flew home alone I never saw him again.

I went to fashion school and now design upscale maternity clothes and am successful enough at it for my standards, admittedly not high, but I have my health and work I love, and that is a life blessed. And if you remember the late seventies or early eighties, you weren't there, but I didn't forget Rudy, and there he was last week at a gallery opening, Rudy whom I hadn't seen in years.

Rudy who? Everyone asked later as I tried to explain his career—he sells real estate now, or software or something—I'm afraid I've already forgotten. *Fires Halfway* was never more than a minor hit, but it's the one that got people to know who I meant. It's still in rotation. Its reputation has grown, if anything.

Isn't that enough to get him a new contract, you ask?

Well, no. Because he didn't actually write it.

Sometimes, I have to admit, I'm still pulled in by the past, by the hopeful love I felt for him that I wonder at now. Neither Rudy nor Lou died, neither there in 1982 in Berlin nor in the twenty years since, although not for lack of trying. And neither did I, or I wouldn't be telling you my story. But enough people have paid the final price, including Serge, one of Rudy's favourite drummers, who OD'd on heroin in a Paris hotel room. You'd think we'd all have seen enough by now, but it seems each new generation falls for the same dangerous lies, for the girl at the opening on Rudy's arm couldn't have been more than twenty-five, and her pupils were big as saucers.

"What's with her?" I remember whispering.

"Orange," he whispered back. "It's so good. Want some? Remember Fan?"

Maybe he should have died.

♦♦♦

"Halfway there," I muttered gloomily, watching his nightly candle. By the third night I felt seasoned, knew what to expect, almost tired of the inevitability.

The dead pull of Berlin. Out of time, out of space. I could stay here forever, I thought.

I could stay here forever
Counting down
And never get to zero
I could stay here forever
With you

Rudy and I wrote a song that week. It ended up making him enough to pay cash for his Toronto house. We were already split up when he next recorded and it didn't occur to me to ask for a credit and he didn't offer me one. It was Hans who tracked me down and told me I should threaten to sue. Which I did, and Rudy sent me a large cheque worth, indeed, half the royalties. I didn't care about my name. He told me to buy rubber spike heels, thinking he was being cute, but at the time I was back in school and put it towards my loan.

♦♦♦

We indulged heavily in room service. We didn't go out, unless he had a gig. His playing was less than memorable, but he looked beautiful. Giggling, we'd take a cab back to the hotel afterwards, refusing all invitations.

"We'll hate each other before it's over," I said, thinking I already did, a little. But I couldn't stop any more than him. Once the candles were over, we experimented with sex on the new Purple and discovered it was not just possible but fantastic, inexhaustibly compelling and inexhaustible every other way, until, at dawn, we'd both want to stop but seemingly couldn't. Sleep, when it came, was always a welcome respite. I felt like we had hormones in an IV drip. It was almost embarrassing.

One night when I was alone I turned on the radio and heard the fire song we'd written together a few nights earlier and had been singing together every day, as we cried or laughed at our plight, or more likely, just made strange love again.

Of course that was impossible; Rudy hadn't recorded it yet. The music was very beautiful. I wished I knew more of music so I could sing him the melody when he returned from seeing Lou (my euphemistic name for his Purple supplier, which I shared with him—he didn't get the joke) and he could write it down, because it was far better than the one he'd written.

But the words were the same, word for word.

What is time? What is creativity?

I felt like we'd been sent out on a space probe, the two of us, to bring back the unearthly answers to those portentous questions, but who could survive that?

Still, waiting for him to come back, I tried to tap it out on the room's piano, but I have little ear for music and I never got it right. When he eventually got back he said, "That's the most beautiful thing I've ever heard you play; it captures so perfectly our eerie trajectory."

"It's a quarter of the original, if that, and many notes misheard. It's the melody to 'Fires Halfway.'"

"'Fires Halfway' already has a different melody. What do you mean, the original?"

"This one's better. I heard it on the radio."

"You're a technology-based Coleridge," Rudy said. "I know you said you'd wanted to be Kim, and I said I'd be happy if you could, but now you're pushing it." Still he madly scribbled notes, and the lost portions he replaced with accessible poppy riffs, not nearly so frightening. It was a good collaboration, the one and only between ourselves and the Sirian extraterrestrials singing to me and only me from the radio. Or so I joked. Rudy winced. I could say things like that and still remember to pick up the dry cleaning; it was before Fan came. Rudy was concerned; he had a lighter grip that week than me. Kim, whom he'd conjured, strange wise beauty, was turning out to be a little more than he could handle.

"How was your meeting with Lou?" I asked.

"Not very productive. Possibly a good thing as I have to play tomorrow night."

"They'll love you," I said. "I was going to go shopping with Katie to buy a dress. Want to go out? We haven't been out for days, except for shows. I'm kind of glad you couldn't get any more Purple."

"Where is there to go? We're past Pluto, Kim."

"You'll have to get back in time for your gig tomorrow."

"Yes," he sighed as if he didn't like it much. "I could spit on them and they'd love me. Why do people worship celebrities?"

"I don't know," I said, wondering whether he was ready to

hear me say he wasn't much of a celebrity compared to Lou but thinking I'd wait.

"Where is there to go? We're past Pluto, Kim," he said again. "And the bars have closed."

"Die Ruine's private and open all night."

"You're not kidding." Rudy laughed a little bitterly and took two dry-cleaned silk jackets off their hangers: one black, one mauve. At least the cuts were different.

♦♦♦

A blonde with dark circles under her eyes told us she loved Rudy's song about Kim and introduced herself as Fan. I recognized her as part of Leni's group from the first night and when she asked us to join her we agreed; the place was standing room only. The three of us drank rye, which is odd as I generally hate it. We were glum and silent, maybe because of the whiskey.

I went to the bathroom; the atmosphere at our table was so claustrophobic I had to escape. There was a hole high in the crumbled wall. I stood on the toilet and looked through, saw two stars like eyes looking back at me, the eyes of God or perhaps the Devil as the tarot reader had said. One of them must be Sirius, I thought. My home planet. I half believed it; we were that far gone. It was an interstellar distance Rudy would have to take on stage tomorrow night but I figured it was almost a requirement in his profession. Lou had likely played from much farther out in space. I got back and told Fan and Rudy.

"There's a dark twin to the Dog Star," Fan said. "Want to go?"

"That's where we've been the last week, since we arrived," I replied.

"Ah. You must mean you have some of the new Purple. I'd like to join you," she said.

"We're lonely explorers. The arduousness of our journey through uncharted territory has caused us to go from love to hate in less than a week," Rudy said.

It was true I wanted more than anything to get away from him; the problem was Purple impelled us toward one another: tiny electric trains about to crash, derail, explode. It always seemed worth it until afterwards. When Fan reached over and fondled Rudy's thigh, I was thrilled at the possibility of dumping him off on her but she had other plans for the three of us.

♦♦♦

Two days later, waking up, curtains pulled against the glare, I glanced at my watch.

"Shit," I said, noticing the date, "we have three hours to catch our plane."

"You go," Rudy said, reaching over and cupping Fan's breast in his hand. "I think I am going to stay here, with Fan."

She nodded solemnly, extricated herself from his fondling, leaned over and submerged his unlit cock in her small mouth. Her long blonde hair veiled the act decoratively.

I put a few things into a suitcase, feeling neither jealousy nor even curiosity. I didn't remember when she'd arrived, or why, and wasn't sure I cared.

"Don't forget this," Rudy said, reaching over to the night table to pick up a silver choker we'd bought in an expensive jewellery shop on the Ku'Damm.

"Oh thanks, I almost did forget it." I popped it into the suitcase. What had we been doing for the last forty-eight hours? The memories came, a little at a time. More or less what Rudy and me had been up to, only there'd been three of us.

"Oh no," Fan said, "you should wear it." She got up, having finished her job, and clasped the choker behind my neck. "Zo baby, you don't think you will stay here with us?"

"No."

"Why not? You find me beautiful, no? You seem to like it with a girl. I could teach you…"

I looked from her to Rudy, a statue in repose. A naked

prince. A young lion. Purple did little for my vocabulary. It had seemed a good thing, once. "I think maybe I have had enough of beauty for awhile, you know?"

"Ah," Fan said, "I never have enough of beauty. Never never never."

"I know," I said. "That's why you're a junkie and I'm not."

She laughed instead of taking offence, whispered in my ear. "I sense that you are a little bit tired of him and I understand. I have a girlfriend, Lucerne, who would be only too happy to take him off our hands. The thing is, we would have to take the credit card. You made him put it in your name too, didn't you?"

"No."

"But you can make his signature, yes? A girl could be a Rudy."

"His name's Rudolph," I said, giving away his worst secret.

She sighed. "No good. How much cash then? And of course, we could sell the dog collar for quite a bit, that is unless you're very fond of it." She was forgetting to lower her voice but Rudy didn't seem to hear, or maybe he didn't care.

"Well, I'm thinking it will make a great memento of this bizarre chapter."

"What? I do not always understand your Canadian English. I lived for a time in London but it is a much different accent."

"Not worth repeating."

"Between two women there is always all the time in the world."

"It's not personal."

Fan wasn't offended. In retrospect I'm not surprised. It was her job, after all, to understand such things. "You get sick even of the best sweets if you eat too many," she said by way of analysis. "Now when we do Purple it no longer fulfils each desire like liquid light."

"Did you write that down?" I asked Rudy. He didn't answer, paging through a magazine.

"I know," Fan continued, packing her own little patent leather case, "we get bored. Too much of the same is not good. There are many things I could teach you. Many different and new games you have not experienced before. We play to amuse ourselves."

"Like dolphins," I said, "or maybe dogs."

She didn't hear my sarcastic undertone, beamed widely. "*Genau!* Dolphins' sexuality is so spiritual, no? Like us."

I had to admit it had occasionally felt like that, playing like dolphins in a flooded old hotel room, sporting a baby grand and drawn mauve curtains. What is it about mauve? It was the only colour I wore then, if I wasn't wearing black.

Fan took off one of her many scarves and pulled it tightly around my breasts. I moaned, wondering whether dolphins ever moaned. "Lie down," she whispered. "Just once more."

I complied.

Lying there, my eyes closed, I heard her charge Rudy two hundred and fifty dollars. "American," she whined. I heard her get up and fish through the wallet he'd left on the night table. "What is this? Don't tell me you don't have any American?"

My eyes slammed open. "You're paying for this?"

"Well, it's actually the first I've heard of it."

"Not true. You agreed to pay me before I came up, and you did pay me half last night, remember?" She winked at me. "It's been amazing. Think of it this way, it's half my regular rate because *Ich finde sie beide sehr* cool, very beautiful. Beauty always pays a lower price, in all things."

Fan and her damn beauty obsession. She was slated for a lot of face lifts some year, that was for sure.

"Are you really going to go?" Rudy asked, looking forlorn. I covered him with a sheet.

"Get a grip, kid, you need it. Although I have to say it's been a ball. If a very strange ball, doesn't bounce like other balls, obeys physics from another dimension."

"It's not my fault, I didn't know. I thought she was a groovy pick-up, just like you did."

I figured him for a liar. And what was wrong with paying a groovy pick-up? Fan had a plane to catch, just like I did, only hers was next week and to Paris.

Still haven't been to Paris.

"You wouldn't have to pay if it was just you," she whispered, lasciviously. Rudy glowered at her, overhearing. "We could make a lot of money. We could go anywhere, travel the world. I have great connections."

"I'll bet." Watching her pack scarves. Would she wash them out in tonight's hotel room? Where did she live, and with whom? Do women like Fan "live" anywhere? Do they have kitchens, or only restaurants? I'd buy her drinks and ask about her life but I knew I wouldn't get to hear her stories unless I joined in them. You hear the best gossip only when you give people something to gossip about. I'd have to earn her trust, she wouldn't give it away for free.

"Well, if you gotta go, go in style." She gave me her black lace shirt to wear, a rubber miniskirt, and net stockings. They fit perfectly.

"I guess you'll be wearing my jeans and T-shirt out," I said, unzipping my suitcase to dig out clothes for her.

She took them and held them up against her long slim body, delighted. "They are a very nice jeans and T-shirt. They will remember you me always."

"Cool," I said and kissed her briefly on those soft soft lips. "Take care. Don't get hurt. There's some crazy people out there, some bad bad drugs."

She smiled, so happy I stopped to think she might be endangering herself. "I am the craziest," she said. "Is no one badder than me." She laughed delightedly, including me in her big secret, the one she depended on to keep her safe from harm. I hoped it would, even if she was the devil.

"No doubt," I said, glancing at Rudy before I left. He was asleep. Would they spend another few days together, Fan steadily emptying his wallet of traveller's checks, or was it over between them too? Who knew, and more importantly, who really cared?

◆◆◆

Katie drove me to the airport, shrugged when I told her Rudy had changed his flight, would be staying on with Fan. When we got to Tegel, I asked whether she'd supplied the Purple. Maybe there'd been a lot I'd missed. Maybe Fan and Katie had cooked it all up together, right from the beginning. She didn't reply, not really, and who could blame her? Katie was way too slick to ever implicate herself; in that way she and Fan were of a type. Instead she asked, "What's with the clothes?" Giving me the once over.

"I've been in Berlin," I said. "What do you think?"

"Did you go to the other side?"

"Yes."

"What was it like?" Katie asked.

"Strange. But good to see it, I guess. To know what's there."

"But you wouldn't want to live there, right?"

"No," I said. "But then, that's what everyone from this side says, don't they?"

She nodded, smiling. "The new song. No one will ever forget it."

Hamilton Beach

OUTSIDE THE DOOR water continues to run. Wraparound workbenches, on every wall but this one, stacked to the ceiling with piles of doll faces. Piled one on top of the other, faces look out of faces like layers of masks. They still have their eyes; blue eyes with flecks of light in them.

Staring up.

I've never been here before.

There's no one else in the room. I stay in bed, looking at the doll's eyes. Sacrilege, those fake flecks of light. Like faking orgasm, only worse. Faking Life.

Who'd I come with? Why don't I remember? Like other wickedly hungover mornings I know it'll return to me. Machine-heads. Virtual sex junkies. They've discovered it's pheromones that keep your memory sharpened. Kids get it from hugs and kisses. Why there's so much more ADD now; people don't get laid any more, and kids cuddle with virtual pets, not their parents or puppies. But I only did it once.

Water runs. My head hurts. Not only do I not remember how I got here, or where here is, I also don't remember where I live, or what I do with myself from day to day. What do I remember?

Martin, my boyfriend. He's not here with me now, although it comes to me that's not unusual, for him. I told Martin about the machine-heads, and he said he'd run with them too. Once or twice, he said. Of course, he's lied before.

I'm wearing my clothes, which gets rid of at least one uncomfortable possibility.

The sound of running water. Maybe Martin's having a shower—a nice thought. If he was trying to duck out on me again he wouldn't be spending so long in the bathroom.

Beside the bed on the floor there's rumpled clothes. A soft old cherry-coloured corduroy shirt. Black jeans. Pointed shoes. Expensive once but beat-up looking now. No underwear and good cotton socks. Are those the kinds of thing Martin wears? What's he look like? What do I look like? What's my name? I look at the work benches, the stacks of doll-faces, glazed eyes staring ceiling-wards. As dumb as them, but a little more mobile, I get up out of bed.

The hall is empty, so empty, and the building is filled with silence. The water is still running; I open the door. A young woman is standing at the sink, painting her eyelids. Her blonde red curls are tied back in a ponytail; the red is dyed. Her mouth sticks out under jagged lipstick, soft like a little kid's. She jumps, ever so slightly, keeps applying purple on purple as if I wasn't there. At last her eyes meet mine in the mirror. Mine are brown; my hair's brown too, short. I'm wearing black jeans and a grey hooded sweat-shirt, look about twenty-three. Am cute in a dishevelled gamine-like way.

But I knew all that, I just forgot.

She gives me a dark look, as though I'm not playing by the rules. I don't know what the rules are, yet. I only just woke up, in a strange building with no coffee machine. "Is there a coffee machine around here somewhere?" I ask. "Like in the lounge or something?" She doesn't look at me. She just paints and paints. "D'you have any Tylenol?" No answer. Her eyelids are getting very thick. "What are you going to be for Carnival?" I try, leaning back on the paper towel dispenser, watching her in the mirror. Funny I didn't forget Carnival.

Bull's eye! "Sleeping Beauty," my girl says. "You?"

"I was thinking of being Darth Vader's girlfriend. Kind of

a spin-off, like *Bride of Frankenstein*." Saying it, I know it's true. Maybe if I talk enough, I'll remember more. Seems to me it's happened before.

"Han Solo had a girlfriend, not Darth Vader. Don't you remember?"

"I thought Darth Vader had a girlfriend too, only they just left that part out."

"Left it out of what?"

"*Star Wars* was a story before it was a movie, too. You see, I have this theory that all the movies were stories first. And before that, just pictures written on an invisible wall somewhere, waiting for someone to take them down. Kind of a Plato's cave thing. And now they're pictures on a screen again, just like they were in the beginning. But a screen on this side, not the other side."

She turns around at last. It's always different seeing someone outside the mirror and not in it. Like seeing a different part of their personality. "You seem to know a lot more about stories than you do about television. That's very unusual. I'm Louise," she says. "What's your name?"

"It's Louise too," I say glibly, because I don't remember that part yet. "I'm looking for my boyfriend but I've lost him. Again."

"You seem pretty mixed up," she says, measuring me with her eyes. "You better watch out: Carnival isn't a game; it's dangerous. That's sort of like *Sleeping Beauty* though, that show about losing your prince."

"Kind of a gender reversed Orpheus. Kind of like Isis and Osiris. Is your prince going to come and wake you up?"

"Maybe. Maybe when we've finished making our show. I'm the star." Louise makes a face, not entirely pleased about it. Some star; her foundation clumsily covers zits around her mouth.

"I think maybe it's Martin's place across the hall. D'you know him? D'you live in this building?"

She opens her eyes, the bluest blue, very wide as if she can't believe how stupid I am. Truth is, neither can I. "Martin with the big purple eyes, the sharp nose, so handsome?"

"That's my man," I say, glad she jogged my memory.

"He's your boyfriend? Really? What kind?"

"How many kinds are there?"

"I mean on this side or the other side?"

"All sides," I say, my head splitting, figuring it's a trick question. She nods, accepting my answer, although it seems to worry her. "Where is he?" I ask. "We said we'd do Carnival together like we do every year, and here it is not even started and I've already lost him and myself. They should call Carnival the Season of Memory Loss."

Louise rolls her eyes, says curtly, "He was in here just before you. But he left."

I want to fill in some more gaps, ask questions, but she's gone, her chunky heels clattering. They're too big for her, like a little girl playing dress-up in her mother's shoes.

"Hey, Louise, wait up," I yell.

She runs down the hall, turns a corner and vanishes. I hear a steel door slam; hear her feet clattering on stairs that lead downwards. Slinging my day-pack over my shoulder I follow her, slowly, down long shadowy tiers of stair wells, to the street door. Look both ways, no sign of L.

I walk, don't recognize any street names. The few other people out walking too are so poor they seem invisible even to themselves. I pass old dry goods stores with locked doors and yellow plastic in the windows. There's not a sign of Carnival, as if the city's biggest party doesn't exist. I buy Tylenol at a drug store, swallow several. Finally I come to a coffee shop called the Dew Drop Inn. I'm starving so I go in. The prices are ridiculously low: thirty-five cents for a cup of coffee, eighty-five for a fried egg sandwich; that's what I order.

The place is empty, huge, and dim. The booths are upholstered in shiny red stuff with flecks of gold in it, just like the flecks in the dolls' eyes, the rips held together with wrinkled silver duct tape; they wouldn't call it gaffer's tape here. A taupe Formica counter with red swivel stools and a green Hamilton Beach milkshake machine behind it. God, how I always loved that name. It's always been like a picture to me, of a perfect place, where you could leave all your troubles behind, where everything would be okay and you'd be happy.

The waitress is in her fifties with bleached blonde hair and pencil thin plucked eyebrows. She sighs, bringing me my coffee. It's terrible, from last week's pot reheated eleven times. I stir in a whole bunch of sugar to mask the taste. I bite into Miracle Whip, not Hellman's, stare a little.

"Are you lost, dear?" she calls from across the room, where she's busy polishing spotless tables, filling full sugar containers, sighing.

"I'm looking for my friend. I thought he might've come in here." Little does she know the half of it.

She carries my sandwich from the kitchen, walking painfully, wrapped in support bandages that go halfway to her knees.

"You must be ready for your break, Denise," I say, now that she's close enough I can read her name tag. Denise or Vera, I'd figured. A fifties name to match the place, her look.

"Well, yes," she says, laughing a little. "It's these damn legs, you know?"

"Sit down?"

"Okay, but I'll get my drink first." She comes back with a can of Tab. Her yellow polyester uniform hisses on the shiny flecked vinyl.

"What is it about me?" I ask, too blunt by half, as always. "People are always asking me if I'm lost."

She reaches out, pats my hand. "The truth is, I think we're all lost. It's just some people try to hide it more than others." She blows smoke rings. "I think the trick is to stay amused, don't you?"

A woman after my own heart. And she can't be a machine-head. They never touch living flesh.

♦♦♦

Three years ago during Carnival I went to this warehouse party alone. Martin was gone again. Thing is, I was really drunk, soooo, on my way out I got off the elevator on the wrong floor and walked into this big eerie room full of machine-heads and their gear. I started turning so I could run, but this one guy asked me if I didn't want to try.

I said I'd do anything once.

He gave me a VR headset and controllers; I put on the headset and entered the space they were sharing, thinking I'd get to do a handsome stranger. But the people in there, our sex partners, had arms and legs made of machines, genital organs that didn't look human at all, but were still sexy in this creepy way: valves expanding and contracting, each black rubber exhalation a sigh. I heard the rasping cries of grinding gears, saw furtive graspings of skeletal robotic hands, all the bones showing. Beneath dirty flesh-coloured vinyl I saw chrome tendons, frayed wiring. Sucking and popping and moaning, the sounds of machines in orgasm. Then as I stayed in, it started to happen to me too; I got replaced, starting with my sex where I was the most connected. Genius embedded in this craftsman's hand. A sad, wicked, broken-faced genius, but all the same: the sound, the texture were so detailed, so rich. The furniture was clipped, the detail in shadows, in excrescences of old pink vinyl, raised and knobby like a keloid scar, in palest conflagrations of mauve in the velvet bodysuit I wore. Sighing, sighing: only velvet sighs like that. Someone was a genius, for sure.

It could've been funny, I suppose, and in some twisted way it even was but it scared the hell out of me. I signed off and jacked out, left to walk city streets, shards of broken ice glinting like starlight. I knew it wasn't real, so what was the matter? The technology's still so new; maybe it's like early horror movies. "The Thing" used to terrify people and now we just laugh.

I walked, turning over in my mind sensations that had more to do with pain than pleasure; the missing parts of myself, the parts I'd allowed to be replaced by robotics had all been screaming faintly, phantom limbs. But it's still a visual medium—how can you remember sensations in VR? I had to have supplied the sensations myself, a shadow of a shadow.

Footsteps running behind me, male footsteps. I turned. One of the machine-heads, Matt, the one who'd invited me. I wasn't afraid. Machine-heads are terrified of raping real women. They'd have to touch.

He reached for my hand, like something long forgotten, and pulled it back, his mouth twitching. It was the first sign he might yet know what he'd lost.

"You don't like it?" he asked sadly. We walked side by side in the frozen night, the Don River snaking below us, full of moonlight. The east end has always been this sad.

"It was okay," I lied.

"Then you'll come back? Not many women come. Give me your number."

"I know where to find you," I lied again. "I'll drop in some time, 'kay?" I smiled up at him, his shaved head.

He said, as if he was quoting: "And all because real people seemed too frightening and the machines promised to take the pain away."

"That's exactly right," I said, amazed, sober. "Who said that?"

"I did," he said, and turned to go. "I know you won't come back. You don't want to come that far in with us again. And I can't come back out anymore to be with you, even if I wanted."

"Touch my hand," I said. "Take your mitt off, touch my hand."

"In the virtual worlds people think they can do anything, darken as much as they want, and it doesn't matter, doesn't have any effect in the real world. Strikes me they might be wrong. A shadow cast from that side to this, staining us," he said, still sounding so lost and poetic and smart. Handsome too, in a rough-hewn way.

"I thought that was just propaganda really, hype, that whole no-touch thing," I said, half meaning it. An outlaw culture's romance, I'd always figured. For it to be true would be too frightening by half.

He waved his wet woolly mitten at me, walked away. His footsteps sounded cold and lonely.

"And where is the one old story now that will tell us the way out of this?" I called after him, but then, I'm always saying that; it's my thing. He stopped, turned towards me, took his mitten off. And touched the icy metal bridge rail instead. It stuck. He pulled it away, leaving behind tiny bits of skin.

"I'm sorry," I whispered, "so sorry," the snot freezing in my nose.

"I guess they lied," I thought I heard him say, walking away again. We were already too far apart, couldn't hear each other anymore.

Broken mirrors. We are all holding pieces of a broken mirror, trying stubbornly to glue them back together. Maybe we should leave it shattered.

It's too bad I couldn't tell him that, he would've liked it. That's the thing; he seemed so nice, much nicer than Martin really, in spite of his preferences. I think about him a lot, of how our hands froze on the railing, looking down at the river. Your tongue would get stuck there forever if you let it. Something so stupid only an ignorant kid would do it.

Denise's cigarette package is red. Du Maurier King Size. She lights her smoke with a real lighter, a fake gold one and not a Bic click flick dick or whatever. She inhales as if nicotine were prana itself.

"Maybe I went to another city last night and just don't remember," I say, thinking what harm can utter frankness do after everything's already gone so wrong?

She looks at me levelly. She's been around the block a few times, this one. Knows the score. "But," she says, blowing smoke rings, "you'd have to do an awful beer and pills cocktail to forget that much, down it with even more tequila." Denise speaks so slowly, as though she has more time than the rest of us, only it isn't very pleasant time.

"Problem is I don't remember if I did that or not. Mind if I have one of your smokes?" I ask.

"Oh, please do. Please do. But finish your breakfast first. It'll help."

But I push my half-eaten egg away, light my butt, don't inhale. I don't really smoke but it seems like the right thing to do; keep my molecules moving so I don't get petrified in the fifties like Denise. And I entertain a thin hope it might make Martin show up, like he used to do to make the streetcar come. He wouldn't have kept doing it if it hadn't worked so often. That's what we were like together: two lost lambs making up our own mythology, taking solace in an urban sympathetic magic, at once invented and uncovered.

"Say, Denise?"

"Yes, dear?" She's staring out the window at the dead buildings, the grey afternoon light.

"Do you know where anybody celebrates Carnival around here? Maybe if I could find Carnival I could find my friend."

"Carnival? They started it up here a few years ago, right? Kind of like down in New Orleans. I've never paid much attention; it's not something for us old folks. But there's a dance at a place called The Aquarium, a week from Tuesday. Somebody left me a poster for it, but I haven't put it up yet." She gets up and walks ever so slowly to the counter, retrieves the poster lying there. Watching her is like watching time itself. A bad time. "Maybe if you go to this dance..."

She shows me the little map at the bottom of the poster. The Aquarium is a club just four blocks away from where we are. My life is like a video game this morning. If I follow the clues I'll find Martin, remember where I am, how I got to be here. "Well, I guess I better get going. It was really nice to meet you, Denise. You've helped me out a lot."

"Okay, dear. Hope you feel better. Do drop in again."

I walk till night falls. I've slept in parks before and would do it again if I had to, but still. The street door is open: relief. The stairs as I walk up are still, so still. I don't hear anything except my own feet, one at a time, although once I hear footsteps running along on an upper floor, but maybe it's just a trick of memory, of desire, like knowing he'll be there. But he isn't, and neither is the red shirt. A stack of boxes is gone, but everything else is the same. I lock the heavy steel door and go to sleep.

♦♦♦

I make myself at home (haha) and wait for more clues.

I look in the mirror; hold a mask to my face. Still, I can't see: eyes in the way. I cut them out with an X-Acto blade but leave the eyelids, so they open and shut, eerily mechanical, over mine. For hours then, I sit at the workbench, cutting the eyes out of a few stacks of dolls. I don't know why, but it makes me feel good. Cut out all those fake eyes, all that sacrilege.

There's a landline and someone calls it while I'm working, orders masks. I have to find x number of a certain type, box them, courier them to her Carnival store. "Make sure all the eye holes are cut out," she says sharply. "They weren't last time."

I tell her I'm strapped, ask if she could pick them up herself, bring cash. She agrees, somewhat surly. If I'm going to be staying here, I'm going to have to have money to eat.

Wherever this is.

She shows two hours later, just as I'm finishing up. Harried and businesslike, she takes the box I've packed for her and gives me fifty bucks. Doesn't bat an eye at my masked face, like she sees weirder every day.

I go to the Dew Drop for dinner, remembering at the last moment to go maskless, order a hot beef sandwich. Thick powdered gravy poured on white bread, a slab of beef and pale peas floating on the surface tension of melted marg. The fifties isn't even my mother's childhood; how come this place got stuck so far back?

I'm the only person there again, and Denise joins me, can of Tab and red cigarettes in hand. I tell everything I know, there's bits that come back just in the telling. "Once Martin and I had this dream we'd get a studio together. In the east end where rent was cheap. We'd work our butts off; he'd be an artist and I'd do the production and management, and then after we got rich we could move somewhere else, like to Hamilton Beach maybe," I explain.

"It didn't work, did it?" she asks, and I have to nod. I ask her where we are and she laughs. I guess she thought I was kidding and I couldn't bring myself to tell her the truth.

◆◆◆

The next morning I take an old motorcycle helmet out of a cardboard box full of junk and trade it for my mask. I look in the mirror. Darth Vader. Could be. Just a little modification on the shape. Dig under all the workbenches; find a box of stuff for working with Plexiglas resin. I learned how to use it in art school, a million years ago, before I met Martin, back when I still had dreams of being an artist myself. What a fool.

◆◆◆

Memory returns very slowly. I haven't had such bad amnesia since I first learned to abuse alcohol when I was thirteen. Where am I? Only the east end could be this sad. It's just a part I never really knew; east of the Don River there are still pockets where the fifties and sixties and seventies live on, bordered now, so locked in misery they'll never be able to catch up to the rest of time. In the store windows there are aspidistras with leaves that need wiping, and the ubiquitous layers of yellow plastic. I don't know what all that yellow plastic is for, unless it's to protect the plants from UV, not that they need much protecting, what with the dank grey skies. Why don't I just get on the streetcar, go back to the west side, our old apartment, our friends, our bars, our jobs?

I can't. We gave all that up, late summer. Came here. It's the in-between part I've forgotten, and I still don't know where Martin is. I go to the Dew Drop for dinner again, order ham with canned pineapple rings. As always, the place is empty except for me, as though only I know the way in. Denise waves distantly, sighing, but doesn't join me this time.

When I get back I see someone's been there while I've been gone, made the bed, worked on the masks. It's happened before. Who?

♦♦♦

I take a westbound red rocket, what they call the streetcars here. I'm full of trepidation, and when the route passes through my old Spadina neighbourhood I don't even get off, my limbs suddenly leaden. Who would I visit? Who even knows me anymore? I feel out of place again, only in a different way. Where do I really belong, or when? It seems like when people or neighbourhoods get stuck, they create little pockets of frozen time around themselves. Denise got stuck in the fifties, even though she's too young for it. At the Dew Drop Inn, I guess the fifties never stopped. I wonder when I'm stuck in. A bad time with Martin, most likely.

I get off the streetcar and stand on the other side of the road, a faint feeling of panic rising in me. The west side looks wrong, gives me a vertiginous feeling as though I've stepped through a mirror and the world's reversed; everything has different meanings. I can barely wait for the streetcar to take me back to the other side, to run upstairs, coat tails flying, sit at my bench and cut doll eyes out.

On the way back from the streetcar stop I see Louise. "Hey, Louise," I say, grabbing her arm.

She shakes me off, glares.

"Where's Martin?" I demand. "I still can't find him. You know him, have you seen him? And how come he never mentioned you? What's going on?"

"Maybe he doesn't like you anymore," she spits. "Maybe you're too messed up for him. Maybe he's got someone new."

"Messed up? That's a joke. He's a way worse abuser than me."

"You don't really have the same name as me."

"Course not. I'm Petra. That was a joke."

"I thought you were her. Where's your lost five months, Petra?" Where?

She's wearing a white satin party dress over her jeans. She doesn't make any sense. Her frizzy ponytail, her strapless dress over her dirty T-shirt and satin old lady pumps. Maybe if I'm nice to her she'll tell me what she knows.

"Look," I say kindly, "you can't even get the zipper done up. How is your prince going to recognize you looking like that?"

"You stay away from me," she hisses. "You've always said you didn't even want to be on this side. And you can't come without your mask."

"What is with your crazy outfit, then?" Some Carnival thing going on this year that I don't understand.

But she snaps her silver purse shut and runs.

She's running again.

What's she so afraid of?

♦♦♦

Can there be such a thing as a wrong neighbourhood of the soul?—a time in life (for all feeling displaces time—although often in unusual and unprecedented ways) when one is continually doubling back on one's tracks, meeting, it seems, none of the right people, everything taking place in fits and starts and going nowhere? And, if so, is there a reason for this, a purpose behind it that we, in our diminished state, cannot comprehend but only intuit? And why is everything a mirror of everything else? And why does my heart quake so unexpectedly and how beautifully the winter light falls across the snow, and that does lift my spirits.

Someone has washed and ironed Martin's burgundy shirt. I see it now, hanging from a rod amidst the clutter on the far side of the room. Martin himself would have ironed only the front and the sleeves—he always wore a vest with his shirt—a paisley brocade waistcoat from a vintage suit, covering the shirt's still wash-wrinkled back.

◆◆◆

"It's the memory thing that bugs me the most. I've lost months, and if I could just figure out what they were, I'd have Martin back." Denise shakes her head, sighs distractedly and looks out the window at the trashiness of the passing parade, humming a dance tune from the fifties. Poor Denise. Still singing the same song, over and over, like a wind-up jewellery box ballerina.

"I think you mean you wonder where you lost them?" she says.

"What do you mean?"

"Seems to me it's a location, much as anything. You were used far worse than she ever was. At least she's awake for it."

Sleeping Beauty awake? I ponder that, ask what she means, but she shrugs, sighs as if I'm a dirty business, she's said too much. I pay and leave, thanking her for the clues, such as they are. I don't know if I should pay her any attention, but then, I'm not getting much help from anyone else. Besides, I like her dottiness: half oracle and half crazy-old-lady, perhaps even something to aspire to. She's my fairy Godwaitress, this time around.

◆◆◆

That night I take the streetcar to my old west side local, the Fishbowl. I don't really want to but I make myself, thinking it'll be good for me. I run into Martin, of all people. I'm so relieved to see him I pretend nothing weird is going on. We talk and drink all night, dancing and leaning our heads on one another's shoulders. It's the beginning all over again, like when we first fell in love.

"Hey listen, Louise," he says. "I've got this really great idea for a mask. I think it'll sell like crazy, for Carnival, you know."

"How come you called me Louise?"

"I did? Oh. Isn't that what you call yourself now? Hey, tell me what you think. Darth Vader. You remember Vader. He's out of an old movie, *Star Wars*."

"Yeah, I know. Funny, but I've been thinking about him too."

"Great minds think alike," he says. Snow falls as we go outside and hail a cab. "You know I love you, don't you, Louise?"

"Sure," I say, closing my eyes, leaning into his shoulder in the back seat. I'm so happy to have him back I ignore his name calling.

Together we tramp up the now familiar stairs. We're dressed alike, in old black sweaters and jeans. His are corduroy. He's wearing the pointy shoes I remember from the first day and when they're lying on their side on the floor I see they have a hole in the bottom. After we've finished making love Martin goes to sleep. I lie there for a while, just thinking. The lingering sexiness carries me into a dream where everything is pleasure, where the moment is all that exists, like at Hamilton Beach. The window high above is turning blue.

In the morning he's gone, but I find I don't much care. I have orders to fill, Denise to talk to over dinner, my lost months to uncover.

♦♦♦

My window is bleak, wintery, star filled. I read old magazines, stir my instant coffee. There is never enough sun in the wintertime, never half enough damn sun. It's so hard to even remember ever having had any other life than this one. You wake up going "Where am I?" and you end up forgetting there ever was a Before. Kind of like life.

I stay in, living on boxed cereal, apples, and instant coffee.

Between mask orders I cut out four-year-old newspaper clippings I don't bother to read and glue them into a scrapbook. With a hot gun yet; no Uhu glue sticks here. Very wasteful. No sign of M.

◆◆◆

When I wake in the middle of the night Martin's there. "I love you," he says, and I hear someone murmur in response. It's Louise. She is here, in bed with him, with me.

It's feeling a little cramped tonight, I have to say.

Rage. Louise the ugly, the misshapen, has my Martin. What can the attraction be? Perhaps she's good for his ego. Perhaps I should tell him how brilliant he is more often. But, I think angrily, I've never really been that kind of girl.

I go back to sleep, hoping I'm dreaming. Hoping they'll go away.

◆◆◆

I stare at the walls, the endless stacked faces. Layers and layers of masks. I've got to start thinking of my costume, and not just how to make it, but what it means. Vader is the exterior. I'll be his inner girlfriend; his anima. But what is beneath the mask, historically? Who was Vader before he was Vader? Dark Father. Hades was dark husband, but then, husband and father are the same in more than one story. Dark incest.

One night I take out the VR headset and realize it's part of the mask. I hot glue it to the motorcycle helmet, carve out a piece of plexi and mould it to the back to get the shape right. It's nice to be using my education for something. I look in the mirror, very pleased with my results. A little matte black spray paint and I'm in business. Too bad I couldn't record the heavy breathing, but a smartphone or even a cassette recorder are things I haven't come across. They probably sell old Vader voice-chips at surplus electronics stores, but I haven't found one anywhere near here. I haven't come across a computer either; I could probably find a sound file of Vader's breathing on the interwebz but the out of time quality here seems to extend to technology.

♦♦♦

Darth Vader. Well.

Fancy meeting you here.

It doesn't occur to me till morning that I'd planned to be his bride and not the man himself.

But the soul reaches blindly, unbidden, for what it needs.

Louise and Martin shared my bed again last night.

♦♦♦

I start wearing my Vader mask on my daily walks. Also a length of black velvet for my cape—it must've been used for photography backdrops. So strange to borrow clothes from people I only live with intermittently, in the middle of the night, for snatched moments of crowding elbows and knees, nanoseconds of overheard lovemaking, as contextually odd as dream, before I drift to sleep again. Always drifting to sleep again in this life. What would it be to wake up for good? It's all too much like wearing a mask whose symbolism you don't understand, have to piece it together from the reactions you get.

Denise smiles but looks worried as I take my helmet off, set it beside me on the red vinyl banquette. "Sometimes," she says, "it's better to forget. Don't you see?"

"I can't see till I cross," I say, "to the other side." Not knowing what I mean, just listening to it. How to follow clues. Eat my Hawai'ian burger, drink my milkshake, not because I like them, but so I can watch the Hamilton Beach machine. I take my dinner reading out: *The Larrousse Encyclopedia of Mythology.*

Denise looks impressed by the size of my tome. I turn it around, show it to her. "I always carry it around in my day-pack this time of year. Some people laugh but it carries so much information about Carnival, about stories. Carnival is like living myth, living fiction. The only problem is every once in a while it feels like we're all going just a little mad. But then, that's what it's supposed to be like, isn't it?"

"Be careful," she says, "maybe you'll get out yet."

I look in the mirror beside the coat rack, at Vader. My eyes stare out. Have I given life to the mask, or has it made me dead, a doll, an only partially alive thing?

Almost like a machine-head.

◆◆◆

People on the street are afraid of me, giving me a wide berth. They must think I'm a machine-head, unafraid to wear my gear on the street. There are jacks in my helmet, the goggle jacks. They are like a question, an anticipation, a challenge. I wait, trying to be open-minded.

What does it mean, to be a machine-head for Carnival, but not in real life? It's like my mother telling me she used to go out as a punk for Halloween when she was young, even though she wasn't one. Wear her hair shampooed green and spiked with egg white, henna tattoos, fake safety pin earrings. For a night.

But I'm living the deconstruction of myth, and not just pretending to it. Besides, I am dangerous: I really don't know much about who I am, brain burned out by drugs, by drinking, by other things I've forgotten or never knew about. But maybe not those things at all. I mean, I've never really been any more excessive than most people I know, probably less. I just use it in a different way. Sometimes you have to forget yourself to remember who you really are. It's kind of funny. I mean, you're supposed to lose yourself during Carnival, but I've really done it this time.

◆◆◆

I love Vader, because he gives me power where I had none before. How does a timid, poverty-stricken, vague, unemployable, confused, and self-abusing but basically good-hearted young woman become so quickly transformed into the terror of the neighbourhood? It could only be because of those whose presence I feel nearby. Everyone thinks I'm one of them. One day I will meet them for real.

What if I decide to join?

I like the power. Still, I know it isn't really mine, although it could be, perhaps should be. It's his.

I know it's a him. I can feel it.

And someday I shall have to pay him back.

Or perhaps wrest back what he has stolen from me.

You know when you pass a store window and see someone faintly unattractive and somehow dowdy looking and then realize with a shock it's yourself, that you look ordinary when you aren't preening in the mirror? Well, that happened to me, but in a different way. I saw a man (I walk like a man now!) in machine-head gear, modified to resemble an evil villain from a kid's SF movie that was popular when my mother's mother was young and still won't go away. In the split second before I got it, I was terrified, a sick shock in my stomach. I almost ran.

Curious to run from yourself.

But why are people so afraid of machine-heads? Is it the self-destructiveness, the memory loss, the outlaw quality? I mean, everyone knows they're terrified of real women. Of touch. Wouldn't rape us if they could.

◆◆◆

I decide to explore the building. I was always afraid to before, but now I've got Vader to protect me. Not a sign of life anywhere ... but at the end of the hall on the top floor the door's open and inside, well, I'm not really surprised ... a VR imaging system.

I put on the glove that's sitting on top of the console, plug in the jacks for my Eyes, settle into a big comfy chair, which, I realize, is an old dentist's chair. It seems somehow appropriate, like pulling the dark teeth of desire. A line for a poem; I'll have to remember it later. Would give it to Matt if I could. Funny how I still save poem lines for him. A machine-head poet: what a combination. As though I'm still waiting to see him again.

I enter the scenario that's already booted up. I know I should be more circumspect; if the system's still running I could be discovered at any moment, but, my helmet and the concomitant by-passers' fear of me has made me brave, even foolhardy.

I myself raping Louise.

I'm a man.

In the act of rape.

She's wearing a white satin party dress, incongruously over a dirty T-shirt and too big satin old lady pumps. Her purple eyelids streaking, purple tears running down her whiteface. Raping a sad dirty clown.

She's acting of course, just pretending she's being raped. These guys aren't pros, just very good amateurs. Who'm I kidding? The details are too fine, too expensive looking, laid over video Louise. Her scarred, toothed black rubber vulva, the antique glow of her copper automaton hands. No one puts in hundreds of hours of bit-mapping without a payoff at the end. Of course they distribute, sell it on the black market.

She is screaming and screaming.

I'm cynical, though, participating in the rape. Because it's not real I'm safely almost enjoying it, perhaps because Louise always seems so stupid. It is the stupidity in her that one enjoys seeing raped. Enjoys raping.

But stupid how?

Who'm I kidding? That could be me up there. Is. A part of me. I can tell. Instead of projecting my personality into the guy, like I'm supposed to, I'm suddenly "inside" Louise. Sometimes that's the best you can do, is say, "I saw it happen." What part of her feels really raped after these performances?

Before it's over I take off the headset and leave.

More reversals.

The phantom limbs in that other scenario I once participated in. This time, a phantom dick. A phantom nasty dick, too; not one of the nice kind. I wonder if I'll ever be able to enjoy sex again.

It didn't work, though. In spite of the technology, I couldn't be him for long.

I leave just in time. I hear footsteps on the stairs, and duck into the open door of an empty unused office. I sneak a peek after he's passed (they were male footsteps) and check him out.

It's Martin.

I remember when I was a little girl, walking home from a friend's house after dark. I'd be frightened, even if it was only five-o-clock, dark already in winter. I'd hear footsteps on the pavement behind me, and not wanting to turn and look, I'd listen to hear if they were male or female. You could always tell. It was always the male ones you feared. Who taught me to do that? What words did they use?

Watch out for bad men.

♦♦♦

I work on my last order, the last before Carnival Tuesday. Everything's changed; I keep the studio door locked, hear footsteps upstairs when I know there are none. What do I fear now? I know only too well.

I fear my lover. I fear he'll want me to act for those things, like she does. I fear how it would change me.

This is why I like wearing the helmet; in it, on the street, I no longer have the fear, walking at night.

Except of course, for them. For him.

Persephone, bride of Hades. Now we can only wear our power clothed in darkness.

♦♦♦

Mardi Gras Tuesday I go to the party at the Aquarium, wearing the Vader helmet. It's like a Carnival warehouse party anywhere, lots of poseurs drinking their faces off and trying to look dangerous in their costumes. Glamorous, like they have exciting lives.

◆◆◆

And some even do. I run into Matt. His shaved head, his lonely boots. We slug beer. He says, "You came in further than you thought."

◆◆◆

"What d'you mean?" I ask. The only way to get people to stop talking cryptic Carnival style gibberish is to ask them straight out, I figure. Even when they're machine-head poets you once thought you could maybe love.

"You were very, very good," he says.

"Good when?"

"Good in your lost months?"

"Good where, good how, what kind of good?"

"Good fuck good. Good on the other side."

"The other side of what?"

"You don't know. That's what I thought."

"Damn right I don't. Getting tired of it too."

"Dope cocktail for months, someone said, I didn't know if it was true. You're the hottest new thing."

At last I do know. "I found the system," I say, "at least one of them. I did see a rape, I mean do it. But it wasn't me, it was Louise."

"Layers and layers of rape. An endless bottomless rape. You only accessed the top layer. Thought it was just her, never you. But what if you'd gone deeper, raped yourself?"

He hands me a smartphone, the first one I've seen. "It's the master. We've just been beta testing it. It has no distribution yet. Get rid of it, get out of here, far out."

"Don't I want to try it first, see?"

His eyebrows go up. As though I revolt him. Funny coming from a guy like that.

"Why are you helping me?" I ask.

"Because you came in one night, just to be nice, to offer company. You didn't have to. You don't know what it's like for us. That we can't get back out. I'd touch you but…"

"You're afraid."

"We're all trapped in there with her, being fetishistically fucked by technology."

"We have to bust Martin!" I cry out. "We have to save Louise."

"Shhh, they're both here." His eyebrows shoot up again; he says, "but don't you see? I work with him, we're on the same side, the other side."

Oh, that other side.

Now who's so stupid, Petra?

♦♦♦

Walk along the Don River. Stick my tongue to the icy railing just to see what it feels like. Pull it away before it gets stuck. Denise tried to help. What little she knew, all rumour and threat, smoke and mirrors. Without getting herself in trouble. Or me in more.

I'll do anything once. But only once.

An oil drum, homeless men and women gathered around the fire. I go up and have a smoke with them, a DuMaurier. I've taken up not just her habit but Denise's brand. I chat, pass out butts and coins as best I can. And throw the phone in, watch it hiss and bubble, the cancerous smell of melting petrochemicals. Walk away, alone, back downriver. Not afraid. They never rape real women. And then remember: they could still jump out from behind a building, chloroform you, dope you so bad you don't know what you're acting in, how it'll be used. It happened to me.

What happened to Louise? Is she there by choice, because she loves Martin, because she thinks she's being hip and noir and cutting-edge? Or are they doing something to her, like what they did to me? But I can't help her, at least not here.

I'm just a little girl, alone, screwed up. When I get back to the other side I'll call the cops, but they'll guess it was me. It's no excuse but some of them, like Matt, don't like where they are, or when.

I'll never know now what Martin truly desires, never know what made me love the dark stranger so blindly for so many years. Only in becoming him did I see enough to fully wake up, get away.

Huge flakes of snow fall from the sky, so big and fluffy and fairy tale looking. For a moment I think I see two alike, have a nanosecond's certainty they aren't real but bitmapped in. VR. But then their tiny spines, their spires, melt and now I'll never know.

I miss Matt, but know I'll never look in there for him again, too afraid I might come face to face with myself, a hidden un-erased copy. Hail a taxi, go back to the west side, where I belong.

◆◆◆

We think what we do on the sleazy side of town is invisible, but it's not. Perhaps it is true, and not just a crazy thought of mine, brought home from Carnival, that what we do on the other side of the screen has an effect in the real world.

I may, for a time, have forgotten my name, my address, even what city I live in, but I remembered this: we have to live as though it is true, no longer Faking Life.

Judy

THAT WAS THE SUMMER all the non-smokers died. It was a hot summer, murderously hot. Everyone who had air conditioning kept it going day and night, so of course the first thing they checked was Legionnaire's Disease.

Frank and I didn't have air conditioning, so we slept through the days with the fan on, and come dusk we'd climb up on the roof with Judy, our cigarettes, a bottle, and Judy's dog, Hamilton. Hamilton didn't smoke and drink like the rest of us, but he survived that summer anyway. The Tobacco Fiasco, as it came to be known, turned out not to affect dogs, but we didn't know that at the time. Legionnaire's Disease didn't pan out, and after that we didn't know anything at all, and tried not to think too much about what we didn't know. That's why we spent so much time up on the roof, getting drunk. Judy was up there with us, but she was thinking.

Right after the Tobacco Fiasco got cleared up we left for the east coast to watch the whales die. It was a strange thing to do, drive all those miles to watch them die. It was Judy's idea; she said she wanted to document it. "Document what?" Frank had asked, like she was crazy.

She was crazy. "We've got to document it," she'd said, like we were crazy. We were, but we listened to her, because she'd been right about the cigarettes. We listened to her even though she stuffed the trunk of Frank's Volkswagen so full of camera equipment that we hardly had room for the tent.

She'd done the same thing when all those people started dying. While Frank and I slept Judy would be out there making notes and taking photographs. In the evenings she'd join us on the roof, and, although she'd already been up all day, she'd spend the night measuring her gathered data against each new theory that entered her head between jokes, cigarettes, and swigs off the bottle.

We ran out of cigarettes around four thirty one of those mornings, and it was Judy who offered to walk up to the 7-Eleven to pick up a deck. She explained that she was the least drunk of the three of us, and not to worry, that she'd take Hamilton with her.

They ran all the way home from College Street. Frank and I couldn't understand it, what with Judy's smoker's lungs. Even Hamilton was breathless by the time they got back up to the roof, and he's a big, non-smoking dog.

Judy waved the pack of cigarettes around like it was a live grenade. It was.

"We all smoke like forest fires till sunrise!" She yelled it so loud she woke the neighbours, but Judy didn't care; she knew she was on to something. Frank and I were too drunk to get excited, but Judy ran downstairs, cigarette in hand, to dial the hot line to the Surgeon General's office. She read them her statistics for at least an hour, and when she got off the phone she came back out on the roof and worked on the second bottle with us. By the time it was finished, daylight had arrived, so we called it a night and all went downstairs to sleep.

The headlines made the afternoon papers. Judy never did get any credit for it, except that people stopped dying. Tobacco prices rose faster than interest rates until the government got nervous and imposed sanctions; they knew it would look bad if people were spending so much money on cigarettes they couldn't afford to eat, never mind pay their taxes. After that, prices levelled off, but by then every backyard in the city was planted with tobacco, and we were already halfway to the east coast.

♦♦♦

They were huge, pale grey things, and they'd come moaning out of the sea in that white light you see only on the ocean at sunrise. Just when you thought you'd seen the last one, another would appear, its cavernous head lunging sadly for the shoreline. Judy would be there to greet it, embracing her tripod as though it was some strange prehistoric tree, counting the seconds till the shot was perfect. Frank and I walked out to the road after three days, leaving Judy on the beach with the Volks, her cameras, and all those dying whales. She hardly saw us go. She didn't even notice when we took Hamilton with us. He was a carnivorous dog, but after three days all those whale carcasses had him as grossed out as we were.

We rented a Toyota in the nearest town and headed for Halifax, intending to get hammered. In Yarmouth we stopped at the Yellow Dog bar for a drink and directions. In spite of the name, they wouldn't let us take Hamilton in, so we left him tied to an elm tree outside. We got inside and ordered a couple of drinks from Eddie. Eddie was the big, friendly guy behind the bar. The second our drinks arrived, Hamilton began to howl like all get out. Eddie looked at us. He waited for the dog to stop howling. He looked at us some more. Finally he jerked his thumb towards the door. "That animal out there belong to you guys?"

Frank and I looked at one another. We both got uncomfortable. We looked at one another too long. Frank looked at Eddie, saying, "Yeah, yeah, it's our dog."

"Then go outside and get it to shut up." Maybe Eddie wasn't such a friendly guy after all. Frank went. Eddie turned to me. "You guys aren't from around here, are you?"

"Around where?" I felt like a jerk. I found myself wishing Judy were here; she always knew what to say to guys like this.

"You from the city, right?" I knew what he meant by the city. To guys like that the city is the city. Any city, but especially the one we were from.

"Yeah."

Hamilton hadn't stopped howling. "You sure that's your dog?"

"What makes you say that?"

"Well, it sure as hell ain't your friend's dog, 'cause if it was, he'd have stopped howling by now. And if it was yours, I'd wonder why you're not the one out there." I sat there, not saying a thing. Some bars are like that. "Let's see, you're from the city, it's not your dog. Makes me wonder. Another thing, what did you say you were in the neighbourhood for?"

"Ah, you know, lie around on the beach. Catch some rays."

"Only one beach for miles around here, fella. And if you've been there you'd know it wasn't the kind of beach you want to do much lying around on."

"Oh." I was running out of snappy answers. Hamilton still hadn't stopped howling.

"Go outside, untie the dog, bring him in. When you get inside you can tell me who the dog belongs to and what happened to them." I did as I was told. Frank came in with me, looking bewildered. Hamilton wasn't bewildered. When he saw Eddie he stopped howling right away. Eddie patted him thoughtfully and brought him a big dish of cool water. "Don't worry, kid, we're getting to it." He looked at me. "You got an answer for me yet, fella?"

"It's Judy's dog, Eddie."

"And you left Judy on the beach by herself?"

"You don't understand, Eddie, she—"

"I understand more than you think. You don't leave anybody on that beach alone."

"Why not?" Frank was starting to sound as stupid as me.

"Well, think about it. She might run out of smokes."

"I hadn't thought of that."

"I'll forgive you, considering as you're not so bright."

"But Judy can take of herself, she's very—"

"She takes care of you, right?"

"Huh?" Frank looked at me, horror stricken.

"What would have happened if you or me had decided to quit smoking last month, before she—"

"Fat chance, Ace, but I get your drift."

"See?" said Eddie. "Besides, that's a bad beach. You shouldn't let people stay there alone. Them whales hypnotizes people."

"Hypnotizes?" Frank laughed.

"Frank," I said, "she was a little, you know…"

"Right," said Eddie. "The drinks are on me. Now you guys clear out and go get your friend. And if you decide to change your mind, just remember how happy her dog will be to see her." Hamilton howled on cue. "Attaboy."

We left. We felt like jackasses. Eddie had put such a fear of the lord into our hearts that we drove like mad, crazed people all the way to Whale Beach, which wasn't a short distance. And then we looked for Judy.

◆◆◆

They were huge and white and towered high above our heads. I kept losing Frank in the labyrinth made by their huge, heaving bodies. The ones that had been dead a few days were starting to make a stench like nothing else. We shouted at each other, and sometimes it seemed as though their bodies were casting our voices like echoes, and Frank would turn out to be where I had least expected him. We didn't find her. We didn't find her strange tree of a tripod; we didn't find any of her cameras. Even Hamilton couldn't find her. He howled forlornly for his lost mistress. Then the sun set. We slept on the beach, with Hamilton between us for warmth. We didn't sleep much, because he would wake up from time to time and howl as though his heart was breaking. With sunrise the mist rolled in.

When I woke up, I was face down in an alleyway that reeked of beer and vomit. It was the cockroaches that woke me up, them and the rats. They thought I was spending too much time in their territory.

I made the rounds of the streets and the bars for days. I was looking for Frank, I was looking for Judy, I was looking for Hamilton, for the Volkswagen, for the rented Toyota. I was looking for anything I knew. I would have been happy if I'd found Eddie and the Yellow Dog bar, but when I asked about it people just laughed at me viciously.

I found Judy's tripod. It stood alone at the far end of the beach, pointed out to sea. What had she been photographing? The camera was gone. I took the tripod with me, that and the huge clean rib of a whale.

I hitchhiked back to the city, where I went to our old house. I set up the sad tripod on the roof, which was as empty as the house, except for the wake of bottles and cigarette packs remaining from the summer. The phone kept ringing, but it was always for Judy. They wanted to interview her about her Tobacco Fiasco research. I always told them I didn't know where she was, and I never did see her again, except for maybe once, on the cover of *Life* Magazine.

Myrtle's Marina

GOD KNOWS WHAT THEY FARMED, Peter thought. Stones, maybe. And turned away from the winter fields towards the water and the marina office: a little brown painted clapboard house with a pitched roof and small casement windows, a screen door, one large and three little rooms inside. It always reminded Peter of the cabins at Camp Wawanesa. He'd go to camp for two weeks in August before the family came here all together, to stay at Myrtle's Marina. Since he no longer used it as the office perhaps he should open a little sailing camp, with rows of bunk beds. The counsellors could smoke up in the store room, looking out at the water, although, he thought, they usually did that in some locked room they'd swiped the keys to, a woods clearing, or beyond a place with a name like Cedar Point, on a scrubby, secluded little beach or island. Likewise where they went to have sex, discreetly, because getting caught meant getting fired. Although the kids always knew, he remembered, gossiping about things they were too young to understand. Had anyone known about Peter and Marti, either the other employees or any of the customers? Probably.

The little house, situated as it was between the road and the boat launch, was intended to be the official entry point to the marina, containing in its large front room a solid brown desk and an equally solid oak swivel chair, the kind Peter remembered only the principal got at school when he was young enough to be impressed by principals. Now he was at an age where he could be one himself, figured it to be just another kind of job; not so different from sailing school really, just fewer water hazards. Better pay, though, and more regular. Peter went inside, sifting the dusty stillness. Nothing happened here, ever. Not since he and Marti used to come here to make love.

The old-timers understood when he told them why he came back. Because it was there, because his great-grandfather built the first version of the marina eighty years before, an eye on tourism as an upgrade from farming the stony unforthcoming fields. His parents and his brother, and even Aunt Myrtle no longer thought the old family farmstead on the water important, so why did he? Maybe because of that, because of them no longer wanting it.

"Our family throws everything of value away," Peter had said, when his father had asked, perplexed; maybe one had to be eighty to understand a thing like that. Yet Peter understood, just as the seniors did. Was he so prematurely aged, inside, to believe something only very old people believed otherwise? "Someone has to stop it," he'd said stubbornly, and bought the land back from the stranger Aunt Myrtle had sold it to. The stranger had taken a loss, sold it to Peter for less than he'd paid Myrtle, who had inherited it, along with Peter's father.

"I wanted nothing to do with it. It going for even less should've been a sign," his father had said, but Peter hadn't cared. He didn't want to be a doctor in Toronto like his brother Mark, who lived in a fancy condominium sixteen floors above Lake Ontario. He'd miss skipping stones from his private beach. What woman who wanted a family could resist this unkempt shoreline, these stony beaches? You'd look after toddlers here and not go stir-crazy, a stone's throw from the lake. But Marti was gone, a goner. And if Peter chose to sell, he'd take a loss too, and lose his shirt. And so he stayed, year after year.

Usually he didn't stay long, going back outside almost immediately to re-caulk the rental boats or back across the gravel road to the farmhouse to do his bookkeeping. He put the new computer on the main house's kitchen table when he upgraded, and not in the little office building at all. He told himself it was so he didn't have to heat two buildings. Most people who wanted him had learned to call at the house phone.

Peter remembered Myrtle telling him the office was spooky when she'd heard he was buying the place. They never saw one another much, although she only lived one township away. But she'd called him up, invited him to dinner when the news had broken of the sale going through. She looked good in her new blue sweater, better than she had when she'd run the marina, running around in old sneakers and an older anorak, her face drawn, always behind on the work and the bills.

"The old people always said it was haunted," Myrtle said over salmon and white wine, "although I never saw or heard anything."

"It's not why you sold?" Peter asked.

"Oh no. It's a money sink; the farmhouse is log. It's never been re-chinked, because the repairs money always goes to the marina buildings across the road, it being the income generator. Ostensibly. And the barn's fallen down so bad no one will ever get it up again."

"Nobody's going to farm, Myrtle. Don't need the barn."

"But you already know all that, you already know we all think you're crazy to want it. Especially because you had to buy it, as me and your dad didn't."

"It's my childhood," Peter said, "and our family history."

Myrtle had just rolled her eyes at his sentimentality. She had a gift shop in Buckhorn now. It didn't make any more money than the marina, but it was a lot less work. Like Peter, she'd never married nor had kids. The marina required a man, and Myrtle'd had to hire them, although Peter had come and helped most summers when he was in college studying tourism, which was probably when he'd cemented his attachment. And then he'd bought it a few years later. Was it the second summer

Marti came, or the third? He should be able to remember a thing like that.

All blonde and blue, like sun on water.

He hadn't thought anymore about the alleged ghost until the old-timers started stopping by. He'd laughed, shrugged, been too busy with the business end to listen to old people's tales of nameless fears. Horror meant, after all, wondering how to pay the mortgage on the property in the winter months when there was no income, hoping his summer savings from all those boat rentals to tourists would stretch till spring. But if the oldsters had been right about one thing perhaps they could be right about two, for today Peter didn't just feel the spiraling sense of dusty, empty mystery he'd gotten used to and learned to enjoy, but something new and a little menacing.

The always present sense of mystery had acquired an extra tone, emanating, Peter was suddenly sure, from the kitchen he'd just left, more specifically from an institutionally painted green kitchen cupboard that he saw through the open door. But he didn't go into the kitchen, not yet, rather just glancing down the hall and through the door, at the cupboard, its door hanging ever so slightly ajar.

Making fun of himself, distancing his own fear, Peter went through the remaining rooms, looking at all the stuff the previous owners had left behind, which, in seven years he'd never brought himself to get rid of. It helped him think, he always told himself, when he was looking for a new angle on how to make a go of things. Objects from before, belonging to strangers, things that retained this alien sensibility of another life, someone's life beyond his own, unknowable, unreachable, yet here, made concrete by abandoned items: huge bags of pesticide, fertilizer; the previous owners grew corn and tomatoes to sell to the cottage folk in addition to running the marina.

Peter looked at the gargantuan, heavy bags leaning in a corner, too heavy to lift, really, even shove aside. What to do with the herbicides, the 5-5-5? He knew he could unload them on local farmers who'd be glad for the stuff, but the thought of it running into the ditches bordering his own land, contaminating his own well water, the well water of his children-yet-to-come, elicited a profound distaste. He composted religiously, had a heap the size of a small shed. The neighbours were covetous, but Peter, who didn't grow a thing, was saving it for the wife.

The newly strange kitchen still called, and so he went back, if only to see there was nothing there. A sink, a hotplate, no refrigerator; he'd taken that up to the main house when the compressor on his own had fried.

"Kitchen cupboards, panelling, click-handle latches that lock and pinch your fingers. Kitchen cupboards that have never belonged to a family, never been tamed by children. The moment suddenly framed and put in a late-night movie where it's difficult to breathe, or maybe like you're under water. You open that door. Your rational mind tells you there's no danger but your instincts tell you otherwise; you can feel your heart pounding, pumping adrenalin. You'd shut it except you've already started opening it, can't stop now. Somehow you have to complete the motion, as though, now, you are in one of those dreams where everything is hyper-real. Open the door. Hand goes in. Hmm. A paperback book."

Late winter and he was talking to himself: suggestible, susceptible, cabin fever taking a wrong turn. He shut up, acutely aware that should anyone walk in on him, which no one would, not in a million years, they'd think him barmy. As if everyone didn't already, a little, simply for buying the place.

But what about Marti? What would she think, if she chose this moment to return?

Peter took the book out of the cupboard. It was called *The King in Yellow,* and Peter remembered Marti reading it. She hadn't brought it with her; she'd found it here. It was strange, she said, like nothing else she'd ever read, but she couldn't stop—maybe he'd like to read it too? He hadn't given it another thought. Every cottage on the lake was lined with musty paperbacks after all, but then she'd disappeared, leaving the book here and not in the shelf under the window with the one-dollar used copies of Agatha Christie and Stephen King and John Grisham.

What could it possibly mean? He turned it over and over, unable to let it go in spite of the fact the book elicited a profound terror, a kind of childhood nightmare panic. His hand shaking, he at last replaced it gingerly, as though he'd been caught going through someone else's cupboards, which in a way he had; he couldn't remember ever cleaning them out in any methodical way. He glimpsed a few plates: green plastic, a tinfoil pie plate, some loose spoons. But it wasn't those objects that gave him the creeps, only the book. Being terrified of a book was even worse than talking to yourself. Thankfully he had no audience unless he included the broken aluminum coffee percolators on the counter, the black-capped chickadees in the cedar outside the little window above the sink.

He left the room, bewildered. It was only a book. He could go back and get it, throw it into the middle of the lake, put it in the trash, use it for kindling in his wood stove. There were a million ways to dispose of it. But he didn't. On the one hand it was too ridiculous, and on the other, he was afraid to touch it again. They'd come and find him, dead of heart failure in the spring, his body frozen. It would be a balm to whoever discovered him; decomposition wouldn't have set in, or at least not much.

Peter sat down behind the heavy, scarred oak desk, made doodles of ducks and frogs on the unused memo pad, waiting for his hand to stop shaking, his heart to settle down. Because of a book. He thought of the warnings of gap-toothed, patched together oldsters dropping by the last few summers, never spending a penny, just wanting to yarn. They told him all the lake's old stories, stories he'd shared with his tourists. Probably some of them kept coming back because of it. Hearing the stories, they'd feel part of something.

And then inevitably, just before the old guys left, they'd ask some version of, "Have you felt it yet?" A knowing grin. "It gets everyone sooner or later; you've just held out longer than most." But Myrtle had never said anything about it getting her, although perhaps she'd been too embarrassed to admit it. Maybe for Myrtle it hadn't been the book but something else. The percolator parts, perhaps, or the tin spoons.

It had certainly gotten Peter, whatever it even was. He drew another duck, another frog. He'd forgotten how intrinsically inescapable fear could be, how impervious to the ministrations of the rational mind. He'd have to remember that when the children came. Night terrors came at age three or four. How did he know that? Had he really spent the winter skimming copies of *Today's Parent* he'd surreptitiously swiped from his GP's office?

He would've liked to leave, to walk down to the marsh bordering the lake west of the beach, say hello to the real frogs, following his usual spring patrol, but it was too early in the year; the spring peepers wouldn't be awake yet. Tiny dogwood-climbing frogs with suction cups for toes. In two months he'd wish he could shut them up, calling for a mate all through the night. And so, without frog songs to keep him company, it was once again back to the kitchen; at least his breathing was normal now. On the cracked and chipped counter there were three bent aluminum coffee percolators, but there wasn't one whole, usable one among them. While the coffee basket that was missing in one was there in another, of course it didn't fit.

For the hundredth time Peter played with the percolators. If he had a stem for the one with the coffee basket that fit, and a lid for it, instead of the twisted, non-fitting mess he held aloft, distastefully, between finger and thumb, he could make coffee, actually work down here instead of up at the house. And then if Marti snuck back through for old times' sake, he'd be there. She wouldn't come to the house, she'd come here, drawn to the bags of 5-5-5, where they'd done it, in great haste, before the boaters returned at sundown. And he'd talk to her, just as now he'd already started talking to himself again, not even aware of it.

"Hate to throw things away that will have a later use. I could buy cheap plastic for the kids when they're old enough to use sand toys, the kind of things I sell and then have to clean off the beach every fall, already split and faded. Truth is, these old metal percolators will be perfect; you can use the coffee baskets as sieves. These will last for years—they already have."

Of course, there was one small snag in this offspring fantasy; you had to have a mother first. And as far as women go, there hadn't really been anyone besides Marti. Not exactly mother material.

He was holding the book again, had removed it from its cupboard nest without even realizing it. He'd been right to be spooked by the mostly empty cupboards, to leave them alone. They were haunted, he was suddenly sure, by the demonic powers of this seemingly innocuous thing he was holding in his hand just now. He dropped it in a hurry, shaking again. Damn. He needed something to keep from talking to himself, from thinking a cheap paperback called *The King in Yellow* was a dimensional portal activated by human touch. As he was thinking now. He needed an extra little job for the winter, when the marina was closed, as it was now. And it would help with the more conventional panic over the bills. Never mind the market gardening; that would be the wife's thing.

He and Marti shouldn't have had sex on the 5-5-5 bags. If they had gone to the house, she'd have stayed. "In our family we throw everything of value away." Weren't those the words he'd used, to his own father? Get into hopeless debt buying back the marina, throw Marti away, as though the property wasn't useless without her. Wifeless. Kidless. Barren.

He'd thought she was that kind of girl, adventurous, finding odd locations a little thrill. And maybe she had; but sex in a store room is the kind you enjoy and then move on from.

It was so stunningly clear; why hadn't he seen it before? "There's always a part of you that knows the truth, however hard you try to shut it up," Peter told the book sadly. Perhaps, he thought, it was the haunting that had value in this place, and not the stony beach, the still blue lake, the loons calling from between the piney islands. "We always throw everything of value away in our family," he whispered again. But not the marina, and not the book. He'd keep it forever now, treasure it for its moment of insight. He hadn't asked her to stay because she was a mess, even though he'd known by then he loved her.

In the storage room there was a wheeled, folded up cot: kept there for the nights you have a fight with the wife, Peter thought, patting the book in his jacket pocket, but really, he didn't know why the cot was there. He and Marti never had sex on the cot, in spite of it actually harbouring a remarkably mildew free mattress

"A bag of 5-5-5 doesn't have a mattress, it just emulates one. Sort of," Peter remarked. "Since the cot is for cottagers too drunk to drive their boats back out to the islands after wandering back from the bar."

He'd never asked for anyone's keys, even the few times he should have. He'd been too intimidated to take keys away from drunks larger than himself, drunks deeply invested in their own competence. Pissed. Blasted. Wrecked. "Note descriptive words," Peter said, "They're very accurate." Every winter they were hauling frozen snowmobilers out of the lake. The sober frozen snowmobilers were often still slightly alive, at least alive enough to be rushed off to the county hospital. But the frozen dead ones had always, without exception, been pissed, blasted, wrecked. And never once a drunk dead female snowmobiler. Home with the youngsters they were, knitting and purling lavender worsted booties. Much too sensible to take the snowmobile out after consuming half a bottle of vodka, complete with exclamations about how well it made her drive. If a man would let anyone take his keys away, it would be his wife.

Peter knew, he'd seen it: the largest, drunkest, most ob-streperous man giving his keys to the teeny, tiny, soft spoken, completely sober wife, wailing toddler in tow. Name was Josie. Got the kid out of bed, wrapped him in a blanket, and drove like hell just so she could snag hubby at the boat launch where Peter let him keep his ancient Snow Cat, said, "Give me the keys." Why hadn't she let him crash through the ice? He just drank the money anyway. Josie had been one hell of a driver, Peter remembered, used to race when she was young, and drive in demolition derbies. If anyone could drive the icy back roads to the marina in the dead of night on bald tires, with a screaming baby in the car seat, Josie could. If she wanted to have a couple of beers and take the snowmobile out on the ice, Peter was pretty sure she'd handle it. But Josie never felt safe enough to leave the baby home with Dad, go out alone on the lake at night, get some air in her hair. Daddy might drink half a bottle of vodka and drop the iron on the baby's head. And not enough money for sitters; besides, he'd be insulted, think she was out of her mind hiring someone when he was in the house.

Would Marti do any of those things? Not bloody likely. Marti, with her bravado and love of self-medication of all kinds, was, like the big, drunk, egotistical man in question, the type who'd tangle herself and the Snow Cat around an island pine. If it was sense that men were after when they looked for a wife, to compensate for their own lack of same, Marti would've been exactly the bad choice Peter had so often told himself she was.

Years younger, she'd been a summer employee. They'd had an affair, and Peter had surprised himself by falling in love. He'd wanted to know her then, had gotten to know her, too, much more than he'd ever known anyone. Had ever wanted to know.

It was March; soon time to open the marina. Or at least, start preparing to open it. Peter discovered he could care less. All the details of management and maintenance he used to obsess over, even enjoy, seemed as turbid today as the water-coloured sky. "Even if I wanted to be like that again," Peter said, "I no longer know how. That part of me is a lost shirt, gone overboard from an outboard, sunk to the bottom. Or gone with Marti, more likely."

Marti's liquid body, made out of stars, arching over him on the floor of the store room, the stars falling out of her body, a dark sea, stars floating in it, five pointed stars he could pick up and stick on the walls of the bedroom to entertain the children when they came: luminous, glow-in-the-dark stars. They jumped out of his hand, sat beside him and Marti on the bed, watched them make love approvingly. Smiled and told jokes to the lovers, in fact.

How terrifying it had been, the surrender required, the hard bitten edges of himself he'd have to give up to say, yes, I want this. Except that he hadn't. He'd pretended it wasn't real. And now he couldn't go back to sleep, no matter how much he wanted to. And he couldn't have Marti, either, because she was gone. A goner.

Faced with the unknown, there was only one thing to do. Ask it what it wanted, feed it. "What d'you want then?" he asked the book, "How do I get my real life back?"

Maybe she'd seen the stars too; he'd never actually thought of that. She'd played the reckless babe for him, lying beneath him on the stony shore of an uninhabited island, her skin smelling of pine woods and salt and wind in spite of the vodka they'd been putting away. Maybe it wasn't a choice; perhaps portals opened each time Marti made love, funneling the lovers into more beautiful dimensions. And perhaps each and every one of her lovers, and he knew there had been quite a few, had closed his eyes to a beauty so much larger than he could fathom. I'd drink too much too, Peter thought, and remembered how, making love on their island, he'd briefly seen their future spread out before him, pretty and comforting as a star quilt. It was the last time, the time before she left without saying goodbye or even leaving a note. Leaving her few things behind. He'd thrown them away. Except for the book.

In his vision Marti had been leaving to go grocery shopping, Peter's list in hand, getting into her rusty little yellow car, her blonde hair tied in two long pigtails. She wore silver dream catcher earrings, a plaid car coat she'd made out of the same material as the worst couches in existence, a knee-length red and white striped skirt, black tights, black ankle boots, a black rolled-brim hat. Somehow, on Marti, this didn't look dreadful but fetching: a country punk chic that managed, impossibly, to be stylish as well as original. Smiling, sure of herself, as he'd never once seen her, she waved goodbye to Peter and Julian, who didn't squall at his mother's departure, solemnly sieving sand through a dented percolator coffee basket, knowing she'd be bringing home treats.

She reversed down the driveway, tires screeching, and Peter sat on the edge of the sandbox with Julian and played with percolator parts, until the real Marti interrupted, asking, "What are you thinking about?" And he hadn't told her, had run his fingers through her hair and smiled. Maybe she'd been afraid to tell him about the little stars, afraid he'd say she was crazy. It had never even occurred to Peter, how his silences might have hurt her.

He'd closed his eyes again and watched as future-Marti hung laundry, drove Julian to daycare, started tomatoes in flats to grow and sell to the island cottage folk. She invented cookie recipes from scratch, mainly successful, although there was one problematic experiment containing canned pineapple that exploded in the oven. When they put it outside the back door, even the usually indiscriminate stray dogs didn't touch it. Peter, who had taught himself how to cook over the years, perhaps also, like saving the aluminum percolator parts, in anticipation of the children, made most of the dinners.

He shuddered with longing. But what if it was her self-destructiveness that he found seductive? The doomed Marti, the Marti who fucked everything in pants and then laughed at them. The one who was as surprised as he was, to find herself loving Peter. The erstwhile coke head, the brilliant drunk? Maybe she didn't share his vision of their lovely possible future at all. Maybe that had been his job, yet another he'd neglected, like taking the keys away from Josie's husband himself, and growing tomatoes, and inviting Marti to stay in the house no matter what people said, and picking a smiling yellow five-pointed star out of the crumpled sheet and putting it in her hand, saying, "Nothing like this has ever happened to me before."

Peter knew he'd never find her, not unless he gave something up, some preciously adhered to delusion or illusion, as much a part of him by now as his hair, which, truth to tell, was less a part of him than it used to be. For some reason this gave Peter hope. If he could lose his hair, perhaps he could lose his self-importance, his stubborn pride. Delusions could fall out each morning, come out in clumps in his comb. Marti had once said he looked cute balding, that he was lucky he had the right shape of skull for it. As she shared her peanut butter sandwich with him, told him the names of wild flowers he'd never learned.

The Dark Lake

I'M SITTING AT MY DESK, writing in a ledger. Aromatic geranium, anise hyssop, flowering amaranth. The moon is blue. I keep writing poetry in the margins of the ledger. Of course, the order sounds like poetry, too. Perennial geranium, hyssop, love-lies-bleeding; the moon is blue, its soft blue night time shadows; night sounds, cat prints, whispering into this office like stringed instruments, cellos, moon shadows. Everyone is sleeping and sometimes I can almost hear the sounds of their breathing through the walls. Katya will have her arm flung over her head, her head turned sideways, facing the damp curling tendrils of her armpit hair. At night her skin releases its scent, like a flower. Katya's flowery vapour fills the room. She likes her smell, too. Her white sleeveless nightgown is covered with small flowers.

I want tea. Katya is not awake to make it for me. I long for her nurturing but I'll have to make it myself. My name is Jim. I am in love. But not with Katya. I have been in love with Katya before and will be again, but just at this moment, it's the dark swamp song of sex I want from her. I don't wake her; I know she went to bed tired.

Plums and tea. I go down the stairs into the dark ticking kitchen, plug in the kettle. I bring my ledgers down with me, to write while I wait for it to boil. It's hot, even at night, in July. In the daytime the bay glisters turquoise. Snake Station. Places here there's still nothing but rattlesnakes and poison ivy.

I write. The ledger is full of blue lines, blue lines that become soft and blurred when wet. I know this because if I leaf back several years, there are places where my tears have fallen and stained the page. Those are the places where I have written letters to Katya in the margins. "Plump beloved, when will you come?" When I'd finished my weeping I blew smoke rings to amuse her. They were only tears, after all. In the morning there was still an order to fill out, to get ready for shipping, although it's been years that I like to work at night. Other places the blue lines are blurred from the sweat splashing down off my forehead, because it was so hot, like today. I think of Katya, upstairs asleep, curtained in flesh and flowery fabric, her long hair tumbled across the pillow. She fascinates me because she is so fat. All that flowered flesh contains secrets, coded in another language. Sometimes, when we are making love, or even when she is just sleeping beside me, her body imparts one of its secrets, almost in spite of itself. Sometimes the flood of orgasm or the pull of a dream softens the edges of her skin so that the secrets slide out like puddles. Out of an arm, a thigh or a knee. And a secret slips into me, my contours softened also from love or dreaming. Because it is only through the skin that these secrets can come. It is nothing you can read in a book, or, say, a seed catalogue. Even if they'd print it, which they probably wouldn't, it couldn't be written. It is an alphabet that only lodges in the flesh.

◆◆◆

The dark lake. It is summer and everything smells. It smells of strawberries and flowers and hay and pollen and sand and rocks and rattlesnakes. I want to be happy. I want a bath. I want the house to be clean, which it never is, unless I do it myself, at two in the morning, before I settle down with my plums and tea, my ledgers and packing slips. After filling my orders I go down to the dark lake and walk around it. Spring fed, it's not much more than a pond really, cut off from the bay proper by a densely wooded hollow. It takes maybe ten minutes to go all the way around. A rocky basin, cut out by a glacier a million years ago. I sit on my rock, looking into the lake. A dragonfly comes and settles on the rim of my coffee mug. I look in and see my face, framed by the mug's rim, decorated by spun gold insect wings. Another face greets me from the lake. The face of a benevolent water monster; I always see her in my mind's eye when I'm here, looking quite inappropriately cartoony and Disneyesque. I feel her presence, always sense she wants to speak to me, but I'm still afraid. I lie on the rock and feel it heat up, feel how the sun warms my back even when I'm face to the heavens on stone. Today I will not swim either, although she calls, and I am almost in love.

◆◆◆

"Plump beloved, when will you come?" Katya reads aloud from my ledger, smiling. Both Katya and my accountant are always entertained by my daydreams, my inability to leave a ledger crisp with numbers, to always muddle it with poetry in the margins, love letters to my wife. He's my therapist, too; he better be, the amount he gets paid. Katya is forty now, tells me she has already been healed of everything that made her small and pithy and outspoken. She reads my notebook, smoking. Now she wears huge flowered tent dresses, reads, tends our children, plays baseball, grows her hair long and extremely curly, and makes weather. She makes the weather for my business, although she doesn't have to do it too often, just once or twice a year. She makes a cloudburst in the summer, when it hasn't rained for three weeks. I could just run the hoses, but I'm a miser for my electricity bill, and besides, I think it's so cool to have a weather-making wife. More importantly than rain in July, she can put off the first killing frost by a day or two so I have time to mulch the delicate perennials or bring them in. She has her store, which I rarely go to; she too: it's only open Thursday and Saturday afternoons, and can only be approached by boat. It's on a river, the same river, Katya says, where she used to eat blue crab with her mother and uncle, childhood birthdays. The river moves through her life, a page at a time. It is always there. To Katya it is not the bay that is important, or the lake, but the river. At the store she plays with the children, and arranges her merchandise. She sells vortices, through which one may enter other worlds at will. No one knows this except Katya and the children and me. I used to think it was a crafts store, full of hand-painted cushion covers, grapevine wreaths, dried flowers, potpourri. Katya's body whispered the truth in a dream: each wreath is a threshold; each person who buys one opens a door to their own possibilities. My wife drives to IGA for steaks and to Stedman's and Bi-Way for an endless stream of things the children need: sunscreen, new sand shovels, ointment for cuts and bruises, hats, sneakers, sandals, UFO shorts, swimming pools, Band-Aids. I stay home and nap on the shield rocks by the lake.

♦♦♦

I sit at the handmade table, writing in the half-light, cherishing the quiet before my family gets up. "Putting food by," I write, quoting the title of a book, thinking of the pears in the orchard behind the house, of how, this year, I really do want to make chutney out of them.

"Space shorts from Bi-Way," I write for my son Sam. They had space shorts in the Bi-Way flyer yesterday, covered with fluorescent planets and space ships and things, three bucks, size two to six-X. My son should have those; size six-X for him. Because I work in these very early morning hours it sometimes seems my whole family is something I dreamed. I'm always sleeping when they are awake. It's as though they are a glossy magazine someone has left on the kitchen table, through which I look longingly at photographs of a plump beautiful wife in flowered dresses, and chubby gleaming children, stubbornly radiant with happiness and health. Yet, by the time they are up I am fast asleep again, exhausted by my nocturnal prognostications, my order filling, my lists, my walks, sometimes accompanied by the cat, to the dark lake. When I get up again, having catnapped, at noon or at one, there is a cheerful note and an absent pickup truck. "Good Idea! Gone to town to get shorts. See you soon. Love, Katya, Sam, Sela." Sam has written his name himself, a child's scrawl.

I'd like to spend more time with them, but it doesn't work. I wake like clockwork at two each morning, like a pregnant woman with insomnia, regardless of sleeping pills, alcohol, valerian. I've tried them all. I've given up, now use the time to work, to walk to the lake at dawn or before. In the afternoon, after I've slept and they are gone, I take the shipments to the post office. I make more lists. I wonder. We meet for dinner.

Creeping thyme, I write. *Phlox subulata*, michaelmas daisies. I pack the plants carefully. Afterwards I throw the I-Ching. It is an old habit, from when I was young. Chen Tui, the marrying maiden.

Thunder over the lake, indeed.

lavender
echinacea (purple coneflower)
comfrey
creeping thyme
bergamot
bee balm

The last two of which are almost the same thing, the first having a greater medicinal value, the second a floral one. My business is in perennial flowers and herbs, plants and seeds. I experiment with the placing of plants, which goes beside which, according to the homeopathic formulas of Rudolph Steiner. Plants and humus, desire and energy. I mutter through the rose beds at four in the morning, pushing aside straw mulch with my feet to see where the new asparagus is coming up. *Mutter*

mutter mutter: the flower and herb beds, all shimmering pale blue and silver in the ghost light. Sometimes they all seem to rise up and speak to me at once. But what do they say? Simple things, most of the time. "Move me," the veronica says. "Where would you like to go?" "Beside the foxglove." And so I do. "Swim with your monster," the dark opal basil says, but I am afraid. I don't think I'm crazy to talk to my plants and hear them talk back, but I am afraid to swim with my monster, afraid the change she might demand would be too real.

◆◆◆

Shambling through the shrubbery, poking our noses into our charges: a little tear here, a sniff, a chew, a pulled weed. Although many of the weeds are left. Being herbs, or flowers. Motherwort, feverfew, cinquefoil, catnip, some of the wild asters and daisies. Compositae. We take out some of the clover and alfalfa, because there is so much of it, and leave some in, because it is a nitrogen binder, and because we like the flowers. The red clover flowers, especially, are said to be a cancer preventative when taken in tea. I pull the ragweed. The pigweed and purslane I weed selectively. The rest I take home to make a salad for dinner.

◆◆◆

Sometimes it seems as though I am always dreaming. And yet, everything seems to get done around me, miraculously. Perhaps I do it myself, sleepwalking. As though that night waking time for me takes place in an alternate temporal stream, one that doesn't belong to my other life, the life I share. My cheerful domesticity, my dinners with neighbours and the friends they bring, hoping to share in our always pleasantly surprising overflow of joy. Time keeps doing funny things around me, as though I have two selves, and they slip in and out of each other, leaving imprints. I sit on the one sandy bank of the lake for hours; I look at fossilized shells; I can't seem to remember ever doing anything else, staring at the fossils of snails, fossiled spirals. Everything in my life is like double exposure photographs.

The pickup truck starts up, and leaves down the driveway.

◆ ◆ ◆

Someday I will go with them, to where they go every day. To Stedman's, to IGA, to Katya's store. But today I take off my socks and shoes—red $12.99 high-tops Katya bought me at Stedman's—my shorts and T-shirt. Today I dive into the cold spring water, come face to face with that other being who lives there, the horned one whose face I've only seen reflected in my coffee mug. She knows I am not in love with my young wife, but with her. Holds that secret for me, tames it. "Rest your heart," she says, speaking soft and clear in my mind, "it will be again."

◆ ◆ ◆

Pictures, words. When I wake at two that morning, I don't go downstairs to endlessly peer into the mirror of my journals, with the excuse of working, but open my cells to my sleeping wife, listen to her with my body's tiny receivers, the ears of the skin, the way Monsty taught me.

Then, from Katya's flesh into mine comes the feeling of eating green ice cream, on a hot dusty day, a million years ago, her feet in plastic thongs and her thighs damp inside her shorts. She sits on a fence, watching men, kicking her legs. Already she feels superior to them. Already she knows she can do what she wants. She chews gum. She kicks her legs. She walks along the railroad tracks, putting down pennies to be flattened by the train as it roars past, so close her hair feels like it is being blown off, so loud her ears hear it for a long time afterwards. Afterwards the pennies are too hot to touch. She goes down the street, to where her uncle has his metal shop in the back of a garage facing an alleyway, and watches in mute fascination as he makes little holes in her collection of flattened coins. She makes earrings and a necklace, and wears them until they get too heavy. She isn't afraid of the drill press. She knows that very soon, maybe next year, maybe even this year, if she is very serious and very good, he will let her use it. She is eleven; in two days she will be twelve.

It is always hot summer when her year turns. It makes her feel special. It is always hot afternoon when everything is still and she walks down the street, her flip-flops going slimy from the sweat, even the wildest dogs lounging in doorways or under cars, their tongues hanging out. She walks to the corner store for more gum, the change jangling in her pocket. Later this afternoon they will go out for dinner, Katya and her mum, who is called Estelle, and her uncle, who is called Randolph, to the place on the river, and Katya will eat crab. There will be a big tank in the window, with crabs swimming around in it. There will be sea vegetables growing from the mire on the bottom; the owner's one concession aside from the tank's relative roominess to the comfort of the crabs.

Randolph gets the creeps from the crabs, but he doesn't say anything. He loves Katya too much, and, as always, admires her feistiness, her bravery. Estelle is wearing a white suit; she looks slim and pure, her brown hair has waves in it. Katya is wearing a clean T-shirt over her shorts and not the green velvet dress which was offered to her by her mother. Her hair is cut in bangs and quite short but not too short, so that it curls under just above her shoulders. Her brown legs under the table are wearing not flip-flops but new white sandals. Randolph: I am not sure whether he, too, is wearing a white linen dinner jacket (where would he get such a thing?) or his overalls over a purple T-shirt, his safety goggles up on his head, where he has forgotten to take them off. He watches Katya with an intense interest. I inject myself into his interest: it is awed, admiring, completely absorbed. Estelle watches, too. She is cool, a little distant; she sips her drink, which tastes faintly of lime Kool-Aid. She is in love with Randolph.

Their window overlooks the river. The window is huge, made of plate glass. You can look straight down and see the river moving; it gives you a funny sensation, as though you are floating, or on a ship, for the restaurant is built on a bridge, exactly on the river. They say it is bad geomancy to live right on the river, and this accounts for the owner's edginess; it is his electromagnetic currents being perpetually out of balance from the amount of time he spends at his business. When you look at him his image slips out of itself, but just as you go to rub your eyes to make sure you aren't seeing things it slips back in.

"Thank God he doesn't sleep here," Estelle says, smoothing her skirt, even though she is sitting down and it's hidden under the tablecloth. I cannot get a clear picture of Estelle; I cannot tell whether or not I like her. I know that Randolph (Katya's father is dead) is essential to Katya's survival, with his pockets full of change, his dogs, and his extremely loud, dirty machines. Estelle plays the other side: her house is cool and clean and crisp; she likes things nice, she plays music in the afternoons. There are always flowers in the window; the sun shines through the vase, and the water, filled with yellow pollen, looks like liquid gold. Katya loves her mother fiercely, but she stays a little bit distant, or, perhaps, merely respects the distance her mother has created with her white curtains, white couch and white rug, and opera music. Because of her mother's sadness. Katya is afraid she knows what her mother is sad about, beyond simple loneliness. Randolph is safer. Randolph is necessary. Randolph offers freedom, dirt, noise, a clear cheerful gruff surface. The uncomplicated superficiality of men: all the messier emotions that turn into complicated neuroses in all the women she knows, absorbed, subsumed, transformed by the noisy, friendly machines the men work with. Men are better. Men are safer. Usually, Katya sides with the men. And yet, if she was to choose one of them, if she had to choose one, Randolph or Estelle, to raise her for the rest of her childhood, she would choose Estelle. With Estelle she sits at the kitchen table at the back of the house, looking out at the garden. Estelle makes her peanut butter and cucumber sandwiches, and lime Kool-Aid. "What did you do today?" asks Estelle. "Was it fun? How is your uncle? He cut me some roses? How nice." Estelle puts the roses in a vase. They are climbers, cut from the bush. Randolph lives in the old house, the Summers' family house, surrounded by old climbing roses. He is Estelle's brother. Katya and Estelle live in a smaller, newer house on the outskirts of town; there is light yellow wallpaper with tiny butterfly prints all over it. Estelle teaches piano. Katya always tries to be out of the house for the piano lessons, in the afternoons.

They are raising her together, by unspoken agreement. In winter she goes to school but work doesn't stop in the summertime and so, all summer long, during her mother's lessons, Katya goes to Randolph's.

◆◆◆

The air in the bedroom glows faintly with illuminated dust; cigarette smoke, pollen, the disintegrated wings of moths, particles of skin. Onto this screen Katya's body projects its secrets, a hologram of emotion. Because of Monsty I am able to insert myself into the feelings of any of the people in the story: into Katya's child-self, into Randolph, even into the happy river that meanders below their feet, day in and day out, page after page.

Estelle is more opaque; the distance she places between herself and the world since her husband died has made her more difficult to read. Or else it's my own temerity. I know beneath her cream linen jacket she harbours pain; the pain of her loss, the pain of being in love with her brother. Katya knew this, even as a child; I can suddenly feel it. Yet she never told me, never shared this, and what other painful secrets? Withholding her trust, feeling she always had to show me only her flowers. She knew I withheld part of my love. I want to give her that part now, the part always held in reserve. It is Monsty who showed me the way. The invisible one, always felt with the wisdom of the body.

Harker and Serena

THE LONG THIN POLES by the water were round, not square. De-limbed and peeled trees, not railroad ties. Gifts from the river, which flooded each spring. Basketballs, pieces of cordwood, plastic planters, actual railroad ties. Serena always figured railroad ties were okay for flower beds, but not for vegetable gardens. Who wanted to eat creosote?

She dragged them home and pushed her found logs into shapes, making raised beds at the foot of the back stairs. A squarish shape. A triangle. She filled them with wheelbarrow loads of topsoil she dug out of the woods. Pushing and pulling one of the logs in hopes of perfecting the corner of her shape, Serena noticed carvings. She tried to decipher the pattern but it made no sense. It wasn't English or Egyptian. It appeared runic, but it wasn't Ogham. Maybe someone upriver had invented it.

After a year went by her teenaged sons Jake and Blake caught two more of the strangely carved poles. Then April was rainy as always and suddenly there were six. Maybe upriver a stack of carved poles someone had left by the bank was shrinking, just as her pile grew. Serena pulled the poles away from the edge of the flood. She began taking Jake and Blake to the river after a big rain or a sunny day had melted more of the remaining snow. She had a hunch the poles might turn out to be worth something.

And after a long winter cooped up inside, spring was mesmerizing. If she were able to walk on water, she would do it in the spring, when water and earth were flush. But of course, they had to be. The water couldn't rise higher than the land, not here, not yet. It could only fill and flatten it, inches of plate glass. One spring the suckers had come up from the lake to spawn, and swum across her lawn, arcing up out of the water, jumping and jumping. There had been so many of them, their arced backs and jumps a series of semi-circles, until she'd had to blink, wondering whether she was looking at a sea serpent. But the strangers who lived beyond the big bend upstream only sent peeled and carved tree trunks, and never animals.

If they sent things at all. Maybe they laughed at the folks downriver so foolish they caught pneumonia standing knee high in the current, trying to reach out and grab the poles that swam past. You couldn't stand in the middle of the river to catch them. The current was too strong; it would pull your legs out from under you. Even Harker couldn't do it easily.

Harker had come from away and told people he was the new head man. People of weak minds believed him for a day or two, until they noticed no one paid much attention. Serena's doctor husband had been the real mayor.

Sometimes Serena had sex with Harker. She missed her husband, who had gone away at first light the morning after she'd noticed the inscriptions on the first pole. He'd taken all their daughters, not yet grown. She never found out where they had gone. He'd never sent word. No one had ever brought her news of him. No wonder, she thought, she'd started sleeping with Harker.

Harker had hair on the backs of his hands and on his big toes, but he also sprouted vegetation. He was bald as a billiard ball, so what grew on his head never came into the equation. No one knew. But when they were in bed together, Serena was able to run her hands though the lichen on his chest. It was a beautiful off-white colour, which was fine with her. Harker grew a few actual leaves too. Just little ones, sprinkled amongst his eyebrow hairs.

"They change colour in the autumn," he told her, when she plucked one out. They were a dark green leaning towards brown, so mostly they stayed hidden beneath the bushy brown hairs. "When they turn red I pluck them so no one will notice."

"If I pluck one in the spring when it's warm and the light is long, it might grow roots. And then, over time, I could grow a new you," Serena said.

"Just hope it never comes to that," Harker said. They lay companionably on her embroidered pillows together.

"What a strange thing to say!"

"Why do you really think the doctor left?" Harker asked, stroking her arm. "You're good looking and you were crazy fertile. Three girls, two boys. Some people wondered if the doctor might have wanted more children and left you for someone younger because of that?"

"That really would be crazy," she said. "But now that he's gone I can't remember my anatomy. What does a kidney do? A liver?"

"They both clean things, I think, but what?" Harker asked. "The blood, the urine..."

"Why does urine need cleaning, if it's leaving the body anyhow?" Serena asked.

"I can't remember either. But I know why the doctor left you."

"Why then, Harker?"

"Because of the poles. Once you had that much magic, you didn't need him anymore."

With the doctor, all Serena's knowledge of medicine had fled. She used to help him clean wounds and set sprains and fractures and sew people up after surgery or knife fights. But, her mind newly blank, she couldn't charge for her nursing, because she couldn't nurse. She grew lots of food for herself and her sons, and worked part-time as a landscaper, but nothing paid like a paycheque. There weren't many to be had since the call centre had closed. Even the feeder high school was only open half days now.

Serena hadn't yet figured out that she could sell the magic poles if only she and her sons were willing to stand in the icy river from late April to early June, grabbing them as they flew past, in water both too cold and strong and deep to stand for long. It was giving her arthritis, she was sure of it. And Jake and Blake regularly came down with bronchitis and pneumonia.

♦♦♦

In the morning she brought him fresh coffee. "Maybe head man doesn't mean reeve or mayor but the man who sleeps with Serena. First the doctor, and now you." Serena smiled to show it was a joke and pulled Harker out the door and to the river. She wanted him working.

He stood on the shore looking out as if he wasn't sure why he was there. Serena pushed him, gently, from behind. He moved into the torrent and grabbed the first passing log. It fought him, like a big fish wanting to escape.

"I like it," he said after he'd wrestled it to shore.

There were hardly any carvings, just what appeared to be a few leaves at one end. The carvings, Serena was starting to understand, didn't create the magic, they only described it. In the upland village, where more things were magic, folks could probably differentiate in ways she couldn't, or couldn't yet. In addition to being carved, the poles were often warm to the touch, and attracted lint and crumbled leaves and other fine debris. They smelled of hot metal, even when they were made of wood, as this heavy, waterlogged log indeed was. She followed Harker out onto the little gravelly beach and slapped his hands away from the pole.

He paused, gazing at her owlishly. "I want to keep it in my room."

She slapped his hands again, harder than before. "It isn't yours." She didn't regret it at all this time.

"But I got it," he said.

"You got it because I told you to. This is my corner of the

river. Everything that comes out of the river here is mine."

Which was a load of rot. *Finders keepers,* or *I was here first,* she knew, were specious school yard arguments. She began to drag the log home.

"I wanted to keep it," Harker mewled, following. "The leaves are like my leaves."

She was glad he didn't know how much the poles were worth, or she'd have to fight him, and she didn't know how to fight, at least not someone so much bigger than she was. Fighting was more dangerous than just being mean, she guessed.

She'd started selling the poles to out-of-towners over the winter. The buyers had appeared out of nowhere, usually late at night. Sombre men in cowls and cloaks, they had offered her staggering sums.

Setting the pole down, Serena massaged her abdomen where a dull chronic pain had turned into a searing one. "What does a kidney do exactly, do you know?" she asked Harker again. The doctor had taken away not just his encyclopedic knowledge, but his encyclopedias. She was fucked, standing in the freezing river day after day. How had her life come to this?

Harker looked at her pleadingly, his leafy eyebrows and big hands still dripping.

"You can keep the next one," she said. "But we have to go back in the river to get it. I hope we didn't miss one, standing here arguing."

She'd seen Harker ring the necks of geese. A full-grown goose can break a man's arm just by flapping her wings, they always said, but Serena wondered whether it was true. Maybe a smaller man than Harker. He gave the geese to poor families. Serena declined them. She wouldn't have, before she began selling the poles.

"You should have the meat tested. The geese might be full of lead from the shot," she said. "Or creosote."

"From eating railroad ties." Harker nodded helpfully.

She thought of how he looked vacant when he snapped the

geese's necks. There was no cruelty in it. It was just something he did.

She studied the pole. Fresh out of the water, it was already covered with a thin crusting of filth. Dead beetles and living. Dirt. Ground glass. Where had it all come from, so quickly?

Maybe the pole attracted crud because it was garbage magic, junk magic, failed magic. Maybe the folks upriver made a heap of their failures beside the icy bank and laughed, slapping their sides, when the spring torrent took the flotsam.

What if she found her way to the village and talked to people? She could ask them how they made the poles. The poles were much more magic than she'd guessed at first. She could sense it more and more as time went by.

Maybe the magic in the poles was what conditioned her to feel it.

She wondered, again, what their purpose was.

And what she might use them for.

Two very different questions.

"Let's go inside," she said, taking Harker's hand. "We can come back out tomorrow. The water's so cold today we'll catch our deaths."

◆◆◆

Serena told Harker and the Akes to keep the poles a secret. The garbage magic was seemingly worth a very great deal on the black market. She figured it for a black market as the buyers came at night, wearing dark clothes. At first she'd wondered whether they were her neighbours from down the street, wearing disguises. But how could her neighbours know what the magic was worth and for when she didn't?

She hid the money. She would use it for her sons' tuition. Or she'd go downriver to search for her daughters, Mildred, Concepción and Agatha, if not their doctor father. Or upland to learn about magic.

They had gone to bed after pole catching, as was their ritual.

It had been warming and companionable but she still hadn't come.

"If I could figure out how to make them work I could cure cancer," she told Harker, running her fingers through his chest moss. "Or I could use them to clean toxic waste dumps."

"You wouldn't bring your girls back?" he asked. "Mildred? Agatha, and…"

"Concepción." It was nice of him, she thought, to have remembered some of her daughters' names. "My daughters will come back if I cure cancer," she said. "I mean, who wouldn't? And you're not supposed to use magic to make people do things they don't want to do."

"How do you know?" Harker asked. "And maybe, secretly, they want to do them."

He touched her hair in that way he had. She loved it but nevertheless moved his fingers back to where they'd do more good.

◆◆◆

It was time to try a few things. She took one of the poles she hadn't sold from behind the couch and dragged it to the middle of the floor. She stared at it, thinking hard. The pole levitated a couple of inches. Not for long. Less than a minute.

"Impressive," her elder son said. Serena started; she hadn't heard him come in. It frightened her; what if one of the neighbours had snuck in? "But what is the point?" Blake asked. "It's like bending spoons. What are you supposed to do with a bent spoon? All the same, try placing a spoon beside the pole, or on it, and send that thought."

"The magic amplifies the power of the thought?" she asked. "Is that how you think the technology works?"

"Your guess is as good as mine," he said, blowing his blonde bangs off his forehead. He went to the dark little kitchen at the end of the house and came back with a handful of spoons. They sat together on the fraying broadloom, examining their sorry excuse for cutlery. "In our house," Blake said, "the challenge is finding a spoon that isn't bent before the experiment even starts."

"Indeed," Serena said, accepting the spoon he offered. It was a nice straight one, sterling even and not plate. "Don't tell Harker," she added, watching the spoon she'd laid on top of the carved log float, eerily, a couple of inches into the air.

"I thought it was supposed to bend," Blake said.

"Is that the thought you sent?" she asked.

"Isn't it what you sent?" Blake asked.

She looked at him.

"Are we going to start arguing about whose thoughts are more powerful?" he asked, laughing. She wanted to hug Blake, and would have, except he was fifteen, an awkward stage. He thought his friends would snicker if they saw, and probably some of them would.

"Jake is ill," Blake said, changing the subject. "We're not sure what it is."

"Bronchitis? Strep?"

"Pneumonia? Maybe all of them." Blake gave his mother a look. It was imploring, like Harker's look the time she hadn't let him keep a pole. It was this pole, in fact, that she hadn't let him keep. It was barely engraved at all, except for the little circles and sprinkles of leaves at one end.

Why hadn't she let Harker keep the pole? It wasn't too late. She could give it back to him. Or she'd sell it for him, if that was what he wanted.

"They're like my leaves," he'd said.

"Can I go see him?" she asked. Jake had always been tiny. She and the doctor hadn't noticed during the years when the children had seemed uncountable on top of unmanageable, and they'd more or less expected Jake to be small because he was the youngest. She shouldn't have ever asked him to go into the cold river, not Jake. And she wouldn't have except he'd been pissing his life away, playing video games. As if theirs being the only working computer in the whole village wasn't evidence enough of the pointlessness of the endeavour. But no, little Jake loved shooting things. She wouldn't have minded so much if he'd shot the occasional real thing, a beaver or wild turkey they could eat as a change from Harker's geese, which she'd stopped declining. Sadly, Jake only shot onscreen things, mostly bad guys, and, when he could, level bosses. He was smart and she'd have sent him to school so he could follow in his errant father's footsteps but there weren't many loans now, and she couldn't afford medical school, even if she remortgaged the house. The sustainable building school was close by and not so pricey. Maybe she'd tucked enough money away selling poles for him to go to that.

"He's staying at Sue's," Blake said. "He's so sick I can't move him."

Serena sighed. "Take the pole," she said. "Lay it beside him when he sleeps. Wish."

"Is that enough?" Blake asked.

"Whose thoughts are more powerful, didn't you ask? Make yours strong. Tell Jake to wish too. He can sleep holding it. It's extremely powerful, the most powerful stick I have ever found."

"There are no carvings," Blake said. "I didn't notice before. Why did you even bring it home? I thought the more carvings there were the more magic there was."

"There are," she said, showing Blake the leaves. "Just different. Harker picked it. It doesn't matter that it's not very carved. Look at the crud on it. The most magic ones are all covered with crud." She brushed the wood lightly. "See, it's hard to get off. And it's not that the sand and leaves are damp, or the pole. It's the magic. It's a magnetic force of some sort, but it can also do things. Like levitate the poles."

She was sure of it now; just spending time with the poles had been a way of learning about them, as if by osmosis. Just having them in her house had changed her. Serena wondered whether she had made a mistake in selling them.

"How much gold would you have gotten for this stick?" Blake asked.

She looked at him. "If I told you, would you sell it now or save your brother?"

Blake said, "It's got to be worth a lot, or you wouldn't have said that. My brother might die anyway. The stick might not save him."

"Sell it after he dies, if you think that." And she gave him the pole.

Would they come tonight or tomorrow night? What would she tell the cowled and hooded men? I have no more magic for you. What if no more poles came, ever? She had to keep the few she had left. Practise and learn.

She wondered what the buyers used them for. Magic imprinted so easily. Down the street, Sue and her parents and Blake would coax Jake to get up for a few moments. They would drink apple cider, one of the big bottles, not one of the small ones, and eat goose they'd bought from Harker.

When Blake had gone to Sue's dragging the leafy pole behind him, Harker came back and led her to the bedroom. The house was empty, her sons out, the way both he and the buyers liked it best.

"I want things," Harker said, removing the butcher's apron stained with goose blood.

"Which things?" Serena asked.

"Many things," he said, and she began them, running her hands through his lichen.

♦♦♦

In the morning Harker was gone, which almost never happened. Serena put on her printed wrapper and went outside, thinking he might be on the porch smoking.

Between the houses and the fields lit by sunrise there was a row of poles, each sharpened to a point, and each sharp point protruding through a head. She retched, recognizing the impaled heads of her next door neighbours, and Harker's head and Blake's. She saw Concepción's, her black hair in a twist around her neck. Perhaps they had found her on the road outside town, the first of the girls to make her way home.

Serena watched a group of men receding on the downland road. One of them turned as if to look at her. His face flickered even though he was nowhere near firelight.

Her youngest came and stood beside her. She took little Jake's hand.

The pole that healed you was sent by the strangers to protect Harker, she thought but didn't say. *He knew it was his, maybe he even made it, but I didn't let him keep it. Now I have you and not him or your sister and brother. What about Agatha and Mildred? Maybe it's not too late to find them?*

Serena recognized the poles she'd sold. Letting go of Jake's hand, she dashed forward and plucked a leaf from Harker's eyebrow. Like the leaves on the surrounding trees, it was starting to turn a russet shade. But that didn't matter. Serena would still take it home and set it in a glass of water. She would put the glass beside his pole, and she would wish.

The Meaning of Yellow

JESSICA LEFT HER JOURNALS on subways, in taxicabs, in laneways bright yellow with the first fallen leaves, soon to be brown and rumpled and smelling of Halloween. It wasn't just drinking with Simeon; she was a forgetful sort. Each time she bought a replacement journal she told herself she'd leave it at home, but she could never bring herself to stick to this plan. She loved writing in cafés too much to ever give it up.

She always imagined the strangers who found her notebooks. Would they take up where she left off, filling the remaining blank pages with their own to do lists, love letters, and scraps of poetry? Would they complete her failed short stories? Would they share her journals with their friends and imagine her as plump and unattractive? Jessica was plump, but her father had told her that to fetishize the very thin was actually a desexualizing of the female form, representing a male fear of womanly fecundity. He could go on. He was a cultural studies professor. Simeon told Jessica how lucky she was. Jessica's father was never going to sigh in a disappointed manner when she showed up for Thanksgiving dinner with dishevelled hair, sans make-up and polished nails. Simeon, Jessica's best friend, was impeccably groomed at all occasions, but this failed to impress his own father, who hadn't yet gotten over (and might not ever get over) the fact that his son was gay.

"Some people are straight," Jessica pointed out, "and some aren't. People should do what they want. Guys who want to wear eyeliner should, although I do think all those chemicals have got to be bad for your skin. And do you know what they do to the bunnies?"

"What bunnies?" Simeon asked.

They were in a student café called The Mermaid, drinking coffee and eating carrot muffins. Jessica had been there since one, Simeon since three. They'd had one refill each. Jessica would've gotten a third, but refills weren't free, and she was out of money. She'd have asked Simeon to pay, but she was always doing that. He got money from home to flesh out his loan. Her own professor father balked at doing this; he thought she needed to learn how to budget. Jessica couldn't budget to save her life. Just now the manager was giving them dirty looks. The place was filling up with the after class crowd, paying customers who'd ordered soy lattés and expensive pastries and were now looking for somewhere to sit.

"The bunnies they perform the experiments on," Jessica told Simeon as they swung out the door. It was cold. She should've worn a coat and not just a sweater.

"Experiments?"

"They wire their eyes open and put mascara on them to see how they react," Jessica said.

"That doesn't sound right," Simeon said. They'd reached the corner where they usually parted ways.

"Oh fuck," Jessica said, patting her alarmingly empty canvas bag.

Simeon started to laugh. He knew what was wrong. Jessica ran back to the café, hair flying. Her clogs made a nice *thunking* sound on the wet October sidewalks. She burst into the door. Her notebook wasn't on their old table, nor was it underneath. The people now seated were all wearing new brand-name jackets. Didn't they have coffee chains for people like that? She asked if they'd seen her book. What she really wanted to do was go through their bags, one by one, as if she were a store owner and they were suspected shoplifters, but they were already looking down their noses at her obvious desperation. She asked at the counter. The pierced and tattooed manager rolled his eyes; it was his rush and he was understaffed. His eyes willed Jessica to disappear.

Back on the sidewalk, she looked around for Simeon. He was gone, home, she supposed. It was raining now, and she hadn't really expected him to wait for her since they were going in different directions.

She set off for her little bachelor around the corner. Almost at her door, her clog kicked something on the sidewalk. She looked down. At her feet there was a hard-cover journal. It was yellow. She picked it up and stashed the book in her shoulder bag. She turned the key in her lock. She walked up the three flights of stairs. Her sweater and jeans were damp and wet. She unlocked the door to her tiny apartment, went inside and sat down on the old yellow couch. She opened the book she'd found and read.

Renee and her friend Neil climbed down the iron fire-escape that led from her kitchen to the roof of the first storey, where she'd planted purple fall asters and canna lilies in halved oak wine barrels. The cannas' foliage lent the roof a tropical feel, and much to everyone's surprise, managed to bloom, displaying huge spikes of glowing red flowers.

It was a perfect description of the back of Jessica's flat.

Was this one of her journals? Maybe she'd forgotten she'd ever even had it, never mind written in it. Maybe she'd been experimenting with autobiographical fiction, and her first step had been to change her own and Simeon's names.

Except the handwriting wasn't hers, so that couldn't be it.

She turned the page and read on.

She and Neil climbed down the second set of iron stairs and cut through the yard of the butcher shop, even in winter stinky from heaps of discarded beef bones, through the alleyway, and back out onto the main street where they'd seen it earlier in the afternoon. It was an enormous brocade couch with a real wood frame and not a pasteboard one, and was henceforth, extremely heavy.

Now she was sitting on it. Stained yellow; round wooden feet, brocade flowers, a missing centre cushion.

Jessica went to the kitchen and put water on for tea. She changed out of her wet clothes while the tea was steeping, sat back down on the couch, and turned to the next page. It was empty. Impulsively she picked up a pen and wrote:

Renee was in shape from swimming twice a week so she and Neil were able to carry the couch down the street, around the corner into the alleyway, through the butcher's yard that always inspired her, for fifteen minutes at a time, to become a full time vegetarian again, instead of a lapsed little-bit-of-chicken, little-bit-of-fish one. They set it down to pant heavily, exuding vast puffs of vapoury breath, dragon like, staring at their frozen whale, the return journey up the fire escape: the hard part. It didn't help that they'd gone to the campus pub earlier and were drunk, or maybe, on the contrary, that was what made them think they could pull it off.

Jessica remembered she'd gotten the top end, being so much smaller than Simeon. She'd asked him to abandon the project because the slats of the fire escape were icy now and slick with sleet. She was afraid she'd lose her grip on the couch and kill Simeon. She told him so but he thought it made more sense to keep going than to take the couch back down. Jessica had hoped they could just leave it on the fire escape, a canted yellow whale.

She put down her pen and turned the page.

The unknown writer continued the story:

Renee learned to hate the couch—she always meant to find a replacement for the missing centre cushion that, if it wouldn't match, would at least fit. She never did. The couch sat there for a year and eventually she called Neil and they lifted it once again and carried it back down the fire escape from whence it had come. They left it on the second storey roof; a place to sit and contemplate unlikely cannas. The young women downstairs appreciated it more than she did. They always drank cold Steam Whistles on its leaf-shadowed squishiness in the afternoon when they got home from their landscaping jobs. Leaf shadows joining with brocade fabric ones, mutating.

Years later, when Renee was happily married, she found a yellow couch at a yard sale that reminded her of the first one. It was as if the couch had followed her. Why? What did it mean? Should she buy it? She pulled out her cell to call Neil and ask him.

Jessica shut the book. She was apparently reading her own future.

It was a good future. She still lived in the apartment; she had nice new downstairs neighbours. She still had the couch. She still had Simeon. And later on, she found a nice guy, and got to keep Simeon too.

There was a tiny part of her, she realized, that had always doubted there would be a later on, for her. She felt reprieved by this story, by whoever had written it.

Jessica remembered her and Simeon's Ouija board phase. Ouija boards were usually a girl thing, but Simeon was Simeon.

Will I find love?

O-H Y-E-S.

Who will it be?

M-O-R-G-A-N.

Jessica spent all of grade eight looking for Morgan but he never appeared.

This was like that, only much worse. Or better, depending on how you looked at it. Except that Jessica wasn't thirteen anymore. She couldn't get excited. It was just nuts. There had to be a rational explanation, and suddenly its obviousness dawned on her. She picked up the cordless and called Simeon. "I found your book," she announced.

"That's great," he said. "I thought I'd have to get a new one! Bring it to class tomorrow."

"Okay," Jessica said. "It was right on the street outside my door. You must have dropped it last time. We drank two bottles of wine, remember?"

"I'm so relieved. They're eighty dollars," Simeon said, "and there aren't any at the used bookstore."

"What are you talking about?" Jessica asked.

"My biology textbook."

"No, this is a yellow hard-cover journal with lined pages. You're writing a short story in it. It's about you and me, and that day last winter we brought home my couch, only you've changed our names to Renee and Neil."

"Not so," Simeon said.

"You're lying to mess with my head," Jessica said.

"That would be someone else," Simeon said.

"But who? No one saw us that day. The description of the roof, the cannas, the fire escape. It's all there, exactly as it happened."

It was Simeon's turn to say it. "You're lying to mess with my head."

"But I'm not. And it even describes our future."

"Oh?" Simeon didn't do too good a job of sounding credulous.

"We're still best friends in a year, and even after I get married. See you tomorrow."

Jessica hung up. She picked up the yellow book, opened it to the page ahead of the last entry. It was empty. Should she write something more? She leafed through the remaining pages one by one. Every single one was empty.

If she wrote something else about Renee and the yellow couch, would another entry appear, one page ahead?

Jessica knew how to find out, but she was too afraid to try. Instead, she slipped the yellow book into her canvas bag. She'd show it to Simeon. He'd admit it was his after all. That had to be it. The part about her writing the missing part of the story was just a coincidence. Pleased with her analysis, Jessica went to sleep.

The next day Jessica went to the café after class to meet Simeon. Her cheque from her little job at the library had finally cleared, and it was her turn to treat. She stood in line at the crowded counter while the manager stuffed two carrot muffins into a paper bag. Someone tapped her shoulder. She thought it was inadvertent; the café was so crowded. The tap came again. She turned around. A young man in a wool scarf and a duffle coat stood there holding out her journal, the black one she'd lost the day before. Everyone had those notebooks. Except that she'd taped a postcard of a Christiane Pflug painting to the cover, "Cottingham School with Yellow Flag." What was it about yellow, anyhow?

She took it. "Thanks," she said. She felt exposed, wondering if he'd read it. She wrote in journals to vent, not to be brilliant. She felt suddenly angry at all the imaginary people who'd found her many lost notebooks and snickered at her.

"Do I know you?" Jessica asked. "How did you know it was mine?"

Maybe he stared at her in some class. Maybe he'd surreptitiously stolen her book so he'd have an excuse to introduce himself.

He smiled. "I'm Morgan," he said, and turned away before it even sank in.

"Wait!" she called when it did.

He was already at the door. He heard her, though. He turned around and said, "I don't think you'll lose your notebooks anymore, Renee."

She pushed through the crowd to follow him. On St. Andrews she turned both ways. He was gone. She felt like someone was performing experiments on her. How would she react?

"Jessica!" someone said behind her, and she started, afraid to turn and look, see the young man again. Except whoever it was had called her Jessica, not Renee. And she knew Simeon's voice, she always had. She was just so disoriented she'd momentarily forgotten. Just as she'd forgotten—or pretended to have forgotten—that the handwriting in the yellow book wasn't like Simeon's, not even remotely.

She reached into her bag to get out the yellow journal and show it to Simeon. But her bag felt, once again, alarmingly empty. Jessica felt as if she'd been captured, and taken on a long ride through inexplicable weirdness—unmoored in space and time, coerced to explore a maze of many new dimensions.

"Oh fuck," she said, and laughed.

"Fuck what?" Simeon asked. "You haven't lost your journal again; you haven't had time to buy a new one since I saw you yesterday." He noticed she was holding it then, the postcard of the Pflug painting still taped to its cover. "Oh," he said. "You found it."

"That's right," Jessica said, still laughing. "It's Morgan's notebook I've lost this time, I'll bet you anything."

For just a moment she thought she saw the yellow flag ripple in the breeze, and then it stopped. "My turn to buy," she said, and they headed back into the Mermaid Café.

"I remember about Morgan," Simeon said, as she'd hoped he would. "So you finally met him?"

"Yes, I did. He's not what I thought, though."

"Is he your true love?" Simeon asked.

"Possibly," Jessica said. "All the same, can you help me throw the yellow couch off the roof this afternoon?"

"Whatever for?" Simeon asked.

"I want to watch it fall," Jessica said.

Trading Polaris

I'D ALWAYS LIVED ALONE until you came, Alia. We hadn't just been lovers, companions; you led me beyond time. With you I was able to watch its comings and goings from the tops of invisible ladders, of trees, its messengers little ghostly animals we'd given birth to while dreaming there, while making love. We spent three summer months together, in my white clapboard house facing the sea. Before you came it was just an empty ballroom where I danced with sea winds.

September came; you had to be home. You lived an eight-day walk above our seaside valley. You asked me to take you part way. On the fourth evening we camped by a rocky waterfall; in the morning our campsite was enveloped in a golden mist. You were gone, our fire dead. I was afraid I'd never see you again, for you'd disappeared into that yellow fog as though into a cloud that might carry you away, to rain you down in a place where you might find smarter lovers.

I left the fire pit and began to walk in the direction I believed your village lay. The flat land swelled into shallow wooded hills, reminiscent of a woman's body, but it wasn't yours. It was Sonia's, but I didn't know that then.

◆◆◆

When I made camp that night I tried to climb the spirit ladder as you'd taught me, up to the starry place we'd gone together. At the top of that ladder it's possible to see into the past and future, to retrieve from the sky what is necessary to the life of Earth dwellers—the trick is to keep your brains intact on your way back down—such as they are. I'd so willingly shucked the husk of self to fly—a husk that seemed, while visioning, irrelevant, but a necessary cloak, you reminded me, for navigating this world, its people. On the way down, my first time with you, I was still so borderless I could understand the speech of trees, the secrets of rivers. I consumed this wealth of new knowledge gluttonously, never thought how there's no use in wisdom if it can't be shared. I understood so many new languages but could no longer speak. Is that why you left me? You said you'd go, part way, but I'd always thought we'd say goodbye first. It was when we descended together I learned how much stronger you were than me, how much more treasure you could carry down the ladder and still remain intact. Did you vanish because I proved too weak to carry knowledge?

Alone, I tried to climb again, the way you'd shown me. Hoped that, could I climb high enough, I'd be able to signal you, call you to return, but four of the ladder's incorporeal steps were missing. I thought perhaps I'd broken them our last time. Who had we left up there, unable to descend? What nameless beasts had we spawned—dream pigs or fishes running amok in a world I couldn't see? The part I could see it with was still up there, perched on a broken rung. I would have to find my own way to knowledge now; the path you'd given me was barred. I'd have to go into the woods alone.

At the forest's edge I camped beneath an enormous rock, standing sentinel, a single child in a short-grassed open place, interspersed with flowering bushes, grazed by goats. I thought of our town park, its monuments and manicured lawns, its planted shrubbery, but this was landscaping by four-footeds. They had planted even the bushes, shitting out guava seeds in the fall. It was places like this, I thought, tamed by wildness, that we'd modelled our first parks after.

I looked at the stars before I fell asleep. For a brief moment it seemed they were falling from the sky, like pieces of quartz singing into my brain. My grandfather spoke to me that night. Long dead, he spoke from the past, but the stars, who had heard him, gave his words to me repackaged in the present, for to stellar beings, who live so long, not a moment had passed between his time and mine.

◆◆◆

My grandfather wakes from sleep and shakes off his dream of being an unborn me. He stands up, sees the blinking distant lamps of ships at sea disguised as fireflies. He wakes to a cold wind and maybe bears in the not so far off woods that might come out to eat him. My grandfather feels safer in the open places, imitating his mind that, like mine likes to travel unencumbered, far searching. He turns and looks at the stone, and at its mouth, into which all the time has gone. All the time in the mouth of the stone. The stone in the shape of a head. It speaks so slowly that to hear it say one sentence would take a lifetime. "Ah," says my grandfather, "It is you I've been listening to all my life; you have eaten up all my time."

My grandfather goes back to our town to find that everyone he knows has died. He waits for his own death, but it does not come. In the café he drinks lemonade and casts shadows in the late afternoon sunlight. His old body, still casting shadows. So many things we can't do in old age but there is a skill that follows us past the grave.

◆◆◆

So he hadn't died camping alone as we'd always thought, even when too old for it. He had returned, but first passed through a stone's mouth, and so came back too late, after even I had passed away. How lonely for him, and, it suddenly felt, for me. The one person in my family who knew what it was to learn alien languages, who sought that knowledge as eagerly and foolishly as me, caught now forever on time's opposite side.

Of course all his words didn't follow me out of my dream, but I woke with that searing insight nonetheless, a comet trail if not the comet itself. I looked at myself to see whether I'd turned into my grandfather as I slept. It seemed possible. I'd come closer to him than I ever had when he'd lived.

It was only then, because I'd seen it in my dream, that I noticed how the stone resembled a rough human head, whether by chance or by human carving it was hard to say. I imagined my grandfather chipping away at the rock as though it was only its lack of human shape that prevented it from being more loquacious. I scratched under the grass until I found the remains of an old fire pit. Among them, a knife blade of his I remembered from childhood, its carved wooden handle rotted away. I broke it, angry he'd disappeared twenty years before, couldn't share what he'd learned on his own strange journey except in dream fragments. Yet I felt my journey really did cross his, if only in a timeless time.

♦♦♦

I was grateful for the woods. There at last I found streams to wash in. There I dwelt on memories of my days spent with you, Alia. Oh Stone, give me back our time.

But the stone I'd left behind hadn't said a thing to me. Like you, the stone thought I didn't quite rate. I thought of going back and smashing it, but I had no sledgehammer with me, no words strong enough to break a stone already so old. And wasn't that what grandfather tried, chipping away at it? As though to give it a human face would make its speech quicker, easier to understand? Perhaps that's when it swallowed him, for having the audacity to try. Oh, Stone, tell me where Alia went.

♦♦♦

A half day's walk past the first forest stream I saw the house. Small, dark, barely windowed, its roof like tree bark for bears to scratch on. A house so odd I didn't know it for what it was till I saw the door and chimney just like in my own white house. The breezes tangoed there partnerless now, had been dancing without me for how long? I longed to be home. This strange little doorway made me miss my own with a sharper pain than I'd yet known. I was afraid of the house and the others that followed in its wake. I slunk through their gardens at night, sleeping under their hedges when the sunlight fought its way through all those leaves.

I'd come all this way hoping to find your village, Alia, but I'd been lost so long human habitation frightened me. I followed hoof prints to streams, afraid of what I'd find on human footpaths. I wandered by moonlight through this up and down country, hoping to find the larger down that might lead me to the coast and home, thinking to forget you after all, or to wait for your possible return. Who could live here, in such peculiar houses? I never thought my own people would be as strange to me, that I'd grown too accustomed to visions, to mouthy stones.

♦♦♦

I made camp one night above a small waterfall, spilling into a pool on either side of which gardens lay. It was chilly and I wanted a fire but was afraid of discovery.

A story came to me then, of a hero returning from his visit with gods. At night he reaches the edge of a town, but decides to wait till morning before making his entrance. It's a cold night, and he freezes in his little camp, too scared of the fire he's stolen to use it. There was no proud homecoming for him like in those other stories, the ones they made up. His people were skittish of foreigners, and so, when the hero arrived in the morning, and breakfasted with the table manners of gods, they ran him right back out of town. Or so I thought before I fell asleep.

That night brought a different dream: I was being slowly eaten by a little she bear. The bear took a bite from my ribs, chewed methodically, took another from my neck. When the bear started eating faster I woke up, afraid of finding myself only half there if I put it off any longer. I woke to the half light of dawn, an absence of bears, the sharp point of a stick descending. When they'd beaten me long enough I lost consciousness.

Just once I woke to see their faces, glowing moons exalted by greed. I forgot to fear for my life, screaming questions, wanting only to know what they were after. Someone else came then, and by the sudden respite in their violence, I knew it was one the others feared. A woman bent over me and I could see her face, luminous like a moon, her skin pale like yours. She sent the others away; already I was calling her by your name. "They'll never tell you why they hate you," she said harshly, and took me to her home, dragging my bleeding body over stones.

She gave me herb tea to make me go back to sleep. In my brief moments of wakefulness she fed me; days of fish broth were followed at last by dried salmon. I chewed on its saltiness as though I was chewing on life. I was: I'd been starving myself as mourners do, my half rotten mind forgetting to eat except for stones.

She moved me outside to the porch and I sat there for days, not moving except to make myself horizontal for sleep on the swing. When the sun shafted through the trees in the afternoons I'd examine my hair for stray greys, pulling them out methodically one by one.

Even after my body healed I was still hearing the trees talk; the mangoes and banyans, respectively proud and full of vanity. She would come home from fishing and I'd babble at her, talking about our summer by the sea. You see, Alia, for the first weeks I mistook her for you, even though she corrected me often enough, telling me her name was Sonia.

Now I think she was your shadow, your reflection. Perhaps if I'd constellated with my own twin I wouldn't have drowned so easily in hers. Discouraged by my name calling, she locked me up in the pig barn, as though the sight of me disturbed her. I scratched at the walls, worried she'd change her mind, return with the villagers, with sharpened sticks.

She let me out a few days later to take me fishing, cheerful and chatty as though nothing unusual had happened. She said she knew secret ponds, hers alone, and blithely added that if anyone were to follow us I'd have to kill them. She armed me with an old fish knife, dull and rusty with neglect. Of course, it reminded me of grandfather's. On the path to her pool she showed me where she'd marked the grave of an intruder. I didn't ask her if it was real; it did my job for me, keeping them away. I knew well enough her people feared her, and not only because she caught more fish than anyone else in her village. It was one of the reasons she lived apart, to protect the locations of her pools.

I felt sometimes as though she kept me as an object for her profanities, her cruelty, yet while she was often unkind, it was still true she'd saved my life. She thought her people suspicious idiots, but kept me in the pig pens just in case. Or was I more amusing there? Poor woman. Her daughter, ashamed of her, had gone to live with relatives in the village proper. "With a mother like you," she'd said, "I'll never get married. " True enough. A mother like Sonia might eat the bridegroom for breakfast on the big day. There were other days I thought she'd saved me just to upset the villagers.

◆◆◆

Willows swept the shores; the musty smell of dead leaves seeped into our clothing. It was a nice change from the pig shed. Sonia's little boat slept on the pool, its stern sinking slowly with the sun as it grew heavier with the day's catch. She'd tell me stories those afternoons, about magic salmon, capable of returning the eater to his own true, lost path. We never caught any, and once I asked her why. You could only find them, she said, in pools more secret, more enchanted still than this one. She did go fishing alone sometimes, but never showed me what she'd caught. Sometimes I was even brave enough to laugh at her. Still, I believe it was true, that she really did; her mistake was to guard her catch too jealously, as though it might protect her from harm. I thought if she'd shared what she knew with her people they'd have been kinder, less hateful of outsiders. She was the only one who'd ever travelled.

But when we fished together a yellow dream fell over us and Sonia would smile. For those hours on the pond I could let my old heart out for a swim and pretend she was my lover as you had been. I wanted her, too, but she seemed so old. In truth she wasn't much older than me, but there was something in her eyes you couldn't go near without hurting yourself. My dreams fell into those eyes, and I was imprisoned again, by a woman who knew too much. It never occurred to me how those eyes must cut the other way, must hurt her also.

She traded fish for silver. She beat the silver into the shapes of little pigs, wearing them on a string around her neck. Fish into pigs, an act of transformation: silver between. Sometimes she'd count them. When there were enough she bought a piglet. I spent a lot of time with the little sow, trying to learn her language, as I'd lost hope for people. I called her Polaris, after the star that is at once the source and absence of all motion, the end of a little bear's tail and the apex of the centre pole around which our sky slowly spins. A big name for a pig, who was after all a pig and not a bear. As I got better I hoped to have someone friendlier than Sonia to talk to in Polaris, but she never spoke to me. I thought it was her revenge for having been given the wrong name, but I knew of no pig stars to name her after. Still, I never stopped believing she was our lost dream child, Alia, that she'd found her way down the broken ladder at last to be with me.

We bred Polaris and when my second spring came she had six babies. I was as proud of them as she herself. Sonia moved me into the house right after that. Maybe she was jealous, or just afraid I'd turn into a pig. I moved up from the pig pens without ever having learned their language.

Sonia taught me how to be a human being again. She made me eat with a knife and fork, seated across the table from her. I'd eaten out of slop buckets so long I accidentally poked the fork into my cheek until it bled. "See what you've made me!" I yelled, but she just laughed, told me to do the dishes. I cleaned the house, wondering how many pigs she'd had before me, but when I was finished she opened a bottle of banana wine. After we'd drunk it she made me come to bed with her. It seemed I was still a human being in at least one respect, but I wasn't quite sure I'd passed the test, as it never happened again.

I tried to run away one night but Polaris woke up and made such a noise before I'd cleared the garden. Sonia tied me to the bed that night and for a week after. I counted pigs to fall asleep.

After two years she told me I could go.

"Where?" I asked, really not knowing.

She laughed and said, "It's not the ladder that broke your mind, but the villagers' beatings. Still, you'll survive, even heal. In three weeks you'll go home."

"The ladder?" I asked. "I never told you about the ladder. You've been up there too?"

"Of course. Once you've been up it shows, others can see it."

She asked me to tell her my story. Night after night we drank guava wine and talked. I told her about life in our village, a coastal fishing village as hers was a mountain one; my months with you; the secrets you'd taught me; the yellow mist that enshrouded our camp the last night we spent together, and into which you vanished.

"Be careful of ignorant villagers," she said. "They ruined your memory, but I'll give it back." She blew into my mouth and I said, "I remember the wind too, that peculiar wind on the plateau that sucks the spirit out and then blows it back in. I remember my grandfather. When I go home, will everyone I know have died too?"

"You mean like this?" she asked, and sucked in her cheeks, her eyes suddenly black and shiny, irisless.

"Stop," I yelled, before she could inhale the whole room, myself included. She laughed and blew me out again. I ran to my room to pack, bolting the door. She knocked, but I wouldn't let her in.

◆◆◆

Sonia bought me a horse to make the trip. "Can you talk horse too?" she asked, making fun of me.

"Horse? I didn't think horses could talk." Yet it was true, in spite of my failure with Polaris, after trees and stones and stars anything still seemed possible.

"Don't say that around him or he'll be insulted." She whispered something in the horse's ear in a low guttural voice and the horse turned and looked at me, his eyes too that shiny dangerous black, like haematite, like obsidian.

"Sonia, please." I turned away, hiding my face.

"Animals aren't slaves," Sonia said. "They're working for us for a while. They can quit anytime they want. We have to pay them for their work, like we pay anyone."

"You don't seem to have the same respect for people," I grumbled, but Sonia rolled her black eyes at me, said, "You pay animals by listening. Pay attention to what they say."

"I wanted it over, all this listening. I'm frightened of madness."

"You'll hear the voices all your life; they'll never be gone. Don't throw away gifts; very few can hear animals, plants, stones."

"It's not insanity?"

"Can be," she said, weighing me with her eyes. "Doesn't have to be. A choice." Her eyes weighed and weighed. "There's something I've been meaning to show you." She gave me a hand mirror she'd made herself, framed in silver. "Look at your eyes, and tell me if you still fear me, your horse."

I took the mirror and looked, already knowing what I would

see. Black. Shiny. Irisless. That was the moment I knew I'd forever be among those who know too much.

◆◆◆

I took the horse and bags full of goods for trading. For my two years of indentured semi-slavery Sonia gave me a present she'd made in secret: a set of silver cutlery with stars on the handles for my house in town. She was as good a silversmith as a fisher woman. Stars, in memory of Polaris.

Sonia told me my horse was called Slipstream. "What's it mean?" I asked.

"A little joke about time. Remember what happened to your grandfather? Be nice to Slipstream or he will, and then where will you be?"

"Rather, when?"

"Good question. Be nice to him if you want your friends still alive when you get home," she laughed. "It's not only your grandfather's stone who knows how to play cat's cradle with time."

With this warning, bursting saddlebags, and food for the trip I was ready. Sonia said she'd take me part way down the valley and as we passed through the village proper people came out to watch us. They bowed and called me Mr. Salmon Woman, but I saw them snicker behind their cloaks. I'd earned a new name for my stay but not much more in the way of their respect. At least they didn't drool at me, their eyes brimming with violence any more, wanting to take me home and beat the magic out of me. Perhaps they thought they'd made a mistake about me. I'd never spoken to one of them.

Strange how the leaves fell in that village, red and yellow, piles of them. It was nearing the end of the dry season; we'd planned our trip to avoid the coming rains. The old men came out, wearing hoods against the damp, to rake the leaves into piles where they were burned. In the market we bought a donkey to carry some of Slipstream's load. Sonia had asked me to return, after the rains were over, with goods from my seaside village, said she'd pay me in silver, in secrets. The coastal villages had never traded with the mountain people before. Sonia said it was time to begin, and I thought perhaps she'd learned something from me after all.

Children ran under our feet, through the little yards that faced the square. Under those red trees Sonia and I were married. I have never felt sadder than at that moment. "Alia was your heart," Sonia said by way of marriage vows, "but I am your mind."

Before we left the village we saw a little girl, drawing designs with chalk in the cracking pavement near the bonfire. She seemed different than all the others, playing with an ardent freedom I'd sensed in no one else. She didn't seem tight and narrow, closed against strangeness, against hope. Like Sonia, she too brimmed with secret knowledge but it was innocent; she hadn't been hurt by it and their was no concomitant cruelty in it yet. I left Sonia's side to go and speak with her, but without warning, one of the hooded old men seized her and threw her into the bonfire. I ran forward to pull the child from the flames but it was already too late. She'd burnt quickly, and silently, making no cries, not struggling, and not smelling of burnt flesh either. I cried but hid my tears in the hood that I too now wore. The men stared, and began to encircle us, their brooms and rakes, cluttered with red and yellow leaves, raised menacingly. Sonia drew me towards her, throwing half her cloak around my shoulders to show I had her protection. It wasn't enough, however, and it was only when my wife made that trick with her eyes and threatened to breathe them all in, only to exhale them forever changed, that they let us pass, whispering and rustling like leaves as we left them behind. I half imagined they said they wanted to come with us after all, see the outside. We walked very slowly out of the square, and onto the one road that led out, to safety. Bears, wild pigs, what could frighten me now?

We began the slow trek down the mountain to a town I no longer believed existed. The pig pens had burned away the memory of my white house, of that sea wind blowing through. So much for my wife being the restorer of memory, but perhaps it was only certain forgotten moments she could bring back, and not the forgettings she'd occasioned herself. We are all fallible.

We camped together above a waterfall that night, just as you and I had, listening while Slipstream and the donkey ate. Sonia had brought along the remaining bottle of last year's fruit wine, a sweet mango. We finished it after our fish, as our little fire burned down.

"We have to make sure it's out before we sleep," she said. "Too dry this time of year, before the rains come."

"Sonia, who was the child?"

"Spirit child, witch child. They hate them almost as much as they hate outsiders."

"But she was so good. I could feel it in her, good in a way they know nothing about."

"Good in a way they're afraid of, because it threatens everything they believe in, their whole way of life."

"She was like you, a bit. Only not so hard."

"Hard is what life among them has done to me. I never wanted to be this way." Sonia reached out and laid her hand on my knee, and as always, I didn't know whether to recoil or embrace her. She had that effect on me. "I'm the only witch they've ever allowed to grow to adulthood."

"Why?"

"They thought they needed one witch to protect them from the eyes of outsiders."

"You were a spirit child then too, like that one? What are they, spirit children? She didn't smell like burning flesh."

"We only harden as we age. If I was to burn now I'm afraid I'd smell just like bacon," she said ironically. Then added, "If I answer all your questions now you'll never come back next year, and I need you to. It's the only way to stop the burnings."

"We don't have witches," I said.

"I know, but you are one now, and you're returning. I'm sorry, husband. I hadn't intended for you to see a thing like that; it's why I kept you hidden."

◆◆◆

When I woke in the morning Sonia was gone, as she'd said she'd go. I went home down the hills without my wife, wondering what lay ahead of me, and whether, by having married her, I'd given up my right to you forever. But my night's dream came to me as I walked the leafy trail, saw at last the sea, the town. A seemingly prophetic dream that filled me with exhilaration and dread. You'd be back, Alia, and I'd marry you as I'd hoped, keeping my other marriage secret. I'd never go back to the mountains to my first bride, never begin the trading that she and I had hoped for so fervently. But you and I would have a child, and it would be a spirit child, the first one ever born by the sea. Sonia's legacy after all, having changed me so irrevocably. Which would be better? To give you up, Alia, my one true love, or to father a child that might be destroyed by a fear, by a hate that had never existed in our town before, that its birth might elicit? Sonia had awakened me to my own witchery, both terrifying and promising. The full saddlebags had been a cover. It was my new fearsome eyes, the child I'd father, that were my real trading goods. But what would I have to bring back to her mountain village to end the cycle, allow people to see the gift and not just the difference, the gentleness as well as the fearsome power?

I prayed to my grandfather, but he didn't hear. He too had tried to open a trade route between the mountains and the sea, had been catapulted for his arrogance into the future time when such things might be possible, destined to end his years in the loneliness of those who can travel forwards, but not back to their home time.

And you, Alia?

You live in the middle, in a secret forest village in the foot-hills. You retain a measure of Sonia's wisdom, and teach it where you can, as you taught me. Still, your eyes are human. You haven't lost the innocence of the sea people, and are thus protected from the fear and ignorance of those who need the protection of witches but fear and hate their power. You wait, wondering whether I'll ever find the path home to you.

Bus Owls

THERE WAS ONE YEAR that southern Ontario was subjected to an influx of Great Grey Owls. They came from the north and for a few months or a year adorned all our fences and posts, watching us, seeing what we would do. Some people watched, photographing and writing about this massive silent invasion, but in the main, it was we who were being watched for once and not the other way around.

Or so Stella thought on her way home from Toronto, taking the Greyhound. In Oshawa the bus always stopped to let people off or on. Stella liked it when her schedule coincided with the express bus, which stopped only at Scarborough Town Centre. But if not, there she was in the 'Shwa again, adding half an hour to her trip home. On the good side, in 'Shwa she could get off the bus and have a breath of fresh air and a smoke. Stella still smoked in those days, the ones she is remembering, the ones she is describing here. It was before everything changed. Now, post change, it is no longer possible to smoke cigarettes, no matter how much she misses them.

Sometimes missing them is akin to heartbreak. Sometimes missing them is like losing her best friend in all the world. Sometimes missing them is like having to grow up forever and never look back. Not even once, for a single backward look would inevitably coincide with the first cigarette. It is like she swore. It is like she made a vow, she isn't sure to whom. It is like she made this vow when she wasn't looking, for had she been looking, she would never have made it. The sacrifice, the murder even of her smoking self is so large, so violent. It is like she made the decision to quit in her sleep.

She remembers how she told herself the new story, this ground-breaking story about art and tears and luck and being young again, and saying goodbye and never looking back, not even once, for you know what happened to Lot's wife. Because of her decision, the stars perform new constellations. Because of her follow through, a new season approaches. Because of her forthrightness, her dog begins to talk. Because she cared, the children all get new ice skates for Christmas, and actually turn off their computers long enough to put them on and go outside to the pond on the point to skate beneath these strange new stars that appear, even, to dance a little above their heads.

In a way she has had to leave two lovers. She and her man were co-dependent, but in a nice way. In the evening they would sit together, discussing books and movies, watching movies and reading, sipping beer and wine and tea and smoking really a lot of cigarettes. She cannot do this anymore. She stares at him now across naked hallways. I do not love you any less. If anything I love you more. Love us more. Love the world more.

Now her evenings are spent blogging on all the world's activist sites. She can't help it. She has so much to say. She always did have so much to say, but she used to say it to him, while she smoked a cigarette. Now she can't do that anymore, so she says it to the world. The typing keeps her hands busy, hands which she would otherwise use for smoking. Typing hands cannot smoke, it is true. She has expanded her audience, now that she no longer smokes. She talks to the world, and not just to him.

She can no longer write anything of any length. A beginning, middle, and end, stretched across ten entire double-spaced pages seem a minor impossibility. The thought of revising her new novel yet again elicits unexpectedly suicidal thoughts. She runs away. Whatever made her think finishing the novel was important? It is true the novel is her life's work, a book she spent thirty years of her life drafting various versions of, a book that really would only require a few relatively short and easy months to fine tune, but no, she balks. She is like a horse throwing its rider. Absolutely fucking not, no way, not ever.

She feels no regret. Yet the pragmatic part of her thinks: thirty years, the thing is good; it seems a pity to waste it. Perhaps she could apply for a grant to hire a nice young assistant to implement the necessary nips and tucks. A young assistant who never smoked, and to whom menopause is so far in the future that she has no issues with her attention span at all. Someone who can sit and write for hours each and every day with no thought of commensurate financial reward beyond a few skimpy arts council grants, if any, and some thought of possible publication. In her spare time the assistant could do the shopping and laundry and vacuuming and make dinner to boot.

The assistant sounds like someone, in fact, quite a bit like Stella herself used to be. Maybe she has been insane all these years only she doesn't know it. Let someone else do the work while she blogs about literacy, uranium, Indigenous land claims, nutrition and brain function, agribusiness, genetic engineering, wind farms, etcetera. The list is endless. She knows a little about everything, just the right length for a blog post, or a comment on someone else's blog. She has opinions about very serious things and also about the Oshawa bus and plastic owls.

You know those plastic owls? You can order them from the catalogues of nurseries that sell objects as well as plants. The big plastic owls are taken home and affixed to garden posts. They are supposed to keep critters away, the sorts of critters that might come at night and snack on all one's nice fresh lettuces.

Before the Change, the only good part of the milk run was you could get off in 'Shwa and smoke. It is just as well she quit, because the new driver, a short blonde woman, told her she doesn't let any Peterborough passengers off the bus in Oshawa anymore, not to smoke or make phone calls or go to the bathroom or anything else. "I used to," she said, "but then I had to go chasing after them when they didn't come back in time."

Stella thought about it later. At the time she was busy resenting the woman for not letting her off to smoke. But later she thought why didn't the driver just leave these rude people behind? The reason, of course, was that they'd complain and she might lose her job if enough people complained.

Sometimes there was a new driver for the second half. Sometimes even a new bus. Once she stood there in an empty station, she remembers, with a driver. They both smoked. There was a post beneath the overhang, the part of the structure that sheltered waiting passengers in case of inclement weather. She is not sure what the post was for, normally. The driver silently pointed at the top of this post, where a large grey owl perched.

"It is plastic," she said. "It is to keep the little brown bats away at night, and the raccoons. They would frighten the waiting passengers. You can buy them in gardening catalogues."

The driver smiled. "Just wait and watch," he said.

She waited and watched.

The owl turned its head and looked at her.

Then the bus came, and Stella got on it. When she looked out the window both the man and the owl were gone.

A Shower of Fireflies

THEY'D GO DAYS WITHOUT BATHING, wear the clothes they'd slept in. She wrote in the margins of the passing years, trimmed the wicks of the kerosene lamps. Was amazed in August by the Perseids, by congregations of moths. She remembers how, when they first arrived, her little son asked where the water fountain was. He couldn't differentiate between this drumlin overgrown with mullein, thistle, and milkweed and the city park he'd left behind. Almost two decades later, he's still living at home. He's handsome and funny and helps out a lot; she wants to give him the world, but she knows she'd miss him.

One summer she found a box of mason jars in the damp dirt basement, so old the glass was wavy and tinged with green. The boy and his cousin caught fireflies and put them in the jars to use as flashlights on their late-night walks. In the morning, the candle ends on the old scarred picnic table would be full of moth wings. Moth bodies. Poems to mature later. She stayed home and nursed, listening for boys' voices coming home over the hill.

The new baby grew round and sturdy, could identify plants at three. She helped in the garden as soon as she could walk, but protested when her mother squashed broccoli butterfly larvae between thumb and forefinger. By midafternoon, the kitchen was lined with mason jars of the green worms. When Margo visited, she said, "Do you know the jars in your kitchen are full of butterflies?" So busy trying to find time to write and keeping the fire going, she hadn't noticed them hatching. Twenty years later the girl is gone. Margo said, "It's the wild one you remember more."

The fireflies lived in those glass jars, year upon year, winking in the bedrooms at night. The butterflies still line her kitchen. Sometimes she thinks they're not in jars at all, but in her throat, made, too, of green glass. Sometimes it swallows you up, all that green, and when it finally spits you out two decades later, you look around and say, this place has changed, and so have I. You have to know how to hold on to things, and you have to know how to let them go. Tonight they'll sit on the back step, she and her son. It's August again, just like it was when they first came. They'll open the jars and let them go. The fireflies will fly up to meet the shooting stars, soon become indistinguishable.

The butterflies will find her daughter and settle on her arms, sink into her skin. Become the tattoo that reminds her who she is.

She wonders what her own tattoo will be. Is glad she waited this long to get her own; maybe she's finally old enough to choose just the right one.

Daughter Catcher

THE WITCH SIENA LIVED at the bottom of the gardens on Vine Street where there were woods, mostly cedar and willow for it was damp. Nature's natural cycle seemed altered there, for the ground was in places knee deep in broken sticks, and littered with the arms of dead trees. It was March, and Siena piled sticks and some old half-rotten clothes into a big heap; the village teenagers might come one day to have a bonfire. No one else came down much, so that the few paths were often overgrown, too brambly to struggle through, and decorated with takeout containers, beer bottles both whole and dangerously broken, and Styrofoam, both in cup and slab and pellet form.

The streets and driveways of the village were swept clean often, the lawns sprayed and weeded and raked and mowed, but no one cleaned up the ownerless woods, unless the witch did it. Siena didn't actually hear what people said about her, but she could guess: they thought she was stupid enough to think if she cleaned up after them they might give her daughter back. Noelle wasn't dead, Siena was sure of that. She'd have felt it if the girl was dead, just as she'd have felt it if her men had died. But her entire family was still alive, Siena knew it for a fact. She just didn't have them near her anymore, the way they were supposed to be.

Early spring runoff filled the lowland gully beyond the fallen trees and piles of sticks. While she gathered bottles, discon-

certed as ever by how many there were that once contained
hard liquor of all sorts, Siena talked to herself. When had she
begun? She knew it didn't help her reputation much, that she'd
spent too much time alone in the raggedy woods. She rarely
entered the village proper anymore except to fill recycling bins
before anyone else was up, as she was doing now. It was very
early on Thursday morning, and Siena was fulfilling her weekly
ritual of carrying sacks of pop cans and bottles up the disused
lane from the woods to the street. Surreptitiously, she tipped
the sacks into the big blue plastic boxes, otherwise woefully
empty. Why, Siena often wondered, was it better to dump
garbage off the bridge at night than to sort it into bins? Why
was that so hard? But the villagers couldn't, wouldn't, didn't.

Siena knew that even before dawn on Sundays the townsfolk
made an opposite trek to her own: they went out, also with
sacks, but they went to the bridge and tossed in their old pillows,
used condoms, empty pill bottles, pornography, vomit stained
sleeping bags, single shoes and sometimes even used toilet paper.
They treated the gully beneath the bridge as an impromptu
landfill in the middle of town. Yellow, green, orange and clear
garbage bags hurled on top of one another made such a nice
sound: a kind of sliding squishing *ker-thunk*. The witch, they
seemed to think, would deal with it. She always had.

And the morning after their midnight purges, Siena thought
bitterly, they could go to church and talk about how disgusting
she was: now so solitary, and untrustworthy because of it,
and because she wove things she found out of old string she
gathered; she knitted spider webs out of the dirty old string,
and hung them from the trees. They were frightening, like
things spiders on LSD might have made, and there were more
each year. Siena made them painstakingly; each intricate piece
of webbing took at least a month to make. It was especially
because of the spider webs, Siena thought, that they could face
the day pretending they were clean nice decent people. But she
couldn't have stopped making them even if she'd tried. They

were a compulsion, like her paranoid and vengeful thoughts. She was sure the villagers looked the other way when their boys bent to reach for stones, even though they knew not one would ever make its mark; Siena knew how to deflect stones even before they flew.

Aside from taciturn little boys, the only other person the witch saw early on Thursdays was a woman who combed the streets looking for things others had thrown away that she might drag home to sell at her weekend yard sales. "Looks like rain," the woman said this morning.

"Yes. Have much luck today?" Siena asked.

"Some old shirts, and two nice lamp stands." She gestured at the lamps, missing shades. Siena had hailed from the city once, and knew the lamps would sell for a hundred dollars each at a trendy retro boutique. But how would the woman get to the city? And how much would the store owner give her for the lamps? And so she just smiled and nodded, and only said, "The lamps are nice." They'd already spoken more than they ever had. Speaking to a real person was actually quite hard.

"Do you want to buy them?" the woman asked, startling Siena out of her reverie.

"No."

"I guessed not," the woman laughed.

Was there a touch of derision in her laugh? Siena couldn't be sure. "Why's that?" she asked, a little belligerently.

"They say you sleep under a heap of odds and ends, other people's garbage and sticks."

It seemed hard to believe she'd survived winter doing that, but maybe she'd been so damaged by trauma Siena didn't even know where she slept anymore. The rag picker looked at her, and Siena waited for the verbal spasm of hatred she knew must be coming, either from herself or from the woman. But they just looked at each other, and finally Siena pointed at the lamps and said, "You'll get twenty dollars for them when the cottagers come to open up."

The woman looked immensely pleased. Siena looked at the black hooded sweatshirt draped over her arm. "My son would've liked that," she said, suddenly not wanting to end the conversation, challenging as it was. She thought it might be the first one she'd had in years.

The woman stared. "You used to have a family once, didn't you?" she asked.

"Yes," Siena said.

"Your daughter was very bad. She sold drugs at the high school and was killed by the bikers who supplied her when she didn't pay. They cut up her body and distributed it in many places, so they could never be caught."

Siena figured then the woman had been so poor for so long it had driven her crazy, and forgave her this new assault. Besides, Noelle had been loud and unkempt and never did anything anyone asked, laughing at them instead, or crying, but that had been the extent of it. "That was Paul Hubert," she said. "I heard that story too. It wasn't Noelle, not at all. And even with Paul, why didn't someone help him, teach him to love himself enough so he wouldn't have to turn to drugs?"

This last line she knew came out of the witch wisdom her own mother had taught her. She hadn't said anything like that in years, was surprised at herself. After Noelle's disappearance, what had any of it mattered? She couldn't believe in it anymore. If her magic hadn't been able to protect Noelle, it was worse than useless.

The woman looked startled. "They said you couldn't even really talk anymore."

"I couldn't. But I had to defend Noelle. Usually I don't hear the rumours. No one says them to my face."

"That was so long ago," the woman said, memory dawning like daybreak on her creased face. But she didn't continue, and Siena didn't know whether she was referring to Noelle, or to Paul Hubert, or to her own demise. "We're not any of us as young as we used to be," she continued, peering into Siena's face. She looked familiar, as if they'd once sat on committees together. They'd baked for the same fundraisers, surely. "Sally," the woman said, stretching out her hand. "Sally Fish."

Ah, the minister's wife. What had happened to her? Siena must've heard, and then forgotten, just as Sally had mistaken Noelle's story for Paul Hubert's. Even in a village, memory was fickle. And what about Siena herself? Did she really sleep under sticks? The village had watched her lose everything, and grow prematurely old because of it. Whatever her life had become, it sure wasn't what she'd planned. Siena shook Sally's hand. "Siena Straw."

"I know who you are, Siena. You had the most beautiful gardens, flowers and vegetables both. You were a really good herbalist and you always looked elegant."

"I was just born with skinny genes, is all. And I was good at putting together outfits from thrift stores. If I had money for new clothes I gave it to the kids."

"It was always so important to them," Sally said, "the right kind of sneakers and jeans at school."

"Yes."

They parted, and the next Thursday Sally wasn't out, nor the next. Siena went back to piling sticks and talking to herself. "The paths through the cedars all grown over with brambles and garbage. The slabs of Styrofoam and piles of old shoes replicating each night so that in the morning there were even more. Why always this bleak blackbadness, inconsolable beyond hope at the core, at the bottom, collecting at the fallen logs. The beads of dirty Styrofoam, disintegrating. Siena thought she might die under the weight of it. But she couldn't; what if her daughter came back and her mother wasn't there? Siena knew at one time or another she'd felt a little of what Noelle might've felt when she'd run through town shouting obscenities at the minister and the principal and the constable. Perhaps what Siena could not speak, the girl had. And so the stones they threw at Noelle had in their way been meant for her.

"Maybe they'll give Noelle back if I take their garbage as well as my own. Heaping it into a higher and higher mound each night after spending hours and hours and hours collecting it. And then burrowing beneath it to sleep, in spite of it smelling rather badly. There, I've just admitted it, even to myself. I'm looking for my daughter's body," Siena muttered, piling sticks. She'd misplaced it somewhere, she knew. "My daughter isn't dead, only mad or missing. Maybe she's not out here at all. I bet they've got her in a basement somewhere."

The week after that the geese were flying overhead in pairs, looking for nesting spots, just as Siena and her husband had come here from the city, looking for a quiet pretty place to raise their brood. The geese flew over her piles and honked derisively, and Siena built herself an actual lean-to out of deadfall and Styrofoam instead of burrowing under her shame pile that night, and tried not to talk to herself so much. Her conversation with Sally had been so short, and now weeks old, but still it had reminded her of the difference. Her husband had often made fun of her constant mumbling. She'd done it even then, when he was still around. But that too had been different. Mumbling to a person didn't get you called crazy; it was just a little rude.

She unwound string from a tangle of sticks and sat down on a pile of other sticks and began to make a spider web, part God's eye, part dream catcher. It was obsessive but she couldn't help herself; when Siena found string she had to make something out of it. Something more or less circular to hang in a tree. Siena told herself she was making magic; it was a witchy thing, not a dream catcher but a daughter catcher. Still the objects never seemed beautiful and powerful as she'd intended when she was done but rather sad and lonely as she felt, and possibly mad. And yet consciousness glimmered on, and Siena survived the spring's windiest gale in her makeshift lean-to. Her shelter looked a little like an igloo from a distance, the water rounded white slabs piled into circular walls. The Styrofoam had good insulation value.

The geese flew overhead several times each day, and at last Siena broke down and cried, missing her husband so badly she couldn't give the pain a name. Geese mated for life, as she'd always felt she and her husband would. As the years passed and Siena outgrew her youthful restlessness, the boredom that came after the first thrill of marriage was replaced each year by joy at discovering its yet undiscovered riches: for each year there were more. She should've gone with him. Then they could've still had a kind of happiness, if not the ridiculous happiness they'd had before. Now she was alone without any of them, cleaning up after people who scorned her.

But he'd left, and their son had gone with him, although the young man was old enough to go out on his own now, seek a wife and a fortune. But he and the old man got along well. Any wife the lad found would have to make herself part of their life more than they'd ever make themselves part of hers. She could do the books and mind the clutter; they had never been high on organizational skills, Siena's men hadn't. They liked the same things: military history and beer. They worked together now, she'd heard back when she still spoke to people, in some faraway town, setting up a shop selling memorabilia of oh, so many wars. But between them they knew most of their facts, would be able to back up each piece of begged or borrowed or stolen or scavenged bit of merchandise with a story, quite likely to be true. Siena missed them desperately. Twice in the woods she had found old old guns, and saved them for her men, should they ever pass back through. But why would they?

And so she talked to herself, and performed her forest cleaning tasks, even though there was always more to do; it was an obscenely endless job. Sometimes she realized she'd thought she was talking to her daughter, and then Siena would start to cry again. She and Noelle had been as close as the old man and the young man, in their way. They'd liked the same things:

poetry and painting and witching. It got you every time, that witching. They should've chosen different professions. A witch would always have stones thrown at her, at one time or another in her life, it was true. Her own mother, a witch also, had told Siena that, trying to herd her to a gentler occupation. But for Siena the witching was the gentlest task she knew, and the most necessary. And so she'd turned her back on her own mother's words, her own mother's tears, sure she and her daughter could together change things, together change the world's view of what a witch was. She longed for the days her mother had told her about: the days when witches were well paid and cared for with kindness, invited to good parties and not forgotten but necessary, and not ostracized in the ragged woods at the bottom of the gardens. Her mother had been right of course, except that Siena herself had avoided the stoning her entire life; and the gossip she'd inured herself against. It was her daughter who hadn't found the strength of will to turn the stones back in midair, or as Siena herself was able to do, before they even flew. She'd been too young, the girl had, and too full of fun and too full of love; that had bothered people.

Siena herself had always been a quiet unassuming sort and so people had largely left her alone even though they knew what she was. And if anyone ever pointed a finger right at her and began to speak of what was wrong with her witchery, how ungodly it was, she knew how to deflect them with a joke, or flattery, or a spoonful of hope for their poor little brokenhearted souls, and so they put down their pebbles and unkind words. But all that had been before they'd stoned her daughter, and Noelle had gone mad or missing or maybe both, and the mildly, as most everyone's are, broken hearts of her men had broken further and they'd left. They'd asked Siena to go with them, but she hadn't.

If she moved and her daughter returned to find her, Siena had to be there, didn't she?

She knitted, wondering as always why her burrowing and her

knitting didn't coerce the villagers to give her daughter back. It was witchy magic, after all. It was supposed to work. Her mother had taught her that, taught her how clear intent poured into the creation of an object would amplify its power to heal.

But they hadn't worked, not one of them, and there were thirty or forty spider webs now, strung here and there in the woods. No wonder no one came down here much anymore, not even the dog walkers. Siena's daughter catchers were disturbing, never mind unsuccessful. Perhaps she'd take them all down. And so she wandered the woods with a new purpose, ostensibly to find and detach and burn all her creepy hanging things. She found and detached and bagged six, and where she thought she'd hung the seventh, she instead found a tall boy with wild red hair, stuffing it into his pocket.

"Why do you want that?" Siena asked.

"Want what?" he asked, his hand covering the bulge in his pocket.

"My spider webs. I made them."

"Oh!" he said. "We thought Noelle made them. They bring luck in love."

"How could Noelle make them if she's gone?"

"Maybe she's a ghost," the young man offered. How old was he? Had he known Noelle, or did they just talk about her, like everyone else? How old would Noelle be now, if she were here?

Siena began to stare and stutter, as if to prove everything he'd heard about her was true.

"You look cold," he said. "Come to the fire for tea?"

"Okay," Siena said, surprised. And she did. There were four or five of them, sitting on logs and stumps and one broken chair arranged around one of her stick piles that they'd set alight. They made tea and gave her some, and when they poured a little rum in their own and asked her if she wanted any, she didn't refuse.

"Just don't break the bottles, okay? I cut my fingers when I clean up down here."

"I wouldn't," the boy said. "What's your name?"

"Siena. You?"

"Peter."

"Hello, Peter. Why aren't you afraid of me?"

"Because you're Noelle's mother."

"Maybe. But I'm evil. And she must've been evil too, or they wouldn't have stoned her." It was only saying it aloud that made Siena realize some small part of her believed it to be true.

"You're not evil, you just went crazy because you lost Noelle. That would happen to anyone. But don't stop making those weird string things. They're magic. They're infallible."

"Who do you love?" Siena asked.

"I don't like anyone in that way, and no one likes me. Although Liz has been my best friend since kindergarten, so I'm not exactly alone either."

One of the girls in the circle smiled at Siena. She had black braids and wore a little skirt that in better light Siena would've known wasn't made of leaves, and striped knee socks and sneakers. "But they've worked for lots of us," the girl said.

Siena smiled to herself, and fell asleep, the fire and the rum so warm. When she woke the moon had risen, the youngsters gone home to their families. Siena too should walk back to her igloo, but on the way she saw a glimmer of water beneath a heap of deadfall. She investigated further, stepping in it, and was shocked; the icy water came almost to her hips. Siena would've fallen as if she'd stepped off a creek bank, which was precisely what she'd done, except the mounds of deadfall and garbage prevented it. She hauled herself out before her muscles could seize up from the cold.

Had there always been a creek here? It was as if she'd forgotten it even existed, but how could that be so? It was so full of garbage it was obliterated from sight, but that didn't account for its absence from her mind.

Siena saw another daughter catcher then, hanging just out of reach as if blown by the wind. She didn't care what the young people said, to Siena it radiated evil. Her thoughts after all were full of malice when she made them; some tiny secret part of her wished terrible things upon the townsfolk because of what had happened to Noelle. But by the old laws of mirrors Siena knew this was a dangerous thing to do, that she brought judgement upon herself when she wove malice into her magic. People would talk about her even more than before, and she'd grow even more bitter and solitary because of it, and weave even more hate into her webs, and the villagers, sensing her hate, would call her an evil witch, and so on, in an unending circle of fear and hate.

Still, she hiked her skirt and shinnied up the tree and pulled it down. There was love in the webs too, the yearning she felt for Noelle, or they wouldn't work to find the kids the love they so craved. She took it home to her stick and Styrofoam shelter. Peter was right, she had gone mad. The villagers were right about her. How could she not have seen it? Still, the shelter was a step up from the stick piles she used to burrow beneath. When had she built it? After she'd talked to Sally, she thought. And after she realized birds took better care of themselves than she did.

In the morning she hoped the youngsters would invite her for tea again, but they would be in school. The same two geese flew overhead. They took a long time to make their decision of where to build their nest, or else they just wanted to drag out their weeks of dinners out and movies and sex, before the long work of raising a family began. Seeing them, Siena wished again her men hadn't left. She wished her husband had stayed behind and helped her dig for her daughter's body.

She wished he'd believed, as she'd believed, that they could still find Noelle, that their love could find a way. Siena allowed herself a little resentment then, towards her missing husband. There was a streak of weakness in him, she'd always secretly felt, an inability to hold on, hold out. If he'd stood beside her it would've been easier to say, "You shouldn't have stoned

Noelle. She was just letting her hair down, letting off a little steam. Things would've felt better for you if you'd done it a little more yourselves." She could've spoken before it even happened, but when she already felt it coming, said something like, "Noelle's a little frisky, it's true, but great care must be taken of the free-spirited; they teach us all that joy is still possible. To judge them is to judge ourselves. We'd do better to imitate than to decry."

But she hadn't. Or if she had, she hadn't done it enough. Or if she'd done it enough, it hadn't made enough of a difference. They'd still stoned Noelle. She'd still gone mad or missing or both.

Siena went to investigate the missing creek, had a memory then, of a time when the creek had been beautiful. One spring it had flooded its banks so that when she and her daughter and her son, maybe nine and eleven then, had sat on the swing at the edge, their feet dangling in the risen water. The current was fierce that spring, and they had slipped into the water and been pulled with huge force around two bends until the place where several fallen trees slowed the stream.

Screaming and laughing, the three of them, laughing because of the speed of the current, screaming because the water was still icy with melt-off. Everything so green. Each spring it felt like that, as if a winter of starvation was being assuaged. Siena remembered how that day had been so much better than the expensive asphalt-paved fair. A better thrill, and free. She and her children had looked into one another's eyes, wide with excitement, barely believing anything could be so wonderful. And then done it again.

How could she have forgotten the creek? It must have been the trauma. But it seemed not only she but everyone in the village had forgotten.

Siena's heart could not break any more than it had already broken; it had calcified, scarred over. The truth was, she no longer had the strength or hope even to leave and try and find the men. But what was there to stay for? She'd never find Noelle. Noelle was mad or missing or both.

"They don't have her in a basement," the girl with black braids said. She was sitting beside the dead fire.

Siena stared at her.

"I heard you say they did one time," Peter's friend said. "You were walking, talking, didn't notice I was here."

"Just like now. So how do you know?"

"It's a feeling mostly, not that that's much help, I'm sure. But it's pretty strong. I'm Liz, by the way." Siena stared at Liz. Was she a witch? Witches were always taught to pay great attention to their intuition. "Do you have another?" Liz asked.

"What?"

"Spider web. My friends took the others, and there weren't any left that I could find."

"Is that why you're not in school? You came down here looking for a spider web?"

The girl nodded.

"What's his name?" Siena asked.

"I've known him since kindergarten but he acts like my brother. I can't get him to see me as potential girlfriend material. Noelle's spider webs are a charm. She's the patron saint of love."

"But I make them, not Noelle."

"You make them for her," Liz said. "So she'll feel your love and come back. So in that way they're still hers. And I bet she makes them work for us, from wherever she is."

"Did you know Noelle?" Siena asked.

"We all knew her," Liz said. "We used to come down here and party. She was a little older. It was a few years ago, back when you still lived in the..." the girl's voice trailed off, as if she were embarrassed for Siena.

"House?"

"Yes," Liz said.

"Who lives in my house now?" Siena asked.

"It's empty. No one will buy it or rent it."

"Maybe if I stop hating them, they'll give her back. I just can't figure it."

"What did your mother say?" Liz asked.

"Don't beat yourself up so much." Siena laughed at the memory. She'd always been hard on herself, and her mother had always told her to love herself. But then her mother had died, and Noelle had disappeared, and then the men had left. Since then Siena had been hard on herself for pretty well every minute of every day.

"Here. I have one in my pocket. If I give it to you will you go back to class?"

"Yes." The girl held her hand out for Siena's gift.

"Did you know there's a creek under all that garbage?" Siena asked as Liz got up to go.

"Really? They're connected, the missing creek, missing Noelle. I'll get the others and we'll clean it."

"Thanks," Siena said.

But what did she mean? Thanks for helping clean the creek or thanks for believing Noelle was still alive?

Liz was as good as her word. Over the ensuing weeks the teenagers came and built igloos out of Styrofoam they could stay in when their parents kicked them out for being lippy. They made stick piles and burned them. They carted bags and bags of bottles to the recycling bins on Thursday mornings, until every blue box in the village was full. Even Sally Fish came to help; occasionally she found an object she could sell at her weekend sale.

"It was time to clean the place up," Sally said. "I had to help, after what they did to Noelle."

So she'd heard the truth at last. Siena was glad, but she didn't make a big deal out of it. After weeks of burning and recycling and land-filling garbage, there was a creek. It was still a little murky, so they planted cattails along the edges. By early fall it ran crystal clear, and there were little brown trout in it, and geese flying in screaming Vs overhead. At first they weren't very good at it, their Vs misshapen; it reminded Siena of when her son had first learned to drive. She missed him terribly and started to cry all over again, even though the creek cleanup had distracted her all summer, the youngsters and their bonfires and tea had kept her warm. So many of them had found love, and all, they insisted, although Siena still wasn't sure, because of her magic spider webs. They brought glue guns and glued the walls of her hut together, so it would be less drafty in the coming winter. Peter brought a little window to set into the side.

But Siena cried, missing her husband. She'd always called him her husband even though they'd never married in a church, but the witch figured God wouldn't have noticed the difference; what he'd have noticed instead, if he'd been looking or cared, which was doubtful, was how she'd poured everything into her family—scrubbing and cleaning and working and growing vegetables and cooking and canning and washing and hanging clothes until she was so exhausted she couldn't even remember what her own dreams had been for herself, or if she'd ever even had any. She hadn't minded; she'd loved them all so much. It had been worth it. And while the family was on the poor side and complained a lot because of it, they were largely happier and more content than they knew. Isn't it always so? Although there were days Siena had noticed how lucky they were, that a tiny bit of heaven had come unglued from the sky to land at their feet, astonishing them, allowing them to live in it. It was like a secret, and she'd taken the best care of it she knew how. Remembering her lost happiness, Siena began to shake her head then, and muttered, "I tried not to talk about it too much, lest someone notice and try and take it away. They were always doing that, weren't they?" She dug first haphazardly and then with more frenzy in her pockets where she thought she'd once put away a little string.

But a hand touched her shoulder then, and made her turn and take a cup of tea, and said, "Maybe they'll return one day, as geese. Remember that story? They'll land and shed their feathers and put on clothes," and again Siena wondered whether Liz might be a witch, whether one could be born into it, and not just trained by one's own mother.

"Why would they do that?" Siena asked.

"Well, if we found Noelle they'd have no reason to stay away," Liz said, and with a sudden abstracted look on her face got up and wandered away.

"I know you won't make them anymore, but you brought so much love into the world making spider webs for her and giving them away," Peter said. "Maybe Noelle's supposed to just be the patron saint of love."

"You can't say that to a mother," Sally Fish said, and again Siena wondered what had happened to the minister's wife. One day she'd have to ask.

"Come here!" Liz called, "I found the most amazing feet!" Peter got up, and when he and Siena got to the creek where Liz was pointing he put his arm around the girl and she smiled, a cat in pyjamas, suddenly.

There were two dead trees lying across the creek, too big and heavy to move. But beneath them in the now sparkling clear water, there were two elegant feet. And the toes, it was undeniable, were wiggling not just with the current but with life. Siena stepped into the shallows at the edge and leaned over to peer under the tree. A young woman was lying on the soft sand at the bottom of the creek, her arms folded across her chest, a fraying daughter catcher held over her heart. Her eyes were closed. Siena reached in and stroked Noelle's feet.

"How do we get her out?" Siena asked the gathered teenagers. "So she can be loved too and not just always create it in other's people's lives?"

"By teaching her to love herself, like you did for us," Liz said.

"I didn't know that's what I did," Siena said.

No Woman Is an Island

K AREN. I'VE BARELY DARED *think of her, thought today of the skirt I gave her years ago. I suddenly realized it was a going away present. A goodbye present: I only saw her once more after that. But which of us was going away?*

And now I can't not think of her, back on Salt Spring after ten years, in this little cabin where we stayed—a sleeping loft, a little cook stove, and, amazingly, the same even more faded blue print curtain on the window.

Karen's son was named Moon. What was Moon's father called? I feel I could retrieve his name, if it was important enough. But it's not.

Homes. What are they made of? After squatting in this cabin and others, working and camping all over British Columbia for years alone, I met Karen and Moon. We hit it off and in the end they lived with me here for almost a year, and then we forged a life plan together. We'd work, buy land, make a family of ourselves. I thought Toronto, my home town, and not Vancouver or Victoria. We didn't even tell Moon's father—Karen had stopped forwarding their address or lack of it after what happened the last time he took his son for a weekend. Finding the child uncontrollable, he'd returned Moon to Karen's doorstep at midnight, not even staying to make sure she was home.

We had little money and hitchhiked, the three of us, with backpacks and rolled tents. It was September. Moon was nine,

I was twenty, Karen was twenty-nine. Moon thought it high adventure to sleep in ditches when we weren't let off near a campground at night; to coax a flame from damp kindling; to strike the tent himself some mornings; to eat beans and scrambled eggs cooked in a pan over a fire. I remember Karen even offered to demonstrate how to skin and cook a roadkill porcupine. "Gross," Moon told me, "but quite edible with onions."

"Must you?" I declined. Now I think it a shame I didn't take the chance to learn this extra life skill.

◆◆◆

Enzo had woken from a dream in which their daughter Katie's fort had red gaillardias woven through the dishevelled pile of kids' sleeping bags, signifying, he knew even in the dream, limitless joy. Ending in a disastrous mood as often as not, but still, he'd had such a great time with Katie and her friends, had been even somewhat lax about nutritious meals and bedtime and teeth brushing but perhaps that was the point. If one stopped obsessing over propriety for a sweet short moment sometimes lasting an entire weekend about their hair their baths their laundry their three square, they let you into their incredible secret, more: would teach you how to participate in infinite joy.

But the next morning, their daughter's amusing nine-year-old friends gone home, Enzo worried again. Right at this moment Azalea might be kayaking in the cold and wet. He was surprised to find no anger in himself at her leaving, ditching him with the kid. He just wanted her home safe. Badly.

◆◆◆

I remember Karen and I walking in the railway lands at the foot of Bathurst Street, a break from job-and-apartment hunting. We came upon an empty old boxcar and found a plastic bag of toiletries and other small items, a sleeping bag, a comic lying open beside it. "Let's sit and read the comic," I said, completely charmed.

Karen replied, "It's their home; it would be rude to go in without being invited," and I was humbled, feeling as always she saw more than me. I so desperately wanted to wear that home as my own, just for a few minutes. I would trespass for the sake of my fantasy, not even seeing how fragile this tiny home was, how doubly important to respect its ephemeral boundaries.

Living in a city again I needed to work so I could pay for rent and food; knew already how hard it would be to save a down payment, not spend it in bars and restaurants, on clothes, anything to wash the feel of eight hours of shift work away. On Salt Spring we'd been able to live rent free in our borrowed cabin, eat off the land, at least to an extent. I loved it. It was Karen who grumbled. She already had a child, even then almost ten years old. He'd be a young adult now. For how long was I oblivious, as she hardened herself against the disapproving gaze?

The cabin is on Crown Land. My old friend Elm pays a pittance for his lease. "What is public land for if people can't make homes on it," Karen used to say, and with what fervent desire I wanted her to be right.

♦♦♦

Why didn't Azalea write or call? It had been more than a week. Enzo read her computer journal, for herself alone. He began at the beginning. Azalea wrote, five years before:

I bought Karen a skirt. I don't know why. We've never felt the need to make showy gifts to one another. We had such dreams, Karen and I. I remember how, after we came east, two months into city life I hated walls already. I missed tents badly; just enough of a roof to keep the rain off. Karen and I worked in clubs at night, and soon all the peace of the forest had gone to noise. But not quite all; so often as I hustled tables,

I was kayaking along a forested coast in my mind, watching for whales.

And now Enzo and I have a house full of appliances. Why? So that our daughter won't grow up to be like Karen. We live as if we believed machines could protect us. Yet Karen grew up surrounded by appliances too, and they didn't protect her. Even more than Karen, I wonder what Moon's doing now.

Before it came back to him Enzo briefly wondered who Karen was. He wondered who his own friends were. Scrolling through pages he saw that Azalea wrote about Karen more than she wrote about him—he could think of no one who took up as much space in his life. Except, of course, for her. Azalea herself.

Who were his friends? His mother, his daughter. Azalea, Enzo had thought, but now he wasn't so sure. Did friends walk away from one another? Was that sometimes a necessary part of friendship? And the question begged asking: abandon one another to what?

And which of them had abandoned the other?

There were old friends from high school and university he talked to once or twice a year. They seemed so far away from his life now, a distance too large to be breached. They wouldn't be able to offer comfort if he called, because he wouldn't tell. Tell them what?

Azalea's gone.

And Karen? She was a single mother, a few years older than Azalea. The two women had travelled the west coast before they came to Ontario, where Azalea met Enzo, did the married thing. Went back to school. They had a child.

But what happened to Karen? And what happened to Azalea, to make her leave?

◆◆◆

I phoned Enzo to tell him I'm not coming home yet, to dependably shop for school clothes, set the alarm, pack lunches for the big day. He didn't tell me I was cruel or neglectful, just told me Katie was fine and asked me when I'd come. Not sure, I said. I felt selfish, yet what about his cruelty? How impassively he sat by while I lost myself in years of laundry and cooking and scrubbed floors and isolation, so often alone with the child. The baby drove me crazy in love and towards desperation in equal measures. I wrote papers for school in the wee hours and broke into occasional sobs of exhaustion Enzo found unaccountable.

I suppose I'm having a bit of a nervous breakdown, leaving as I so suddenly did but without crying jags, temper tantrums, or an inability to get out of bed. This time I just bought a plane ticket instead, without warning Enzo. Looking for some peace, wanting to be alone. And now I am alone, yet not feeling isolated at all. Funny, that.

◆◆◆

Enzo began a journal, after Labour Day weekend came and went, after Katie chirped through Cheerios and scrambled eggs, onto the school bus.

8 September: The man who lent her the cabin then still lives in the same house in Victoria; she called him, asked if she could use it again. Was happy he remembered her. He works in broadcasting now, calls himself Elmer again.

Perhaps, right now, Azalea sits at the wooden table, writes by kerosene lamp, for (I imagine) it's a heavy overcast day. She listens, awed by how happy she is, to the surf on the stones outside the window. Yesterday, kayaking, she saw orcas.

It was his first journal entry, ever. Suddenly, he was like Azalea. And Karen too, he'd bet twenty bucks; he suddenly remembered the two women talking: how soothing they found their journals. Azalea gone, no longer reminding him where his car keys were, his memory quickened. Funny how that worked.

◆◆◆

Why is this the only place I can talk about God, even to myself—far from any neighbours, not even a road, only a kayak to go coastwise around to the village? Because my life here is so potentially dangerous I need one. As are all our lives, every day, but we hide behind machines so we don't have to look. Dangerous, yet beautiful, and most importantly what seemed necessary: the right to make a small home out of small things. Wash each night one cup one spoon one pan.

My computer is an appliance that doesn't wash dishes or clothes; instead, it rinses my soul. I wonder whether Enzo has booted up my journal at home—it's not password protected. If he was away, and he kept one, would I be able to resist? It terrifies me to be possibly so exposed, even to my husband. Enough complaints in there about him to be sure, gentle as he is. And perhaps better there than spoken aloud always—for I'm no paragon myself. Yet part of me is relieved by the possibility: at last he'd know all.

I remember the night Karen and I traded journals, read our way through one another's lives and minds by lamplight. It was the next morning we decided we could buy land together.

◆◆◆

By early October, Azalea still wasn't home, although she'd called twice more from the village, so Enzo knew at least she was alive. He worried alone now over the list of possible calamities as they usually did together at the beginning of each cold season: chimney fires, power failures, frozen pipes. So much for calling themselves suburban; they were still technically in the country, at the edge of the little town north of Toronto. The faceless minivan shame of living in suburbia, without even the town services that made it worthwhile. Continuing with his snooping, he read an entry near the end of Azalea's first year's diary:

Reading back through the whole year on New Year's Day it strikes me this journal literally saved my life. Must remember to tell that to the next suicidal person I talk to. For, sigh, there will be one as surely as there will be another winter. And Karen? I hope she's well. I haven't seen her in months. She didn't seem well when we saw her last.

Karen again.

Enzo felt terribly guilty for reading, but couldn't stop. Reading her journals was like eating soup made out of Azalea.

◆◆◆

I remember fifteen years ago a squatter friend telling Karen she was bourgeois to want a house. She said: "I want to rest. I want to retreat from this life. It's too harsh. I want my son to have a roof."

I can hear her saying it, clear as day, just as I can hear his scornful reply: "Cop-out."

And Karen never got her house, least not when I still knew her.

Our Toronto apartment had a working fireplace. I remember one winter night I went to Alexandra Park and collected deadfall. It felt peaceful, a country thing, akin to our old life on the islands, gathering rosehips. I remember a passing man stopped, stared at me with pity and scorn, thought I was so poor I couldn't afford twelve-ninety-eight for a fire-log, wrapped in plastic, printed in four toxic colours, from the corner store. Leave the deadfall to rot until the parks department guys came in their green trucks to clear it away. I was so offended. Yet it couldn't have been the first time I suffered the disapproving stranger's gaze: surely, before, I just didn't notice, too scornful myself, a reverse contempt that suddenly, that snowy night, was no longer there to protect me. A fallen shield.

I'll go home next week. But who is home?

◆◆◆

They lost touch with Karen. Azalea was busy with the baby, with part-time classes, with starting a daycare centre in their village. Karen frightened them, each year poorer and more unkempt, skidding from restaurant work to welfare. But they didn't say it, even to themselves: we are walking away from her, hand in hand. Not looking back.

Enzo fantasized he'd find Karen. A coming-home present for Azalea, so she'd stay. He knew real life didn't work that way. And saw it then: he'd find Karen, give her the spare room, and still Azalea wouldn't come. A shuddering laughing thought.

◆◆◆

Thanksgiving morning.

Coasting in a borrowed kayak I found the cabin last night; my memory hadn't failed me. It is still here, not fallen down. Someone has come, one year or another to make repairs. More importantly there's kerosene in the lamps, stacked wood outside.

Someone has been here recently: strings of wild rosehips hang in the window, drying. Yet they've gone again: the ocean-facing windows are shuttered.

There's a journal lying open on the table—I wonder whose it is? I'm writing in it but haven't read it yet. If overly secretive, they wouldn't have left it here lying open. I will read it tomorrow, a Thanksgiving present to myself.

I look out the window, see a witch's moon, a crescent horned moon. My mother would have liked it, in the years before. It reminds me of the moons on that skirt her friend gave her. Stole it out of the household money Enzo gave her for groceries: fifteen dollars a week until there was enough; she didn't dare tell him she wanted to buy a hundred-dollar skirt for my mother. She told me, though; I think I was twelve. She wasn't working then; new motherhood had already burned through all her savings. Funny how I remember these details; surely these people have forgotten me entirely, and yet when I was a child they were so important.

I lived here when I was very small, when my mother was still happy. Used to watch her chop kindling while I strung rosehips for a useful game. Her friend took care of me when

it was my mother's turn in the kayak. What was her name?
Oddly I remember her husband's name but not hers.
A flowering bush.
Rhododendron?
My mother was happy here. Here she had a friend.
It is only here that the moon is my namesake. Writing helps.

◆◆◆

In a boxcar in the decommissioned railway lands south of Richmond Street a woman sat wrapped in blankets. Reflexively she rummaged through her belongings for the little packet to see how much was left. Promised herself again that tomorrow she would find a detox program, check in.

She wore three layers of skirts, the bottom skirt a hippie treasure, an expensive item given her years before by a friend: midnight blue silk with stars and crescent moons printed in gold. The stars and moons were nearly washed away.

The woman never wore this skirt on the outside, but only as the bottom layer, next to her skin. She felt that as long as she never wore it on the outside, the street layer, she wouldn't be murdered. Never reveal your true name.

What was the woman's name, her friend who gave her the skirt? She didn't remember.

A fat orange moon rising in the southern sky, through the open door of the boxcar.

Years ago, she lived in a place so different from this. They had a kayak, she and her friend. They took turns paddling the ocean waters, looking for whales.

Once she had a friend.

Once she had a son.

She remembered the son's name.

My Mother's Skeleton

MY DAUGHTER AND I SIT in the shade of wild apples, watching tiny garden snails. They are so small one feels a giant watching them, or perhaps as though one has microscopes for eyes. These tiny snails are lost in the vastness of a plank laid across the purple-stemmed cacophony of rhubarb.

I gently put the snails back under the rhubarb. "Snails need to be moist and slimy," I tell my little daughter, "or they'll dry out." Rhubarb Hollow is our magic shady place beneath the wild apples. Sometimes I bring a notebook when we come out here to play even though I hardly ever write in longhand anymore, but on the first of June I am still too surprised by green's return to sit in the dark computer room upstairs, even just for half an hour. I treasure this moment because next month or next year Annie won't like this game anymore and because soon I must go inside and resume preparations for our party.

It is our annual Victoria Day weekend camping party. The hours blur by until, just after midnight, I sit with my sister Alice and our friend Sandra at a fire in a fieldstone pit, perhaps a hundred years old. We discuss the unknown purpose for this carefully made pit—a large bread oven perhaps, but why so far from the house? Or maybe it's the foundations of a ruined grain silo. The hills are decorated with tents, some glowing like luminous mushrooms. The folks in the tents are late night readers or they're afraid of the dark and think a flashlight left on will keep them safe from wild animals, which there indeed are, especially this far from the house. My black mutt Asteroid sits between us, keeping guard.

While other children went to church on Sundays we were marched to the art gallery, having required an equal amount of scrubbing as the churchgoers. We were expected to be very quiet, clean, and respectful, as if in the presence of the sublime. My father still has this religious hush when looking at large expensive art books, full of costly reproductions. I feel I know what it was to be raised religiously, yet art didn't become my religion. That was something I was still in the process of discovering, or maybe rediscovering.

At twelve, Leni and I spent a summer on a farm near Sudbury. The land was rented by family friend Kerry McFarlane and his brothers, all working in the mines so they could buy land. Often that summer we built bonfires on huge outcroppings of shield rock, and sat around them half the night. We walked endlessly in woods and fields, canoed in rivers that seemed so miraculously different from Toronto as to participate in an alien landscape, one that would require a new language, a new metaphor, to divine. For instance, we saw moose.

My father sometimes mocks my choice to live in rural eastern Ontario, a place that after all isn't important. Not the way Europe is allegedly important. It is true the towns are full of empty storefronts and video stores and submarine franchises, and lack four-hundred-year-old churches and art museums. At least our own: yet there is a four-hundred-year-old church and art museum nearby, the Anishinaabeg Teaching Rocks. One cannot visit them and not feel taught. And in spite of his mockery, my father comes and looks at my perennial gardens in disbelief each June. I never let him go home without greens or squash.

My mother is not here; we mourn her still. This is one thing I have learned: to mourn properly is a lifelong task. From time to time I try on her beautiful velvet shoes. I've been saving her nicest size elevens; they don't fit me yet and my feet aren't growing anymore. A human's growth isn't indeterminate, stretching through a whole life like the beaver's. Up north, farther north in Ontario, she used to sit under the birch trees, doing drawings in such miniscule detail, of deadfall, ferns. She must've had microscopes for eyes.

Later this summer we will go back north, take the Polar Bear Express to Moosonee, my father, my husband, and all our children, his and mine. I should like my children to ride a train before all the passenger trains are gone. Like we did, coming home from that Sudbury farm, with my aunt Prunella, the year before my mother died. Eating snack bar food and playing crazy eights all night long while the train rattled and clacked through the forests and swamps of Ontario. My sister and I had never stayed awake all night before, but were brave and persevering, helped by card games and sweetened snack bar coffee. Staying awake through the half-numbed navigation of Toronto's cavernous Union Station, the walk along impossibly bright King Street to eat bananas and cream in a greasy spoon. Greasy spoons don't serve bananas and cream anymore—only upscale breakfast bistros for the urban trendy do that. Another thing lost.

When it is still night Alice, Sandra, and I hear coyotes. What seems like hours but is perhaps only a few moments later, we watch the last of the luminous tent mushrooms wink out. Now that dawn is coming our campers feel safe enough to turn their lights off. My sisters and I stand on the hills, the lonely fields far from the house cloaked in pockets of mist—the sky striped lavender and pink. Time collapses and I think of all the years when we were young travellers, staying up around fires, surrounded by forests that stretched farther than the eye could see. We did it in many countries, sometimes together, sometimes separately and for a brief moment all those other dawns, other fires, other journeys collapse into one. What are these, I wonder: fire, night conversation, dawn? They exist to remind us how unknowable and mysterious life really is. The next day you see each other and feel: this one I will call friend forever.

I have been living inside my mother's skeleton for twenty years. It's quite roomy and comfortable so most of the time I don't even realize my confinement. As though it had grown, her huge ribcage spread out on these hills like the skeleton of a whale. I remember turning fourteen east of here, listening to spring runoff under two feet of snow on a farm in Lanark County. Our friend Ben sat in shirtsleeves, his jacket beneath him on a melting snow bank, playing the double bass while snowmelt also sang in underground rivulets. A series of phone calls at dusk; Kerry driving a blue pickup to the city; premonition soaking through me like darkening twilight.

♦♦♦

My mother was born in Europe, where she learned to live for art. But she died here, in a still forested land, sitting for hours under birch trees on Kerry's farm, drawing with a botanical exactness, but also an awe: what is this landscape, what does it say, what are its secrets? My mother came across the sea, all the pain of Europe's war in her pocket. In her other pocket, two seeds: two children. Beneath the truly weird, almost fluorescent green of the forest canopy, up north in Ontario, she planted us, so that we might live.

Decades later we still live in the shelter of her ribcage. The rain comes through, but we don't mind: at night we can see the trails of shooting stars, and the smoke from our cook fires wafts through the slatted bones. I may never find another place to live now.

Acknowledgements

Thanks to the Ontario Arts Council, the Canada Council for the Arts, Doug Back, and the editors of the publications in which these stories first appeared, including: Jo-Ellen Brydon, Julie Rouse and George Kirkpatrick, Lorraine Filyer, Candas J. Dorsey, Sally Tomasevic and Marcel Gagne, Keith Brooke, Darrell Lum and Eric Chock, Karen Correia da Silva, Sharon Hamilton, Bruce Kauffman, Rose Lemberg and Shweta Narayan, Bruce Boston, Claude Lalumiere, Silvia Moreno-Garcia, Hal Niedzviecki, Joe Pulver Sr., Rich Dana, Rhonda Parrish and Greg Bechtel, Justin Isis, Brendan Connell, and Michael Callaghan. Thank you also to my faithful beta readers including Jan Thornhill, Kate Story, Anita Buerhle and Tapanga Koe. Thanks to Luciana Ricciutelli, Val Fullard, and Renée Knapp, my amazing team at Inanna Publications.

"Mother Down The Well." *Dead North Anthology.* Ed. Silvia Moreno-Garcia. Holstein, ON: Exile Editions, 2013.

"The Lonely Planet Guide to Other Dimensions." *ELQ The Exile Quarterly.* Ed. Michael Callaghan. Forthcoming, 2020.

"Big Ears." *Transversions: An Anthology of New Fantastic Literature.* Eds. Sally Tomasevic and Marcel Gagne. Toronto: Black Orchid Press, 2000.

"A Room of His Own." *Tesseracts 21. Nevertheless, Optimistic SF Anthology.* Eds. Rhonda Parrish and Greg Bechtel. Calgary: Tesseract Books, Edge Fantasy and Science Fiction, 2018.

"Washing Lady's Hair." *Strangers Among Us.* Eds. Susan Forest and Lucas Law. Calgary: Laksa Media Groups, Inc., 2016.

"Seeds." SF text accompanying a video installation by the author. Windowspace '91, a Peterborough windows show. Curated by Jo-Ellen Brydon.

"As If Leaves Could Hide Invisible Beings." *That Not Forgotten.* Ed. Bruce Kauffman. Brighton, ON: Hidden Brook Press, 2012.

"The Dreams of Trees." *Bibliotheca Fantastica.* Ed. Don Pizarro. Ithaca, NY: Dagan Books, 2013.

"On Fire Bridge." *The Peterborough Review,* Volume 1, No. 3 (Winter 1995). Eds. Julie Rouse and George Kirkpatrick.

"Castoroides." *Stone Telling Magazine.* Eds. Rose Lemberg and Shweta Narayan. Online: Summer 2012.

"One Day I'm Gonna Give Up the Blues for Good." *Prairie Fire* (SF issue). Ed. Candas J. Dorsey. Winnipeg, Summer 1994.

"Kaolani, From Kaua'i." *Bamboo Ridge # 91.* Eds. Darrell Lum and Eric Chock. Honolulu: Bamboo Ridge Press, 2008.

"Fires Halfway." *Drowning in Beauty: The Neo-Decadent Anthology.* Eds. Justin Isis and Daniel Corrick. Sacramento, CA: Snuggly Books, 2018.

"Hamilton Beach." *Obsolete #9.* Ed. Rich Dana. Cedar Rapids, Iowa: Obsolete Press, . 2016

"Judy" *This Magazine*. Volume 7, No. 4 (October 1983). Ed. Lorraine Filyer. Illustrated by the author.

"Myrtle's Marina." Original title, "Stones, Maybe." *Cassilda's Song*. Ed. Joe Pulver Sr. Ann Arbor, MI: Chaosium Inc., 2015.

"The Dark Lake." *The Peterborough Review*, Volume 1, No. 1 (Summer 1994). Eds. Julie Rouse and George Kirkpatrick.

"The Meaning of Yellow." *Write: The Magazine of the Writers' Union of Canada*. Volume 40, No. 3 (Winter 2013). Ed. Hal Niedzviecki.

"Trading Polaris." *Infinity Plus*. Ed. Keith Brooke. UK. Online: March 2003.

"Bus Owls." *The Link*. Ed. Sharon Hamilton. Campbellford, ON, March/April 2010, No. 152.

"A Shower of Fireflies." *Star*Line*. Ed. Bruce Boston. Ocala, FL: SFPA Press, 2008 (reprint).

"Daughter Catcher." *Over the Rainbow* anthology. Eds. Derek Newman-Stille and Kelsi Morris. Holstein, ON: Exile Editions, 2018.

"No Woman Is an Island." *Gulch Anthology, Steel Bananas*. Eds. Karen Correia da Silva et al. Toronto: Tightrope Books, 2009.

"My Mother's Skeleton." *That Not Forgotten*. Ed. Bruce Kauffman. Brighton, ON: Hidden Brook Press, 2012.

Photo: Andy Carroll

Ursula Pflug is author or editor of ten books including novels, novellas and story collections. Her fiction has appeared in Canada, the U.S. and the UK, in award-winning genre and literary publications including *Lightspeed, Fantasy, Strange Horizons, Postscripts, Leviathan, LCRW, Now Magazine* and B*amboo Ridge.* Her short stories have been taught in universities in Canada and India, and she has collaborated extensively with filmmakers, playwrights, choreographers, and installation artists. Her fiction has won small press awards abroad and been a finalist for the Aurora, ReLit and KM Hunter Awards as well as the 3 Day Novel and Descant Novella Contests at home. She lives in rural Peterborough County, Ontario.